No. 1 *New York Times* bestselling author **Christine Feehan** has had over ninety novels published and has thrilled legions of fans with her seductive Dark Carpathian tales. She has received numerous honours throughout her career, including being a nominee for the Romance Writers of America RITA and receiving a Career Achievement Award from *Romantic Times*, and has been published in multiple languages.

By Christine Feehan

Torpedo Ink series:
Judgment Road
Vengeance Road
Vendetta Road
Desolation Road
Reckless Road
Annihilation Road
Savage Road

Shadow series:
Shadow Rider
Shadow Reaper
Shadow Keeper
Shadow Warrior
Shadow Flight
Shadow Storm
Shadow Fire

'Dark' Carpathian series:
Dark Prince
Dark Desire
Dark Gold
Dark Magic
Dark Challenge
Dark Fire
Dark Legend
Dark Guardian
Dark Symphony
Dark Melody
Dark Destiny
Dark Secret
Dark Demon
Dark Celebration
Dark Possession
Dark Curse
Dark Slayer
Dark Peril
Dark Predator
Dark Storm
Dark Lycan
Dark Wolf
Dark Blood
Dark Ghost
Dark Promises
Dark Carousel
Dark Legacy
Dark Sentinel
Dark Illusion
Dark Song
Dark Tarot
Dark Nights
Darkest at Dawn (omnibus)
Dark Whisper
Dark Memory
Dark Hope
Dark Joy

Sea Haven series:
Water Bound
Spirit Bound
Air Bound
Earth Bound
Fire Bound
Bound Together

GhostWalker series:
Shadow Game
Mind Game
Night Game
Conspiracy Game
Deadly Game
Predatory Game
Murder Game
Street Game
Ruthless Game
Samurai Game
Viper Game
Spider Game
Power Game
Covert Game
Toxic Game
Lethal Game
Lightning Game
Phantom Game
Ghostly Game

Drake Sisters series:
Oceans of Fire
Dangerous Tides
Safe Harbour
Turbulent Sea
Hidden Currents
Magic Before Christmas

Leopard People series:
Fever
Burning Wild
Wild Fire
Savage Nature
Leopard's Prey
Cat's Lair
Wild Cat
Leopard's Fury
Leopard's Blood
Leopard's Run
Leopard's Wrath
Leopard's Rage
Leopard's Scar

The Scarletti Curse
Lair of the Lion
Murder at Sunrise Lake
Red on The River

CHRISTINE FEEHAN
Dark Joy

PIATKUS

PIATKUS

First published in the US in 2026 by Berkley,
An imprint of Penguin Random House LLC
First published in Great Britain in 2026 by Piatkus

1 3 5 7 9 10 8 6 4 2

Copyright © 2026 by Christine Feehan

The moral right of the author has been asserted.

*All characters and events in this publication, other than those
clearly in the public domain, are fictitious and any resemblance
to real persons, living or dead, is purely coincidental.*

All rights reserved.
Penguin Random House values and supports copyright. Copyright fuels creativity, encourages diverse voices, promotes free speech, and creates a vibrant culture. Thank you for buying an authorized edition of this book and for complying with copyright laws by not reproducing, scanning, or distributing any part of it in any form without permission. You are supporting writers and allowing Penguin Random House to continue to publish books for every reader. Please note that no part of this book may be used or reproduced in any manner for the purpose of training artificial intelligence technologies or systems.

A CIP catalogue record for this book
is available from the British Library.

Hardback ISBN 978-0-349-44567-0
Trade paperback ISBN 978-0-349-44568-7

Printed and bound in Great Britain by Clays Ltd, Elcograf S.p.A.

Papers used by Piatkus are from well-managed forests
and other responsible sources.

Piatkus
An imprint of
Little, Brown Book Group
Carmelite House
50 Victoria Embankment
London EC4Y 0DZ

The authorised representative
in the EEA is
Hachette Ireland
8 Castlecourt Centre
Dublin 15, D15 XTP3, Ireland
(email: info@hbgi.ie)

An Hachette UK Company
www.hachette.co.uk

www.littlebrown.co.uk

For Joy.
Thank you for being in my life.

FOR MY READERS

Be sure to go to ChristineFeehan.com/members/ to sign up for my private book announcement list and download the free ebook of *Dark Desserts*. Join my community and get firsthand news, enter the book discussions, ask your questions and chat with me. Please feel free to email me at Christine@ChristineFeehan.com. I would love to hear from you.

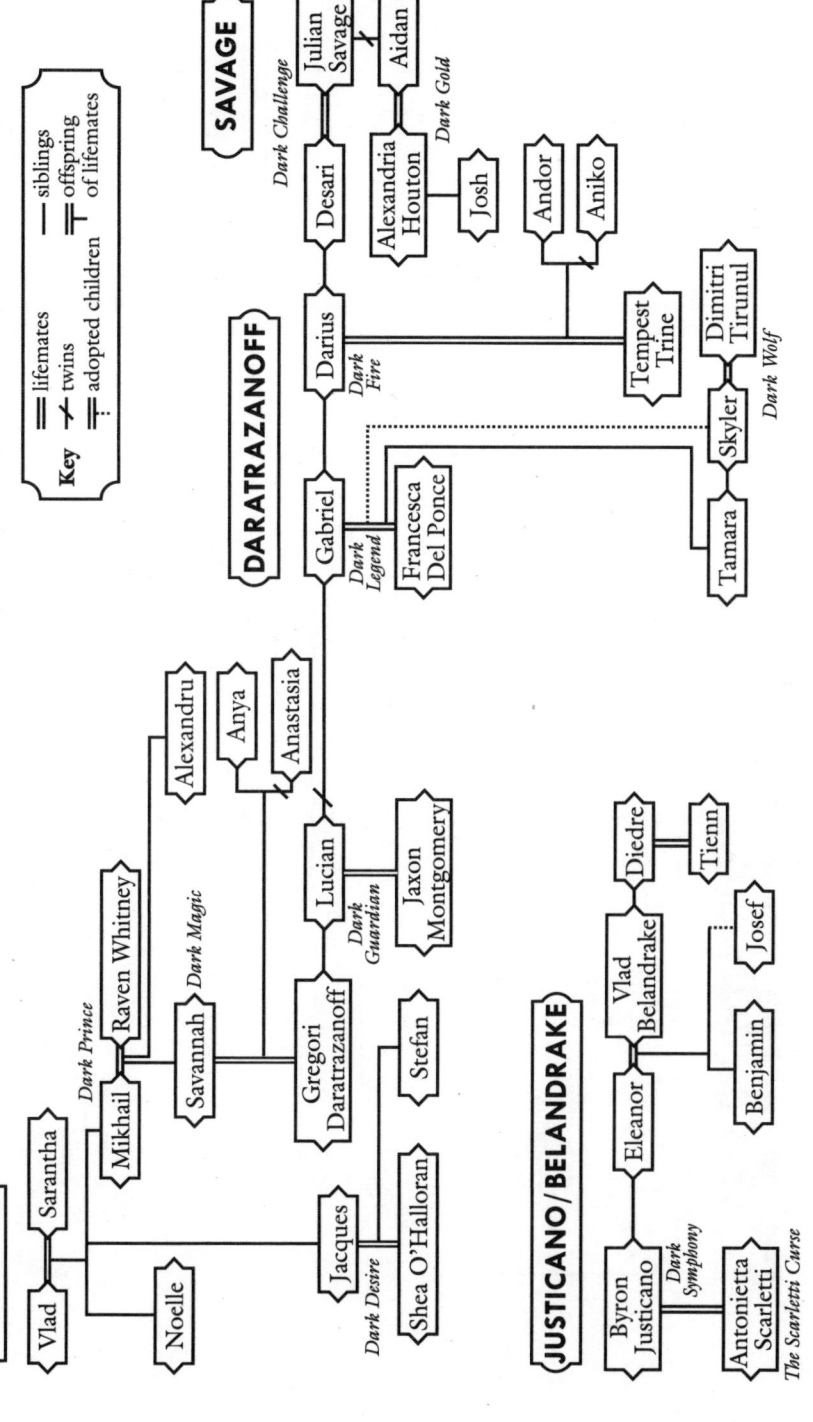

THE CARPATHIAN FAMILIES

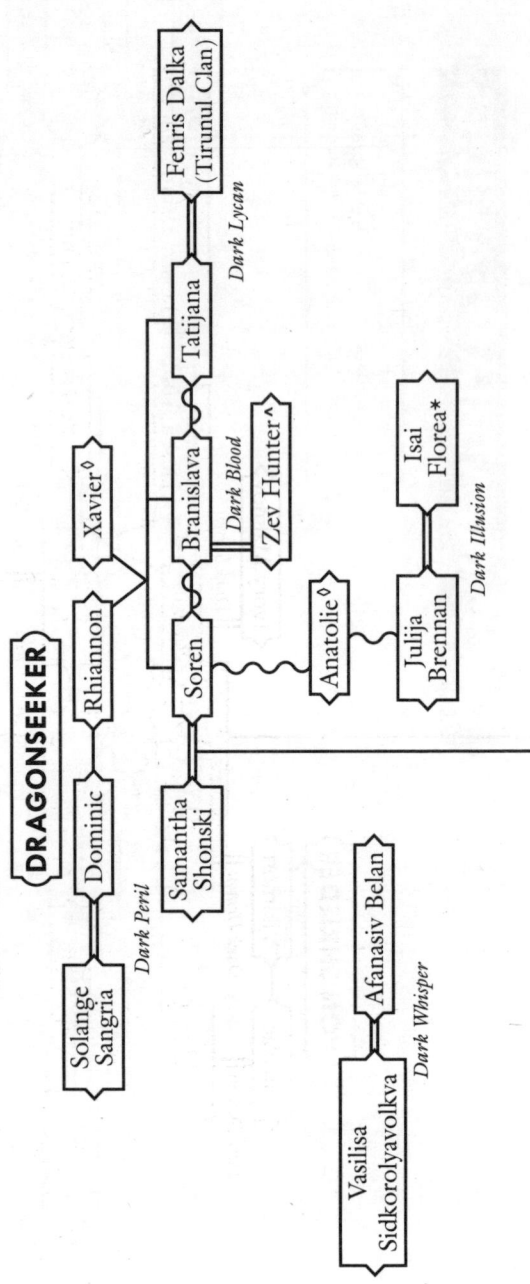

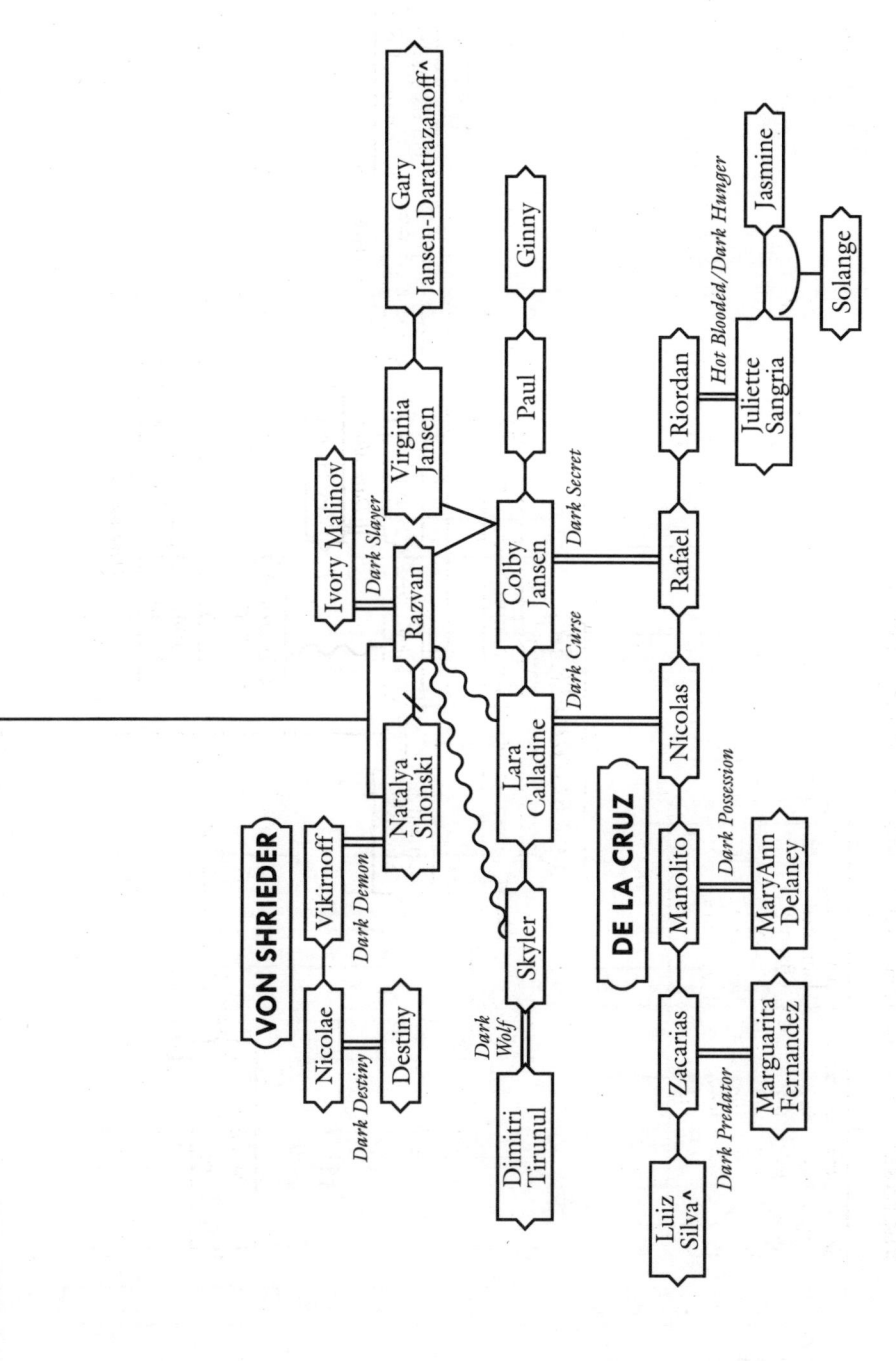

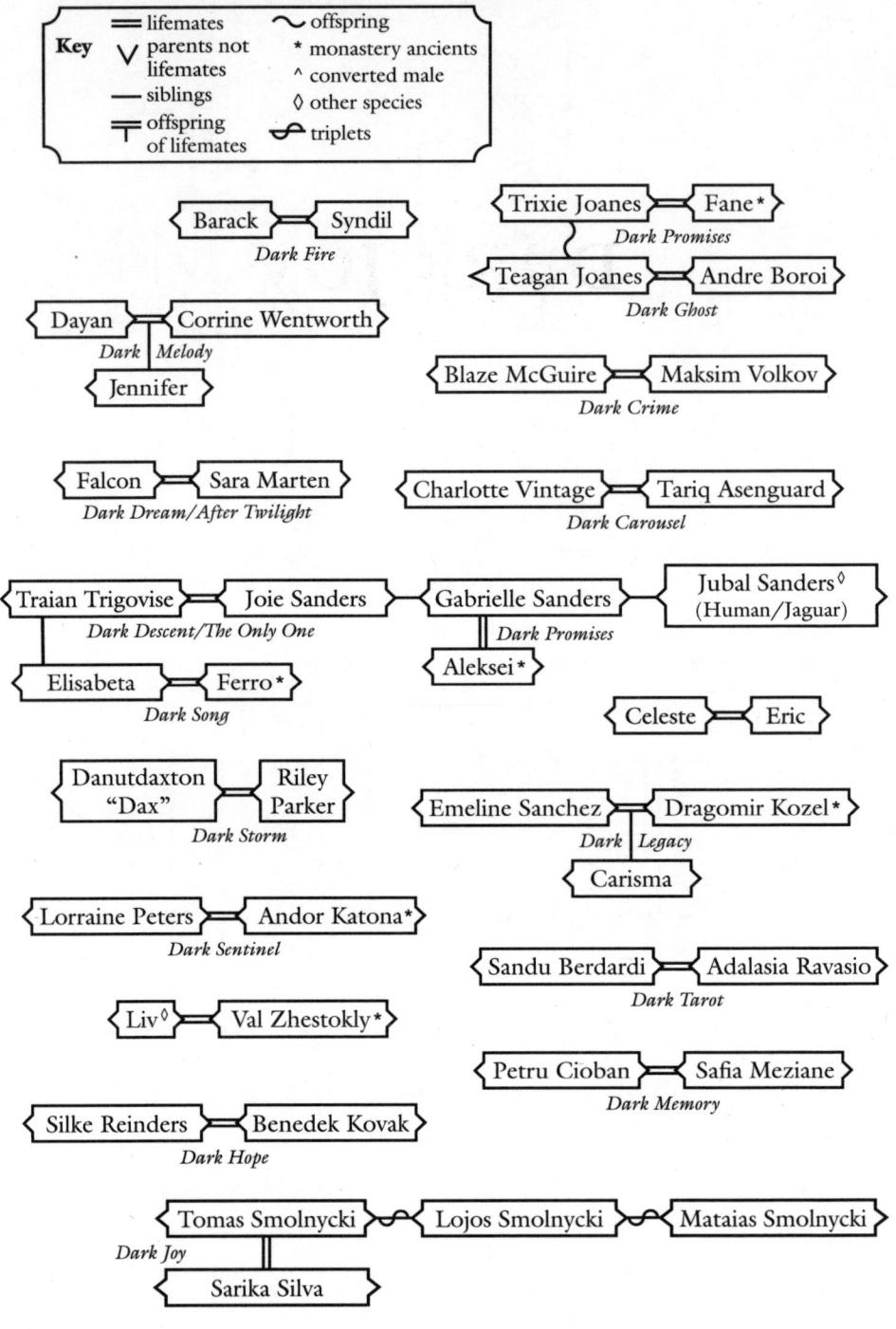

dark joy

CHAPTER 1

Just past sunset, a cool breeze slipped through the canopy as Sarika Silva stood on a boulder and peered up at the umbrella of branches far above her head. There was little light on the forest floor, and few plants thriving, yet there were hundreds of years of debris. Ferns and some smaller bushes managed to grow in the dark, dimly lit atmosphere.

She could hear the scurry of lizards and mice, of voles and beetles as they hurried back and forth preparing for the night and the host of predators emerging. She drew in a deep breath, taking in the amazing scents surrounding her. Scores of tree frogs of various species called back and forth to one another.

She held herself very still, trying not to attract attention. She had an unfortunate trait she hadn't yet found a way to rid herself of. All manner of wildlife found her fascinating. She reciprocated the feeling, which was fine at home when dogs and cats sought her out. Or the occasional bunny. But in the various rainforests she'd visited, the animals had been diverse and often quite dangerous.

It wasn't in her best interest to draw attention to herself. She'd had monkeys, sloths, capybaras and even gorillas seek her out. There had been ocelots, orangutans and countless other animals that showed up in camp or found her on the trails. Once a Bengal tiger. Herd animals followed her.

The rainforest was moody. Eerie. Mysterious. Beauty and danger went hand in hand in the rainforest. Sarika had spent time working in several around the world. This was her first visit to Peru, and to her shock, she felt as if she'd come home. The emotion was overwhelming, so much so that when she'd first stepped off the boat onto solid ground and made her way to the designated meeting place arranged with her guide, she had felt tears welling up. Her heart accelerated, and every single nerve ending came alive.

Alive. That was the true feeling. She felt intensely alive. It was such a weird, unexpected reaction when she'd spent several years studying the various rainforests. Her interest had begun when she was a little girl. She would read everything she could get her hands on, reading far above her grade level on conservation and especially jaguars and the way they were slowly going extinct. She wanted to find a way to save them, and it became the driving purpose of her education. Never once had she regretted her decision to save the jaguars.

Her hero was T. Smolnycki Sr., the leading expert in the field she was most interested in. She'd read everything he'd written, every paper he had produced. He was a conservationist, a biologist and a mammalogist. No matter how long she'd searched, she'd never managed to find a photo of him—or his son. His son went by T. Smolnycki Jr. When his father retired, he took over his work and became her new hero.

The father and son had worked tirelessly to establish conservation for the rainforests, but more importantly to her, they were passionate about the preservation of large cats, including jaguars. That passion came through in the various articles they had written and the worldwide organization they had founded. She found it interesting that Smolnycki Jr.'s papers sounded so similar to his father's writing. They had the same turns of phrase, the same eloquence. The research was always impeccable and had held up through the years, as had their conservation ideas.

When she was eight years old, she wrote to Smolnycki Jr. To her shock, he had answered her. They established a correspondence of sorts over the years. He had always encouraged her in her dream of saving the jaguars. He seemed to take her ideas seriously, never chiding her for suggesting various plans to him. At times he would point out very gently why a particular idea wouldn't work; other times he seemed excited about an idea she'd come up with.

T. Smolnycki Jr. often disappeared for months at a time. He would emerge from the wilderness to write another paper or pertinent article or spearhead the drive for the jaguar corridor spanning countries across the globe. His father had been her idol, and while she respected and admired him, she felt Smolnycki Jr. was more of a friend and mentor.

Sarika had gone into the same field as the two men. As she furthered her education, she became a veterinarian for exotic animals, specializing in cats. Along the way, she rounded out her education by becoming a biologist and conservationist. In the years she was getting her education, she made numerous trips to rainforests around the world, volunteering, studying and working, but she'd always avoided Peru.

Peru was home. Peru was where she'd been born into the world of jaguar shape-shifters. She should have been raised there, but instead, when her mother died in childbirth, her father had kept his son but sent her to be raised by his older brother, who lived in the United States.

Her uncle Alois and aunt Gemma had never been able to have children, and they'd welcomed her. Surrounded her with love. Given her every advantage. They had raised her in Maine, far away from others. To get to their estate, they used a Cessna to fly in and out, landing on the lake for access to their home. In a dense forest, they were surrounded by old growth, the little that was left from the days of intense logging.

She knew how to fly the Cessna and often would view from above the abundance of the many varieties of trees. There were dense populations of fir, spruce and pine. Yellow birch, paper birch, sugar maple and aspen dominated the stands of hardwood. What she loved most was the diversity of wildlife making their homes in the heavy tree-rich forest surrounding them.

She often flew the plane low enough to catch sight of moose, black bears, foxes, bobcats, deer and lynx. There was an abundance of raccoons, coyotes, porcupines and fishers. She always got a thrill when she spotted the local wildlife. When she backpacked and camped in the forest, many of the animals sought her out. Even then, she had to be careful that no one else witnessed the way animals seemed to want to be with her.

Mostly, what she loved about her life was the way her aunt and uncle taught her to shift from early childhood. She was a jaguar shifter, and her female, Coh, loved to run free in the haven of the forest. That was the reason her aunt and uncle had chosen to live in such a remote location. As jaguar shape-shifters, a very secretive species, they were careful never to allow anyone see them shift. As jaguars needed the forest to roam and stay healthy, her aunt and uncle had found the perfect place to live so that their animals could thrive.

She'd lost them both, first Alois and then Gemma. She loved them dearly and missed them every single day. Without them, she was lonely and felt vulnerable without the stability of a home. She'd traveled all over the world, was away for months, but they had always been there waiting for her. Now she was alone. She felt compelled to come to Peru and seek out her last remaining relative, hoping they would make a connection with each other.

Sarika inhaled deeply, taking in the scents of the Peruvian rainforest. So many. The earth smelled raw and musky. The flowers climbing the trees were fragrant and exotic. The explosion of color against the bark of the various species of trees was stunning. So many vivid colors of green interspersed with the brilliant colors of trumpet-shaped flowers, spidery flowers, orchids and so many others.

Despite the waning light, she found herself drawn to the interior. While the dense canopy overhead protected the forest floor from wind and even, to some extent, storms, the interior felt heavy with moisture. It seemed as though the drone of the crickets and cicadas never stopped. The darkness turned the jungle into an eerie, moody world.

She knew better than to walk too far into the interior. She had a very good sense of smell, especially if she shifted—which she was prepared to do. If necessary, she could utilize all the jaguar's abilities as well. Still, walking into an unfamiliar rainforest was sheer madness.

It was possible remnants of the male shifter jaguars were still around, men her adopted parents had warned her to always be leery of. She knew better, but she couldn't stop herself from moving deeper into the jungle, drawn by the magnificence and the feeling of coming home. She'd never once experienced that nearly euphoric, wondrous feeling of belonging until that moment, not a single time in all the various rainforests she'd visited.

The dark, moody interior called to her. Buttress roots formed giant fins beneath the trees, nearly as tall as she was, anchoring them against the winds. Aboveground, the storms could be wild, but the thick canopy kept the forest floor dark, humid and calm.

She took her time, going from tree to tree, examining the draping orchids and wild trumpets winding their way up the trunks. Sheer beauty. She was familiar with the various plants and their uses. So many were able to be used to make medicine. Others were poisonous. All of them held a beauty that drew her like a magnet.

A sudden chill slid down her spine, and she froze in place. Something—or someone—was watching her. Her radar went off, and it was never faulty. She judged how close she was to the riverbank. She'd wandered quite a distance examining the plants and trees, lost in her world of discovery when she should have been concerned for her safety.

From deep in the interior, a throaty cough sent adrenaline rushing through her veins. Her heart instantly began to pound. There was something about that sound that had goose bumps rising all over her skin and the tiny hairs on her body reacting. She became aware of every sound. There was a rustle in the leaves littering the forest floor straight ahead of her, and she remained unmoving, straining to hear whether it was a small rodent, a lizard or the whispery tread of the jaguar.

The jaguar, whether a shifter or a true cat, was the fiercest predator in the forest. Sarika found the formidable, elusive cat elegant and stately. It was also watchful and extremely wary. One didn't walk up on a jaguar and surprise it. It was the same with the jaguar shifters. Both species had excellent vision and hearing. The large cats and their shifter cousins hunted by sight and sound. In any case, that strange attraction animals had to her could be the reason the jaguar was closer than it should have been.

Sarika glanced behind her uncertainly. The jungle had closed behind her, cutting off her view of the riverbank. She knew the way out. She had an excellent sense of direction. As a shifter, she had that same ability to hunt with sight and hearing. She gleaned information from everything around her, but knowing a jaguar was on the prowl, most likely hunting this time of day, filled her with trepidation.

She'd spent far too much time studying the large cats to dismiss a hunter, although there were very few unprovoked attacks on humans. Still, they were deadly predators and certainly capable of hunting a human. Scary and fearless, the jaguar has the strongest bite of all cats, including tigers and lions. They have the ability to pierce through bone with razor-sharp teeth.

The intensity of the silence was broken by a sawing call. She was well aware that both the male and female jaguar could roar. When they greeted one another, they made a sound similar to a snuffling. They hunted day or night and killed with a powerful bite, usually to the back of the skull. The sound abruptly turned into a snarl that lifted every hair on her body. Then came the growling roar she most feared.

As apex predators, jaguars were at the top of the food chain with no natural enemies, other than their own species being a danger to them. Sarika was well aware she wasn't the largest person in the jungle.

Even if she tried to make herself appear bigger, she doubted if that would work.

If this jaguar was female and she had a den nearby, going forward could get her in trouble. It would be far better to get out of the trees. Sarika found herself hesitant to do that. Shifters were a secretive species. It had been drilled into her from the time she was a toddler that she could never reveal her true nature. Better to shift if she needed to defend herself there in the rainforest, out of sight.

It was just that . . . she had no fighting experience. That sawing roar was troublesome. It wasn't a greeting. It was a clear warning. She had a healthy respect for the powerful cats, and she would never want to endanger, hurt or kill one. She also thought it would be impossible for someone as inexperienced as she was to defeat a fully grown cat with fighting experience.

She was well aware jaguars could easily climb trees and leap long distances. She wouldn't be any safer in the water than she was on land. Jaguars were excellent swimmers, loved lakes, rivers and wetlands. They hunted in water.

"Not the smartest thing I've ever done," she murmured aloud.

"No, it wasn't." A male voice came from the darkened interior.

The unexpected reply set her heart pounding. She had concentrated so much on the jaguar that she had no indication a male was anywhere in the vicinity. She should have scented him. Sarika inhaled deeply, expecting to find out how close he was to her, but she got . . . nothing.

"I told you to stay out of the forest. To wait by the river for me." Now that voice was pure male, quiet but powerful. Velvet soft and compelling, but there was no mistaking the absolute authority.

"Luiz?" she asked. "Luiz Silva?"

"Luiz De La Cruz," the voice corrected.

Her heart skipped a beat. Fear washed over her. She certainly knew the name De La Cruz. They were notorious in both Peru and Brazil.

They owned more land than legal, their ranches expansive and guarded carefully. It was said they were ruthless. Enemies of the De La Cruz family tended to disappear.

"I thought I was corresponding with my cousin, Luiz Silva," she said, imposing strict discipline on herself. For some unexplained reason, she felt threatened. She couldn't say it was the voice exactly. He spoke in a low tone. It wasn't even the words he spoke or the fact that he'd identified himself as a De La Cruz. He felt dangerous. Powerful. She hadn't even seen him yet, but the warning that had preceded the jaguar came through just as clear. Maybe more so.

Sarika stood her ground, doing her best not to shake. The atmosphere had grown heavy. Threatening. The insects suddenly ceased their continuous noise. Monkeys screamed warnings and raced away, using the treetops.

"I have gone by the name of Silva," the voice informed her.

She blew out an exasperated breath. He could have just said that in the first place and not tried intimidating her with the De La Cruz name. Okay, he'd succeeded in intimidating her, which just annoyed the holy hell out of her.

"Seriously? You couldn't have led with that?" After all, if he was telling the truth and his name was really Luiz Silva, he was her cousin. She might be intimidated by the name De La Cruz and even a wild jaguar, but if he was her cousin, she wasn't going to allow him to scare her into submission. She wasn't that easily intimidated.

There was no real sound to warn her, not even the whisper of boots on leaves, but Luiz De La Cruz was suddenly standing in front of her, almost as if he had teleported, like in some science fiction movie. What was wrong with her? She should have been better prepared. She didn't like using a weapon, but she knew how and always carried something on her to protect herself. She'd traveled all over the world, studying in many different, very dangerous environments. Being a conservationist had taken her into many situations such as this one, and she'd always gone prepared.

Around her waist, she had her belt with a sheath containing a very sharp knife. While she was proficient in the use of it, the blade was her fail-safe, the last resort, should she be attacked by human, shifter or wild predator.

His eyebrow raised. "If you were going to use that, you should have already been prepared. What possessed you to come all this way and meet me alone?"

She didn't need him to ask her that question; she was already asking herself. She decided to be casual. "I travel alone to many countries and meet guides."

He studied her face, feature by feature, with a predator's stare. His eyes were intense, a vivid green flecked with gold, the irises ringed with amber. He had presence, appeared rugged, but there was something about him that was charismatic. Some quality that drew her to him, and she knew that same magic would work on others, male or female, he was around. At the same time, the predator in him was so strong that she knew he was far more than a man standing in front of her.

Luiz De La Cruz was mesmerizing, and that was scary. She felt almost frozen, the way one did when looking into the eyes of a large cat hunting. Her body reacted on its own, recognizing the extreme danger, yet couldn't move. Every hair on her body reacted; goose bumps rose. She had to work to keep her heart and lungs under control. A predator smelled fear. Hearing was acute. He would know she feared him; he most likely already did.

"Do you think that's such a good idea?"

She tried a brief smile, hoping to connect with her cousin. She was certain he was her uncle's son. She'd never met his father or this man, but it wasn't like she had much in the way of family. As far as she knew, Luiz was all that was left after the deaths of her adoptive parents. "Not at this precise moment."

"You're safer with me than you've ever been in your life."

Arrogant much? She didn't say it aloud. And she almost believed he could make her safer than anyone else she'd ever been around—unless he changed his mind and decided she was a threat. Then, all bets were off.

"You were raised by Uncle Alois, my father's oldest brother, and his wife, Gemma. I'm very sorry for your loss."

For some reason, that simple sentiment had a lump rising in her throat. She choked it down. It was an odd way of expressing sympathy. Other than her, Alois and Gemma had been his only relatives. She decided to address the issue immediately.

"Yes, my father sent me away when I was not yet a year."

"You were happy?" He sounded as if he really wanted to know.

"I have absolutely no regrets, although it would have been wonderful to meet my father and brother. I have always been extremely happy in my life with my aunt and uncle. They surrounded me with love, even during my rebellious teenage years. They allowed me to pursue all my interests and get an excellent education, and gave me as many advantages as they could."

"Perhaps they should have instilled a deeper sense of self-preservation in you."

There was no reprimand in his tone, but she took *great* exception to his critique of her aunt and uncle. She narrowed her eyes at him. "They took me in when my father didn't want to keep me. I was surrounded by love. They gave me everything. Don't you dare say one word against them."

Silence followed her outburst. It seemed as though the jungle itself held its breath right along with her. It wasn't as if his expression changed. He didn't appear angry. He simply watched her with the intense focus of a jaguar. He might say he was a De La Cruz, but he was also a predatory cat. There was absolutely no doubt in her mind. Luiz might be her cousin, but he was a stranger to her, and she was hissing at him like an outraged female jaguar—which she was. But she had brains, and she was alone. It wasn't the smartest idea to challenge a male jaguar shifter. He was at the top of the food chain there in the rainforest and very used to being the complete authority. That was stamped into every line of his face.

"Perhaps there is a small misunderstanding between us," Luiz said. "I didn't mean to imply my uncle and aunt hadn't given you a good life or education. It's clear to me that you feel at home in the rainforest. My comment was more about you and your lack of self-preservation."

She couldn't argue that she'd taken all the safety precautions possible. She hadn't. She'd allowed the jungle to close in behind her. She wasn't as prepared as she could have been to shift. She'd even come alone to meet a guide she had never met. None of those things were intelligent.

"It is also necessary to correct a misconception regarding your father, Uncle Javier. I was eighteen when you were born, so very aware of what happened during that time. Your brother was sixteen. Your mother had difficulty with pregnancies, and no one thought she would have another child after sixteen years, least of all Uncle Javier. Our world was ruled by a very savage and clearly insane shifter. We referred to him as Brodrick the Terrible. He changed the entire history of our people and nearly drove us to extinction. He was aided by vampires and mages, but he was responsible."

Sarika lifted an eyebrow at the word *vampire*. She wasn't about to interrupt him when she wanted to hear the history of her family. She wanted to be ready to learn everything she could about who she was and how she could help her people as well as the wild jaguars slowly facing extinction. That was the reason she had waited so long to come to Peru. But vampires? Her uncle and aunt had never once mentioned vampires to her.

"Please continue."

"The women were being rounded up and killed if they didn't have the genetics Brodrick felt they should have. It didn't matter the age of the female or if their jaguar had shown itself."

"What was his reasoning? Without females a species would die out."

"He felt too many females had mixed children. Many of the male shifters weren't staying with the females to help raise their young. Many of our women turned to human males to have a stable home. Brodrick wanted every child of those unions killed if he could prove they couldn't shift. He either forced the women to have shifter children or he killed them. It was a very brutal time, and you were born right into that mess."

Sarika knew there had been some kind of conflict going on with the jaguar shifters. She thought it was a power play to take over leadership. She didn't know a great deal about the politics of the shifter world. She was raised with a strict code of honor and discipline. She assumed most jaguars were raised with that same code. Evidently, she was wrong.

"Your mother died in childbirth, leaving your father with a newborn child. A female. Uncle Javier and my father were part of a small coalition trying to stop Brodrick. That put you in direct danger. As a female, you were the one most at risk, and Uncle Javier knew that. He didn't want Brodrick to know of your existence. Our lineage was one Brodrick sought for females."

"So my father sent me away to protect me."

Luiz nodded slowly. His gaze never left hers. Never left her face. Looked directly into her eyes. It was impossible to think he was being dishonest. The thing was, there was no inflection in his voice, just that soft, velvety purr that was mesmerizing. He was dangerous in so many ways. He could make anyone believe anything he said—yet she knew he was telling her the truth.

"Your father and brother tried to rescue several females being held prisoner, and they were killed on that raid. My father was killed two years later on a similar raid. I spent months healing from wounds. I wasn't the only one, but after those battles, fewer males would join us. Things were very ugly for several years."

She had been safe in the United States, living a good life. No, a great life. Here, in this beautiful rainforest, a war had taken place.

Worse, it was an internal war, their species being destroyed from the inside out.

"Many of the jaguar males became aggressive and felt it was their right to take any female they wanted. Brodrick's example gave them permission to become worse than animals."

"Is it still going on?"

"Brodrick is dead, but there are still a few jaguar males who haven't realized they are going to be hunted if they attack one of our females."

She couldn't detect a change in his voice or demeanor, but she shivered. A cold chill went down her spine. She had the feeling he would bring jungle justice to any jaguar he found attacking a woman. That should have made her feel safe with him, but he gave off a vibe that was just plain scary. She also didn't like the way he put that—*still a few jaguar males who haven't realized they are going to be hunted if they attack one of our females*. As if those males didn't know right from wrong and would only avoid attacking a female if someone was watching and willing to hunt them down to administer justice.

It wasn't as if a female shifter could go to the police. Shifters lived under shifter law, not human law. The women couldn't go outside their species for aid. That left them at the mercy of their rulers. If the ruler was corrupt, his people would follow his example. She tried to hide the delicate shudder his revelation had produced.

"On a happier note, you came at just the right time," Luiz continued.

"I did?" She pounced on that. She needed a safe, happy subject to regain her equilibrium.

"There's a large celebration being planned right now, and several of the women have arrived to help with preparations."

"A celebration?" She echoed his announcement, mainly to give her mind time to process the switch from dangerous jaguar males to celebrations. "Shifters?" She would really welcome meeting others. She had so much catching up to do. She had counted on her cousin to give her the history of the shifters and jaguars in the Peru rainforest, but

Luiz didn't seem as if he was going to be that accommodating. In fact, he seemed as if he would give her lectures and leave her to her own devices. Or force her to leave.

"One of the women, Solange Sangria Dragonseeker, is pregnant. She's shifter royalty, and her lifemate, Dominic, is . . ." He broke off abruptly, for the first time giving her the impression he was hesitant as to how to explain Dominic Dragonseeker.

Sarika wasn't positive why she thought he was exasperated with trying to impart information to her because his demeanor hadn't changed at all, nor had his tone. Still, she was good at reading people, and he was a bit at a loss.

"Did Alois talk to you about Carpathians?"

Was there a note of resignation in his voice? Or judgment of her uncle? Alois had been his uncle as well. She detested admitting she knew nothing of Carpathians because she was certain Luiz would disapprove.

She tilted her chin at him. "I'm aware of the Carpathian Mountains, but no, we never spoke specifically of their inhabitants."

Luiz held up his hand and examined the surrounding forest in a long, slow perusal. Sarika hadn't detected a change in the drone of insects or the fluttering of wings as birds settled in for the night. Several monkeys screamed but then fell abruptly silent, sending chills down her spine.

She'd always had an awareness when she was in a jungle. She was a shifter, regardless of living most of her life as a human. Her jaguar was always on alert in a rainforest, yet she didn't feel the warning until Luiz alerted. Suddenly, she was very certain there were eyes on them. All along, she had thought the threat emanated from Luiz, but now she felt that same warning blaring through her body, her cells going on alert. Luiz hadn't been the threat. There was something else out there watching them.

"We've stayed here too long. I'm going to take you to my home. I don't stay there, but you'll be safe and able to rest. Tomorrow evening I will take you to meet Dominic and Solange."

She looked carefully around. "Something is out there." She was absolutely certain she'd felt the danger all along and attributed it to Luiz.

"A male jaguar. He's been creeping closer for the last fifteen minutes. He was stalking you as I came up on you. I warned him off, but he didn't leave."

That had been the sawing roar she'd heard. Luiz telling the jaguar to back off. It hadn't.

"Is he animal or shifter? Is it possible for you to tell the difference?" She didn't think she could, but it was clear Luiz was at home in the rainforest. He'd lived his entire life there. He certainly could have developed a way to tell. Scent didn't give it away, and she didn't know any other way that might discern the difference unless she . . . Her hand crept up to cover the amulet she always wore against her skin.

"Yes, I can even identify him specifically. His name is Percy Rios. I've had my eyes on him for some time. He's been prowling around very close to Dominic and Solange's territory. Solange has relatives who visit her often. In fact, they're expected very soon. Juliette Sangria, her cousin, is lifemate to Riordan De La Cruz. They're on their way. Her cousin Jasmine is married to Jubal Sanders. Both women and Jasmine's daughter, Sandrine, are jaguar."

"And you think this Percy Rios is looking to acquire one of them for himself." She made it a statement.

"He's stalking you."

That was his answer? That made no sense. "How would he know I'm a jaguar shifter?" She wasn't challenging his judgment so much as really needing to know. She thought she'd come prepared, but she was fast learning she didn't know the first thing about the environment or the species she'd been born into.

"You smell like a female shifter."

She winced. She didn't like the sound of that. "That's just lovely." Her voice dripped with sarcasm.

He didn't so much as smile. She had the feeling emotions like humor or sarcasm were lost on him. There was no faint smile in his eyes. Nothing at all. No emotion. Just those flat, cold eyes that were so intense that although they felt like ice, the ice burned wherever his gaze touched.

"No disrespect intended, Sarika. Were you aware Sarika was your mother's name?"

She had been, but her aunt and uncle had never really talked about her mother, other than to mention in passing that her birth father had named her after her mother.

Luiz's attention appeared to be centered solely on her, but Sarika knew it wasn't so. He no longer scanned their surroundings for evidence of the male jaguar. He knew exactly where the large predator was. Deliberately, she raised her face to the canopy and inhaled the scent of flowers, shrubs, trees and the forest floor. Along with those scents came the information on the multitude of wildlife around them.

The jaguar male had to be downwind, but she caught enough hints of him being close enough to raise the alarm. She couldn't pinpoint his exact position.

"How do you know where he is?"

"I smell him as well."

"He's downwind," she protested. "He has to be, or I would smell him."

Luiz didn't look impatient, but she felt his impatience. "I am not only a jaguar shifter, I am also Carpathian. We will discuss what Carpathians are once I have you safe in my home."

Did that mean Carpathians could smell even better than shifters? Carpathians were born in the Carpathian Mountains, weren't they? He wasn't making any sense. She could believe that he was of another species entirely. Was that what he was implying? That Carpathians were another species? It wouldn't be so difficult to believe, after all—no one would ever believe in shifters, yet she was one.

Luiz Silva De La Cruz was her only living relative. She wanted to have a decent relationship with him. It made no sense that she was irritated with him. What had he said or done to cause her to be so nervous in his presence?

"I have all my things in my backpack," she announced, deciding to risk it. She hadn't come all this way to be a coward.

"I will carry you. It will be much faster that way."

CHAPTER 2

"True black is the absence of light," Tomas Smolnycki told his brothers, Mataias and Lojos. "Technically, it isn't a color."

Mataias gave an exaggerated sigh. "At least you aren't lecturing us on saving the rainforest and all its inhabitants."

"That's coming," Lojos warned. "You know how he is."

The three were triplets. Tomas and Lojos nearly always had opposite points of view, and Mataias was the peacemaker. Down through the centuries, their discussions had become habit more than anything else. By taking different sides of an argument, they were able to look at situations completely rather than just one-sidedly. They always gave input on every subject to one another. Many times, throughout the centuries, those varying points of view had saved their lives.

"I find, as the years go by," Tomas said, "that the two of you are becoming more contrary than ever. And perhaps you're losing your faculties. Slipping just a bit."

"It makes no sense that, as Carpathian hunters who have lost the ability to see color, we see gray and not black, if black is the absence of color," Lojos said.

"He does have a point, Tomas," Mataias pointed out. "We do not have the side of our souls that provides light. We are wholly dark and without color or emotion other than remembered, so how is it we see in gray rather than in black?"

Tomas heaved a sigh. "Seriously? Because we see in gray versus black doesn't negate the fact that black isn't truly a color. It's the absence of light."

"So you say," Lojos said.

"It's a science-based fact. I didn't just make it up," Tomas said.

"Everything with you is supposedly science based," Lojos protested. "How many times, over the centuries we've been alive, has science proven itself wrong? Everyone is told one thing as absolute fact, and then a century later someone disproves that theory, because it turns out it wasn't a fact after all. It was a theory."

Tomas paused in his argument to take a slow, careful scan of the dark forest around them. *We're being stalked.* He used the telepathic communication the three brothers had used for centuries. *Three in the trees ahead. Three coming up behind us. Three in root systems of the trees to our left and right.*

He continued their conversation in a mild, even tone. "You probably are still going to give me your ridiculous theory on why the earth is flat, not round."

It isn't Justice. Mataias named the beast they hunted. He wasn't quite vampire. At least as far as they could ascertain. He was *more.* Much more dangerous than a vampire—or a Carpathian hunter. Justice had been one of the legendary ancients, the one about which stories were handed down through the centuries.

"It wasn't my ridiculous theory," Lojos objected aloud, not giving away the fact that they knew they were being hunted. "I merely told you about it."

Do you think it is possible Justice recruited the undead to stop us? Lojos asked his brothers, staying to the telepathic means of communication when asking pertinent questions. *He knows we're on his trail, and he knows we won't stop until he is dead—or we are.*

"You did defend it," Mataias contributed.

We don't yet know what he's capable of, Tomas answered. *I wouldn't think he would have had the time. Nicu went to warn the prince and to help guard him, but we set out immediately after Justice. But again, we don't know his full capabilities.*

Tomas was several steps ahead of his brothers, taking the lead, which he normally did when they were hunting the undead. He was the bait. A man wrapped up in his philosophical discussion and seemingly unaware of his surroundings. Tomas always looked the part of a scholar when he became the bait.

The triplets wore their chestnut-colored hair long and pulled back at the nape of their necks. All three had peculiar aquamarine-colored eyes. Tomas had teardrop-shaped scarring from the edge of his hairline to his jaw on his right side. Sometimes, like now, when he wanted to lull his opponents into a false sense of security, he wore black-framed glasses to enhance the first impression of being an easy target.

The three in the tree roots are beginning to grow restless. They haven't gotten the command from their master to attack, but they won't be able to hold much longer, Mataias warned.

Tomas gave a fleeting thought to the possibility that Justice had turned vampire and had recruited these lesser vampires. He had no doubt that when Justice turned, he wouldn't go through the disorienting stage most Carpathians did when first turning.

The brothers had hunted the vampire for so many centuries it seemed like child's play to them. In the world of Carpathians, they had a certain reputation, but all three knew from their vast experience that battling vampires was a dangerous business. Not that they thought about the danger. It was their job. They gave little thought to wounds, mortal or otherwise.

They were Carpathians, ancient hunters of the vampire. Throughout the long centuries, even their prey had changed, developing the ability to band together and fight as a unit. That hadn't changed the ultimate goal for the hunters—keeping others safe from the undead. It did, however, change strategies. They learned from each battle.

"I wasn't defending such a ludicrous theory, I was merely informing you so you had ideas to make your head explode," Lojos informed his brothers. "We've traveled the world numerous times, and we've never fallen off the edge."

"We've never even come to an edge," Mataias said. "Seriously, Lojos, how would you ever endorse such an idiotic theory?"

Tomas didn't look skyward, but he began to build a storm, the dark clouds drifting across the sky, slowly blotting out the stars and moon. In a few of the darker clouds, veins of lightning sparked jagged lines, coloring the dark gray with a lighter shade.

"Are you going to deliberately misunderstand me, adding to the discussion on the world being round or flat? There are numerous theories. If Tomas wants to play the part of the mad scientist, then I think he should be aware of every theory before he decides which one he ascribes to."

The earth is shuddering. Those attempting to conceal themselves in the roots are poisoning the ground, Lojos warned the others.

Perhaps it is best to draw them out. I had hoped to wait until they are surrounding us completely and we know exactly where their master is, Tomas replied.

You do like things easy, Mataias said.

As easy and as efficient as possible, Tomas agreed.

He deliberately allowed his hand to brush against the thorny bark of one of the tall kapok trees. The spines, or conical thorns, gave the giant tree a menacing appearance. It was also perfect to feign cutting one's hand carelessly as many visitors to the rainforest did. A Carpathian wouldn't have gotten cut, but if he did, he would have closed the wound immediately.

Tomas had assumed the role of a professor, one he was quite familiar with. Swearing, he brought his injured palm to his mouth and then shook it as if it stung. As he did, he flung tiny droplets of blood into the air. Improbably, at that precise moment, a breeze seemed to drop through the canopy, setting off several small eddies of leaves and twigs on the forest floor. At the same time, that slight wind dispersed the drops of blood throughout the air. The droplets appeared like tiny rubies glittering in the weird streak of light that shone through the canopy.

Mataias kept his hand close to his chest as he manipulated the still air, producing the slight breeze that would send his brother's ancient Carpathian blood straight to the concealed vampires. No vampire, not even a master, could resist the lure of ancient blood. He had stepped in front of Tomas, right into the pathway of the three vampires concealed just ahead of them, ready to spring their ambush.

Lojos paused for a moment, bending down on the pretext of tying his boot, putting his body right in the middle of the three trees whose root systems housed the eager vampires. Deliberately, he didn't look at the jutting fins of roots, rather fussed over meticulously tying the cords on his boot as if to tighten them.

Tomas dropped back from his brothers, putting his hand to his mouth as if the stinging wound could be soothed that way. In truth, his healing saliva closed the tiny laceration. He stood swaying a little, looking around him at the trees and shrubs, studiously avoiding looking behind him.

Evil had a smell. A presence. The undead weren't simply pure evil; they were abominations. Nature shrank from contact with them. Their poisonous touch caused every living thing to wither and die. The ground groaned and trembled when their feet touched it. Trees split in two. The leaves and fronds on brush and fern turned black and broke apart. The undead delighted in killing. It mattered little if it was plants, wildlife or human. They lived for cruel torture and the destruction of all living things.

Movement in the roots. The three are emerging, Tomas warned Lojos. *I still haven't located their master.*

Tomas, like his brothers, was pragmatic about not always knowing exactly what they were up against—or who. It mattered little. Over the centuries, they had been forced to battle and dispose of friends, and even family. Cousins. They had learned from experience that vampires could not be recovered. The Carpathian they once had been was long gone—dead to their world. It was only an evil entity left behind in a rotting body.

The trees shivered and shook. Leaves tumbled to the ground as branches cracked ominously, splitting apart so that dark, poisonous sludge oozed in thick streams down trunks. The large fin-shaped roots shuddered and creaked in protest. The ground rippled, then rolled and pitched as if trying to dislodge something foul from its depths.

Lojos stood slowly, turning to face the three vampires as they emerged from the root system and spread out in an attempt to surround him. Long tongues, like those of lizards, darted out in an attempt to capture the droplets of blood that had been dispersed in the air. The three were dressed similarly, in dark trousers and lighter shirts. To Lojos, they appeared in shades of gray. Their attire didn't impress him any more than their hair. They looked as if they wore ill-fitting wigs.

The strange thing was their faces were oddly familiar. Or at least, they had the appearance of being triplets—triplets that imitated Lojos and his brothers' features. They didn't come close by any means, but the resemblance was there—faintly, but there. To his knowledge, they didn't have cousins who were triplets.

Take a look at these three, he advised his brothers. *Do they remind you of anyone?*

Change your appearance, Lojos, Tomas ordered. *All of us should. They look too much like us for it to be coincidence. Try to engage them in conversation. We need to know what they're up to.*

Does our hair look like that? Mataias asked.

I certainly hope not, Tomas said. *That hair is more appalling than their twisted faces. Surely, we don't look as bad as that lot.*

If we do, our brethren should have warned us, Lojos said.

Tomas turned away from the three vampires to face the new ones hurrying behind them to seal off any retreat. They emerged from three different locations, their attire far too similar to the three accosting Lojos. Only their faces and hair were different. He stared at them for a moment, aware that their appearance had thrown him off.

When he had advised his brothers to change their appearance, he had done the same. Looking at the three vampires rushing to cut him off from the others, had it been possible for him to feel astonishment, he would have. Not wanting his brothers to turn from their tasks, he sent them images of the three he faced.

The vampire on his left wore his atrocious hair falling to his waist in what appeared to be a bird's nest of tangles. Worse, clumps were missing from his scalp, while other places had far too much hair shooting up in a ridiculous manner like sprouts.

He is definitely attempting to look like Benedek. He named an ancient they had been traveling with a week earlier. *Thank the stars we know Benedek's hair is not so hideous.*

Good grief. Why would they want to appear as such buffoons? Lojos asked.

Look at this one, Tomas advised, showing the vampire approaching from his right. *His hair is worse than Benedek the imposter.* He sent the image of the vampire to his brothers. *He must be imitating Petru.*

Petru was another ancient who had found his lifemate in the hills above Dellys, Algeria, on the Mediterranean Sea.

His hair is exploding out of his head like a whitish-gray pelt found from roadkill, Mataias observed. *Good grief, you don't suppose he ran across a dead animal and tried to use its fur for hair?*

What has hair that long? Lojos asked. *And why is it lopsided on him?*

I do wish I could take a quick picture and send it to Petru, Tomas said. He held up his hand to stop the rush of the three vampires. "Hold. I recognize you as our legendary ancients." He did his best to pour awe and respect into his voice.

The three imposters stumbled to a halt, giving him time to show the last image to his brothers, that of the vampire who had been heading straight at him. *This one is a very poor replica of Nicu. His hair is likely supposed to be black—you know, that absence of color. Looks gray to me and as if it has never been washed. I swear there are maggots in it.*

"I am here with my traveling companions hunting vampire. We never expected to run into ancients such as yourselves."

My adversaries have arrived, Mataias said, sending the images to his brothers. *Again, they are impersonating ancients.* The three had stumbled to a halt as Mataias bowed low in greeting.

The first image Mataias sent his brothers was of a vampire with a face that could have been that of one of their ancient brethren, Dragomir. Dragomir had found his lifemate, Emeline, and certainly hadn't turned vampire. The horrendous display of hair on his head was nearly Tomas' downfall. Tomas wished he had a real sense of humor. By staying together, the triplets had retained a semblance of humor. It was more remembered than real, but he knew the situation and the appearances of the vampires impersonating ancients would have been hysterically funny. He was definitely going to keep the images in his head so that when he came across his friends, he could show them.

The fake Dragomir's hair was parted in the middle and slicked back from his head with some oily substance. Several chunks hung from the scalp as if the vampire had used a toupee and haphazardly glued it in place.

The second vampire Mataias faced was no doubt meant to be Valentin Zhestokly. He resided in the United States, as did Dragomir. Val's lifemate, too young to claim, lived in San Diego, and the Carpathian hunter would never leave her without his protection. The body was nearly emaciated, and again, the hair was atrocious. Only aspects of the face allowed them to recognize who the vampire was attempting to be.

The third vampire was no doubt meant to be Ferro, another ancient who had found his lifemate, Elisabeta, and resided in the States.

Any ideas on why they would be impersonating ancients? Lojos asked.

It would have to be their master's idea, Tomas mused.

Justice, then? He would know every ancient, although not what happened to them or where they would be, Mataias ventured.

Tomas kept his attention centered on the three vampires, who were sniffing the air and testing it with long, chameleonlike tongues. The reptiles could have tongues up to forty-seven inches in length, and the tongues testing the air for droplets of Carpathian blood seemed that long or longer.

He gave a short bow toward the three vampire imposters cutting him off from his brothers, doing his best to appear respectful and not quite bright. "What service may we offer you?" he asked.

The three imposters exchanged gleeful looks. The one pretending to be Benedek answered in a voice that was more a growl than an actual voice. "We have been hunting these long nights and are near starving after our battles."

"Offer freely of your healing blood, brother," the imposter Petru said eagerly.

You believe Justice has finally turned vampire? Mataias asked.

Tomas hoped not. It would be difficult enough to track and kill the beast, let alone a combination of beast and vampire, but his reluctance had nothing to do with that. He would do his duty to his people and humanity without question. Justice was a legendary Carpathian. He had followed his code of honor for more centuries than any other. In the end, he had sacrificed his life and sanity for his brethren, saving them and condemning himself to a torturous existence in the very bowels of hell.

It is possible he has turned vampire, but more likely he persuaded the nine to impersonate ancients to throw us off. After all those centuries of living by his code of honor, Tomas believed Justice might be insane, but he doubted if he would become vampire. Maybe he just wanted to believe there was still hope for his brothers and himself.

To what purpose? Lojos asked. *What would he believe he could gain from such a parody?*

A delaying tactic? Tomas ventured.

We do not know it is Justice, Mataias said. *If it isn't and a master vampire is close, we will have to be prepared for his attack.*

It was unnecessary advice—they had been battling vampires for centuries—but those continual reminders aided them in never becoming complacent.

The imposters spread out, circling each of the ancients, sniffing the air, trying to find the trail to the elusive scent of ancient blood. They swayed back and forth, long, hard nails clicking together, feet stomping into the ground in a locking pattern very familiar to the ancient hunters.

"Come to me," the Benedek imposter ordered. "Give me your blood to sustain me on these endless hunts."

Obediently, Tomas bent his head toward his wrist as he stumbled forward two steps and appeared to trip. At once, the three vampires rushed him.

Out of the corner of his eye he observed the three vampires nearest Lojos swaying and chanting, their hands in the air.

A locking spell, Lojos, he warned.

His brother would recognize the mesmerizing patterns the imposters created to hold Lojos in place, making it less dangerous for them to approach, but the warning would serve to remind his brothers, as well as himself, of the various tricks vampires often used.

The three vampires facing Mataias didn't bother with niceties or pretending to be civil. They rushed the ancient, confident they had him trapped and helpless.

Tomas slid across the ground seconds before the three imposters reached him. As he did, he targeted the legs of fake Benedek, hitting at full speed with centuries of experience striking his target. He knew exactly where to hit on the body to do the most damage. His heels slammed into Benedek's knees, shattering them. It only takes eighty pounds of pressure to break a kneecap. He applied far more than that.

He moved with lightning speed. As Benedek began to topple, screaming and shrieking, Tomas drove his fist into the imposter's chest, fingers seeking the withered, desiccated organ. The momentum of the heavy body crashing to the ground aided him in dragging the decayed heart from the chest. He leapt behind the writhing, cursing vampire and simultaneously tossed the heart into the air while calling down the lightning.

The jagged bolt answered his summons, piercing the blackened heart dead center as it tumbled from the sky. The trajectory of the bolt continued, unerringly finding the Benedek imposter, reducing him to tiny ashes.

In the ensuing shocked silence, Tomas streaked through the air straight at the vampire impersonating Petru. The vampire hadn't even fully turned to try to comprehend or react to what had happened in the mere seconds it had taken Tomas to destroy fake Benedek. Tomas slammed his fist through the rib cage, found the withered heart with strong fingers and began to extract it.

Imposter Petru shrieked and buried his talons into Tomas' chest, ripping great gouges of flesh away—or he tried to. Tomas had armor in the thin material of his clothing, a kind of natural silk that was strong enough to break the thick talons the vampire was trying to use against him.

There was no way to stop the acid blood pouring over his hand and forearm as Tomas extracted the heart. The acid burned through flesh and muscle straight to the bone. Tomas cut off all feeling of pain and jerked the heart free, swinging fake Petru's body around as he did so in order to place the vampire between him and the one impersonating Nicu.

The shrunken heart made a terrible sucking sound as it was extracted from the body. The sound accompanied the earsplitting screams of the vampire as he thrashed and fought to get away from Tomas. Tomas shoved his body into the imposter Nicu as he threw the heart into the air and called down the lightning.

Black blood spurted onto the fake Nicu's chest and face, thousands of parasites wiggling over him as the vampire impersonating Petru fell backward. Nicu landed on him, face down, screaming and beating at the vampire, tearing at him with his teeth.

Lightning incinerated the heart in midair and jumped to the jerking, thrashing body just as Nicu shoved him off and to one side. Foul smoke rose in clouds as the body blackened and turned to ash.

The imposter Nicu rolled and rolled to get away from the burning vampire, yelling for his master the entire time. He spun around onto his belly, digging claws into the ground as he tried to crawl away from Tomas.

Tomas leapt after him with lightning speed, landing on his back, driving him into the ground, knees planted firmly as he drove his fist through bone and muscle to find the heart. It was a much more difficult route going in through a vampire's back, but Tomas had perfected the technique over the centuries, and he was relentless.

Ignoring the way the vampire's body contorted in an attempt to shift, Tomas pushed his fist deeper in an effort to extract the heart. He had disposed of the first two vampires in record time. Not two minutes had gone by, and he'd killed two of the undead. The shock value was apparent, disorienting all the vampires who had been expecting easy prey.

The vampire imitating Nicu continued to scream for aid, and in answer, vines of thorns burst through the soil to stab into Tomas' legs and shoulders, anywhere the venomous plants could reach. While trying to pull Tomas off the imposter Nicu, the vines had no way of knowing which body was which. They stabbed and wrapped up Nicu right along with Tomas. The fact that the master vampire had answered the call for aid gave Tomas a direction.

He didn't flinch or try to remove the vicious vines, but he immediately shared with his brothers the impression of where the master might be concealed.

He is closer than expected. As always, he was steady and calm. No one would ever have known he was being attacked, the vines trying to imprison him.

The thorns are acting as needles. Be careful of these vines. Stay away from the ground if at all possible. The vines themselves seem to be tubes.

The thorns stabbed at him over and over in an effort to penetrate his armor.

Clearly, the goal is getting my blood, not aiding this foul one the master has tied me to. What he did not consider is that those tubes are easily followed right back to him.

He does not expect you to live, Lojos said. *It still hasn't occurred to him that he is dealing with some of the ancients he had his minions impersonate.*

Is it time to allow him to see who we are? Mataias asked.

Tomas didn't look at his brothers. He was well aware each of them was fighting the three vampires who had targeted them. Ignoring the black blood coating his arm and fist, Tomas relentlessly stayed to his goal.

My vote would be to hold off until I dispose of this one and am able to hunt their master. When he realizes we are ancients, he may run, he said.

I think that would be best as well, Mataias agreed. *Lojos?*

I'm all for waiting.

Tomas turned his full attention to extracting the heart. He managed to get his fingers around the pulsing organ and began to remove his fist from the chest. The vampire did his best to slam his head against Tomas' forehead, but the vines holding him prisoner didn't allow for much movement.

The thorns penetrated the vampire's arms and legs. The insidious vines wrapped around imposter Nicu's neck and began to pull tight while the thorns stabbed him everywhere. Each time those vines tried to curl around Tomas' neck and chest, he countered with flames hot enough to force them to retreat. It was a delicate balance, allowing the vines to wrap the vampire up and yet keep himself free of the worst of them.

The moment he extracted the heart, he tossed it in the air and called down the lightning. Then he summoned his dragon.

Tomas had created the dragon from stone and given it a color that allowed the huge reptilian to fade into the background just as Tomas and his brothers were capable of doing. Tomas' dragon was colored phantom violet.

The creature was aggressive when it came to protecting Tomas and fighting vampires. It loved the battle. Where Tomas didn't feel emotions, his dragon did.

The dragon's secret name was Kinta, meaning "mist of fog." He thought the name was very appropriate. With his brothers, he had created stone dragons for several children when they needed them to fly them to safety. After that, the children would fly their dragons for fun, learning combat through games. The more they were on the dragons, the more the creatures came to life. It had been the same with Kinta.

His dragon was a fierce opponent. He had learned from sharing Tomas' combat skills as well as consulting with other dragons they had run across in their travels. The dragon exploded out of the sky, roaring with rage, shaking the ground and letting loose a steady stream of flames over the vines. As the vines shriveled into long blackened threads, dropping away from Tomas, the dragon began to dig deeper into the soil, uncovering the tubular roots, which he proceeded to ignite.

Tomas could see the long, exposed roots leading deeper into the forest. He took a moment to bathe his arms and hands in the white-hot lightning to remove the acid from his body. There were two punctures where the vines had managed to get in between his armor to penetrate, which meant he would have to rid himself of parasites. That could wait. Now, he had to follow those tubular roots back to the master vampire.

He swung onto the back of his dragon, and Kinta immediately rose, using his powerful wings to lift them from the ground. Tomas didn't have to give Kinta orders; the violet dragon was connected to him and knew what Tomas wanted. Tomas never discounted Kinta's input; he had learned battle technique and strategy from the few ancient dragons still existing. Those dragons had been willing to share knowledge, and Kinta had taken full advantage.

Tomas caught sight of Lojos below him. Lojos was a direct fighter. He always took the battle straight to his opponent. Watching him, at first one would think there was little finesse, but Lojos was poetry in motion. There was a distinct artistry to the way he took down his enemies. He might rush them without saying a word, using blurring speed and going straight for his prey, but when one slowed down the way he moved and actually studied it, Lojos flowed across the ground. There was no wasted movement. Tomas had always admired the way Lojos conducted himself in a fight.

One vampire was incinerated, and Lojos was elbow-deep in the second of his enemies' chests. He kept the imposter resembling himself between him and the vampire that faintly resembled Mataias. Kinta blasted a trail of fire between Lojos and the remaining vampire.

The fake Lojos slammed his fist into the real Lojos' chest, racing to try to extract his heart before the hunter could slay him. The imposter shrieked his hatred, the sound echoing through the forest. The birds in the canopy lifted from the branches, taking to the sky, and monkeys called hysterically to one another in warning. The floor erupted with hundreds of scorpions crawling out of the decaying vegetation to rush Lojos.

Out of the trees, a second dragon, one colored an ever-changing green, charged. One moment it was part of the jungle, and then the nearly transparent dragon shimmered like a phantom, almost impossible to spot even as it streaked toward Lojos.

Tomas continued forward to check on Mataias, knowing Lojos' dragon, Fantoma, would aid him—not that Lojos needed it. Tomas had every confidence in his brother's ability to win against any odds.

Mataias was the thinker of the family. The calm strategist. His brain worked at top speed, and he went through each move dozens of times in a rapid evaluation of any situation. Having been born first, he was the one who led his brothers. He took his role seriously, the same way he did everything in his life, including taking down their enemies. He was methodical and relentless. Mataias appeared to be the most laid-back of the triplets, but he was lethal as hell.

At the moment, he was engaged in a battle with all three vampires. The imposters looked ludicrous beside Tomas' brother. Mataias appeared strong and fit against the undead, who were trying to tear his body apart. He moved in a circular fashion, almost a balletic dance, a beautiful, deadly tango. He moved in and around the three vampires, striking first at one and then at the other, so fast and smooth, he couldn't seem to be touched.

The frustration level of the undead engaging with Mataias reached a fever pitch. All three shrieked and cursed at Mataias as he moved in and out and around them, each time inflicting damage on the vampires. That was his brother's methodical fighting technique, whether there was one or multiple he was up against. He was constantly in motion, never giving the vampires time to set themselves.

Tomas leaned over the neck of his dragon to study the forest floor and the exposed tubes running from the vines toward the interior. The tubes suddenly disappeared as the earth erupted into dozens of wildly spinning mini-cyclones. The leaves and dirt and debris were thrown into the air, temporarily blinding him. When the vegetation settled, there wasn't a single sign of roots or the thorny plants.

CHAPTER 3

"Wait." Sarika held up one hand defensively. "I don't understand." Her cousin was going to *carry* her? Like a sack of potatoes through the jungle? She'd been told many things about her looks, including that she looked ethereal at times, but she'd never been called fragile. She wasn't a delicate hothouse flower. "I find that offer rather insulting. I've traveled all over the world on my own and managed to get through every jungle I was in by walking on my own two feet."

Luiz raised an eyebrow, but his expression remained exactly the same. "We can travel much faster if I carry you. I have only this night to give you. During the day, I will be sleeping. I thought you wanted to talk. To discuss the history of our family and learn as much as possible about the shifters in this area. Was I mistaken?"

His tone was mild. Pitched low. She had no idea why he raised her alarms—and irritated her at the same time. He hadn't really said or done anything wrong. She was so out of sorts. Her breath caught in her lungs. Out of sorts. That wasn't her personality. Arguing and getting irritated with males wasn't in her personality. She found the men she traveled with on her trips down the Amazon and throughout the world's rainforests a little amusing. She respected them and what they did, but they often tended to act superior—until they realized she could pull her weight on the treks. That realization usually changed their attitude toward her.

The moment she recognized that she was not in her usual state of mind, alarms shrieked at her. Her jaguar female could *not* go into heat in the rainforest. Not when she knew it was occupied by male shifters. That would be a disaster. A total, absolute disaster.

When jaguar females came into heat, they were extremely vocal in looking for a mate. She'd experienced the heat of her jaguar female on more than one occasion, and it had been very uncomfortable. She hoped she wasn't coming into heat now. That scent would call every male shifter for miles. Jaguars could mate up to a hundred times a day in the wild. When she'd been in heat, she'd felt as if she could have accommodated a man at least that many times. Instead, she went into the woods alone and ran until she was so exhausted she couldn't stand. The last thing she wanted was to go into heat here in the jungle with male shifters around. She gave a fleeting thought to leaving the rainforest until she knew for certain, one way or the other.

She sighed, trying to decide what to do. She'd counted on finding out about her history. It was important to her to learn where she came from and what had happened for her to be sent away. Having a living cousin had been exciting to her. A relative. Someone she hoped to have a relationship with.

"Are you concerned that I mean you harm?"

Startled, she raised her gaze to her cousin's face. For the first time, there had been a change of tone. Still low and mild, but there was a hint of gentleness in his voice that hadn't been there before. Perhaps that was what had been wrong all along. He seemed so indifferent to her, as if it meant nothing to him that she was his family. He didn't seem to care one way or the other that she was related.

"Sarika?" he prompted.

She'd taken too long to answer him. "I didn't come to be a burden on you, Luiz. I wanted to meet my only relative. My parents made it very clear to me before they died that they wanted to know I had someone in the world." She tilted her chin at him. "I'm a grown woman. I've been well educated, and I'm certainly capable of making a living for myself. I wanted to meet you, but if you have no interest in an acquaintance, it is best to say so, and we can be done with this."

Never once had his piercing gaze left hers. It was difficult to meet his strangely colored eyes when he had the direct focus of a predator.

"I have given you the impression I am unhappy to meet you?" Again, a note of gentleness crept in.

She didn't see a change of expression on his face or in his eyes. He looked as dangerous as ever, yet there was something appealing about his tone. Maybe she was just so anxious to believe someone other than her parents wanted her. Until that moment, she hadn't realized that knowing her father had kept her brother but sent her away had made her feel as though she was unwanted. She'd been isolated to a great extent growing up, mostly through necessity, but aside from her adoptive parents, she'd never been close to anyone.

Sarika tried to make light of her insecurities when she didn't feel that way at all. "I don't wish to be a burden on you, cousin. I'm very aware you had little notice before my arrival."

Those artic-cold green eyes didn't blink but remained fixed on her so she couldn't possibly look away. "Have I indicated in some way that you are a burden or that I am unhappy to meet my only family?"

"I must be misreading you," she admitted. "Or perhaps I have a chip on my shoulder because my father sent me away while his son and you were wanted. You did explain his reasoning, but that explanation doesn't negate a lifetime of feeling unwanted by family."

It was his lack of expression. He had said he was sorry for *her* loss when he spoke of her adoptive parents, but that loss had been his as well. Alois and Gemma were his only relatives other than Sarika, and now they were gone. Granted, he hadn't grown up around them and hadn't had a chance to develop real feelings for them, but Alois was his father's brother. Surely, his father had spoken of Alois to Luiz. Alois had certainly regaled her with tales of growing up with his two brothers in the rainforest and how mischievous they had been. She had grown fond of those memories of her uncles and their antics with Alois.

"Family means a great deal to me," she confessed. "Maybe too much, since we don't know each other. I didn't like the idea of being alone, but that doesn't mean I'm incapable of being alone."

She knew she'd tilted her chin in that telltale gesture her parents had called her on more than once. In fact, often.

"How did I give you the idea that you are unwanted by me? I made every effort, despite some difficulty, to reach you when the sun set so we would have as many hours as possible to get to know each other. I am told I do not show enough emotion. Is that the problem?"

He'd called her out, just as she had done to him. "Family trait?" she murmured, flashing him a little half smile.

"I would imagine the two of us have quite a few traits in common. Stubbornness might be one of the foremost traits we share."

Sarika gave a little shrug. "I know I'm stubborn. That particular characteristic might be considered a negative one, but it got me through some difficult times."

"Such as?" he prompted.

It was the first question he'd asked her about herself that showed real interest. She could tell he really wanted to know. He was so low-key, his mask impossible to read. No real inflections when he spoke, but the flare of interest was there in his eyes. So brief, she might not have caught it had she blinked.

"I've spent a good deal of my time working on conservation in the world's rainforests. Several of the expeditions I went on went awry due to numerous causes: weather, war, poachers, any number of reasons."

"Determination," he corrected. "Not stubbornness."

She burst out laughing. "You say that now, but once you have to deal with me, I believe that you'll decide the determination was stubbornness after all."

Sarika expected a smile, even if it was only a brief one, but his tough features didn't change expression. Apparently, she wasn't nearly as funny to her cousin as she was to herself. She repressed a sigh and hung determinedly on to her smile.

"You say you worked on conservation in the various rainforests—did you do so alone?"

The tone was mild, not at all condemning, but Sarika felt the reprimand and instantly reacted. Like a porcupine, with every hair on her body rising like quills, she actually felt prickly. She couldn't imagine being friends with Luiz, no matter how long she knew him. He didn't look judgy, but it seemed as if he was judging her. He looked indifferent. No, not even that.

She sighed, wishing she weren't so prickly with him. She made every effort to keep her tone even, with no trace of annoyance. "There were others I met going on the expeditions. While I was in school, I went on a few, and that allowed me to meet others interested in conservation. Once I was out of school, I joined several organizations for the preservation of jaguar habitats and was accepted on various treks. We set up cameras and tagged a few of the jaguars. The idea is to open a corridor for the jaguars so they aren't interbreeding. By enlisting the aid of locals, we have a much better chance of success. So far, the program has been working." Animation crept into her voice. She believed in the work. She knew that without intervention, the jaguar species would become extinct.

"You joined total strangers trekking into the rainforest?" Luiz repeated it as if he couldn't quite comprehend.

"Are you having a problem with my choice of career?" she challenged. She tried as hard as she could to tamp down the belligerence, but there was just something about him that set her off.

"Do you think it was safe for you to do such a thing?"

"Is it safe for you to live here? Or any of those you say reside here?" This cousin thing wasn't working out quite the way she had envisioned.

"You were raised in a far different environment than me or any other shifter, male or female, residing here," Luiz said. "You're trying to save a species of wildlife and not considering that jaguar shifters are dying out as well? Without women and children, the jaguar shifter species will be extinct in a few years."

"Just because I was raised differently doesn't mean I wasn't taught how to protect myself." She did the chin thing again before she could stop herself. Alois and Gemma always warned her that little gesture of defiance would get her in trouble someday. They emphasized that she needed to appear serene and feminine, as if she were an easy mark. They had told her never to give away the fact that she could protect herself because that took away part of her advantage of sheer surprise.

Luiz didn't react to the challenge of her chin tilt the way several of the men had when she argued with them on the various treks she'd gone on. The men had automatically assumed they would lead, and she would follow quietly along, even in the discussions. She eventually earned her reputation for intelligence. That didn't negate that things were usually awkward in the beginning.

The rainforest seemed to reflect Luiz's silence. Those gold-flecked green eyes seemed to pierce right through her, as if he could see every mistake she'd ever made.

One moment Luiz was several feet from her; the next he was behind her, one arm locked around her throat and the other holding a knife to her chin. "How do you protect yourself from an attack such as this one?"

His voice was that same mild, expressionless tone. His body was relaxed, but she felt every muscle. He felt like a stone column, not a physical flesh-and-blood man. Although he held her in a very dangerous hold, she didn't feel nearly as threatened as she had when he was standing in front of her—which made no sense at all.

"I see what you mean," she said, because she did.

The moment she acknowledged that she wouldn't have been able to stop him had he cut her throat that quickly, he released her, stepping away from her.

"How did you move so fast?"

Luiz's gaze went past her, looking over her shoulder. His expression was inscrutable, but the danger emanating from him increased tenfold. One hand very gently settled around her arm, and Luiz guided her behind him. It was done so smoothly and firmly that she didn't have time to think about what she was doing. Nor was she alarmed. She actually felt safe and protected.

A man sauntered out of the brush off to her left, facing Luiz straight on. He moved with an easy assurance in the jungle, as if he'd been born there—as, undoubtedly, he had been. He was a little shorter than Luiz and very compact, his chest dense, his muscles apparent. His hair was a tawny color, and his eyes were the rounder golden eyes of a jaguar. They held that same particular focus as Luiz's gaze did. It took discipline to keep from wrapping her hand in Luiz's shirt and holding on because those eyes were on her. And they were hungry.

"Percy," Luiz greeted.

That cool tone brought the jaguar shifter to a halt. He switched his gaze to Luiz with an obvious effort, almost as if he had dismissed the threat in order to get to her. She took one step back to give Luiz fighting room if it came to that, but she remained behind him.

"Luiz. One rarely sees you anymore."

That sounded like an accusation to Sarika. She immediately had the feeling that Percy didn't care for Luiz—or was leery of him. That wouldn't sit well with a man like Percy. She had been around so many men in the jungle and had learned to read body language. Percy was a man with supreme confidence. It was possible he had every reason to be confident.

Several times his gaze slid from Luiz to Sarika as if he couldn't help himself. Each time it happened, she had a visceral reaction to that almost greedy, hungry stare. Her stomach dropped, and she wanted to flee.

Each time it happened, as if he knew how uncomfortable she was,

Luiz shifted his body slightly—the tiniest of movements, but it instantly drew Percy's attention back to him.

"I have been around, Percy. I often choose not to be seen."

Sarika had gotten used to her cousin's voice, so mild as to be nearly gentle, yet he managed to convey a threat. And there was a threat to Percy. The animosity between the two men was palpable. She didn't fully understand why Luiz would dislike Percy so much. He put her on edge because she could feel his interest was totally sexual. She feared he would have taken advantage of her being alone in the forest, just as Luiz had warned could happen.

"I see you are claiming the one female shifter available," Percy said, a snarl in his tone.

Luiz lifted an eyebrow. "I have not claimed her. I believe a woman has choices."

He was being deceptive. He didn't believe that way at all. Sarika didn't know how she was aware of her cousin's viewpoint, but she was absolutely certain he was deceiving Percy and misleading her. She took a second step back, still keeping her cousin's solid body between her and the male jaguar shifter.

Something stirred in her brain. A strange fluttering, a buzzing, faint at first, and then she felt Luiz pouring into her mind. If she thought he'd felt powerful and dangerous before, feeling him in her mind allowed her to know for certain how lethal he truly was.

Don't move. I'll give you all the answers you need when you are safe within the walls of my home. Have no fears, you are safe from Percy, but I wouldn't want to kill him in front of you. You're already afraid of me.

She wanted to deny she feared him, but she did. She wanted to like him. To be close to him—her only living relative—but she didn't get the feeling that connection meant anything to him.

What she should be doing was questioning how he could talk to her telepathically; instead, she tried to relax, to remain calm. If he was in her head and could read her, shouldn't she be able to read him? She might get a real understanding of him as a person. If she was going to trust him with her safety, she had to know he would look out for her. Know it. Not just want it because she had a fantasy about having a family.

Percy chose to ignore the threat emanating from Luiz, which in Sarika's estimation made him arrogant and a little ignorant. Maybe he had a death wish. As fast as Luiz had moved to prove his point that she wasn't safe just minutes earlier, she didn't feel as if Percy had too much of a chance in an all-out fight with her cousin.

"I am Percy Rios," he introduced himself, once more looking past Luiz's stocky build to settle on her. "You are?"

"My cousin," Luiz answered for her. "My family. Under my protection."

That was as clear a warning as could be possible. Luiz hadn't withdrawn from her mind, and she felt the utter resolve to keep her safe. The terrible tension in her began to ease.

Percy didn't look at Luiz; he continued staring at her with that focused, hungry gaze. He was so locked onto her she feared he would ignore Luiz's presence and attack her. In that moment, she felt sorry for all the female shifters the males had done this to, especially if they had no protection. Percy was driving Luiz's point home to her.

"Your name?" Percy persisted. "What harm is there for me to know your name? I'm merely attempting to be friends with you."

Luiz's movement was subtle, but it was enough to bring Percy's attention back to him. Those vivid green eyes flecked with gold locked onto his opponent instantly. Sarika's stomach knotted.

"Why would you want to be friends with my cousin, Percy? I hadn't noticed you were attempting friendship with me," Luiz said. "Or is it simply because she's a woman and you thought it would be easy to acquire her?"

Percy shrugged. "You aren't the kind of man one has as a friend. Backup in a fight, but not as a friend."

Sarika had to admit the man wasn't backing down. She thought him a little crazy to challenge Luiz—or maybe he was desperate. Desperation could make people behave in ways that were totally out of character. She knew the shifter race was dwindling at an alarming rate. Luiz had just revealed to her that the jaguar males had followed their leader and contributed to the downfall of their race.

Percy switched his attention back to Sarika. "Since Luiz is your cousin and admittedly has no claim on you, I would very much like a chance to get to know you."

Before she could reply, Luiz did. "I'm very old-fashioned, Percy. My cousin is under my protection and will not be getting to know anyone without my consent."

"You would stop her from finding a mate?"

Sarika winced at his choice of words. She identified more as human than shifter. She didn't like the word *mate*. *Partner* was much more to her liking. She was giving Percy the wrong impression. She wasn't submissive, and she certainly didn't allow others to make decisions for her. If he was basing their compatibility on her silence, she needed to put a stop to his false impressions.

Don't speak to him yet, Luiz cautioned. *I want you to see his true colors. He will attempt to come around when I am unavailable. I want you to know he is dangerous to you, not just take my word for it.*

How do you know for certain? It was surprisingly easy to answer her cousin.

I can read his mind.

"I understand you follow Brodrick's ways, believing it is your right to take a female without her consent. To impregnate her and force her to have children you may or may not accept. If you don't accept them, you slay them."

Luiz said it so casually, without malice, his tone so matter-of-fact, it took a moment to sink in. Sarika couldn't stop her audible gasp of horror.

They kill babies?

They wait until the child is old enough to shift. Unfortunately, not all jaguars reveal themselves early. Brodrick made many mistakes and killed young girls who might potentially have shifted had he not been so eager to kill.

Percy looked outraged. "I've never killed a child. Never."

He's telling the truth, Luiz informed her.

"But you were with Brodrick when he committed such crimes." Luiz made it a statement.

"I was a teen," Percy defended. "I couldn't stop him; no one could."

"A lot of good men tried," Luiz pointed out.

"Yeah, and they're all dead," Percy snarled. "You should know—he killed everyone in your family."

"I do have my cousin left," Luiz said, his tone even softer.

"You were torn to shreds. No one knows how you survived." Percy's expression turned sly. "What did you do, Luiz? Lay under the dead and dying?"

"Stop," Sarika whispered. "Don't say any more."

Luiz didn't appear affected, but she saw the images in his mind. Just for the briefest of moments, a terrible battle, his friends and family dead and dying, just as Percy said. Then another battle, this one horrendous, Luiz trying to save a woman. The memory was a flash and then gone. He dismissed them as if they didn't matter, as if he couldn't feel, but she felt that terrible grief for him.

"You took the name De La Cruz," Percy declared with contempt, ignoring Sarika as if she hadn't spoken. "You traded your life for servitude. Knowing you bow down to the De La Cruz brothers turns my stomach. You turned on your own kind just so you could live."

"Is that what you believe? So I could live? Do you believe the De La Cruz brothers are alive? Do you think I am?" There was a trace of amusement in Luiz's voice, but Sarika was in his mind. He didn't feel amused. He didn't feel anything at all. But she sensed he was even more deadly than he had been.

"I want to leave this place, Luiz," she said. "There is no need to remain. I don't wish to continue this ugly conversation." She turned a cool gaze on the shifter. "We are not in the least compatible. In fact, the way you treat my cousin disgusts me."

Percy's eyes went a malevolent yellow. A dark flush rose beneath his skin as he took an aggressive step toward her. "You don't know your cousin, but I do."

Step back, Sarika, give me some fighting room. If I have to do this, look away.

Don't. Please. Let's just go. Get me out of here. He's . . . slimy.

He's more than slimy. He's a vile man who believes it is his right to have you or any other woman if he desires her.

"Step back, Percy," Luiz said.

"Or what?" Percy challenged. "Look at him. Ask him what his intentions are. Killing comes easy to him. He has quite the reputation. That's what he's threatening. His answer is always to kill." He leveled his malevolent gaze at Luiz. "Do you have any idea how many of his own kind he's murdered?" His penetrating stare swung to Sarika. "You don't know him at all."

What he is saying is the truth, and yet not, Luiz whispered into her mind. *There was no murder. I tracked any man who took a woman. Sometimes three or four shifters would be together. They didn't give her up quietly, and yes, I took their lives, but they had their chance at killing me.*

Again, she caught glimpses of brutal, vicious fights and massive wounds on Luiz before the memories disappeared, as if he weren't aware of or affected by them. She had no idea why he didn't acknowledge his past, but his mind appeared totally calm. Even knowing he could be in a fight to the death with Percy didn't change his tranquility in the least.

"I am not going to get into a debate with you," she said aloud. "I'm leaving with my cousin. I can't say it's been enjoyable meeting you. I am fiercely loyal to family, and hearing you deliberately try to turn me against him is upsetting."

Percy's demeanor changed instantly. "You misunderstand. I am doing my best to protect you. I've lived here my entire life and am dedicated to the welfare of all shifters despite what your cousin says about me. Yes, as a teenager, I did follow Brodrick, but out of fear, not admiration. If you intend to make your home here, there will be others attempting to make your acquaintance. I believe if you give yourself a chance to know me, you'll find I've made mistakes I readily admit to, but I've done my best to make up for them." He poured absolute sincerity into his voice.

"I traveled a long way to spend time with Luiz, and right now, I'm extremely tired from the journey. Luiz, I would like to go home, please."

"Of course," Luiz said.

"I will see you again," Percy said firmly.

She didn't respond, not wanting to encourage him. They both watched as the shifter faded into the deeper brush.

Is he going to follow us? Sarika found she'd been telling the truth—she was suddenly exhausted. She wanted to find a very comfortable chair and put her feet up.

Most shifters are aware of my home and know it is off-limits. He will not be able to keep up with us.

"I wasn't lying when I told him I am tired. I don't think I'm going to be moving very fast, Luiz," she admitted.

"I am going to carry you. I have many things to discuss with you, and we will need the privacy of my home." *When I took the name De La Cruz, it was because I became a De La Cruz. In one of the battles with shifters, I was wounded. Mortally wounded. The De La Cruz family saved my life. In doing so, they had to give me their blood.*

Sarika thought Luiz meant the De La Cruz family had given him transfusions, but that wasn't what she saw in his mind. What she saw there seemed to be something out of a fictional horror movie. She found herself backing away from him.

He is watching, little cousin. We have to walk the opposite way and get to the heavier brush, where he cannot observe us.

She found herself complying, although she didn't know why. If she had any sense at all, she would have run.

The man you say saved your life appears to be a vampire. There. She said it. She thought it, and now she'd challenged him to tell her the truth. She was rather proud that she wasn't screaming.

The De La Cruz brothers are legendary hunters of the vampire.

Great. Vampire. Male shifters trying to kidnap women, and now Luiz had to throw in vampires. It wasn't his first time. She didn't want to believe him, but he was too matter-of-fact. There were vampires. She continued walking along the narrow trail, averting her face so he couldn't see her expression. What she should do was get back to the river and summon a boat. She didn't belong in her cousin's world.

Yes, you do.

She looked up at him. Not just that soft whisper in her mind, but the feeling he gave her was one of being adamant. Certain. As if he had no doubts about her.

She looked around them when he stopped abruptly. "What makes you think that?" She kept her voice low. Sound traveled at night, but the dense foliage would muffle her words.

"You didn't run."

"I thought about it."

For the first time, he gave her what could have been a real smile. "That shows you have good sense, little cousin." He turned to face her, standing only a foot away from her. He reached to take her hands. "I am fully Carpathian, Sarika. I have my jaguar, but being a male, when I converted, the ancestors of my family poured their knowledge into me. It is as if I am a true ancient. Not as if," he corrected. "I am a true ancient."

"I don't know what that means."

"That is an explanation best left for the privacy of my home." He hesitated. "We're going to fly. I don't want you to freak out on me."

Her *horrible* sense of humor got the best of her. "Seriously? How can you claim to be ancient and use a term like 'freak out'?" Humor was her go-to when she was nervous. She wanted him to be a little insane to think he could fly, but she feared he was capable. She just didn't know how.

"I'll shift into a large harpy eagle and carry you to the house. It is much deeper in the interior. Once you're inside the walls, you'll be totally safe, even from Percy or any other shifters should they become aware of your presence."

"Won't Percy tell them?" She was stalling. She could shift into a jaguar. It seemed Carpathians could shift into other species.

"He wouldn't take a chance that you would connect with one of them or that they would kidnap you."

There was no keeping him talking. Right before her eyes, Luiz shifted with lightning speed into a magnificent—and terrifying—harpy eagle. The upper side of the enormous bird was covered in slate-black feathers, while the underside was mostly white. Striped feathers covered the legs. The head of the harpy eagle was gray and crowned with an enormous double crest.

A normal-sized eagle had talons as big as a grizzly's claws, but this predator looked as if it could easily take down a grown man. The talons looked lethal. She couldn't imagine being gripped by those. Still, she held her ground. Running from a man as powerful as Luiz De La Cruz was ludicrous. She might seem impetuous to him, but she weighed her decisions carefully.

The harpy eagle's enormous wings fanned the air, creating a miniwindstorm, and then the bird rose into the air. Her stomach dropped as it flew in a circle around her and then dove straight for her. At the last moment, Sarika closed her eyes. Tight. She even pressed her lips together so she wouldn't scream.

The talons settled around her waist, snatching her as it flew. Shockingly, he had cushioned her body to prevent the hooked yellow toes from penetrating her skin. She had no idea how he managed to do that so quickly—or at all—but he'd protected her, and that made it easier to trust that he would keep her safe on the flight back . . . sort of.

You don't have a nest full of chicks you intend to drop me into so they can feast, do you? She clutched at the bird's legs, trying to keep her grip as light as possible so she didn't accidentally break one. The harpy eagle had a black beak, wickedly hooked, and looked like it could eviscerate her in seconds. She thought it prudent not to get on its bad side.

Did you know harpy eagles mate for life—just as Carpathians do? Luiz asked in his expressionless, casual way.

The same can't be said of most shifters, Sarika answered, thinking it was insanity to have such a conversation while she was in a fantasy world of harpy eagles flying her through the rainforest at a dizzying speed.

That, sadly, is the truth, he agreed. *As for harpy eagles, they won't mate until they're between four and six, and when they do, they produce two eggs. After the first hatches, the other egg is neglected and as a rule doesn't hatch. They breed every two or three years, so that one eaglet is extremely important.*

Laughter bubbled up. *Are you saying you're contemplating dropping me into the nest?*

You're small enough to fit. The harpies make their nest anywhere from fifty-two feet to one hundred forty-one feet aboveground. You certainly would fit. The nest can be four feet deep and over five feet wide.

I should have made a better friend of you, Sarika said.

Open your eyes.

How did you know I have them closed?

You've been fighting with yourself to open your eyes since I removed you from the ground. You've always wanted to fly.

Reality sometimes doesn't live up to one's dreams, she informed him. Cautiously, she lifted her lashes very slowly, just a tiny bit at a time.

Everything is moving too fast. She closed her eyes as tightly as possible, her stomach lurching. She wasn't afraid of heights; at least, she didn't think she was all that afraid. Her cousin seemed to be protecting her just as he said he would. She didn't want to miss the experience.

I'll slow down.

If Percy is watching, won't he think this is crazy? Because I do. Very cautiously, she opened her eyes.

Luiz had slowed their progression, so the dizzy feeling abated.

He cannot see us. I'm shielding us from his sight.

Of course you are, because anyone can do that.

Any Carpathian *can do that,* he corrected.

CHAPTER 4

Slow down, Tomas advised his dragon. *We are dealing with a master. I believe he may be an ancient.*

We are dealing with scum, Kinta informed him. His voice, in Tomas' mind, sounded filled with contempt. *It matters little what else he is.*

Tomas shook his head. His dragon had always had very strong opinions and had no trouble expressing them.

Knowing who he is can be important to the way we approach the battle, he reminded.

Kinta, like Tomas' brother Lojos, believed in the direct method. His tactic was to press an attack and keep pressure on the enemy until he was slain. The dragon cared little about injuries. When in battle, his only thought, only purpose other than protecting his rider, was to slay the enemy.

Tomas studied the ground and the surrounding trees. Ancients were very adept at hiding themselves, even as vampires. This didn't feel like Justice. Not once in tracking the ancient Carpathian had he felt they were close to him, not that he knew exactly what Justice would feel like. He was probably the most powerful ancient in their world. He knew an ancient such as Justice would be able to fly under the radar of hunters. He would be low-key, so much so that no one would be able to feel his presence. But when they did, he would be overwhelmingly powerful. Dangerous.

Just as you are, Kinta said. *You have those same traits.*

Tomas didn't want to think too closely about that. When a Carpathian lived too long, becoming vampire wasn't the worst he could do.

No one on this earth is as powerful or as knowledgeable as Justice, he cautioned his dragon.

He has been imprisoned hundreds of years. You have not, Kinta reminded placidly.

That was so like his dragon. Kinta was certain Tomas could do anything. Right now, the most important thing he could do was hunt down the master vampire and rid the world of evil. He studied the forest, not the ground. The rainforest was a living entity. A vampire was undead and therefore an abomination against nature. No matter how clever the vampire was, no matter how powerful, nature would retreat from the vile creature.

Tomas inhaled, taking in the scents of the woods, brush and flowers. The abundance of vegetation on the forest floor had its own smell. He noted that the thick debris was crawling with insects—far too many of them, as if they had been disturbed. When he urged Kinta to fly as low as possible so he could sweep along the ground to find definitive traces of the master vampire's passing, the dragon did so with reluctance. He preferred fighting from the air. Flying low meant both rider and dragon were within reach of an inventive vampire's attack.

Just ahead, the trees shivered slightly. There was no wind moving across the forest floor, yet the roots of the trees trembled.

Kinta, there is a trap just ahead. Keep moving but don't continue forward. His piercing gaze quartered the area as his dragon made a circle just in front of the group of trees.

The trees they were weaving in and out of were closer together than many of the others, the branches intertwined. It would be easy enough for a shifter to race along those branches.

Why is Justice going through the rainforest at a snail's pace, using the ground and trees rather than taking to the sky and covering ground much faster? He posed the question to his dragon and his brothers. *If he has a destination in mind, he certainly isn't going the quickest route available to him.*

His brothers were used to communicating back and forth even during a battle. It was Mataias who answered first. *Perhaps he is merely reacquainting himself with freedom.*

He knows he is hunted, Lojos ventured. *He could be playing a game of cat and mouse.*

Tomas thought that over. *Honing his skills? Finding the undead, leading us to them and setting a trap. Is it possible he can persuade the undead to do his bidding? Benedek could use his voice to compel the undead.*

He knows we travel together, Mataias said. *Having the undead take on our appearance could be a tactic to throw us off.*

Tomas shook his head. *I doubt that. He knows we are ancients, riding the edge as he was many centuries before he was forced to sacrifice himself. He had to have gone mad being alone so long in the depths of hell.*

But he wasn't alone, Lojos reminded. *Lilith stole a Carpathian child centuries ago, and it was confirmed she was taken below. She grew up with Justice protecting her. They spoke Carpathian together. Several have heard them.*

But she is not his lifemate, Mataias pointed out. *There is no saving us without a lifemate, no matter how strong we are.*

Tomas knew that was the truth. They could only keep their honor for so long. The longer they lived, the more they evolved into something else. He thought of it as if they were becoming a beast—one living for the joy of battle. A vampire felt a rush when they killed while feeding. Vampires got high from the fear they induced in their victims. The crueler they were, the more depraved, the more of a rush they got from tormenting those they preyed on.

Tomas knew there was scarring on his soul, not just tears and holes a lifemate could repair when they bonded together. This thick scarring was different, and nothing removed it or the results of living far beyond their time. He had gone from not feeling emotions, not seeing in color and hearing whispers of temptation for hundreds of years, to sudden silence. Not even the whispers were there to plague him, and he found the silence far worse. That lasted several centuries. And then came the need for battle. The rush and joy he experienced engaging in a fight to the death with the undead. Did that make him a monster?

With those newer feelings, and he'd had them for the last couple of centuries, he worried about his ability to be a decent lifemate, especially if his woman was born outside the Carpathian species. What was he offering her? She would be forced to give up her identity, her very humanness; she would have to die to be reborn Carpathian. It wasn't a pleasant process. He'd witnessed it more than once, and it was extremely disturbing to him.

All the time he was contemplating why Justice might associate with vampires instead of slaying them, he was assessing the trees and terrain around him.

Allow me to get to the ground, and you appear to fly away, Tomas said. *You know what to do.* Kinta was very adept at fading away, becoming like a soft violet smoke or fog drifting through the trees, impossible to see despite his bulk.

The ground is a trap, the dragon reminded Tomas. *As are the trees ahead. You said so yourself.* Kinta believed in an all-out war. He didn't want Tomas on the ground when he could better protect him from his back.

I intend to get information from the master vampire. It's imperative to understand why he chose to use our likenesses when they confronted us.

Truthfully, the eagerness for battle was on him, just as it was on Kinta. Not just eagerness, it was a need—an actual need. Just feeling that emotion, having a need versus his duty, was nearly euphoric. He felt emotion when he fought his enemies. It mattered little what he felt, just that he could. That he did.

His brothers were like him. They slipped in and out of one another's minds without thinking about it; they'd been doing it for centuries. That ensured they shared all information. He liked that they all had different points of view. That meant more knowledge and more ways to think about everything from battles to conservation.

Tomas appeared to be walking on the ground, but in fact, he was gliding above it, an easy trick he'd used a thousand times over the centuries. Nearly every vampire had fallen for it, even master vampires, who had been around nearly as many years as he had. Each footstep appeared to sink into the thick vegetation on the forest floor. There was the rustle of leaves and even a slight echo through the ground, a deliberate attempt to lure any creature, or the master vampire himself, into attacking.

He appeared confused as he looked around him, as if he thought the vampire was close but had no real direction for him. Sometimes the same battle played out hundreds of times. Having lived so long, Tomas had seen it all.

Just as he knew would happen, the ground around him erupted into many small geysers as thorny vines burst through the forest floor, all reaching for him like six aggressive snakes. Each attempted to wrap around his arms and legs to prevent movement. Simultaneously, the vampire erupted from the ground directly in front of Tomas, his fist punching forward toward Tomas' chest.

Tomas dissolved into thousands of molecules, streaking behind the undead so he appeared to vanish. The master vampire turned in a circle, muttering spells, his hands in the air as he did so. Tomas recognized the ancient spell compelling the vampire's enemies to show themselves. The vampire wasn't especially strong at compulsion toward a hunter, but Tomas felt a slight tug.

He materialized in front of the creature, with only a small distance between them. He nodded his head. "Gustov, I am rarely surprised by anything, but I hadn't heard you had chosen the way of the undead. You were always strong." He allowed a tinge of admiration to creep into his voice, admiration and questioning shock.

He had perfected the art of speaking to the undead over the centuries, knowing the right tones to use, the right things to say to flatter and put them at ease. Going into battle with one of them felt as if it were a part he'd stepped into and knew the role so well he never had to think about what to say or do any longer. That was dangerous, and he recognized it as such. There was no room for complacency even when hunting and slaying a newly turned vampire.

The master vampire regarded him without moving, his red-rimmed eyes flickering with malice and hatred. He appeared quite handsome, his clothes tailored to his fit physique and his dark hair slicked back. Unlike those impersonating the ancients, his hair looked real. Tomas was aware that if a woman saw him, she might very well find him attractive.

"Tomas?" A flicker of apprehension showed on his smooth features and was gone quickly. "I heard you and your brothers were far from here."

"You obviously heard wrong." That simple statement revealed the vampires were keeping track of him and his brothers. Because the vampires attempted to use the other ancients' faces and hair, did that mean they were watching them as well? Worse, sharing information with one another? It was imperative he find out.

"Your informant was clearly wrong, old friend." He spoke as if they were friends; in the old days, growing up, Gustov had followed him everywhere. He was a few years younger, but those years didn't count once both hit fifty. Over the years, Gustov had been a formidable vampire hunter. He had lived far beyond the expectation of a hunter. He had lived with honor.

Fleetingly, Tomas wondered what had happened inside the Carpathian's mind, his heart, which switch flipped to allow him to give up his code and become the very thing he'd hunted for centuries. He had to let that go for the moment. Gustov had always been extremely intelligent and skilled in a fight. It mattered little how much experience he had in battles with vampires if he wasn't paying attention. Master vampires were always up to something.

"Do you have an enemy who wishes you gone?" Tomas sounded solicitous, worried for his old friend.

"The one I follow believes I am capable of handling even the strongest of our enemies," Gustov responded. His voice turned sly. "Join us, Tomas. Call to your brothers. At long last, we have the means to defeat the prince, to wipe him and the Dubrinsky line from this earth. We will hold reign over all species."

Ordinarily, Tomas would pay no attention to anything a vampire said. Nearly every word out of their mouths was a lie. For some reason, he heard truth in Gustov's voice. Instantly, despite the fact that his brothers were in battles of their own, he opened his mind to theirs. They needed this information should he be defeated by the master vampire.

"No one can defeat the prince, not when he has so much power." Tomas spoke cautiously and even looked around him as if he feared the forest had ears. "And there is always a Daratrazanoff guarding the prince. Gregori. You and I both know that combination can set fire to the earth. We would all be annihilated if we went after Mikhail directly." The way he worded his protest made it sound as if he wanted to destroy the prince but feared the power of Dubrinsky and Daratrazanoff. It was well known to the Carpathian people that if Gregori amplified Mikhail's power, it was worse than any nuclear bomb detonating.

Gustov's mouth, a slash of darkness, pulled into a macabre grin. "That's just the thing, Tomas." He looked around the forest and lowered his voice, taking another step closer.

Tomas held himself in place, knowing that Gustov very well could be setting up to attack using his whispered, confidential conversation to distract him.

"There is an ancient weapon known to my master. He is not yet one of us and stays that way, so no hunters will come after him. But he is . . . more."

Tomas schooled his features to appear shocked and interested. He, too, looked around and kept his voice very low. "He is not yet turned?"

Gustov gave him another macabre grin, showing stained, jagged teeth. "He reprimanded me and said I should have waited, that I would be more powerful than a vampire. I didn't believe him, but he defeated every one of the skilled fighters I sent against him, even when he was truly outnumbered. He spared me because he has a mission. He explained how he spent time in the underworld and he learned of a powerful weapon that had been broken apart. The three parts link together to form the weapon. Dubrinsky and Daratrazanoff cannot hope to defeat this weapon. It was made by ancients with the metal falling from the sky."

Gustov believed every word he was saying. If Tomas could feel alarm, he would have been broadcasting warnings immediately. As it was, he registered that Gustov was telling the truth, trying to persuade Tomas to join their cause.

"You're positive your master was telling the truth?" he pushed. He could feel his brothers' concern in their stillness.

Gustov looked gleeful, certain he had persuaded Tomas to their side. Tomas and his brothers were known to be fierce fighters. They were phantoms few saw if they desired to remain unseen. His brothers always traveled with him. The triplets would be a tremendous asset, and Gustov was certain they could persuade other ancients to join the cause.

"He was definitely telling the truth. He knew the weapon was in three parts and fit together. He had an idea of where each piece was and how he could acquire it. Once he has all three pieces, he will rid the world of the Dubrinsky and Daratrazanoff lines and he will be in power. Every species will have no choice other than to do as we demand." Now Gustov sounded triumphant.

"Where in his vision of a different world do we come in?" Tomas asked.

"We will be his army. Ancients, like you, if you resist becoming vampire, will have the highest positions. Then I and others like me will run his army of the undead. His plan is well thought out."

When we were in the States with Tariq Asenguard, do you recall Ferro claiming Elisabeta? She had been held captive for centuries. At first, it seemed as if everything was fine, but then there were undertones, a threat to Elisabeta. That threat came from Gary Daratrazanoff, and it was very real, Tomas reminded.

He protected an ancient counsel, one that ensured the prince would not go insane from the madness that runs in his family, Mataias said.

That was the explanation, Tomas agreed, *but it never made sense to me. Why would he be willing to destroy an innocent Carpathian woman, risking her lifemate to turn, especially when he is so powerful?*

What are you thinking, Tomas? Lojos asked.

Gary became one of us in the most difficult way possible. Ancient warriors from the Daratrazanoff line poured their knowledge and skills into him when he was reborn. Is it possible Gary is aware of an ancient weapon that could destroy our people? That he thought Elisabeta might know where those pieces are?

He kept his attention on Gustov. "You say this weapon your master seeks is in pieces. How does he know where to find those pieces?"

For the first time Gustov looked annoyed. "He refused to say, only that he knew the ancients had such a weapon and that it was made from material that fell from the sky several thousand years ago."

We know that meteorites have been used by the ancients for everything from jewelry to weapons, Tomas informed his brothers. He was the accepted scholar in the family, but all three shared information constantly. What one knew, so did the others.

"Did your master give you his name?" Tomas ventured. More and more it sounded as if Justice had made a wrong turn. No one could blame him. He'd lived a legendary life and sacrificed for his family, condemning himself to the underworld in order to keep his family out. He'd been there for centuries, locked behind gates. Carpathians kept him there. That alone would be viewed as a betrayal after all he'd done for his people.

Gustov looked crafty again. "There is no need for names; he is legendary."

For one moment, Tomas felt every year of his long life on earth. Justice. He hadn't allowed himself to really believe the man had turned against his people. It wasn't just that it would be nearly impossible for a lone hunter to bring down a man with Justice's centuries of fighting experience; it was that Tomas had held out for far too long. If a man as strong as Justice had succumbed to the dark side, did anyone have real hope? He knew Ferro still felt those stains, the scarring on his soul that even his lifemate couldn't remove. Was it really too late for all of them?

Tomas knew he continued to evolve just as his brothers and the other ancients did. Was Ferro still changing despite having a lifemate? Was that a curse given them because they had lived far too long? Hunted too many? Killed so often?

Gustov shook his head. "We do not speak his name. We do not take the chance that hunters will go after him until he is ready. At long last we have the ability to destroy the Dubrinsky and Daratrazanoff lines. You must join us, Tomas. You can see how we will triumph."

"The weapon is in three parts and the master knows where each of those parts is located?" Deliberately, Tomas used the term "the master" instead of "your master." Gustov would take it that he was persuading Tomas to his side.

Gustov frowned, shaking his head slightly. "He knows locations but not exactly where the pieces are. He was very vague deliberately. I questioned him, as did others when he brought us together to tell us his plan. But I am certain there is such a weapon."

Sadly, Tomas believed there was such a weapon as well. More and more he was coming to believe that Gary Daratrazanoff knew such a weapon existed. The prince had to be protected at any cost. If he was killed along with his lineage, the Carpathian people would eventually cease to exist. For Tomas, it was the only logical explanation for Gary's behavior toward Elisabeta. He suspected she knew about the ancient weapon. It would have been Gary's duty to ensure the safety of the Carpathian people, no matter how repugnant the carrying out of that would be. Gary had a strict code, and endangering a female Carpathian, especially one whose lifemate had claimed her, would have been a terrible dilemma. Gary had to feel as if he were betraying that code and that he was without honor. Tomas would have.

He doubted if there was more information he could get from the master vampire. Gustov was beginning to exhibit signs of becoming irritated with him. It was clear he had been given the assignment to recruit others to the cause of his master—and acquiring ancients would be a huge coup—but Gustov had to work at patience. Few vampires had much in the way of patience, even during a fight to the death.

He sighed as he regarded the vampire. Gustov had put himself within striking distance, close enough that he should have known better. Clearly, he believed he had lulled Tomas into a false sense of security.

"Do you know what a phantom is, Gustov? The true definition?"

Gustov was taken aback by the sudden question. "Why should I care?"

"I just thought it would be pertinent for you to know in the next few minutes. You're gearing up for an attack, but you seem to have forgotten why my brothers and I are referred to as phantoms. Just to make it clear, our dragons are as well."

Gustov gave a snort of disdain. "Dragons. You conjure up dragons and think they are invincible. You think you're invincible."

"As are my brothers. Where are your servants, Gustov? Where are my brothers? It seems fairly quiet, and yet your pawns outnumbered Lojos and Mataias. Do you see them? Do you feel them? You don't because, like me, my brothers are phantoms. Impossible to kill. If you're waiting to attack me until your servants can help you, they are gone. Carpathian hunters destroyed the undead, sent them to the afterlife, where they can bear the consequences for their choices in this life."

He'd never talked so much in his life before a battle. He preferred to wade in, strike fast and get it over with, but if Gustov provided even one more scrap of information, the tedious wait would be worth it.

Already Tomas could feel the need for battle taking hold. That addiction to the rush of feeling he couldn't prevent. It wasn't a good thing, the taking of life, but there was nothing else for him. He was a hunter, and he had been for centuries, and that meant finding the undead and destroying them.

Secreting himself away in a monastery, even for a short period of time in order to find a way to cope with the loss of evil whispers, hadn't stopped the scarring that covered his soul. He was a scholar, a conservationist and an environmentalist, but first and foremost, he was a hunter—a killer. Nothing was going to change that, not even his lifemate.

He didn't take his gaze from Gustov. The vampire swayed, his feet moving slightly, a dancing rhythm meant to subtly mesmerize his prey. It might work on humans, or even new hunters, although Tomas doubted it. Gustov was calling up some hideous pattern and chant that was meant to keep Tomas from moving.

He'd warned Gustov, and the vampire knew his reputation, yet he didn't heed a single word Tomas had said. When Gustov made his move, rushing Tomas with blurring speed, Tomas appeared to stand his ground. The clawlike talons Gustov tried to dig into Tomas' chest met with no resistance. The claws found empty air as Gustov's forward momentum continued, so his body moved straight through the apparition that appeared to be Tomas.

Gustov roared with rage as he stumbled forward, unable to stop. Tomas appeared behind him, slamming his fist into the undead's back, shattering bones and ripping through muscles. Acid poured over his arm and fist, burning past skin to bone. Tiny parasites tried to burrow under his fingernails and into the cuts inflicted by the razor-sharp bones he tore through.

Gustov spun in a circle, fast, in an attempt to dislodge Tomas. As he did so, thick roots burst through the ground, dangerous wooden vines carrying poison as they struck at Tomas over and over like a nest of vicious snakes. All the while Gustov hurled himself in a blurring circle, he screamed and spat so a multitude of parasites hit the leaves and debris on the forest floor. The moment they did, they rushed toward Tomas.

Tomas was relentless, not allowing the vampire to shake him off, no matter how fast he spun or how deep Gustov's claws dug into him. The vampire nearly contorted in an effort to find a target with his wicked talons. Tomas' feet stayed just above the ground, although it was impossible to avoid the striking vines and roots. The spear-like heads drove again and again into his thighs and calves, but the master vampire was spinning so fast the heads snapped off, which aided Tomas.

His fingers found the withered, blackened heart, wrapped around it and began to rip it free from the whirling, fighting body of the vampire. All the while Gustov chanted command after command, directing the roots on the ground to do his bidding. One of the vines reared up as they spun toward it, the spear-shaped head stabbing Tomas viciously in the back.

Unbidden, Kinta roared out of the forest, spouting a steady stream of flames, completely engulfing the roots and thick vines striking at Tomas. That was one of the things Tomas liked most about his dragon. The creature seemed such an extension of him that he didn't have to give commands as a rule; they tended to be in sync when they went into battle. He rarely shared with other hunters that he even had a dragon or that his brothers did. One never knew who he would have to pursue in the future. It wasn't always an easy way to live, but having his two brothers with him throughout the long journey of their lives had helped to alleviate the worst of the temptations they'd encountered. The dragons, as companions, had aided them as well.

He continued the relentless pull of the heart through Gustov's back while the master vampire raged, twisting to strike at any part of Tomas that he could reach. Claws hooked into him multiple times, but between Kinta's fire and Tomas' determination, he managed to extract the withered black organ that had once been a heart.

The vampire whirled around the moment he was free, desperate to take the heart from Tomas. He slashed viciously at Tomas' face and neck, going for the jugular. Hot, fetid breath, poisonous with just the fumes, blasted Tomas in the face. He didn't allow his concentration to be interrupted even for a moment. He tossed the heart high into the air, a stellar throw when the heavy canopy gave very few openings. At once, the jagged bolt of lightning slammed into the blackened heart, instantly turning it to ash.

Tomas leapt away from Gustov as he directed the lightning at the body of the vampire. Gustov tried to dodge the lightning spear, but Tomas' aim had been perfected over hundreds of years. Gustov was instantly incinerated.

It took time to deal with the ashes before Tomas bathed his arms and hands in the white-hot glow of the lightning whip, removing the acid before he took the time to push parasites out of his body through his pores. It was always a messy business ridding the body of the parasites, which entered when the hunter was wounded. They couldn't afford to miss one.

His brothers joined him as he was dealing with the mess that was his legs, where the vines had struck over and over. Mataias immediately worked on one leg while Lojos did the other. It wasn't long before they were moving as quickly through the forest as possible, hoping to pick up the trail of Gustov's elusive master.

"Did you believe the reading of the tarot cards for each of us?" Tomas asked his brothers as they followed the game path into the deeper jungle, searching for tracks—anything at all to indicate their quarry was in front of them.

Lojos cast him a quick look and then went back to examining the animal track they followed. Tomas felt that measuring look. He knew his brothers. He could feel Mataias' penetrating stare as well. He kept his gaze fixed on the faint animal track.

"It isn't as if I didn't believe what they said was true, that our lifemates are somewhere in this century waiting for us, but it's more as if I wonder if you believe we have the right to claim them."

That was met with intense scrutiny. He didn't look at either of his brothers as he proceeded to examine the foliage around him for the slightest clue that something—or someone—had come before them. Just feeling the heavy weight of their gazes was enough to know they didn't think like him.

"I'm not sure what you're saying," Mataias ventured, a question in his voice.

"You took a vow with us to stay strong and endure no matter how long we had to wait for our lifemates," Lojos said. "We're closer than we've ever been, and we know we will be able to find them if we stick together and follow the dictates of the cards."

"Hints," Tomas corrected.

"Then you *don't* believe the cards," Lojos clarified.

The rotting vegetation on the ground on either side of the narrow track had piled up, even more than usual due to the passage of larger animals on the thin pathway. In a few places, there was a tangle of vines forming tunnels, but they didn't miss a step, simply shimmering into molecules and passing through with ease before reforming.

"I do believe the cards," Tomas clarified. "I saw them work for others. It isn't that. We're beyond the time we were supposed to have lived. Like the other ancients, I believed it was our duty to hold on for our lifemates and to keep the world safe from the undead. Knowing we are becoming something else—and we are—there is most likely a reason that we've survived far too long."

The game trail wound around several trees with massive trunks. He paused to study the crooked limbs, most thick enough to support jaguars as they used the arboreal highway to traverse the rainforest.

"We are tracking Justice, and as far as I can tell, he is no vampire, but he is no longer Carpathian. The danger he represents is very real to every species," he pointed out as he continued to examine the branches, looking for the smallest detail out of place.

"Benedek is the oldest of us," Mataias said softly. "He was closest to becoming the beast, closer than the three of us, and yet has found his lifemate, and they seem happy together."

Several flower petals were crushed against the thick bark on the trunk approximately thirty feet up. The branch extending toward another tree was wide and thick, very strong.

"Do we know if finding our lifemates stops us from continuing to evolve into something other than what we were born to be?" Tomas posed the question deliberately to his brothers.

They were getting away from his original question, but since he appeared to be the only one wrestling with the ethics of binding a human woman to him without her consent, he decided he could contemplate the morality of it alone. Because he was very certain his lifemate was not Carpathian.

"What have Ferro or Benedek said?" Lojos asked.

"Or have Petru or Sandu spoken of any concerns?" Mataias wondered aloud.

"No, but I didn't ask them directly," Tomas said. "I should have."

"We all should have considered that possibility," Mataias corrected.

CHAPTER

5

Sarika was shocked that the inhabitants of the forest ignored the huge harpy eagle as it wove in and out of trees with shocking precision. The eagle flew straight toward the darkest grove of kapok trees. The trunks were quite thick, and the heavy branches were high off the forest floor. The dull whitish-gray fungi growing up the trunks seemed to become larger and much rounder in shape the higher they flew. As they traveled deeper into the dark grove of trees, the coloring of the fungi seemed to change, blending in with the surroundings, making it difficult to spot them despite their size.

Many branches, thick and sturdy, curved upward and reached outward. Others were very straight, stretching out toward neighboring trees. Some grew skyward, providing a canopy to shelter the entire grove. She noticed the foliage and vines grew thicker and heavier, covering the trees to hide the trunks as well as the strange fungi that seemed even larger.

The harpy eagle set Sarika gently down on a particularly thick branch very high in the canopy. Almost immediately, Luiz shifted and turned to place his foot on one of the wide, round pads of fungi. Sarika cringed a little as she followed him. To her shock, the fungi pad wasn't spongy. It was hard, not in the least like mushrooms. It was so hard that it acted as a stepping stair. That gave her a little more confidence to follow Luiz higher into the canopy.

The round pads widened the higher she climbed until they appeared to be a small terrace or several terraces climbing upward until Luiz stopped at the entrance to what had to be his house. The building was very skillfully hidden between two extremely broad trunks and supported on thick, sturdy branches. The house was much larger than she'd expected, being essentially a tree house. It was open in design so that she could look right inside. A fringe of hanging vines appeared to be the front door.

The openness of the design and the hanging vines making up a door made her uneasy. How would she be safe here unless he was with her? He claimed he wouldn't be. She had no doubt that Percy would find his way to Luiz's home.

She didn't voice her protest but followed him through those thick woody vines. Despite her reservations, the moment she entered, she felt as if she were home. That feeling was the same as when she'd entered the rainforest. Extremely strong. She looked around her, noting Luiz remained silent, giving her the chance to see his home.

There was no sense of pride or relaxation coming from him. Luiz maintained that low energy but continued to give off an aura of danger. It was clear to her that just because he was in his home didn't mean he'd let down his guard.

She forced herself to take her mind off her cousin and really look around his home. A half wall of wood made up the outside, allowing the structure to blend into the canopy. The polished hardwood floors gleamed. There were benches made of strong woven vines set against screens that made up movable walls. Behind the screens could be a bedroom and closet. Maybe a kitchen.

Overhead, the ceilings were almost cathedral. Branches from the tree were high up toward the ceiling and curved in and out of the open design. She could see how a jaguar would have access to the arboreal highway, but just as someone in the home could quickly escape, that openness meant other jaguars could easily enter.

Chairs made of vines were in what she considered the main room. Between them was a small table. Behind one of the screens, she glimpsed a table large enough to seat two for dinner. She glanced at Luiz to ensure he didn't mind her snooping, and when he continued to remain silent, she stepped around one of the gorgeous screens to find a wide hammock hanging from the ceiling.

Sarika smiled at Luiz. "Your home is quite beautiful and practical. I can see that without full walls, the breeze can easily flow through the rooms, keeping the heat and humidity at bay."

He waved her toward the chairs. They looked inviting, and she immediately sank into one, thankful to be off her feet.

"Take your shoes off," Luiz encouraged. "I'll give you slippers to walk around in. My home is protected against insects, but the occasional one might slip through."

She tilted her chin at him. "Are you still reading my mind?"

He shrugged, not looking in the least remorseful. "I find it expedient to do so."

"Well, stop. It isn't very comfortable knowing you can read every thought I have." She flashed him a small smile. "Especially since I haven't made my mind up about you."

His eyebrow shot up, making him appear a little more approachable. "What exactly is the problem?"

She burst out laughing. He was so . . . ridiculous.

"I'm still reading your mind."

She didn't bother to conceal that she found him funny as hell. How could she when he was reading every thought in her head?

"Do you really think that shifting into a giant harpy eagle and flying me through a rainforest is normal? That's just a little whacked. Not only that, but you're talking to me telepathically when I'm certain I'm not telepathic, and you just said you could get me slippers when I'm fairly certain you don't have any my size in the house." Deliberately, she looked at his feet, which were decidedly larger than hers. "None of this is normal. Not one single thing."

"You are telepathic, and this is normal for me," he said.

That made her laugh more. "I suppose it is, but I have no idea how." She wasn't touching his assessment of her ability to speak telepathically.

"I am not simply a jaguar shifter; I became a true De La Cruz, with the blood and memories of those who came before, when I was reborn."

She threw her arms into the air. "Right there, Luiz, that's nuts. Something out of a science fiction or fantasy novel. I'm a scientist, very practical. This Carpathian conversion seems a little far-fetched, if you ask me."

His eyebrow shot up again. "Practical? You consider yourself practical? You travel the rainforests with perfect strangers and assume you're safe. And you're a shifter, whether you like it or not. In most circles, that isn't considered normal."

She was surprised the chair was so comfortable, and she snuggled down into it even deeper. "Unfortunately, I can't say you're wrong." He had a point. There wasn't much practicality in the things she did.

"Tell me all about this very fascinating new life you have, cousin." Deliberately, she reminded him of their relationship. Despite him bringing her safely to his home, she still needed reassurance.

"I cannot say it is fascinating, but perhaps looking through your eyes, I will be able to view it the way you do," he said. He sank into the chair across from her and indicated her shoes.

Her feet hurt like hell, so she didn't protest, just leaned down to remove her boots.

"Carpathians lose all ability to see in color or feel emotions after a number of years. They hear the whispers of the undead calling to them, telling them if they kill while feeding, they will once again feel. They live in a gray world, where only honor keeps them from turning vampire. After hundreds of years, it is . . . difficult."

It sounded difficult. And did that mean he had no feelings whatsoever for her? That saddened her. She didn't know him, but she welcomed him as family. She'd been very excited to learn of his existence and get the opportunity to meet him. She was fully prepared to embrace him as family.

"It's complicated to explain," Luiz conceded. "I know my emotions are somewhere inside me—several of the Carpathian women have told me they feel them when they are close to me—and I know I would protect you with my life, but I can't say I actually feel the emotions I should—or want to—feel."

Her heart hurt for him. He didn't sound in the least bit distressed by his revelation, as if he'd accepted his fate long ago.

"Don't feel so bad for me, little cousin. Unlike many other Carpathian hunters struggling to stay honorable, I know I have a lifemate. She is far too young now, but there is an end in sight for me." He steepled his fingers and looked at her over the tops of them. "I have only to protect her and keep her safe. Her parents aren't as thrilled as one would think they would be."

"Are they Carpathian?"

He nodded. "Riley was human at one time, before Dax converted her. She has the human way of thinking—that a woman should choose her partner."

"You don't feel that way?"

"I am very ancient, Sarika. The ancient warriors poured memories and regrets into me. I saw thousands of battles and so many good, honorable men succumb to the tragedy of never finding their lifemate. There is only one for these men. If she were to have a choice and, in her fear, reject him, he would suicide or become vampire. He would have no other choice. Once he claims her, he is sworn to make her happy, and from everything I have witnessed with lifemates, he does."

"What is claiming? How does he claim her?"

"Carpathian men are imprinted with the binding words before their birth, when their soul is split apart. He speaks the words to his woman, and if she is his true lifemate, they are bound together. Married in more human terms but for eternity. The words bind their souls."

"You believe that?"

"I know it is so. I have seen it. Once uttered, it cannot be undone."

"He can just say these words, and she will have to comply, whether she agrees or not?"

She had always tried to have an open mind. Carpathians were clearly a unique species with a completely different set of rules. Every species had its policies it had to follow to survive. As a conservationist, she understood that. She thought in terms of rights for all living creatures, female or male. Young or old. The truth was, in many worlds, the rules were very different and had to be. But being able to bind another being to you without their consent was difficult to take.

"Yes, binding them ensures the hunter does not turn vampire. Guarding the soul of a Carpathian hunter is an enormous task, even if one isn't aware she is doing so. Should our enemies find out, they would do anything to acquire her in order to take the soul of the warrior. More than one of our women are legendary for the lengths they had to go to in order to keep their lifemate's soul safe."

She ran her hand over the smooth surface of the table made of vines. She felt Luiz in the wood. He had been the one to construct the table. How did he manage to get the wood so smooth? She looked around her. "You did all of this?"

He nodded. "It was my home before I became Carpathian. I come here often."

"Why?"

"It is close to my lifemate. I am better able to appear more human to Maureen."

"You said Riley was human at one time. Doesn't that mean she's Carpathian? Wouldn't she understand your need of a lifemate? Surely, her husband, or lifemate, whatever you want to call him, claimed her." She didn't know why she felt a little indignant for Luiz. She didn't believe a man should be able to claim a woman without her consent.

"Dax. We call him Dax. Riley thinks like a human. How could she not? I'm grateful she's protective over little Maureen."

She caught a brief smile in his mind, but his expressionless mask didn't change.

"She was born in a rainstorm. Dax wanted to call her Stormy, but Riley objected strenuously. They settled on Maureen."

"You were there when she was born?"

"Riley had no one close when she went into labor, and there were complications. I have a reputation as a healer, so Dax called for me."

"Is that when you found out the baby was your lifemate?"

"I knew before she was born. I had been given the information, and several times during Riley's pregnancy there was a problem. I spoke to the baby often, convincing her to fight to live. She's strong-willed."

"Something she'll need to be if she's with you," Sarika said.

That earned her another small smile in his mind. "No doubt."

"Are the Carpathian women raised to believe they only have one lifemate? Do they accept them easily?"

"From all the knowledge I acquired when I was reborn, the answer is yes. I also have observed Carpathian women accepting a lifemate. Although I don't believe it is always as easy as it appears on the outside, because the hunters have survived hundreds of years and can be set in their ways. Often the women have also survived hundreds of years, and they, too, can be set in their ways. I would imagine that would make it extremely difficult in the beginning of the relationship for either of them."

She liked that he considered it wouldn't be easy. She suspected many of the Carpathian males might believe they had the right to impose their will on the woman.

"If a woman says no, what can she do if he still says the words to bind them?"

"Learn to live with her partner."

There was absolute in his voice. Luiz wasn't about to give his lifemate a way out. That was obvious. She told herself not to judge. She had no idea what kind of bleak existence these men endured. A short discussion that included a tiny portion of the culture of Carpathian life didn't make her an expert. Fortunately, she wasn't a Carpathian woman.

"I cannot stay much longer and will be gone during daylight hours. When close to you, I can use telepathy, but I will be beneath the ground in the paralyzing state of our kind. The only way I will be able to hear you is if you allow me to take your blood."

Sarika's fingers curled into two tight fists as her breath caught in her lungs until they felt raw and burning. It took a minute to compose herself. "Take my blood?" she echoed. "As in, bite me? Like a vampire?"

"More like a Carpathian. We need blood to survive, but we never kill when feeding."

"That's quite nice of you."

Again, she felt that small flash of amusement in his mind. It didn't show on his face. "I believe that is known as sarcasm."

She wasn't going to allow her cousin to lull her into a false sense of security. "How do Carpathians become vampires exactly?" It took great restraint not to cover her neck with both hands. Just the thought of having someone tear into her neck or throat made her stomach turn.

"You've seen too many movies," he said.

She glared at him. "Stop reading my mind. Especially now. I'm becoming nervous around you, and I don't particularly like letting on. I have a reputation for being calm, cool and collected."

"You just made that up."

She shrugged. "Maybe, but in my head, I'm those things when faced with adversity."

"I'm the one taking the blood, not you, cousin," he pointed out.

"I'd rather be the taker than the takee," she argued.

"There's no such word."

"It's becoming a sensation," she said.

"You're stalling."

She was. Absolutely, she was. "Your friends, the ones you'd like me to meet . . ." She trailed off, unsure how to be delicate about her concerns.

"Some of them are Carpathian, and some are not. No, you aren't going to be used as food by any of them. If they tried, they know they would answer to me. I'm your cousin and only family. Not only are you protected by me, but my brothers and their women would protect you as well. The name De La Cruz carries a certain reputation. You will be perfectly safe."

He kept saying that. She had always felt relatively safe in every jungle she'd gone to, worldwide, but for some unexplained reason, this place, although it felt like home, also seemed very dangerous to her.

"I think I'll just say no to you taking my blood this time," Sarika said in her politest voice.

She was fairly certain she would say no for the rest of her existence. The idea of him biting into her neck and then being able to read her from a distance was extremely disconcerting.

"It is rather imperative for your safety. Percy knows you're here. He'll do whatever he can to acquire you."

"I thought you said this house was safe," she pointed out, doing her best not to stick her chin in the air. She was definitely drawing the line at allowing him to take her blood. In reality, with no apparent walls and a door made of dangling vines, she couldn't imagine how the house, as cool as it was, could possibly be safe.

"I will place protections—safeguards, Carpathians call them—around the house. There are some always in place so no one can enter when I am not here, but with you in residence, I'll add to them. If you invite someone in or cross the line to go out, there will be little to protect you."

"I have no reason to leave, although I'll be hungry."

He shrugged. "I will provide food. There is a small icebox filled and another lockbox with staples in it. Everything in the kitchen works."

"How? How do you get electricity here?"

He lifted his eyebrow again. "Are you paying attention to anything I tell you about Carpathians? I can generate the electricity you need for the house. The same with providing fresh, pure water."

She swore he moved, a blur only. She blinked rapidly, and he was sitting without moving across from her. His expression was exactly the same, but she knew he had done something horrible. She lifted her hand to her neck, searching for telling signs. She didn't feel anything, but she was a little dizzy and *very* suspicious.

"Did you just take my blood?" she demanded.

"Don't ask questions you don't really want answers to. I told you I wouldn't lie to you."

She didn't hear a single note of remorse. Not one. There was nothing on his face, in his eyes or in his mind.

"Why would you do that when I expressly said no?"

"It was necessary."

"I said no."

"You were being unreasonable out of fear. I knew it wouldn't harm you. What tipped you off?"

"I saw you move from your chair and then you were back in it."

He nodded. "That's good, Sarika. Few would have caught that, even shifters. You have excellent instincts. Those instincts will develop even more here in the forest. You also have tremendous gifts. I can feel power in you."

He was so matter-of-fact, as if she should just ignore what he'd done because it somehow was for her own good. "Praising me isn't going to negate what you did, Luiz."

He shrugged. "I didn't praise you to get out of trouble. I don't mind your being upset with me when I know I'm right. Taking your blood is a necessity to keep you safe. And just so you know, I don't say things I don't mean."

He was the most frustrating man. "Are all Carpathian males like you?"

"In what way?"

"Just make decisions regardless of what someone says?"

"Would any of them have taken your blood? Yes."

"Lovely. Just lovely. I have jaguar males prowling around, believing they have the right to kidnap me and force me to have children, and Carpathian males who'll take my blood without my consent anytime they feel justified. This place is looking better and better."

He stood up, once again looking dangerous with that fluid motion. "There are groceries in the kitchen. The water will be hot when you wish to shower or bathe. In the bedroom, there are books to keep you occupied. My suggestion is to sleep as much as possible."

Something in his voice, in his mind, alarmed her. "I suppose you can help with that as well?"

"Of course."

"Well, don't." She was prepared to throw things at him.

He gave her a brief flash of amusement—once again, in his mind only. "Do not leave these premises. Don't invite anyone inside. I will be back as soon after sunset as possible, and we'll go to meet some of the women. They'll be very welcoming."

Sarika wasn't certain how he could possibly know the women would welcome her. Maybe he just commanded them and they did his bidding.

"More sarcasm," he observed aloud. "I'll take my leave. Relax and enjoy the music of the rainforest."

She blinked, and her cousin was gone. He hadn't moved. She knew he hadn't. She'd kept her gaze fixed on him just in case he wanted more blood. He'd simply vanished.

In a way, it was a relief to be alone. She spent a great deal of her time alone, especially since losing her adoptive parents. She hadn't realized the toll it could take being in a stranger's company under such stressful circumstances. She had placed herself in danger simply because she so desperately wanted a family. It wasn't the most intelligent decision she'd ever made.

She wandered through the tree house, marveling that despite being very minimal when it came to furniture, it felt luxurious. The bedroom consisted of a huge hammock for a bed. Covers were folded neatly in it. The bathroom in particular was very nice, and she immediately started water running in the deep bathtub. She had no idea how Luiz had managed to get clean running water to the tree house, but he'd done it. She would be forever grateful.

Truthfully, the lack of walls despite the presence of screens made her feel vulnerable.

You can see out, but no one can see in.

The intrusive, annoying voice poured into her mind. Glaring, she whirled around in a circle seeking the owner of that voice. *Will you go away?*

Just making certain you have everything you need.

I do, with the exception of peace and quiet.

Again, she felt his amusement but had the feeling he didn't, which made no sense to her at all. This world was strange and exciting, but it also was terrifying.

I can't take a bath until I know you're truly gone, she added.

Again, she got the impression of male amusement. *Gone,* he confirmed.

She lay in the bathtub, thankful to soak her aching body in hot water, grateful to Luiz for providing the shelter for her while she contemplated what to do. She'd traveled the world, visiting tropical jungles and exotic rainforests. She'd loved every single experience and repeated those visits as often as possible, but she'd never felt awakened. Alive. Not like she did the moment she stepped off the boat in her present location. That feeling had been brand-new and exhilarating. But . . .

Sarika closed her eyes and allowed herself to relax into the hot water while she ran over the list of pros and cons of remaining there in the forest. She wanted to stay. She wanted family. She loved the rainforest and the inhabitants. She knew shifters lived there, and she was a shifter. It would be so nice to become friends and soak up as much information as possible about her history, her capabilities and the traditions and laws of her people.

But then there was the certain danger of male shifters like Percy, who clearly had his own interests at heart. Instinctively, she knew he wouldn't give up his pursuit. Eventually, there would be a showdown between him and Luiz. One of them would be killed. She had the feeling it would be Percy, and she didn't want that. She wanted it less for Luiz, even though her cousin could make her want to pull out her hair in sheer frustration.

It wasn't safe to stay—that was the bottom line. She had the feeling that the people Luiz planned to introduce her to were Carpathian, just as he was. She wasn't down with donating blood anytime they decided they wanted to take it. Under normal circumstances, she doubted if she would have known Luiz had taken her blood, but her senses continued to be heightened since she'd entered the rainforest.

Sarika sighed as she made up her mind that she would have to leave. That meant getting Luiz to escort her out of the rainforest after making arrangements to get downriver to civilization, where she could take a boat and then a plane back home.

She listened to the sounds of dawn arriving. Wings fluttering as birds settled. Monkeys calling to one another. The drone of insects and scuttle of lizards and voles in the debris on the forest floor as they scrambled for last-minute meals before seeking shelter. An owl screeched, an early hunter, the call indicating it missed its prey.

Her hearing had always been acute, but now it seemed as though it was even more so. Just in the short hours she'd been in the rainforest where she'd been born, she felt the difference in her—and in her jaguar. Forcing herself to leave the bathtub, she enveloped her body in the large, fluffy towel Luiz somehow managed to have in his tree house home. She realized it was like he'd read her mind and provided her with every single thing she desired for her stay. Was that possible? How could he conjure up towels out of thin air? She had the scary feeling Luiz was capable of just that.

"I'm so in over my head," she whispered to the dawn. "I want to stay more than anything I've ever done, but I'm not prepared for this place." It was an admission of sadness. She'd studied and worked hard, interned all over the world just so she could come home and be of use to her people and the animals that inhabited the forest.

Still, as much as she wanted to make up her mind decisively, she thought it would be wise to sleep before completely making her decision. She'd spent days traveling to get there, and she was exhausted. Sarika pulled on a long tee she often slept in and dragged up the cover before dropping the mosquito netting around the hammock. As a rule, she wasn't bothered by insects, but she thought it prudent just in case. She wanted a good night's sleep so she would have every brain cell working when she made her decision.

The sounds of the day were far different from the night, but she was so exhausted she fell asleep almost immediately.

She had no idea if it was minutes or hours later when she woke to a growly male voice calling her name. Instantly, her heart began to pound with alarm. Clutching the blanket to her, she sat up slowly and looked carefully around.

"Sarika." There was a demand in that voice. Impatience. A clear warning.

Now was the time to believe in her cousin's word. Danger prowled outside the tree house in the form of Percy Rios. Forcing calm through deep breathing, she got up slowly to help orient herself and went to her pack to pull out clean clothes. The bath had definitely helped with the aches from traveling. Her internal clock, one that had always been fairly accurate, told her it was nearly six in the evening. She had managed to sleep most of the day.

Entering the kitchen, she ignored the demands coming from around the house. Percy was circling it, looking for a way in. The fact that he hadn't already breached Luiz's home went a long way to easing the tension in her. She made herself a cup of tea. She always carried her favorite tea with her, something she found soothing at the beginning and end of the day. Wrapping her hands around the cup, she made her way into the main living area so she could look over the short walls to observe Percy.

The male shifter appeared very agitated. Twice he banged his fist on what appeared to be a transparent wall. Transparent for her, she remembered, but Luiz had said no one would be able to see in. She was beginning to think her cousin knew what he was talking about. It was strange to go into a room with a low wall where she could see the extensive deck and massive tree limbs where Percy prowled back and forth, but even looking straight at her, he didn't appear to be able to see her.

No jaguar could do that. The ability had to come from Luiz's Carpathian side. She didn't understand exactly what he was talking about, but she knew no one should have that kind of power. No one. If they did, sooner or later, power corrupted. She believed that. She'd seen it in every corner of the world. Just talking with Luiz, it was apparent he wouldn't take no for an answer if he believed he was right. Even if he did know exactly what he was talking about and she didn't, he had no right to make decisions for her—and he had. If the power he'd displayed was because he was a Carpathian, she knew she would never fit into that world.

Percy snarled again and again, slamming his fist against the transparent wall. Then suddenly his voice turned soothing. Pleading. "Sarika, you can't trust Luiz. Let me help you. He's locked you in, and you're his prisoner. Can't you see that?"

She hadn't tried leaving, and she wouldn't with Percy prowling back and forth on the deck, but what if Percy was telling her the truth? That Luiz had closed her inside, and she thought she was secure and protected, but she really was a prisoner. Not that she wanted anything to do with Percy or would ever trust him.

She sipped her tea and watched the jaguar male become even more agitated. Several times he threw daggerlike looks over his shoulder as he shook his head. She set her teacup down and stepped closer to the half wall. Something—or someone—else was out there with Percy. She couldn't see who or what, but she knew the shifter male wasn't alone.

Sarika forced her breathing and heart rate under control. There was no way in hell she was staying in the rainforest. She didn't trust any of these men. Percy wasn't there to save her, and he wasn't alone. She suspected there was more than one male shifter waiting for her to emerge. And Luiz . . . She had no idea what Luiz wanted from her, but she was certain he had an agenda she wasn't going to like.

She had always trusted her instincts, and they were screaming at her to run. To get out. She might have to rely on herself to make her way out of the jungle back to the river. Her jaguar could easily do that. That would mean she would have to make it past the jaguar shifters and find a way to stay ahead of Luiz. The man could fly, which meant he would be far faster than she was. If, for some reason, she was his prisoner, she needed to figure out a way to leave, especially while he was in the ground. She didn't trust anyone in the rainforest. Not a single person.

A child's scream suddenly penetrated her thoughts, and she hastily rushed to the low half wall to try to see into the forest. She heard an unfamiliar male shout, and Percy whirled and leapt from the wraparound porch. The child screamed again, this time calling for help.

Sarika forced herself to slow down and replay the sound. Was it a legitimate cry of a child, or was someone mimicking a child? She was certain it was a female. Very young.

"All right, baby, we'll figure this out." There was no way she could stay safe in the tree house if the jaguar males had kidnapped a child.

CHAPTER

6

Sarika assessed her advantages and disadvantages as she made her way through the forest using the arboreal highway. She stayed in human form but wore breakaway clothes and had a small bundle secured around her neck containing leggings and a long tee. She had made it through Luiz's safeguards, or whatever he called them, more easily than she had anticipated.

She'd felt a slight wrenching, a wave of distortion, that sent a feeling of nausea to the pit of her stomach, but it quickly passed. Whatever the safeguards were, they were there to keep others out, not her in. That gave her the tiniest hope that her cousin was really on her side.

Luiz had said he could come to her at sunset, that he was locked in the ground until then. Since he'd told her the truth about the safeguards, she would believe him about his inability to move before sunset. That left her on her own to try to rescue the crying child. A female for sure.

The little her cousin had told her about the fall of the jaguar shifter species had left her appalled and shaken. She wanted nothing to do with the male shifters, especially not the one she'd met. She didn't trust him at all. Luiz had warned him off, but the moment he knew Luiz was out of the picture, he'd come sneaking around.

Sarika knew she might have to try to summon Luiz. He wouldn't be happy with her after he'd gone to all the trouble of ensuring her safety and warning her to stay inside. She was fully prepared for the consequences if she managed to save a child. Of course, she had no idea what the consequences might entail. She didn't want Luiz to ever take her blood again. Not ever. She felt very firm on that stance.

One of her greatest assets was her ability to feel her surroundings and read the energy of every living creature in close proximity. At least, it had been, until she met her cousin. She hadn't been able to read him. She still trusted her instincts, and right now, she was heading on an unerring path straight to the child and the male shifters confronting her.

Her main disadvantage was that her jaguar had never been in a real fight against another jaguar, particularly a male. Experience counted. But she also knew the males would be very reluctant to injure her too badly if the plan was to kidnap her. Needless to say, she wasn't about to be taken by a mob of males and subjected to what sounded like rape. That meant timing and being extremely careful were important.

As she ran lightly along one branch after another, she sent out waves of calming energy to assure the forest sentinels that she meant them no harm. She'd always been good at connecting with animals—another asset. But her absolutely greatest asset was her voice. She could sound as if she were coming from any direction, which would help keep her position hidden. More than that, her voice was compelling. She had to find the perfect wavelength that each person—or animal—responded to, and then she could subtly influence them.

Her voice wasn't a huge gift, the way she suspected Luiz's was. That was one of the reasons she found herself so uneasy around him. She *never* used her gifts for personal gain, only for the safety of herself and others. That didn't mean she hadn't practiced often to strengthen her abilities. She had. She was very disciplined, and she made it a habit to work on her skills all the time.

Voices became louder, filtering through the trees. She was fairly high up, the dense canopy hiding her as she approached the confrontation below. A powerfully built man had his hand wrapped around the arm of a squirming child, easily pinning her to him while his attention was centered on a beautiful woman who faced him. One of her hands was up, palm out, as if trying to pacify him. She looked terrified but determined.

Another very muscular man circled around behind the woman, his movements stealthy. Sarika recognized the smooth craftiness of a shifter. He didn't make any noise, and the slight breeze was blowing toward him, not away. She doubted if the woman was aware of him. There was something about the second man that struck a note of fear in her. The way he moved. His absolute stealth. The way his energy, despite the situation, remained so low it was nearly undetectable.

And then there was Percy. He was in the shadows of the tree, observing the scene, his muscles locking him in place with what could have been the first step of a freeze-frame stalk. She couldn't tell if his attention was centered on the woman or on the man with the child. She doubted if she had an ally in him, but she would do her best to persuade him he wanted to be aligned with her.

"Let Sandrine go, Rud," the woman said, her voice more pleading than demanding. "She's just a baby."

The little girl appeared to be four or five. She had a pixie face and wild gold-and-silver hair, much like her mother's. She appeared to be a sturdy child, and she clearly was a fighter.

"She's jaguar, same as you, Jasmine. You have no business holding yourself and this female away from the males," Rud snapped. He sounded ferocious. His voice seemed overly loud and overbearing. He was supposed to be in command of the situation, and yet he seemed extremely belligerent.

Steroids? Did male jaguar shifters use illicit drugs? Rud reminded her of someone who was jacked up on steroids and had taken them for a long time. She couldn't imagine that this far out in the rainforest, Rud would be able to get his hands on that specific drug, but he wasn't right. Not by a long shot.

"Let her go and I'll come with you without fighting," Jasmine offered.

Jasmine was really quite beautiful, with the long, thick hair that marked the shifter's species. Her hair was golden, very shiny, and cascaded to her waist. She had the most striking eyes. Cat's eyes, but a vivid emerald green. She was thinner than most shifters, but that didn't detract for a moment from her regal lines.

Rud's expression changed to one of cunning. To leering. "I like a fight with a woman," he said. "We're taking both of you."

Sarika decided it was time to insert herself into the scenario. "Who is your friend, Rud? The one skulking behind Jasmine?" She threw her voice to the opposite side of them, as if she were in the lower branches of the kapok tree there.

Jasmine whirled around to spot the man, who had gone very still. She didn't indicate that Sarika's easy familiarity was not known to her. All three male shifters scanned the trees and surrounding forest in an effort to find her. Sarika felt very, very lucky to have the ability to send her voice from any direction. She didn't like the expressions on the three men's faces. Well, two of them. The third shifter, the one behind Jasmine, was as unreadable as Luiz had been.

"Bacus, I should have known you would be here," Jasmine said. "You and Rud always travel together." She took several steps to her left so she could include the shifter in her line of vision.

Bacus didn't react, but he stopped moving toward Jasmine now that he had been spotted. He didn't even edge closer to her. That worried Sarika. Bacus seemed the most dangerous of the three men to her, and she didn't want to forget he was there. His very stillness allowed him to fade into the background.

"Who's your friend, Jasmine?" Rud demanded.

Sandrine suddenly bit down hard on his arm, and he swore, releasing her. The little girl streaked toward her mother, but Rud was far too fast. He was on her in less than a second, catching her by her wild hair and shaking her.

"You'll pay for that, you little brat."

Jasmine took a step toward him. "Don't you dare hurt her." This time she didn't sound in the least pleading. She sounded fierce.

"Stop, Jasmine," Sarika cautioned, alarm coming through in her voice. It was enough to freeze Sandrine's mother in place. Sarika had been so concerned that Jasmine would get too close to Rud that she didn't know if she had successfully projected her voice from the trees opposite her. That would have been a major mistake.

"If you want her, you'll have to come take her from me," Rud challenged.

"Don't move, Jasmine," Sarika called out, once more throwing her voice from the trees opposite where she was located. "Percy has arrived. He's a friend and will help you and your daughter. Percy, I'm so thankful you're here."

Jasmine's eyes widened in alarm, and she gave a brief shake to her head. Sarika ignored the warning. She was putting Percy in the position of having to choose, looking like a man who would rescue women from dangerous male shifters or letting her know he was solidly with them. She didn't doubt for a moment that Percy ran with the two other males and participated in their despicable deeds. She noted Rud sent a secretive, triumphant smirk toward Bacus. That solidified in her mind that Percy was an enemy. The knowledge didn't deter her. She'd assumed that would be the case just by the way Percy had acted toward her, as if he were entitled to her.

The best way to stall for time was to get them talking. They would believe they could easily handle two adult females and one child. The two men visibly relaxed while Percy tensed.

"Rud and Bacus would never hurt the little girl," Percy said. He stepped out of the shadows and cast a careful look around. "Come out and we'll talk this through, Sarika."

She realized he had deliberately used her name to show the other two shifters that he knew her. He wanted to impress them, but now, as they stared at him, wariness and suspicion crept into their expressions.

"What's there to talk about? Jasmine needs to take her baby home. Your friend Rud needs to let go of her." She paused for a short moment and then let out an alarmed gasp that could be heard throughout the trees. "Is he some kind of pedophile? If he is, you know that Luiz will never stop hunting him."

Jasmine lifted her chin. "The De La Cruz family will never stop hunting any of you, nor will Solange. You're making tremendous enemies with your behavior, Rud. You know how they all feel about children."

"A death wish, then," Sarika said, interjecting, keeping her voice calm and steady. Musing aloud. Stalling. "How sad. Surely, you have things to live for." This time she poured sympathy into her tone, hoping to throw him off. She didn't want Rud, or any of them, thinking about how close the sun was to setting.

"Who are you?" Rud's face darkened at the implication that he was deliberately inviting death. That he couldn't possibly handle Luiz, his family or a woman named Solange. Rud swung his gaze to Percy. "Who is she?" That was a clear demand. A command to an underling.

Sarika saw Percy wince at that tone. He didn't like being made to look small in front of the two female shifters.

"She is cousin to Luiz."

There was silence following that particular revelation. Even Jasmine sent a wary glance around. Apparently, her cousin had somewhat of a reputation. Not only did the men look uneasy, but Jasmine did as well, and the little girl stopped fighting the shifter. Suddenly, it felt very good to have Luiz as a cousin.

"I wasn't told Luiz had a cousin," Rud said. "A female at that. Can she shift? With those bloodlines, she should produce shifters. Percy, were you trying to keep this woman for yourself?" Rud's tone was threatening.

"Percy was trying to help me. We just met," Sarika said quickly, jumping to the shifter's defense. "I don't know my way around the forest as of yet." She thought it best to look as if she were protecting Percy. He would like that, and Rud would become even more suspicious.

"I am ruler of the jaguars," Rud announced. "You should have made yourself known to me. Percy should have told me of you immediately and brought you to me."

She thought it significant that he used the term *ruler* rather than *leader*. There was a difference, and Rud didn't seem to know what it was.

Sarika took a chance of looking around again, doing a quick sweep of her surroundings. To her consternation, Bacus had disappeared. He had shifted back into the shadows, no doubt intent on searching for her exact location. Now she really worried that she had made the one small mistake with her voice when she'd been alarmed on Jasmine's behalf.

Sarika couldn't worry too much about that at the moment. She had to continue to stall for time. She was careful when she spoke to put only the smallest of compulsions into her voice and to ensure her voice seemed to come from the direction of the trees opposite to where she was secreted, hoping to confuse Bacus along with the others.

"You'll have to forgive me, Rud. I wasn't raised in this forest and know nothing of our people and their customs. Percy ran into me as I was making my way off the river and was trying to explain when my cousin objected, um, *strenuously* to our conversation. He refused to allow Percy to speak to me." She put the smallest note of annoyance in her voice, as if Luiz had really irritated her with his orders, removing her from Percy's care.

Once again, Jasmine's eyes had grown round, and she shook her head, attempting to warn Sarika, without speaking aloud, that the shifter males couldn't be trusted. There was no way to acknowledge Jasmine's warning, so she didn't try.

Rud's thunderous expression eased. "Show yourself to me now. I'm done with these games." That was a clear order.

"You haven't released Sandrine," Sarika pointed out, keeping her tone mild but allowing suspicion to creep in. "She's frightened. What ruler would frighten a child?" She allowed her voice to swing dangerously out of control with concerned emotion. "Are those bruises forming on her arm?" Deliberately, Sarika poured even more anxiety into her voice. "Percy, is he really the ruler of the shifters? He doesn't act like any leader I've ever come across."

Again, she turned to Percy rather than Jasmine, as if she already relied on him. She'd even softened her voice. There was no flirty note, but this wasn't a flirty situation. More as if she were relying on the male shifter. It was difficult to play the part of the submissive female needing to be saved, but if that was what it took, she was an exceptional actress when it was needed. If Percy believed he could have her to himself, he might be more willing to come to the child's aid or at least argue with Rud to give Sandrine back to her mother.

How long until the sun went down? It felt like every passing minute was a good hour long. It was necessary to keep stalling and, at the same time, drive a wedge between Percy and Rud. Her worst fear was Bacus. She'd lost sight of him, and it was necessary to figure out exactly where he was.

She found she was too tense to be balancing on a tree branch and trying to manipulate the situation to the females' advantage. Her first goal was to separate the child from Rud. More and more, she was coming to believe he would actually harm the little girl if he didn't get his way.

Jasmine and her daughter were putting out waves of distress and fear, nearly swamping her. Percy was confused, yet she felt the undercurrent of determination and that slightly tainted feeling that always was a warning to her. Rud was all belligerence and fight. An arrogant, angry alpha male intent on destroying anything or anyone he couldn't control. With Rud, she felt his borderline insanity. But Bacus . . . His energy was low. Very low. He wasn't giving anything of his emotions away, and that made him difficult to locate and, in her opinion, the most dangerous of all three shifters. And he was hunting her.

She was scared. She allowed herself to feel and acknowledge that emotion. These men apparently thought nothing of raping women to impregnate them. She had the feeling Jasmine knew all about that just from the tremors that were visibly going through her body. So, okay, she was more than scared. She was leaning toward terror. Just the fact that Rud, the leader of the shifters, would threaten to harm Sandrine, a little girl, for no reason other than he was being opposed, put him in the realm of a madman.

She could easily track Rud and Percy, but Bacus would be especially difficult to track. She didn't want to move. That could entail disturbing foliage. The slightest hint of a leaf going against the wind would give her position away to a hunter. She had no doubt in her mind that Bacus, of the three males, was the true threat when it came to tracking. The more she allowed that thought to loop in her mind, the more fear she felt. Fear had an odor. He could, perhaps, track her just through scent. Jaguars had unbelievable abilities when it came to smell.

Rud was arrogant, demanding everyone respect him and treat him as the shifter in charge of his species. That made him weak—but dangerous. Percy was cunning and tried to get what he wanted through a combination of male demands and cajoling. In her estimation, he was also weak, but dangerous in a different way than Rud. But Bacus . . . He didn't posture. He didn't make demands. He remained quiet in the shadows, observing. He gave nothing of himself away. His energy was so low-key it would be very easy to overlook him. That made him a little terrifying, especially because he was hunting her. She had to stop obsessing over it.

Percy hadn't answered her question immediately. In fact, he was silent for so long Rud roared with rage. "You tell her I'm the leader, Percy," he demanded, very belligerent. He even took an aggressive step in Percy's direction. Sandrine cried out when his fist tightened around her bicep and he gave her a little shake, dragging her with him.

"Rud." Jasmine held up a placating hand. "She's very little."

She sounded pleading. Trying to appease his anger. It was exactly what Rud wanted and needed to feed his tremendous ego.

Sarika couldn't imagine Luiz making such a mistake as hurting a child in front of everyone and demanding another proclaim him the supreme ruler. Even if Percy endorsed Rud's leadership, anyone hearing the exchange could be forgiven for thinking Rud had intimidated him into complying. Rud was no leader in any sense of the word. She despised him just for the way he was treating the child.

"He took over leadership," Percy said, his voice quiet. Thoughtful. "He expects all shifters to follow his lead. And he believes that he has the right to any female shifter, old or young. Brodrick, the previous leader, taught that concept during his reign."

"Women were meant for breeding," Rud stated. He drew the child closer. "Jasmine doesn't have a clue who the father of this little brat is. But we know he was a shifter. That means she is one. We know she can shift. Eventually, if she doesn't cooperate and show us her jaguar, we'll beat it out of her."

Sandrine had burst into tears the moment Rud said her mother didn't have a clue who her father was.

"Baby, we know exactly who your father is," Jasmine whispered. "Don't you doubt it for a minute. Jubal will come for you. Rud and Percy and Bacus are not going to want to fight him because your father is strong and brave and decent. He'll come for you." There was complete conviction in her voice.

"Jubal is at the market. Did you think we weren't keeping track?" Rud sneered. "He can't possibly make it back in time, even if word got to him that his precious brat was gone along with her slut of a mother."

"Call me whatever you want, Rud." Jasmine lifted her chin at him. His accusations appeared to steady her. "Just let Sandrine go."

Rud swung the little girl into his arms and took another step away from Jasmine. He narrowed his gaze at Jasmine, looking more sinister than ever. "I'm taking her, Jasmine. If you want to come, that's your decision."

"Oh my God, Percy, he is a pedophile. That child is a baby." Sarika poured alarm into her voice, sent it winging through the forest, her voice a compulsive tool, powerful when needed.

The surrounding jungle seemed to hold its breath. No movement. No sound. And then it erupted into a wild cacophony of protest. Overhead, monkeys screamed and leapt up and down on boughs, shaking the trees. Birds took flight. Colorful frogs and lizards skittered up and down the trunks. Snakes raised their heads and hissed. Vines shivered and undulated in protest. Flowers climbing the trees closed their petals.

"What the hell?" Rud snapped, looking around him warily. "It isn't yet sunset."

Just that observation voiced aloud told Sarika that Rud was leery of her cousin. He seemed aware that Luiz wouldn't join them until the sun had set. It wouldn't be much longer. She needed to distract him. To stall. He had no idea that the strange reaction in the forest was because of her compelling voice.

"You'll need to reveal yourself to him if you want to keep him here long enough for Luiz to show up. If he takes that child, he'll kill her." The whisper reached her, and at first, she just froze, trying to analyze it. Close. Very close.

Bacus. Now she knew where he was, and it wasn't a good scenario. She hadn't even felt the shiver of branches as the heavier male climbed into the tree. The male voice came from above her. The thread of sound didn't carry beyond the tree she was in, leading her to believe he could direct his voice in any direction, as she could.

"Why would you help us when you're playing second to him?" She directed her voice solely to him. He already knew she was capable.

"I don't take children from their mothers."

"But you haven't challenged him."

"I have no desire to lead the jaguar people. I attached myself to him in order to try to stop his worst crimes." There was no inflection in his voice. No way to use his tone to determine if he was telling the truth.

Did she believe him? Could she? If he was capable of manipulating his voice, he could sound truthful when he was a liar. She didn't trust him. She didn't trust anyone, not even Luiz. This forest was a labyrinth of deception and depravity due to its inhabitants. She didn't understand why Jasmine resided there with her daughter when, clearly, they were in danger every moment they stayed.

"Don't trust Percy. You can't trust any male associating with Rud," Bacus continued.

"You associate with him," she reminded and then raised her voice. "Rud, I'm coming down to talk to you about this situation. I can't believe a man who has leadership over such difficult shifters would harm a child for no reason. Give me a minute. I'm in human form, and I don't know the forest yet or the easy way through the trees."

"Show yourself," he shouted. He'd taken two steps toward the interior, swinging Sandrine onto his hip. "You better be still," he hissed to the child, "or I'll break your neck and then kill your mother. Do you understand me?"

He spoke softly, directing his voice to the little girl, but he didn't have Bacus' talent. Sarika heard every word. She was fairly certain everyone heard. Jaguars had excellent hearing.

As far as she was concerned, Rud was the worst of the worst. She couldn't believe anyone would follow his lead. He was a monster.

The child went absolutely still, her terrified gaze seeking her mother. Jasmine gasped, one hand going to her throat. She looked at the surrounding trees. Sarika couldn't tell if Jasmine was praying the woman they all wanted revealed would show herself or if Jasmine wanted her to run. She was running, all right, but to join the fray.

Sarika sprinted along the outstretched branches, leaping from tree to tree, not bothering to hide her route from the male shifters. In any case, Bacus followed her. He was silent and didn't make the trees so much as shiver, but she was tuned to him now and felt him behind her. Close. Too close.

How long until sunset? Every minute seemed to drag by. She didn't want Rud or the other two male shifters to think about the time. As she ran, she tried to come up with a plan to continue stalling.

She dropped from the tree nearest Jasmine but allowed several feet between them so it wouldn't be easy for the male shifters to get their hands on either of them. She expected Bacus to leap from the tree behind her, but he didn't. Again, she had no idea where he was. He'd been running easily on the branches behind her, and now he was somewhere back in the shadows, something else for her to worry about.

Rud's expression changed as Sarika slowly straightened. His eyes went dark with lust, his face flushed. Percy stepped closer to Sarika, only two steps, but Rud instantly held up his hand to indicate for him to stop moving.

"You can shift." He made it a statement.

Jasmine's breath hitched, and she shook her head. "Don't say anything to him. Don't give him any information."

Sarika smiled at her, keeping her expression calm. Jasmine's anxiety had grown, not lessened, with her having shown herself. Even though she had a child and the circumstances seemed dire, she clearly was opposed to Sarika putting herself in danger. Sarika liked her all the better for that.

"Jasmine, I'm Sarika Silva. My uncle Alois and aunt Gemma raised me. Uncle Alois was the oldest Silva brother." Deliberately, she tried to impart information that wouldn't be harmful, but so Rud might allow the interaction to go on for a couple of minutes. That was all she wanted. Eking out time, minute by minute. She willed Jasmine to follow her example.

"I'm Jasmine Sanders. My husband is Jubal. He's also a shifter, and he comes from a royal line." She looked down her nose at Rud. "If he desired, he would be leader."

Rud sneered. "Jubal doesn't have the balls to lead the jaguars. He would never do what it takes. It offends his sensibilities."

"Be very careful, Rud. You haven't seen him when he's riled," Jasmine cautioned. "You can tell yourself a million times that you're faster and stronger than he is, but bloodlines provide remarkable gifts. You know that. Just look at Solange."

Sarika wanted to kiss her. She clearly understood the mission and was willing to engage with the male shifter as long as possible.

"Solange?" Sarika deliberately questioned. "I'm afraid I am unfamiliar with that name." She was certain Luiz had mentioned Solange but just in passing. She didn't really know much about the woman.

"She's a legend, isn't she, Rud?" Jasmine challenged. "She single-handedly rescued female shifters over and over. She fought and killed several males to do that. She strikes fear in the hearts of the male shifters. Not only that, but Brodrick the Terrible was her father. She killed him, freeing many females until Rud took over."

Sarika swung her gaze to Rud. His face had darkened to pure rage. "She single-handedly drove our species to near extinction. Brodrick was a great man. A true leader."

"He was a mass murderer. A madman who tortured and killed his own people," Jasmine countered. "You may admire him all you want, but you know it is absolutely the truth that he murdered young women and even men in his rages. Children. Very, very young children. I know you're following in his footsteps because you threatened to kill Sandrine."

Sarika pulled in her breath sharply. It wasn't a good thing to remind Rud of the child when he was obviously furious.

"Children who couldn't shift. Those women were betraying our kind, sleeping with humans, having their children instead of doing their duty to our people," Rud said righteously.

"Babies," Jasmine emphasized. "He even tried to kill Solange, believing she wouldn't be able to shift. He thought he'd killed her, but he was wrong. He was wrong about quite a few of those children, but he slaughtered them all the same."

Sarika stroked her fingers down her throat, her breath catching. The things Jasmine was saying followed the history Luiz had given her, just from a different perspective. This Solange had to be a powerhouse. A part of her wanted to stick around to meet her, but she knew that would be crazy. As far as she was concerned, the quicker she got out of the rainforest, the better off she'd be.

She had all but forgotten Bacus in the ensuing conversation, but Rud made a small gesture with his chin. It appeared as if he was signaling someone. That someone could only be Bacus.

"We're getting off track," Rud said. "You need to answer the question of whether or not you're able to shift."

She was carrying a small pack with her, one easily identified by shifters. She thought it would be better not to lie to him. "Of course I can. I told you, I'm Luiz's first cousin."

"How is it no one has ever mentioned you?"

She shrugged. "I wasn't raised here. I told you my uncle and aunt raised me in the States. I'm just visiting Luiz. My stay will be very short."

"Not anymore," Rud decreed. "We need female shifters. It's your duty to provide offspring for our people."

His attempt at sounding clinical failed completely, mostly because looking at her even affected his breathing. It was clear he was aroused—and entitled. She studied him carefully as he slowly put Sandrine on the forest floor. He retained his hold on her arm, but he didn't appear to be hurting her.

"I don't fall under your rule," Sarika pointed out. "I'm a visitor, not a resident."

"You were born into our realm, and that makes you subject to the rules." He gestured toward Jasmine. "Just as she is."

"It sounded to me as if Jasmine has a family. A male, a father for her child. Are you saying that she should be with other men?"

"She needs to provide other children for our species," Rud said.

"Can't she do that with her man?"

"It isn't right that she is only with one man when so many others suffer," Rud answered.

"Still, she provided Sandrine, and she's capable of providing more. If her man, this Jubal, has royal bloodlines, wouldn't it be preferable for him to father any children?" She tried to sound as though she were asking an innocent question.

Rud looked annoyed. His patience was clearly wearing thin. Sarika's heart rate nearly doubled. She knew she had only a few more minutes, if that, to keep the shifter from attacking her or Jasmine. Where was Bacus? Why couldn't she spot him?

"I don't like that your friend Bacus is nowhere in sight," Sarika said. "What are the three of you planning?"

Percy edged closer to her. "You know I'm your friend. Nothing is going to happen to you, Sarika." He tried to sound soothing.

"If you were my friend, you would be removing that child from Rud after the casual way he talked about killing children. *Any* children, let alone those of our species." She meant that. If Bacus was listening, she meant it for him as well. Who would take a chance on a child's life when Rud spoke so easily of murdering children?

She turned her head to look directly at Percy. She was unsure of him. She felt he was in solid with Rud, following his lead, able to enjoy all of Rud's castoffs. That didn't mean he was. She didn't care for the cunning look of superiority that came over his facial features or crept into his eyes when he'd spoken to her earlier. And on Luiz's verandah, he'd been scary and demanding.

Just not like Rud. Rud felt completely off. Oily. Slimy. On the verge of insanity. Drunk on his own power and importance. Like the former leader they described, she had no doubt Rud would contribute to the downfall of their society—even the extinction of their species.

Once again, Percy edged closer. Now he was within striking distance of her. She knew how fast the shifters could move. Bacus suddenly emerged from the shadows, once again behind Jasmine.

Rud gave them both a superior smile. "I have claimed this female shifter, as is my right."

Before the other two men could respond to that declaration, Sarika did. She was outraged that these men believed they had a right to her body without her consent.

"You can go to hell. That isn't going to happen."

Rud's hand around Sandrine's arm transferred to her throat, fingers lengthening to sharp talons. Jasmine gasped and took a step toward him. Bacus put a restraining hand on her shoulder.

"You will surrender willingly, or this child dies right here. Right now," Rud decreed.

Out of the corner of her eye, she saw Percy shake his head, whether to warn her or to disagree with Rud, she wasn't certain. It didn't matter. She felt she had no choice but to attack the leader of the jaguar shifters. That meant getting closer.

When she took what appeared to be a reluctant step toward him, Percy exploded into action, catching at her arm to restrain her. Simultaneously, Bacus shoved Jasmine out of the way, hard enough to send her sprawling to the ground behind him.

Around them, in three places, the ground erupted. Dark geysers of whirling dirt, rotted vegetation, leaves and twigs rose high into the air. Everyone froze as a man emerged from one of the geysers. He stood directly in front of Rud, facing him.

Two others were suddenly there as well, one standing to the side of Percy and her while the third man aided Jasmine to her feet. He did so gently and just as gently put her behind him so his body was between hers and Bacus'.

CHAPTER 7

Sarika found her heart pounding nearly out of control when the three men came up out of the ground. It was clear the troops had arrived, just not the one she was expecting.

All three men were clearly related. They looked like triplets, but it was the man standing directly in front of Rud she found imposing. She wasn't the only one. Everyone's attention was riveted on him—even Bacus'.

The aura he gave off was one of extreme power. Of total command. Of absolute calm. He was tall and broad-shouldered like the other two men. All three had long chestnut-colored hair and brilliant, glittering aquamarine-colored eyes. Those eyes betrayed intelligence and the cunning of the highest predator. There was no doubt in her mind that they were facing three extremely lethal beings.

What was even scarier to Sarika was that the three men *felt* like they were one person to her. They seemed to move in synchronization. They felt like lethal predators, giving off a vibe so much more powerful than Rud or any of the other jaguars.

Strangely, she couldn't take her eyes off the man confronting Rud. No one could. To her, he was the most gorgeous man she'd ever seen. He looked all man, nothing soft about him. Every muscle was sleek and defined. When he moved, those muscles rippled powerfully under his skin, but when he was still, it was almost as if he could fade into the background, becoming a phantom. He had tear-shaped scarring on the right side of his face from hairline to jaw. That should have detracted from his good looks, but she doubted if anything could.

The surrounding jungle had gone eerily silent. The familiar drone of insects she'd found comforting was no more. There were no wings fluttering overhead or the scream of monkeys. Snakes, frogs and lizards seemed frozen to tree branches. The tension was ratcheted up so tight that not a single mouse, vole or salamander scurried through the leaves on the forest floor.

The glittering aquamarine eyes focused on Rud. "Gentlemen." Those eyes shifted for the barest of moments to rest first on Jasmine and then Sarika before they softened when his gaze touched Sandrine. "Ladies."

His voice was the most compelling thing Sarika had ever heard. A wave of unexpected heat rushed through her veins. She could only stare at him with wide, shocked eyes. He'd come out of the ground right in front of her, and with one look, he commanded everyone. She waited, counting her heartbeats.

"Tomas," Rud identified the stranger. He seemed frozen to the spot.

"I believe you are scaring young Sandrine, Rud." That voice was pitched low, with no challenge, no warning, yet the threat was very clear.

She had no idea if the stranger was familiar with Jasmine and Sandrine, but by calling the child by her name and the way the little girl was looking at him, she believed he knew them—that he hadn't just overheard her name.

Rud cleared his throat. "This is a jaguar matter, Tomas. Not Carpathian." He took a quick look around, as did Sarika. Tomas' brothers had faded even more into the background.

"I will have to respectfully disagree with you, Rud. I have an aversion to harming women or children, and it isn't ever going to be done on my watch. It is best you remove your hand from around that child's neck before one of us will be compelled to take action." Again, he spoke in that low, calm voice. Almost gentle. But there was nothing gentle in his slashing eyes or the building waves of sheer menace coming from him.

Rud glanced at Sarika and then flexed the long stiletto-like claws until one rested over Sandrine's jugular. "Do you think you're fast enough?" he challenged.

Sarika stepped toward Rud in protest. Percy's hand slid off her arm. He didn't make a move. Tomas shot her a single look and she froze in place.

He turned his predatory gaze back to Rud and slowly inclined his head. "Faster, yes. I'm Carpathian, as are my brothers. Should you do the child any damage, we have ways to heal her. She is in no danger from you. You, however, are in tremendous danger."

Luiz. Sarika reached for her cousin. *Why aren't you here? You said you would come, especially if there's trouble.*

Her cousin answered her immediately. *By chance, Tomas, Lojos and Mataias happened to have taken rest beneath the earth where Rud decided on a confrontation with Jasmine, you and little Sandrine. As they were closer and more than capable of handling the situation, I have sought sustenance.*

The reminder made her shudder. *So you're out feeding yourself and leaving my safety and that of Jasmine and her child to perfect strangers.* She wanted to strangle him.

There was a short silence. Once again, she had the impression of male amusement that didn't quite register with him. It was there, she felt it, but he didn't.

The impulse to strangle must be a genetic thing, he said. He sounded lazy. Not in the least concerned about her safety. *I have the urge to strangle you for putting yourself in this position after I gave you specific orders not to leave the house.*

She was not commenting on that. The entire time she was chastising her cousin, she kept her attention centered on Tomas. How could she not? He commanded the situation with his quiet authority. She didn't like his solution—that if Rud succeeded in puncturing Sandrine's artery, the Carpathians would simply heal the laceration. It wasn't that easy, that simple, to stop someone from bleeding out when there was arterial damage.

Tomas looked utterly confident. Almost too confident, as if the entire situation bored him. She studied him and realized, not through looking at him but feeling him, that he *wanted* Rud to challenge him. Tomas fascinated her. Mesmerized her. She had thought Luiz was terrifying; Tomas was frightening to her in a different way. She just wasn't certain what that was.

Rud glared at him and then shot a look at both Percy and Bacus. "You dare to interfere with our species? Do you really believe you can get away with challenging the leader of our people?"

Tomas inclined his head. "Yes. If you prefer formality, Jasmine, would you tell me what Rud is doing with your daughter and what he intended to do with you?"

"He planned on kidnapping Sandrine and forcing me to go with him. If I refused, he said he would kill her," Jasmine said. Her voice was barely above a whisper. "He intended to use both of us for breeding purposes."

"As is my right," Rud snarled. "There is no interference between species."

"And you?" Tomas turned those brilliant aquamarine eyes toward Sarika. His gaze settled on her. Held her captive. Compelled her to answer him. "I do not believe we've met."

She lifted her chin. She didn't know why she felt it was important she didn't look frightened. Inside, she was quaking. It was difficult to control the tremors in her body. "I just arrived yesterday to visit my cousin, Luiz Silva."

It was an innocent enough statement, delivered in a calm, low voice. She was honest. Direct. But the moment she spoke to him, Tomas' entire attention focused on her. His expression didn't change, but his eyes did. That powerful predator was suddenly fixated on her. Not only him but his brothers as well. She felt the weight of their scrutiny like a laser piercing through skin and bones to the very heart and soul of her.

She had no idea what she'd said to cause the three Carpathians to focus on her with their strange, piercing eyes, but she wanted none of it. She found their intense scrutiny to be more difficult to deal with than Rud. Rud she could fight. She had a chance of besting him using her brains—her greatest weapon. She had discovered, just by observation, that he could be manipulated. Not so, the three Carpathians. Worse, she feared, even though they hadn't touched her or taken her blood, they were able to read her thoughts.

"Your name?" Tomas' voice was low, but this time it was all velvet smooth. More intimate than anything she'd ever heard in her life.

For a moment, she thought to stay silent. Defiant. Self-preservation was strong.

"She is my female, a jaguar shifter, not Carpathian. You have no authority over her or any of us," Rud snapped. "Don't you dare tell him your name."

She detested being told what to do, especially by the likes of a disturbed, misogynistic, arrogant would-be dictator. Every time the man spoke, he set her teeth on edge.

"Sarika Silva."

Tomas seemed to study her for a long moment, and then his attention was back to Rud. "You have not let the child go. Sandrine, close your eyes now."

Sarika blinked. That was all. She blinked. She missed everything with that one single motion of her eyelids. When she raised them, Rud was on the ground with blood spurting from his throat, and Sandrine was clinging to Tomas, both arms around his neck.

"Percy, Bacus, it is best if you dispose of your leader's body in the proper manner," Tomas advised, but already, his attention had swung back to Sarika.

That fast. That easily. Tomas had killed Rud without any fanfare. He'd done it while she blinked. So casually. She had never witnessed someone being killed. Bile rose as she stared at Rud's body.

Her throat closed. Her lungs seized. She feared she was going to faint from lack of air, but she didn't know why. She had always stood her ground. She had traveled extensively all over the world, and she'd learned not to show fear. To always appear calm and in control. There was no controlling her heart rate or breathing. She felt dizzy with fear.

Tomas waited for Percy and Bacus to go to their fallen leader, pick him up and leap into the trees, the foliage hiding their retreat. One of the brothers waited a moment, and then his body shimmered and disappeared altogether. She knew that he followed the two men. She didn't know for certain if Bacus was a good or bad guy, but she knew Percy wasn't good. And he wasn't intelligent. She was afraid he would do something utterly ridiculous, such as return and try to challenge Tomas.

Once his brother had completely disappeared, Tomas crossed the uneven ground to Jasmine to carefully and gently transfer her daughter to her.

"Thank you, Tomas," Jasmine said as she hugged Sandrine to her. She looked over his shoulder to Sarika, who found herself edging away, back into the shadows. "Sarika, I will never be able to repay you. If you hadn't put yourself in jeopardy, I couldn't have stopped Rud and the others. I don't know why you risked yourself for a complete stranger, but I will forever be grateful to you. I hope you have Luiz bring you to my home to meet my husband. Solange and Dominic will want to thank you in person as well. There is Juliette and Riordan who will want to do the same. Please give us the opportunity."

Tomas had half turned, his molten gaze finding her in the shadows. Her stomach did a strange flip at the burning intensity of his eyes.

She moistened her lips and called up every bit of courage she had. "There's no need to thank me, Jasmine. Truly. I couldn't let that horrid man take your daughter or you. I knew Luiz would come at sunset, although he decided he wasn't needed." She was going to have a few things to say to him. "I don't intend to be here long." She was running as fast as she could. Like right away. She was good with directions, and she could make her way to the river and get the hell out of the insanity that was this rainforest.

Tomas raised one eyebrow. The way he looked at her with such intensity freaked her out. She wasn't the type of woman to fall at the feet of an attractive man and say she wanted to have his babies, but if she was around him too long, that just might happen. And she'd just seen him kill a man. Well, she hadn't seen him do it. It wasn't like she could testify in court that she'd witnessed him killing someone.

She didn't look at the blood on the ground. That just freaked her out even more. How could she be attracted to a man who could kill so casually and then look at her with such focused intensity? He terrified her. Her neck throbbed and burned, and her hand crept up to cover the artery protectively.

"Jasmine," Tomas said without turning his head to look at her. He kept his gaze fixed on Sarika. "Mataias will escort you and Sandrine home. We wouldn't want to take any chances that Percy or Bacus are waiting out there for you."

The way he was looking at her, more predatory, *hungry*, made her heart thud out of control.

"Thank you, Tomas. I'll let Jubal know to expect you."

Since Tomas hadn't said he was paying them a visit, Sarika thought that was very brave of Jasmine. Jasmine sounded sweet, but the expectation was that Tomas would comply. Sarika couldn't imagine him doing anything a woman told him to do. For that matter, he wasn't going to listen to men, either. Tomas was a man to go his own way.

Sarika watched in horror as Jasmine turned away from them, Sandrine in her arms. Mataias, the other brother, reached over and took the child from Jasmine. The little girl went willingly, displaying complete trust by putting her arms around his neck and laying her head on his shoulder. She could tell Mataias was whispering to her. Sandrine's giggle floated back to her.

There she was, suddenly alone with Tomas. She pressed her lips together, gathered her courage and forced a smile. "I'd like to add my thanks to Jasmine's. You came at the exact perfect time, when we needed you desperately."

He gave a slight bow. "Why do you fear me when it is apparent I aided you?"

It was the last thing she expected him to say, and it threw her off-balance. She couldn't tell him the truth—she didn't even know what the truth was. She allowed her gaze to drop to the blood on the ground. It was her only out. "I've never seen anything like that before. I've never seen anyone killed." It was the truth, so if he could read lies in a voice, she would sound honest.

He studied her for too long, so long that she found herself squirming. Color began to creep up her neck into her face.

"But you didn't see it. I made certain that you, Sandrine and Jasmine were protected."

He made the announcement like it was a good thing that he could somehow make all three of the females look away at the precise moment he took Rud's life. How was that possible? Luiz had explained about taking blood and being able to reach her at any time. She suspected he was able to do far more than that—such as control her like a puppet. But this man . . . He hadn't taken her blood, yet he had forced her to blink. To miss the action. The idea that he had that kind of power was terrifying.

"You made me look away?"

"I protected you," he corrected, his voice low and compelling. Like velvet brushing over her skin. He gestured toward the thick grove of trees to her right. "Let's get you somewhere safe. Luiz will want to talk with us."

Stubbornly, she shook her head. "I'm not going back to my cousin's place. I was going to head for the river so I could catch a ride on a boat."

"I think it best if we go talk to your cousin. We'll need to explain things to his satisfaction."

She didn't like the sound of that. Luiz had already indicated he wasn't happy with her choices.

"I am going to the river," she declared decisively.

"Sarika." His voice gentled even more. "Boats have regularly scheduled arrival times in other places. Not around here. They only come here if someone has hired them to bring them or pick them up."

That wasn't good at all. Now she had nowhere to go but to Luiz. She didn't want to be in the company of two Carpathians. What if they both wanted her blood?

"I can make my way to my cousin's," she said. "There's no need for you to be put out."

"I think we both know if I left you alone in this forest with Percy and Bacus on the loose, I would be answering to your cousin. He's a De La Cruz. You might think Silva, but he was reborn into the De La Cruz family, and they are . . . unique."

She gave him her best scowl. "I will not believe for one moment that Luiz, or anyone else, can take you to task successfully for any decision you make."

Luiz was intimidating, but Tomas was equally so. Both men were very sure of themselves. And Tomas might have an advantage in that he had two brothers traveling with him. They seemed, to her, to act as one unit.

Tomas gave her a gift . . . and she knew it was a gift . . . the briefest of smiles, but it was genuine, and for a moment those brilliant eyes lit up, looking for all the world like bluish-green diamonds. The bottom dropped out of her stomach. It was insane how susceptible she was to him. The knowledge that he didn't give others a genuine smile came out of nowhere, but she knew it was true. She couldn't stop herself from taking a step back, once more covering her neck with her hand. She didn't like or trust her reaction to him.

"You have no reason to fear me, Sarika. If there is one person on this planet safe from me, it is you. I give you my word of honor I will escort you safely to your cousin's home. I will need to have a few words with him."

"I've found that having words with Luiz isn't a very good idea," she warned. She didn't even know why she warned him, other than she didn't want the two men to argue over her. And she believed, for some reason, they would.

"I apologize for allowing you to see the body and the amount of blood. I could have hidden it from your eyes. I didn't realize it would affect you so negatively."

Her teeth bit down on her lower lip. She didn't like lies, even if she told them for self-preservation. "It didn't bother me as much as it should have. I believe he intended to kill Sandrine in front of Jasmine. I could feel his hatred of her. He smoldered with it. That's the best way I can describe it." By giving him the truth, she didn't realize what she'd revealed to him. Not until he cocked his head to one side and studied her carefully with those piercing eyes. Eyes that saw far too much.

"If it isn't the fact that I killed Rud, what is it about me that frightens you?"

He queried her gently. So softly, his voice pitched low, and again, she had the sensation of velvet brushing over her skin. For a moment she was so caught up in the strange sensation she almost didn't hear his question. When it finally registered, she felt heat rush under her skin. She despised the fact that she blushed. Did other jaguar shifters blush? It seemed childish. Teenagey. A dead giveaway.

She took a breath, common sense telling her to avoid answering, but her weird reaction to him demanded that she tell the truth. And that was it in a nutshell.

"I don't understand my reactions to you," she admitted honestly. Maybe that wasn't the brightest idea, but she felt compelled to tell him the truth. "Clearly, you're Carpathian. I had never heard of your species until Luiz and I met. It was our first time meeting. My first time being here in this rainforest. My first time encountering other jaguar shifters. None of it has been good. The things Luiz could do so casually were frightening."

Once again, her hand crept up to cover her neck, and his gaze locked in on her trembling fingers. She was giving herself away, not only blurting out truths like an idiot but reinforcing them with silent gestures.

Tomas nodded, his eyebrows drawing together in a slight frown. Expressions, she decided, were important. He'd had such a mask earlier, and that contributed to her rising fear of him. Most likely because Luiz wore a similar mask and both men were intense. She'd rather read what they were thinking than guess at it. Now that no one was around, Tomas seemed to be more relaxed and willing to show her what he was thinking or feeling—at least a little bit.

"Do you mind me asking you what your cousin did that has you so afraid of Carpathians?"

If she said the word *blood*, would that be some kind of trigger for him? Why was he looking at her as if he knew her? As if he knew everything about her? Was he reading her mind? He hadn't taken her blood, and from what Luiz said, that was a prerequisite for that ability, wasn't it?

"He took my blood after I absolutely told him I didn't want him to. And he did it without my knowledge. Well, I suspected and asked him. He was truthful, but he still went against my wishes, and he didn't feel in the least remorseful."

Tomas nodded, his eyes going soft. Gentle. "And then I made certain you didn't see me kill Rud. That must feel like a takeover. I had to make a split-second decision, and I wanted to spare you any real fear. I can see I only added to your concerns over our species."

Tomas crossed the short distance between them. At once she was aware of the difference in their heights. Up close, she felt his power even more. He wasn't touching her, but he was close enough to feel his body heat. He indicated the forest.

"We need to get moving. It is always possible Rud's enforcers will attempt to retaliate. I would prefer that you were out of harm's way."

"He has enforcers?" Her voice came out as a squeak. The idea that those male shifters might be anywhere near her galvanized her into action. She began to walk toward one of the largest trees with low branches.

"Sarika." He said her name in that low, gentle way he had. "No shifter will touch you. Luiz would come at my call—or yours—as would my brothers if I thought I couldn't handle them myself. There's no need to panic."

She despised that she looked like such a coward to him. She'd never been one to retreat in the face of an enemy, but she was so out of her depth. She didn't look at him. She couldn't. She knew she looked weak, and it embarrassed her.

"Is there a way to contact the boats so I can arrange to go home?" She didn't know where home was anymore. She'd hoped it would be here in the rainforest, where she'd been born. Where her family had died. Where there was Luiz.

She crouched low and leapt to the overhanging branch. She didn't want to give him any ideas, like Luiz, of turning into a bird and carrying her back to the tree house. She was decisive about her leap. He made no sound when he leapt behind her. She didn't feel his weight on the branch, but she knew he was there. She felt his body heat. More, she had that shivery feeling inside that she was so unfamiliar with but only he could produce.

"The moment I heard your name, I knew who you were. So did my brothers. I didn't say anything because I didn't want anyone else to know our connection."

She stopped moving and turned to face him. He sounded as if he was being honest, but she would have remembered him. No one would forget meeting Tomas or his brothers.

"How?"

He smiled down at her, that same brief, genuine smile that curled her toes and sent heat rushing through her veins.

"I am T. Smolnycki Jr. You wrote to me for many years."

Her breath caught in her throat. T. Smolnycki felt like an old friend. *T* had to be for Tomas.

"We do not allow photographs, and we do not keep letters, anything that might betray our species, but I have every one of your letters."

As confessions went, it was profound. There was no way to misinterpret what he was telling her. Their connection meant as much to him as it did to her. That was both wonderful and even more frightening. She was *so* susceptible to him. It also explained the scary, intense focus all three brothers had turned on her when she'd given her name. That made her feel a little better. They'd been so completely focused on her in the middle of a dicey situation it had amplified her fears.

She didn't like a lot of attention. She'd learned, traveling as much as she did to other countries, to stay in the background as much as possible. That didn't mean she didn't give her opinion, and she always stood up for herself, but she was careful. The less she was noticed in some circumstances, the safer she was.

"I never thought I'd have the chance to meet you," she confessed. "You and your ideas on conservation have had such an impact on my life." She hero-worshiped him, although she wasn't going to tell him that. Now that she'd met him in person and realized she was physically attracted to him, something that just didn't happen, she was even more confused and embarrassed. She didn't want him ever reading her mind.

She turned back in the direction of Luiz's tree house, thinking it was safer than spending too much time with him. Just knowing who he was, remembering every word of every letter exchanged over the years, only added to the deep attraction she had toward him.

"I'd like to ask a favor." Now she didn't know what to call him. He'd first introduced himself as Tomas, and everyone had referred to him as

Tomas. "I don't know if you're capable of reading my thoughts . . ." It was a question.

"I am."

She closed her eyes briefly, but she was walking fast along a tree branch, and that wasn't such a good idea. "You don't have to take my blood to read them?"

"No."

"And your brothers and Luiz can read my thoughts as well?"

"Yes."

"Without taking my blood," she clarified.

"In close proximity it is easy enough to pick up thoughts. I believe you are capable as well. If we wish to communicate from a distance or check on a specific person, we would have to take their blood." He spoke matter-of-factly, as if it were normal.

"I can't read thoughts," she denied.

"Then you're very adept at reading body language. Your timing was perfect each time you intervened with Rud when you were stalling, waiting for the sun to set."

"You heard us, even when you were in the ground." She kept moving from branch to branch, picking up the pace just a little in order to get back to the tree house. She didn't know why, but she felt she would be safer.

"It just so happened that Rud made his play above our resting places. Bad luck on his part."

Was there a slight trace of amusement in his voice? Or like Luiz, was it in his mind? The moment the question came to her, her breath caught in her throat. Was she catching glimpses of other people's thoughts? That would be invasive. Intrusive. Horrible. She wasn't the kind of woman who invaded other people's privacy, yet it was possible she was catching glimpses of their emotions.

"Do you feel?"

"Feel," he echoed.

This time, he sounded wary. So much so that she stopped and

turned to face him, wanting to see his expression, but he wasn't wearing one. His handsome face was an inscrutable mask. Her heart skipped a beat.

His gaze was hot as it swept over her. More than hot. Hunger was there. A fierce, possessive element crept into his gaze. "Yes." His answer was curt. "Emotions are new after centuries of not being able to feel, so I'm still struggling to get used to them. At times, they feel overwhelming."

She wasn't certain what to do with that admission. The worst was Luiz had told her only a lifemate could restore emotion to a Carpathian hunter. That meant Tomas Smolnycki Jr. had a lifemate, and if the indications were anything to go by, he lusted after her. Men cheated. She was disappointed that her hero was a man who would cheat on a woman who had guarded his soul and restored his emotions. She knew jaguar shifters weren't faithful. Apparently, neither were Carpathians.

She turned away from him, feeling inexplicably sad. He'd been her hero, her mentor, the one person she'd stupidly poured her heart out to. She'd told him everything about her life—other than the fact that she was a shifter. She'd told him her hopes and dreams. She'd shared her ideas on conservation with this man.

True, her first letters had been childish, but as she'd grown up, throughout her college years, and with each internship in the various rainforests she'd traveled, she'd written to him to get advice. After, when she'd returned home, she wrote to him detailing every aspect of her trip, the others who had traveled on the journey with her, what she had learned from them and what her takeaway was. He had always been encouraging. It often took months before he'd reply, but he always did.

Not only did Sarika feel sadness; she felt betrayed. The entire exchange added to her feelings of loss. Of the need to run. She wanted to retreat somewhere safe, to some hole she could crawl into, where she could lick her wounds in peace without the worry she might be giving too much away to anyone.

"You don't want me to read your thoughts, *sivamet*, but you're giving off an alarming emotion, one I am having trouble dealing with. If you don't confide in me what's wrong, you will leave me no choice but to do the very thing you don't want me to do. I see no reason for your distress, yet it is overwhelming."

"Thoughts should be private," she said without turning. She picked up her speed. They were much closer to the tree house and, hopefully, a place for her to hide, just for a short while. She needed respite from the terrible mantle of sorrow that pressed down on her. She had lost everything. Her hopes. Her dreams. Her cousin. This place was a labyrinth of deceit and danger. She didn't understand it, and she didn't want to be a part of it.

"That is the way of human beings and shifters, not Carpathians," he pointed out gently.

He was close. So close. She was running lightly on the branches of trees, and suddenly his warm breath was on her neck, just below her ear. His tone was low and intimate, causing that rush of heat through her veins she couldn't control.

"I should point out, I'm not Carpathian," she said, pouring snippiness into her voice. Not just snippy attitude but as haughty as she could make it. Irritated. Annoyed. She made it as clear as she could by body language that he was to back off and quit breathing on her.

"Perhaps you need to understand more about our species," he murmured in that velvet tone, the one that stroked over her skin and gave her goose bumps and—if she was being honest—all kinds of erotic ideas she'd never once in her life considered.

If Carpathians had playboys in their species, and clearly, they did, Tomas had to take the prize. He was very skilled at seduction. Thankfully, the tree house loomed ahead. Ignoring the man following so close, she leapt for the series of fungi that were actually steps leading up to the wraparound porch.

Luiz leaned over the railing, watching her, studying her expression and body language. He straightened slowly, his gaze resting on Tomas. He wore that mask of his, but there was something very unpleasant in his eyes.

That gave her pause, mostly because that blatant warning didn't seem to faze Tomas in the least. When she cleared the railing, he was right behind her. She stopped abruptly, not wanting her cousin and Tomas to square off, which they clearly were about to do.

CHAPTER 8

How had she gotten into this mess? Sarika took a deep breath and faced her cousin. Already her head was pounding. It hurt just to move. She was prone to migraines when she was stressed. *Stressed* was a silly word that did not in any way encompass how she felt.

Tomas should have stayed beside the railing, but he didn't. He stood just behind her and slightly to one side. She knew he wasn't looking for a confrontation between Luiz and himself; he was, in some alpha Carpathian way, declaring to Luiz something she didn't understand but scared the hell out of her.

"Luiz." Tomas used his easy, casual tone. He stepped around her, stood face-to-face with her cousin and clasped his forearms. *"Én jutta félet és ekämet."*

"Veri olen piros, ekäm."

Tomas stepped back. "I have," he said in English. He moved to stand behind and to the side of Sarika. This time, he put a very gentle hand on her shoulder. When she tensed, he tightened his fingers in warning, and she subsided.

"Perhaps you could tell me what you said to one another," she invited, leveling a challenging gaze at her cousin. She was far too aware of Tomas standing close, his body heat she couldn't ignore, an amazing scent that called to her. His hand was no longer on her shoulder, but he was so close that she felt his breath on her neck.

"We greeted one another as warriors. As brothers," Luiz explained. "He said to me, 'I greet a friend and brother.' He did so because we have known each other for years."

She lifted her chin. "Luiz, that's lovely, it is; but what did you say in return?" Whatever he had said to Tomas had changed the dynamic between them the moment Tomas had murmured, "I have."

Those two words had ratcheted up the tension between the two men. Luiz's gaze had swept over her, and she read alarm in his thoughts. Or feelings he claimed to her that he didn't have.

"I said to him, 'Blood be red, my brother.'"

She blinked. "I have" was not an answer to such a greeting. She didn't understand; whatever she was missing was huge. Her head hurt worse than ever. "I'm afraid you'll have to interpret that for me. I have no idea what that means."

Luiz's gaze jumped to Tomas. "The meaning is clear to all Carpathians. Blood appears red. We don't see in color unless we find our lifemate. I explained to you, there is only one. Figuratively, the greeting means *find your lifemate*."

Sarika froze like a cornered mouse. Tomas had replied, "I have," to that greeting. That meant he had a lifemate. She couldn't stop the fine tremors moving through her body as she turned her head to look up at him over her shoulder. "You have a lifemate. That's why you feel emotion. You said those feelings were difficult to process."

He nodded, his eyes holding hers captive. That focused stare was very much like that of a predator. She'd faced wild animals. She'd certainly faced big cats. They could be terrifying when they targeted someone, but this look was as scary or infinitely worse.

"When you have not felt any emotions for centuries and everything pours in at once, the sensation is overwhelming. I have to learn to sort through what I'm feeling and distance myself when necessary.

It is the same with colors. They actually hurt my eyes. I have to dull them in order to see without them blinding me."

He wrapped a curl around his finger, looking almost mesmerized as he lifted it toward his face. "This color is beautiful. All colors of red and gold. Amazing colors. The same with your eyes. Very vivid green, like gems, very intense."

The way his voice played over her, wreaking havoc on her senses, added to the tremors until she was visibly shaking. She was far too susceptible to him. That meant something ominous.

She had to find a way to breathe. Both men were waiting, allowing her to figure it out on her own. She stepped away from Tomas and, on shaky legs, made her way to the nearest piece of furniture, a hand-carved glider. Dropping into it, she shaded her eyes with her palm, not wanting either man to read her.

"You're mistaken if you think I'm your lifemate," she told Tomas. "I'm a jaguar shifter, not a Carpathian."

"You have gifts," Luiz said, his voice gentle. "I could see that the moment I laid eyes on you. The shifter males saw it. Why do you think Percy was so interested, so much so he was willing to go against Rud?"

"I know this is new and frightening to you," Tomas said. "But you know me. It isn't like I am a total stranger. We've been corresponding for years. We have enough between us to build on."

He didn't state it hopefully or suggestively; he decreed it. Commanded it. Made it sound as if it were a foregone conclusion. Now her head wanted to explode.

She ignored him and turned her accusatory stare directly at Luiz. "I'm here under your protection. You gave me your word of honor, and I believed you. You told me I would be perfectly safe. I'm not. I want to leave here as quickly as possible, and I'd like you to arrange that for me." She poured steel into her tone when she felt so fragile she was afraid she might shatter at any moment.

Luiz and Tomas once again exchanged a long look. Instantly, the air around her became charged with danger. It was no small danger; it was a threat unlike any she'd ever felt, not even when Rud held the child by the throat. This was vicious. Violent. The air so heavy she could barely take a breath.

A slight breeze stirred the leaves dripping from the vines at the doorway, and a man materialized out of the air. She recognized him immediately as Tomas' brother. His face was clear of the scars Tomas had, but she could see a webbing down his exposed arm all the way to his hand. His aquamarine eyes took in each of them, and then he gave a small courtly bow to Sarika.

"*Sisarke*, I trust these two are treating you well. I'm Lojos, Tomas' brother." His gaze shifted to Luiz, and his mask slid into place. "Well met, brother. I understand you're Sarika's cousin."

Luiz sent him a sardonic look. "What I understand is you're stalling to allow Mataias to get here."

Lojos gave him a slight bow, acknowledging his statement was true. When he did so, fog rolled in and out of the porch, leaving behind a tall, broad-shouldered man with unusual-colored eyes. They were a metallic green and seemed to change color when different light hit them. He had a web of scars down his face and arm from what she could see. This was definitely not Mataias. This man looked every bit as intimidating as the others.

The tremors began all over again. Now her head felt as if it were being squeezed in a vise. There were too many men surrounding her, and all of them appeared menacing.

"I am Dominic Dragonseeker," he announced, his gentle gaze on her face, taking in every detail, including her shaking hands. "I'm Solange's lifemate. Jasmine told us what you did for her and our Sandrine. We will never be able to repay you."

He looked menacing, *felt* that way, but he sounded completely different. She tried a tentative smile but feared she looked as freaked out as she felt. "I'm Sarika Silva."

"My cousin," Luiz said.

"My lifemate." Tomas was equally as firm.

Dominic raised his eyebrow and glanced toward Luiz for an explanation of the standoff.

"I gave her my word of safe passage. She wishes to return home."

Before Dominic could reply, Tomas did. "There can be no interference between lifemates. That is a sacred rule. If broken, it carries a death sentence."

Luiz didn't so much as blink. His expression didn't change, but Sarika could see a flame building in his eyes. This was bad. Very bad. She sat there like the mouse she was beginning to think herself, her mind numb. Her fear amounted to terror. These men were predators. Every one of them lethal. She didn't understand how her innocent visit, the visit she had planned for years, had turned into a battlefield. Especially since she didn't understand exactly what was happening.

"I have my honor to consider," Luiz said. "Sarika is my only family, and I'm entrusted with her safety."

"No longer." Tomas didn't give an inch. "She is my lifemate."

"He is correct, Luiz," Dominic said. "Perhaps one of the women will talk with Sarika and explain things."

"He has not claimed her, Dominic," Luiz said. "She wishes to leave."

"If that is all that you require, I will do so now," Tomas said, his voice with quiet menace but so firm she had no doubt he meant what he said. She didn't know what claiming was, but it was very clear that once he accomplished that task, she would be worse off than she was now.

She looked up at him. "Don't." Her voice was pitched very low, hopefully for him alone, but she knew the others heard. It wasn't a firm command, the way she wanted it to come out; she was too scared. She was unable to keep her voice from pleading with him. In front of all of them, she was terribly humiliated that she couldn't sound stronger.

Tomas' eyes, a storm of vicious rage, turned soft. He curled his fingers around the nape of her neck and bent at the waist until his mouth was against her ear. "We do not want a war started here."

"There doesn't have to be a war, does there?" Looking at him made her feel as if she were drowning.

"Not when we can prevent it."

Lojos moved very subtly, but the moment he shifted positions, moving away from her and Tomas, putting several feet between them, all eyes jumped to him. Mataias emerged next, his slashing gaze taking in her, his brothers, and then Luiz and Dominic.

Like the others, he addressed her first, giving her that elegant, courtly bow. "*Sisarke*, it is an honor to make your acquaintance. I am Mataias." He didn't wait for her reaction but immediately turned his attention toward Luiz and Dominic. "Gentlemen. Is there a problem here? Tomas' lifemate is radiating fear so strong that I felt it miles from here. Between here and where I was, the forest is in an uproar."

"She doesn't want to be claimed," Luiz said. "She wants to go home."

Sarika knew instantly that the triplets exchanged a private conversation in seconds. Without warning, there was the brush against her mind, a light touch, but she knew someone was invading, and it wasn't Tomas.

Mataias and Dominic exchanged a look, and she knew immediately *both* had invaded her privacy. That was so unfair. She detested that they could do that so casually, without giving a thought to whether she wanted to give them permission or not. These were beings far too powerful for their own good. Power corrupted; everyone knew that. She didn't even bother to glare at them. What was the use?

"She is merely fearful," Dominic said to Luiz. "Under the circumstances, that would be acceptable and normal. She knows little of our species and nothing about lifemates. I believe having one of the women come here and speak with her will take care of the problem."

Sarika didn't want to talk to one of their women; she wanted to demand Luiz take her home. Get her out of there to somewhere safe, where no jaguar shifter and no Carpathian male could ever get to her.

She looked at her cousin. Reached for him, mind to mind. *I want to go home. You promised me.*

Luiz's gaze flickered over her. She felt the conflict in him, but she wasn't going to relent. She needed out of the situation, and the only way out was through her cousin.

You are truly his lifemate, Sarika. He is telling the truth.

I am not Carpathian. I will fight this every step of the way. I counted on you to keep me safe. You can't just give me to him like I'm some toy you can pass around.

He didn't like that at all. He actually winced. His reaction wasn't outward, but she felt him; she was so tuned to him.

That isn't how it works, Sarika, Luiz told her cautiously. *You are putting me in a terrible position. We would have to fight our way out of here.*

I didn't put us in this position. She was absolutely certain of that. When dreaming of this place and meeting her cousin, her only living relative, she had never once conceived of a catastrophe such as what had taken place.

Tomas' shadow suddenly engulfed her, and then he was towering over her. "You will not speak with your cousin mind to mind when you refuse to do so with your lifemate."

"Choices," Lojos said, his voice very gentle. "Isn't that your belief, brother?"

"Sun scorch that idiocy," Tomas bit out. He reached down and caught a fistful of Sarika's red-gold hair. "Eyes to mine."

It was a command, the kind she found infuriating, but she couldn't stop herself from obeying. The moment their eyes met, she saw the terrible storm building there.

"*Te avio päläfertiilam.* You are my lifemate."

She tried to shake her head in denial, because as far as she was concerned, she wasn't. His fist tightened in her hair, preventing movement.

"*Éntölam kuulua, avio päläfertiilam.* I claim you as my lifemate."

Not one man moved. Around them, the forest animals fell silent, as if they knew something huge was taking place. Her heart began to pound so hard her chest hurt.

"*Ted kuuluak, kacad, kojed.* I belong to you. *Élidamet andam.* I offer my life for you."

His gaze didn't waver from hers. Those brilliant, slashing eyes held her captive. Revealed too much. His stark, raw passion. His total commitment to the path he had taken.

"*Pesämet andam.* I give you my protection."

She put up her hand to stop him, so afraid of the way he was making her feel inside, as if a million tiny threads bound them together. Strong threads. Unbreakable. "Luiz can protect me." That was a plea if she ever heard one. She wanted to break eye contact and look at her cousin, but she was helpless to do anything but stare into his eyes. It was a little like being mesmerized by a cobra. Lethal. Frightening. Shocking. But she was frozen to the spot.

"*Uskolfertiilamet andam.* I give you my allegiance. *Sívamet andam.* I give you my heart. *Sielamet andam.* I give you my soul."

With his free hand, he captured her outstretched palm, pressing it against his chest, right over his heart. His fingers began to move in slow caresses over the back of her hand, right over her bare skin. That was soothing. Gentle. So at odds with the raging storm in his eyes.

"*Ainamet andam.* I give you my body. *Sívamet kuuluak kaik että a ted.* I take into my keeping the same that is yours."

At his declaration, she shook her head, horrified that he thought she would share her body with a man who was a stranger. Letters be damned. She didn't care how gorgeous she found him or if their attraction was off the charts; she wasn't going to just give herself to him.

"*Ainaak olenszal sívambin.* Your life will be cherished by me for all time. *Te élidet ainaak pide minan.* Your life will be placed above mine for all time. *Te avio päläfertiilam.* You are my lifemate."

Sarika had been paying attention to the declarations as he uttered each one. The effect on her body was more frightening than anything she had ever experienced. She had a mad desire to jerk away from him and leap over the railing, taking her chances in the forest. There were too many men between her and the railing, and she knew it would be humiliating if she made a break for it and didn't make it.

His thumb, stroking back and forth on her skin, left a trail of heat that seemed to just get hotter as the blood first rushed through her veins and then pooled low.

"*Ainaak sívamet jutta oleny.* You are bound to me for all eternity."

Eternity? The word horrified her. The way she felt so connected to him, as if her soul and his were one and the same, was even worse.

"*Ainaak terád vigyázak.* You are always in my care."

The moment the last words were spoken, she felt tight bands snap into place inside her. Ties so tight there would be no getting away from him. Somehow, he had really bound them together.

"You have to undo this," she whispered.

"I fear that is an impossibility." He said it calmly.

Screw calm. She leapt to her feet, slamming both palms to his chest to knock him backward, away from her. "You undo it right now. Right this minute. You don't get to take away my freedom of choice. Or any of my freedoms. I don't care what kind of scary badass you are—undo it *now*."

The fact that she hit him as hard as she could and he didn't so much as rock backward added fuel to the fire. Her temper erupted, and she swung her fist at his face. He caught it in midair. As he did, she caught a brief flash of amusement, not just his but shared with his brothers. That only infuriated her more.

"If I were you, I wouldn't close my eyes when you put yourself in the ground," she hissed. "You never know what's going to find its way to your bed." She stuck her chin in the air and tried to pull her fist out of his hand. "It isn't going to be me."

"I think your woman just threatened you," Lojos said.

"She's got fire, that one," Dominic said. "That's a good thing. She'll need it to stand up to you, Tomas."

"She doesn't need to stand up to me." His voice was velvet-smooth again, and he looked straight into her eyes as he raised her curled fist to his mouth. "She can trust me to guide her through our customs."

That strange fireball he seemed to be able to produce rushed through her veins and settled low again. That was so disturbing, when she wanted to kick him in the shins and maybe do even worse to him. She really didn't like that he shared his amusement with his brothers.

"You aren't going to guide me through anything. Do you really think your taking away my choices in any way endears you to me?" She leaned into him. "It does *not*. Just because you did this doesn't mean I'm giving up my plans to leave this place. Every single one of you is insane. The whole lot of you."

"*Sivamet*," he said, using that same velvet voice so it not only stroked over her skin but ignited every nerve ending in her body. "You know you're speaking from a place of fear. I'm well aware you have every reason to be afraid, but there is no need. You trusted your cousin to protect you; you have three of us now."

She lifted her head to glare at Luiz. "I trusted him and look where it got me."

Luiz lifted an eyebrow at her. "Our laws do not allow interference when it comes to lifemates."

"So if he decides to abuse me, there is nothing any of you would do? All of you act so righteous, as if you're better than those horrid male shifters, but you're basically telling me I have *no* rights because I'm a woman. What's the difference between them and you?"

She was furious. More than furious. She was terrified. She despised being weak. She detested that she'd practically had a breakdown in front of these men. Mostly, she hated that she wanted to burst into tears and cry for hours. She was so close, struggling to hold on to her anger so she wouldn't fall apart in front of them.

She didn't know what being a lifemate entailed, but she was fairly certain Tomas was going to take her somewhere away from her cousin. Luiz might say he believed one couldn't interfere between lifemates, but he was a family man, and if he thought for one moment Tomas was hurting her, she was certain he would come to her aid.

"Sarika." Dominic drew her attention with his gentle voice. "It is impossible for a Carpathian lifemate to, in any way, harm his woman. She is his world. He protects her at all costs and sees to her happiness. She is his first priority."

She pounced on that. "So if Tomas is seeing to my happiness, then he will escort me to the river and see to it that I get safely on a boat so I can leave this place. That's what would make me happy." There was pure challenge and triumph in the look she shot Tomas.

His answer was to wrap his arm around her and pull her close to the heat of his body. He felt rock solid. Immovable. He also felt like a tower of strength. It was strange how her body reacted to him when her brain was nearly paralyzed with fear. She felt the burn of tears behind her eyes, and she stiffened, one hand going to his rib cage to push him away. She could not break down in front of these men.

Tomas didn't so much as rock back. She could feel them all staring at her. She decided her only out was to test him. "I have to go into the other room for some alone time. I really, really need you to let me do that."

His palm cupped the side of her face gently. Too gently. The first tear spilled over before she could stop it. Instantly, he swung his body completely in front of hers, blocking the sight of her from the others as if he knew she would despise them seeing her cry. One thumb slid over her cheekbone, erasing the wet mark.

"If you need to lie down for a little while, you should do that. I can feel how tired you are." *Don't be distressed. We'll work this out the way we've been doing for years.* His lips brushed the top of her head, and he walked with her, using his body as a shield to keep the others from seeing her face.

"Did you know when we wrote letters that you were connected to me?" She whispered the question because suddenly his answer was very important. Had she been lured to the rainforest? Had Luiz conspired against her?

You insist on thinking the worst of me, little cousin. If Tomas makes you miserable or ever raises his hand to you, I will kill him. It wouldn't be easy, and his brothers would retaliate, but I would never allow my family—and that's who you are to me—to be abused in any way.

She'd gotten to Luiz. Gotten under his skin. At least she meant something to him. She didn't understand why he hadn't come to her defense and stopped whatever Tomas had done before she was bound to him, but at least now, she knew she mattered to Luiz.

"I didn't know we had a connection," Tomas answered her question. "Having said that, the longer we wrote to each other, the more I felt a connection. I was a hunter incapable of emotion, yet I looked forward to every single letter."

He took her elbow and gently steered her through Luiz's open floor plan to the bedroom behind the screen. The hammock looked inviting. She suddenly needed to lie down more than anything. She was exhausted.

Sarika sank down onto the hammock, and Tomas crouched in front of her, lifting her right foot to remove her shoe. Once he'd pulled off the right shoe and sock, he massaged her foot, his strong fingers bringing instant relief to her sore muscles.

"I have never been a man to be jealous. It is a very unseemly emotion and quite an ugly trait in a man."

Her gaze flew to his face. He raised his eyes to hers as he placed her foot on the floor and lifted her left foot to remove the shoe and sock. There was no levity on his face. None. What he was saying meant something. Was important. She got the impression it was difficult for him to say this to her, and that both intrigued her and made her like him more. Admitting a character trait in himself he didn't like made him appear vulnerable to her.

"I am struggling with new emotions. They come in waves and are difficult to process when it comes to my feelings for you. I did not expect them to be so strong. And they are, Sarika. Stronger than anything I've ever felt. I'm going to make mistakes with you because this is all new to me. I have never felt these emotions for a woman, not in all the centuries of my existence."

Her heart skipped a beat. He was crouched at her feet, his strong fingers massaging aching, tired muscles while he made his confession. It had to be said; she thought him devastatingly beautiful.

"Part of the problem is that we aren't settled yet. I'm intelligent enough to know that and to know the fault lies with me. Unfortunately, I am a very dangerous man."

He didn't have to spell that out for her; she knew. Anyone looking at him knew. She had a difficult time equating this man with the letters he'd written to her. She understood why there were no photographs of him. Aside from the years he'd lived, if anyone saw his picture, they would question what they knew of T. Smolnycki Jr.

"I know I have no right to ask favors of you, not after claiming you without your consent, but perhaps our past interactions might earn me one." His hand slipped into her hair, fingers caressing her scalp.

"Tell me what you need from me." She had no idea why she'd blurted that out. She was exhausted. Scared. Angry. Holding back the need to dissolve into a little puddle of self-pity. Still, her heart reacted to his confession.

He gave her that brief smile. This time it lit up his eyes. Only a small flash, but it was there. "You have a tremendous amount of compassion in you. You're soft inside, *sivamet*. That will be something I'll bend over backward to protect."

She knew he was right. She felt emotions intensely. She had from the time she was a child. His fingers in her hair wreaked havoc with her senses. She was too tired to fight her body's reaction to him. She was going to crash hard. She knew she was, and she just didn't care. She did care about what he needed from her.

"Say it," she encouraged. "I'm not making promises, but I'll try to help you."

"I will warn you it is an unreasonable request, and I'm well aware of that fact."

He was stalling. This confident, bordering-on-arrogant man was stalling, reluctant to tell her what his unreasonable request was. She could tell it meant something to him.

He straightened in one graceful move, a fluid, easy movement. Muscles rippled beneath his shirt, fascinating her. He very carefully removed the pack she still had around her neck and tossed it to the little table close to the hammock before shimmering nearly transparent and then materializing completely in the middle of the woven threads. Easily, he caught her around the waist and eased her body beside his.

She should have fought that far-too-intimate position, but she was just too tired. Instead, she cuddled up to his warmth, and when he took her wrist to draw her arm across his waist, she let him.

"I would very much like you to help me out by not speaking mind to mind to Luiz, or any other man, without inviting me into the conversation."

She closed her eyes against the ominous burning behind her eyes. She didn't want to cry. Tears were useless, and she was so exhausted she nearly forgot what she wanted to sob her heart out over.

"I don't really understand why it would bother you that Luiz talks to me. He is my cousin. Believe me, I know when a man is interested, and he most certainly is not."

"That doesn't matter. I need your help to deal with this while I'm learning to handle the emotions."

As if he knew her head felt like it was stuck in a vise, he began a slow massage of her scalp. She had to admit that felt nice.

"I'm not telepathic." It didn't matter that Luiz had said she was. She had never spoken mind to mind to anyone before her cousin. She tipped her head to look at Tomas. "I would help you if I could, but Luiz bridges the gap between us. I wouldn't have the first clue how to invite you in."

"It is easy enough to establish a connection between us."

She nearly came off the hammock, but one arm locked around her waist as if he knew she would attempt to bolt.

"Absolutely not if your solution is the same as Luiz's. I'm not okay with any of this. It's crazy. The entire lifemate thing. It isn't just crazy, it's scary and wrong. I don't like anyone taking away my rights as a human being. Or as a woman. You don't get to make my decisions or tell me what to do."

He waited, unmoving, not responding until she lay back against him and relaxed. His fingers settled on her scalp, and he began that slow massage that was taking away the headache from hell.

"I would like to promise you that I would not make decisions for you, or that I wouldn't tell you what to do. For instance, I told you I wouldn't enter your mind, but your head is hurting. I can easily take that away. I *need* to take the pain away. You're my lifemate, and that means I see to your care. I've held off in order to get your consent, but I know, if you do not give it to me, I will still remove the headache."

As confessions went, it was straightforward. He was being honest with her. She didn't like what he said, and yet she did. She didn't know if she was confused and conflicted because she was too tired and couldn't think logically or because her head pounded and she feared she might start throwing up. Maybe that would send Tomas packing. A vomiting lifemate. Lovely.

"Woman, you're too much sometimes." There was definite amusement in his voice. "I don't have to read your mind to know your thoughts. When you're tired, you broadcast fairly loudly, at least to me. I would like your permission to take away the pain in your head."

What was the use of saying no when he'd already informed her he would simply do it anyway? And it would be wonderful if the migraine was gone. Sometimes they lasted for days.

"Have at it. Both of your brothers called me *sisarke*. What does it mean?"

"It is a term of endearment meant only for family. It means *little sister*. The three of us always wanted to have that. You are already in their hearts and minds. They consider you family and hope that one day you will feel the same about them."

That felt nice, to be thought of as family by his brothers. She knew she couldn't get complacent, but she was exhausted, and she was willing to take anything good at this point.

She felt warmth moving through her head. Weirdly, it felt good. And just like that, the pain vanished. It was completely gone.

Sarika closed her eyes and took a deep breath. "You do have your uses." She'd give him that. No meds, the migraine was gone, and the relief was tremendous.

His hand went to the nape of her neck, and he began a slow massage of her shoulders and neck, helping to ease the tension from her. Her exhaustion settled around her like a heavy blanket. She felt the weight of it, the physical and emotional toll on her. As a child, she had never been in the best of health. Her adoptive parents had worried far too much about her, but she refused to allow anything to slow her down. She went after the education she wanted and went from country to country interning in as many places as possible in order to learn as much as she could to become better at taking care of the animals and their habitats.

"I'm going to have to fight with you later, Tomas. Right now, I just want to sleep," she confessed.

"Good plan, *sivamet*."

She hadn't asked what that meant for a reason. Whenever he called her that, his voice softened. The velvet deepened, stroked over her, got inside where she didn't want it. She didn't want T. Smolnycki Jr. inside her anywhere. Not her head, not her body. Still, she turned into his warmth, wrapped one arm around his rock-hard abs and drifted off.

CHAPTER 9

"Is she okay?" Luiz asked the moment Tomas emerged from the bedroom.

Tomas nodded. "She's finally asleep."

He glanced at his brothers. Sarika believed they couldn't read her thoughts unless they took her blood or were standing very close to her. In truth, for him, it was easy to read her. When he did, his brothers were just as aware. They'd been sharing information automatically for centuries, and it wasn't going to stop anytime soon.

Sharing his new emotions, they had almost been as upset as he had been. As he still was. His lifemate knew zero about Carpathians, and the one man, her cousin, who was both jaguar and fully Carpathian should have filled her in.

"You had to have known there was a possibility of her being a lifemate to one of us," he said, pinning Luiz with his flat, cold stare. A demon lurked in him. A dangerous monster, one that lived for battle and blood. He knew Luiz was a De La Cruz. In their world, that name was nearly as powerful as Dubrinsky and as powerful as Daratrazanoff or Dragonseeker.

That Luiz didn't do right by Sarika infuriated him. He tamped that down. Emotions had to be swept aside, put away, if he was going to handle this the way a lifemate should. Calm. In control. Making a statement that couldn't be mistaken.

"I did," Luiz conceded. "Although I thought only of her as my cousin. My only living relative. I saw her in that capacity, not as a potential lifemate. That came later, when I took her blood."

"Knowing she was a potential lifemate, she should never have been allowed to leave the safety of this house."

"The safeguards were secure. Percy would never have been able to get in."

Tomas wanted to fly across the room and rip out Luiz's heart. So much for compartmentalizing his emotions. Control was fast disappearing. He seethed with the need to punish Luiz, who answered every question with that same arrogant attitude that must have made Sarika crazy.

Tomas. Mataias, the oldest triplet and their acknowledged leader, was a breath of fresh air, blowing through the ragged, dark thunderclouds in his mind. *You have not had time to process these emotions. Shut them down completely.*

I won't lose her.

You aren't tied to her through unfamiliar emotions. You're bound together. Your soul is one. Let them go completely before you start a war. Luiz might be one of the oldest ancients, but he feels something for his cousin. He will fight, and every one of the De La Cruz brothers will back him. That won't matter if it becomes necessary, but it is not at this time.

Mataias was always the voice of reason. Tomas usually was as well, but he'd been shaken from the moment he laid eyes on Sarika. The instant she spoke and he heard her voice, his world had changed. Color poured in, blinding him. Right in the middle of an intense standoff with Rud. Right when he needed to save a child. He couldn't see clearly. Worse, he hadn't been able to think clearly. Every sensation that filled him was too intense, especially anything having to do with Sarika. Evidently, he was still feeling those emotions with that same intensity.

Tomas took a breath and slammed the door tight on all feelings, so he faced Luiz with the calm and control of an ancient Carpathian. "But she could still leave, and she did. That wasn't securing her safety."

Luiz regarded him with that same expressionless mask. He was a De La Cruz, and there was no reading him. He suddenly inclined his head.

"I made a mistake earlier with her. It was a huge mistake, and I knew it. I took her blood after she adamantly said no."

"You needed to take her blood," Dominic said. "You were going to be in the ground when she was vulnerable. What other way would you have of being able to prevent trouble to her should it happen? You would have to be able to see through her eyes if she was attacked." His metallic-colored eyes rested on Tomas. "You would have done the same. Any of us would have."

Tomas inclined his head in agreement. "Of course."

Luiz sighed. "That wasn't the mistake. She's a female shifter and my first cousin. She knew nothing of Carpathians. Not one thing. Percy was breathing down our necks, but I had to go to ground. The solution was to weave safeguards and take her blood." He reached behind him and caught his neck in the vise of strong fingers. "She shouldn't have known. I'm fast. I relied on my speed. She has a way of knowing when someone is invading her mind, no matter how delicate the touch. So I relied on speed and the lightest of compulsions for her to turn away. Just for a moment." He broke off, shaking his head.

"She knew," Tomas murmured aloud. "She somehow knew."

"I think she saw me. Enemies can't see me, but she did. She's extremely gifted, and those gifts are becoming stronger with every minute she spends in the forest. I should have paid attention to the fact that her lineage is the same as mine. I was proud of her for catching me, but she'd specifically told me she didn't want me to take her blood. When I did, against her wishes, she was horrified. It was genuine. Not manipulative. She was already on the verge of flight. She didn't trust me and was entertaining the idea that I was holding her prisoner.

When I wove the safeguards, I made certain she could exit if she felt it was necessary. I did push her toward sleep, but it was a light push. I didn't think she would need much. She'd been traveling for days with little sleep. I thought she would stay in bed until the sun went down."

"We all make mistakes," Dominic said. "I certainly have made my share of them. I have Solange, and she's a force of nature. Independent. A total warrior. Keeping her safe has never been easy. She puts herself in the middle of any battle and never hesitates. It is a difficult balance when it comes to family. I can imagine that seeing Sarika in person, when you believed you had no one from your side of the family, had to be a shock."

What is he doing? Mataias asked his brothers. *Luiz is older in his soul than all of us. He cannot possibly feel.*

It is clear he did feel, Lojos said. *Emotion causes mistakes. He should have bound her to this tree house, made it impossible for her to leave.*

Had he done what he normally would have, Rud would have taken that child. In fact, Tomas mused, *I believe the shifter would have killed Sandrine.*

He needed to make that admission and end the tension that had built up between the Carpathians. "In a roundabout way, Luiz, you saved Sandrine's life. It was meant to be that Sarika was able to stall all three of the shifters until sunset." He looked the man straight in the eye. "Forgive me. I am dealing with very unfamiliar emotions and finding it difficult after so many centuries."

"Strangely, I am also dealing with the unfamiliar," Luiz admitted. "Sarika has gifts I have not seen. She was able to feel my emotions even before I took her blood, although I cannot. Or I should not. Being close to her, I found myself able to discern sentiments I lost long ago."

The Carpathians exchanged long, puzzled looks in silence. All were far too old not to have come across every type of gift or ability, and yet none of them seemed to have encountered anyone exactly like Sarika.

"She is unaware of her uniqueness," Luiz said. "The sad part is, she isn't trying to hide it, and yet I was slow to pick up on it."

"There are a few women in our world who can share emotions and lighten the burden with ancients," Dominic ventured. "She is possibly one of these women."

Mataias inclined his head. "More than likely."

"There is more to it than that." Luiz spoke with conviction.

"I agree," Tomas said. "I waited until exhaustion overcame her before I used a sleep compulsion. I wanted her completely out before I made a blood exchange. I thought it best that she stay unaware until I have time to explain Carpathian customs and rituals to her."

Not one man disagreed with his way of handling the situation with Sarika. She was afraid, but they knew she would be happy with Tomas once she accepted that she was his lifemate. The bond would take care of that.

"When you say 'exchange,'" Luiz ventured, "do you mean enough to begin the conversion?"

There was no challenge in his voice, no disrespect or even disapproval, but Tomas felt the weight of those things regardless. "I thought it best. She is in jaguar shifter territory, and the males are aware of her. With all of us in the ground, she will have little protection should they manage to get to her. The faster she is converted, the safer she is." He kept his gaze steady on Sarika's cousin. "Do you have an objection?"

Luiz once again raised his hand to dig his fingers into the back of his neck as if he hurt. That gesture bothered Tomas. *He shouldn't feel pain. And if he does, why isn't he healing himself?* he asked his brothers.

"I would have done the same. I believe she needs to be converted quickly and have as many protections in place as possible, yet I believe by making that decision, there is every possibility that you have made your life much more difficult."

Tomas' eyebrow shot up, mostly because he'd come to that same conclusion. "Don't know anything about relationships but will do my best. I know she's family to you." He gestured toward his brothers. "I swear to you, I'll do everything in my power to make her happy."

Luiz seemed to accept that declaration, so Tomas deemed it time to move on. "We have a larger problem. We have been attempting to track Justice. He escaped from the underworld and is loose on the world. He isn't vampire, so there is no way to track him as one would the undead. He's a shadow. Very hard to track a shadow."

"He's recruiting vampires and attempting to bring in ancients." Mataias took up the story. "He doesn't necessarily want the ancients to turn. He's building an army against the prince. Gustov was running the ambush, and he spoke of a weapon his master—that's what he called him—was searching for. I understand it is in three pieces, and the pieces are in different places, far from one another. They were fashioned centuries ago, before our time even, out of metal from the sky."

Lojos indicated Luiz. "Technically, you are the oldest of us. Every De La Cruz warrior ever born and who has died throughout the centuries poured their memories into you. The only two Carpathians that I'm aware of that have this advantage—"

"Disadvantage," Luiz corrected. There was a grimness to his voice. And an edge that told the others the weight of the warriors he carried added to the terrible burden every ancient shouldered the longer they were alive.

Tomas could understand it. He still worried that he had lived far past the time he should have. He knew he was evolving. He hoped his lifemate would stop the process because where he was going wasn't good. He had thought to give her choices until the moment he heard her voice. Saw in colors. *Felt.* There was no going back from that. Whatever was taking place inside him, she would have to come to terms with it as well. Did that mean he had already lost his honor as a Carpathian?

"In this case, Luiz," Dominic said, "you may be the only one to answer the question of what this weapon is and if it really is capable of destroying our prince. If that is the case, we will need to know where each piece is located and what it is we're searching for."

Luiz's fingers squeezed the back of his neck hard. It was all Tomas could do not to go to him and heal him. Why was Luiz enduring something that should be easy enough to get rid of? They healed incredible wounds on their bodies after a battle. He had seen Luiz fight. The man was lightning fast, deadly, and his restorative abilities rivaled some of their best healers.

"When I took Sarika's blood, she was wearing a chain around her neck with an amulet on it made of ancient metal," Luiz informed them. "I had never seen anything like it."

The others looked expectantly at Tomas. "She was wearing it," he confirmed. "It had the raised image of the face of a jaguar. It would be good to examine it closely and ask her where she acquired it. She has traveled extensively. She could have picked it up anywhere."

"Including," Lojos said, "on the internet. You can order anything, even a custom necklace."

"This was made of ancient metal," Luiz said. "I felt the older vibrations it gave off."

Tomas could confirm that as well. "Very strong."

"It warrants looking into," Dominic said. "Sarika could be what drew Justice here."

"Or a piece of this weapon is somewhere close. The ruins aren't far from here. The temple is still standing, along with a few other buildings," Luiz added. "If I had gotten hostile vibrations from Sarika's amulet, I would have ripped it off her."

"I am uncertain anything destructive could be against Sarika's skin," Tomas said. "She has rare gifts, and one is protection." *The blood exchange was not easy,* he confessed to his brothers. *Even under compulsion, exhausted and asleep, she resisted. When I had her take my blood, it felt for a brief moment as if there was a power struggle.*

Both his brothers refrained from turning their puzzled gazes on him. They were used to looking expressionless around others, no matter what they discussed.

We are ancient, Tomas, and extremely formidable, Mataias stated. *There should be no contest between a young female shifter and any of us. What exactly happened?*

Not exactly a power struggle. He tried to explain the strange thing that had happened. *She was lying in the hammock, looking fragile and lost. I shared that moment with you and Lojos because the way she looked in her sleep tore me up, and I needed the two of you to balance the overwhelming emotion I was feeling for the first time. Each emotion seems a first, and the need to inspect it and understand it after the blow of feeling it is strong.*

How did one explain a miracle to his brothers? He had tried to show them just as he shared his emotions with them. Just as they had shared everything for centuries. Information was valuable—one of the most valuable things in their world, they'd discovered. It gave them even more power and made them far better hunters of the undead.

Dominic and Luiz talked in quiet tones, discussing the women and Dominic's lifemate, Solange. He heard Dominic say, with humor in his voice, that it was a good thing she wasn't present. She had been converted and was Carpathian, but like Luiz, she retained her jaguar. Solange was all about women's rights. Their choices. She would *not* be down with taking Sarika's blood or claiming her without her consent.

Tomas had believed he thought the same way as Solange until the moment he realized Sarika was his lifemate and she'd been in danger. Nothing else mattered to him but keeping her safe. He wasn't sorry to claim her or start the conversion process, especially when he realized Sarika was very conflicted. She might actually take it in her head to make a run for it. He would follow. His brothers would follow, and they had a duty to their people. They were on the trail of one of the deadliest Carpathians living, and they had to get to him before he turned his attention to mass murder.

Tomas. Mataias brought his attention back to his brothers and what he was trying to convey. Tomas decided to open his memories to them, although it would be giving a great deal away from the lack of control, not only of his emotions but of his body's reaction.

Every protective instinct I possessed kicked in. Instincts I didn't know I had, not like that. I have always been protective of you two, we have of each other, but feel what I felt. He invited them to share his memories.

He allowed the memory to surface, complete with every uncontrolled, wild emotion that raged through him at the time. They had to know what it was really like. The tarot readers had predicted that their lifemates were in this life cycle. If they found them, it was necessary for them to know that they very possibly could go temporarily insane. After centuries of nothing, colors and emotions were almost too much to take. It felt as if he were in a thrall, one he had no control over. But Sarika lay there, so fragile and lost, so *his*, that he needed to ensure he could protect her. He needed to do that even more than he needed to smooth their relationship.

It most likely wasn't the right decision, but his always logical brain was in total chaos. He drew Sarika gently into his arms and pulled her onto his lap. That might have been a mistake. He had an unexpected and unacceptable response to the feel of her bottom sliding over his groin. The response was instant steel.

It was exhilarating—and painful. Not in the way of a battle wound, but something altogether different. He hadn't thought he would have to fight his body for control right along with his mind, but he did. He shared all of that with his brothers.

This is what happens. This is the feeling and the emotions. It is very complex and intense and unlike anything we've had to deal with, he told them.

At least it is a new experience, Lojos pointed out. *I could use a few new, unique experiences.*

This is just the beginning, Tomas warned.

He had wrapped his arms around her, reveling in the feel of her soft, feminine body against the hardness of his. Her hair slid like so much silk over his face and arm. With a single thought, he removed his shirt, the need to feel her hair against his skin overwhelming, too strong to deny himself.

He wanted to be very cognizant of the fact that he was doing this without her consent and should protect her from the unfamiliar desire, the raging lust that rose like a firestorm he couldn't seem to tamp down. He allowed his brothers to feel that as well, although it shamed him. He was a man of honor, and he both respected and revered his lifemate. His job was to protect her—even from himself.

He had taken a deep breath, let it out and bent his head to her neck. He would have preferred her blouse open so he could really feel her soft skin and the luxury of her feminine curves, something he was very much looking forward to, but it felt wrong when she didn't know what was happening to her.

He reminded himself he had a code of honor and he was already pushing it to the very limits by taking her choices from her. He shared those thoughts with his brothers.

She is the most important thing in your world, Tomas, Mataias reminded. *That makes her the most important thing in our world as well. You have kept your honor under difficult circumstances.*

He could always count on his brother to tell the truth as he saw it. Mataias held all three of them to a high standard. The longer they had survived, the higher those standards had become. All three were very aware of the demon growing inside, the one eager for the next bloodthirsty battle, because along with the battle came the rush. The only real feeling the triplets could count on. They'd grown to look forward to it, although they were aware it wasn't a good thing.

Tomas moved the hair from her shoulder to expose her slender neck to him. The feel of all that thick, curly silk in his hands sent heat rushing through him. The sight of her bare neck and the pulse point open to him caused that heat to pool low until he was aching and full. Around her neck was a chain, and he took a moment to feel his way to find the pendant hanging between her breasts. The raised head of a jaguar gave off vibrations that told him it was very old.

He took his time to bend his head toward her bare skin. His heart sped up. The heat became a fireball rushing through his veins. The feeling was both exhilarating and disturbing. A pleasure he'd never known and a pain that was a continual aching reminder this woman was his. The one. His heart needed her. His body, his soul.

He ran his tongue over that beating pulse in her neck, tasting her, absorbing the faint, unique flavor that was Sarika. That taste, that scent, moved through him, producing a wave of pure pleasure. He found himself kissing that delicate spot, his teeth sliding into place. He bit down, tying them together in one of the most intimate ways of his people.

If he thought the taste of her skin was amazing, her blood was pure aphrodisiac. A thousand tongues stroked over his body. Her blood spread through his system like a slow-moving molten lava. The sensation was unlike anything he'd ever felt, and he didn't want it to ever end. She moved, a small moaning protest that brought him back to his senses. He'd taken more than enough blood for a true exchange.

With great reluctance, he pulled back, sliding his tongue over the brand of possession he'd left behind on her neck. He wanted that mark there. He knew it wasn't a good idea. It would be better not to tell her immediately that he'd done their first blood exchange. He knew it wouldn't go over very well, but lifemates didn't lie to each other. Not even by committing the sin of omission.

He gathered her closer, whispering to her, telling her the truth, that he'd never thought it would ever be possible to find her. That she was his personal miracle. That after centuries of searching, of relentless duty, there she was, the one person that made his sacrifices worth it. She was what every Carpathian hunter was promised, and she was more beautiful than anything he could ever have imagined.

He whispered the command to her, and just the soft demand to take his blood set his heart pounding. One fingernail lengthened. He drew a line over the heavy muscles on his chest, his breath catching in his throat. Bright red ruby beads appeared and slowly began to drip down his chest. He fitted the back of her head into his palm and pressed her toward his chest, keeping up the whispered command because she seemed just a little resistant. He didn't want her to be uncomfortable or feel fear. He kept his voice soothing, soft, a compelling temptation.

Despite Tomas being an ancient with a vast amount of power, and he was very used to being one of the strongest, most dangerous of the Carpathian hunters, his woman didn't respond the way she should have. She had been sitting relaxed in his lap, but now she pushed against the lock he had across her back. She sat up straighter and tried to turn her head away from his chest.

The fact that she could resist his compulsion shocked him. Not just surprised him, shocked him. It had never occurred to him that this could happen. He shared that moment with his brothers, replaying the exact moment she seemed aware of what was happening and began to fight him.

I know you're wondering why I didn't simply take over her mind and force her acceptance, he said to his brothers.

It would have taken you seconds, Tomas, Lojos objected. *Seconds. She wouldn't have been upset because she wouldn't know.*

Tomas knew that was true. If he invaded her mind and shut down all resistance, he could see how her mind worked, look into her memories and figure out how she came to be strong enough to resist an ancient warrior's command.

She asked me not to go into her mind without her consent. I didn't make a promise, but it was important to her, so it was important to me. He knew his brothers wouldn't understand. To them, they considered it a protection for Sarika, and that action would also give Tomas more of an understanding of who his lifemate was and how she thought. What her abilities were. All very important since she would be traveling with them as they attempted to track Justice.

I didn't want her to wake, and she was in danger of doing so. I deepened the command, and she resisted for one short moment before she succumbed.

Then her mouth was on me, and I swear my entire world imploded. I have never felt such a deep, intense need as I did in that moment.

The rest was too personal, and he held it back, merely showing that he had insisted she take enough blood for a true exchange. That had been an exercise in control. He'd never expected his body to be raging at him simply because his lifemate was taking his blood. It was a ritual as old as time, but no one had ever shared the feelings and emotions that swept through him like a tidal wave. He understood. It was far too intimate, too personal to share, even when trying to give his brothers a heads-up for when they hopefully found their lifemates.

I sent her back to sleep without examining her memories. I know I should have, but I wanted her to share with me. I wanted her to give me her consent.

Tomas glanced toward the screen and then switched to speaking aloud so Luiz and Dominic could hear him. "We can weave the safeguards to protect her and keep her inside this time. I will have to wake her long enough to explain what will happen and what she'll feel should she wake before sunset."

The five men stood together and began a complicated weave to encompass the entire tree, including roots and the above canopy. The safeguards were individual ropes that twined around one another until they were so strong they were unbreakable. It would be impossible for any enemy, including mages, to unravel that weave when it was constructed by five ancients. They had been weaving safeguards long before Xavier, the mage, had shared his secrets with Carpathians. Not a single one of the weaves had come from the dark mage.

By the time the five ancients had finished their task, the safeguards were so thick and impenetrable that there was no access to the tree house and no way to destroy it, not even with fire or magic. Tomas was astonished at the degree of relief he felt. His lifemate, should she awaken, would be unable to leave. She would be safe from any type of attack.

Luiz ensured there was plenty of food and drink for her, although

Tomas hoped she wouldn't need it. The blood exchange would make it difficult for her to be apart from him. He had been told the separation was extremely hard on the woman aboveground. Their prince, Mikhail Dubrinsky, had been the first to realize a human psychic woman could carry the other half of a Carpathian's soul. Their species had learned many lessons through his lifemate, Raven.

"Bring her to meet the women," Dominic suggested. "It will be good for her to see other lifemates and realize they are happy with their men."

"We are on the trail of Justice," Lojos reminded.

"We've lost that trail," Mataias admitted. "Tomas can't leave Sarika behind. She must be fully converted to travel with us. I think we can take a short time out in order to allow her to get used to our ways."

Tomas didn't think it would be that easy. His woman seemed highly resistant to becoming his lifemate. She felt the vows said between them. She knew but didn't understand there were ties. She had no comprehension that the soul she had guarded was once more back where it belonged, and it was one soul. Light and dark once more woven together. There was no Tomas without Sarika. There was no longer a Sarika without Tomas. How did his brothers expect her to understand and accept that concept in a few short days?

To them, it was a fact of life. They had a duty to perform; therefore, there was no question that Sarika would comply with their wishes. He was certain they were wrong.

He made his way through the house as the others left. He had always been comfortable with the night, and now he had a new appreciation of it. Of the various shades of colors that had been a relentless dull gray for so many centuries, he had forgotten what color was. The steady drone of insects and various calls of frogs filled the air. He detected the sounds of voles, lizards, mice and other small creatures rushing around beneath the vegetation on the forest floor to find as much to eat as possible before retiring. He knew the placement of every monkey, snake and bird within yards around the tree house and examined each to ensure none were spies for vampires.

"*Sivamet*, wake up, just for a few minutes, and then I promise, you can go back to sleep." Tomas leaned over Sarika, inhaling her feminine scent. He was already addicted to the way she gave off that faint natural perfume.

She looked beautiful lying in the hammock, on her side, one hand tucked under her cheek, the other arm stretched out, fingers wrapped in the hammock's strong weave. Her lashes fluttered, drawing his attention to the length, thickness and slight curl to them. Even her lashes seemed acutely feminine.

She looked up at him, her vivid green eyes blinking as she tried to clear the fog in her head.

"This is important, or I wouldn't disturb you. You have to know what to expect while I am in the ground. The lifemate bond is strong, and should you wake, you could have problems if you're unable to reach me."

The faintest smile curved her lips for just one moment, but it was enough to center his attention there. She had a gorgeous mouth. In all the centuries of his existence, he'd never noticed anyone's mouth before. He hadn't taken note of the way the bottom lip curved or the top one formed a perfect bow. These were details he savored, tucked close to his heart and kept to himself. They were his. Sarika had given him that gift.

"You think I can't be alone for a few hours?" There was a wealth of feminine amusement. "I've spent a good deal of my life alone, Tomas. I like solitude. It gives me peace."

She was imparting information that mattered. That meant something. He needed to hear her because what she just gave him wasn't about his statement.

"Why do you need peace?" His fingertips skimmed over the skin around her throat and neck, touched his marks of possession and found the thin chain holding the amulet. He followed the chain down to where the raised jaguar head nestled against her skin. The moment the pad of his thumb stroked across the face of the cat, he felt the surge of power emanating from the amulet. The source felt feminine and yet old world. The thing was protective of Sarika, even identifying with her as if it had been made for her all those centuries ago.

Was it a weapon as well? A weapon powerful enough to destroy their prince and his second-in-command? Tomas didn't feel that large of a threat from it, but it was difficult to predict. He wouldn't want to be the one to try to remove it from around her neck. It would fight back, and so would Sarika. The object and his lifemate were that connected.

"Sometimes my brain won't slow down." A little frown flitted across her face. "I have nightmares of ancient rites. Of blood sacrifices. Of terrible things that happened to me and to others I loved, and then I can't get them out of my mind. Places and people can trigger them." She sounded as if she expected him to make fun of her.

"How long have you had these dreams?"

"Nightmares," she corrected. "For as far back as I can remember, even as a toddler. Once they're in my head, it takes being alone and a great deal of meditation to quiet them."

"And this amulet? Where did you acquire it?" Once again, he slid the pad of his thumb across that raised surface, tracing the features of the jaguar.

"It was something my mother apparently wore, and when my father sent me to his brother to raise, he told my uncle that she had wanted me to have it. She had made that plain to him from the moment I came into the world. He said she put it on my chest and said it belonged to me. I don't take it off."

"You stood up to the jaguar males, Sarika. You were afraid, but you faced them down. You travel the world and encounter all different tribes and people, even other species, and you accept them, yet you say you'd never heard of Carpathians until Luiz first told you about us. And you fear us. Every one of us. In your nightmares, were there Carpathians that harmed you or your family? Did they participate in these ancient rituals?"

Frowning, she pushed herself into a half-sitting position and then shoved at all the hair falling around her face. He liked that she didn't dismiss the idea but rather gave it serious thought. "I don't know. I blocked out a lot of it because it was gruesome and scary, and once it's in my head, I can't seem to get it out for days."

Her gaze clung to his as if seeking reassurance. She didn't realize their lifemate bond was already working. She trusted him whether she realized it or not.

"Now that you've considered it, you can let your brain figure out the puzzle," he said. "If it continues to bother you, I am capable of reading your memories if needed to help you." He didn't make it an offer, just casually told her he could.

She slid back down into the hammock. "I'm so tired, Tomas. I can't continue the conversation with a functioning brain. I'm sorry."

"Don't be sorry. You traveled for days and had a very traumatic experience. I just want you to listen to me for a couple more minutes, and then you can sleep. Can you do that?"

She nodded but lowered her lashes as if she were drifting off. He wrapped a length of hair around his fist and gave her the information as matter-of-factly as possible.

"These are only possibilities, and I hope you sleep until I come to you, but if not, you may feel sorrow. Overwhelming grief, and think I'm dead because you can't feel or reach me. If that happens, know I am *not* dead but sleeping a rejuvenating sleep."

She didn't look amused this time, only thoughtful. She didn't open her eyes. He continued. "You may have trouble eating or drinking. Don't try to eat meat. Stick to fruit and water or a mild natural tea."

"I'm not even going to ask why, but I'll expect an explanation tomorrow."

"You'll get one. Just know I'm alive, and no matter what, I'll come for you. Can you do that for me?"

"Anything to get you to let me sleep."

There was that slight quirk to her lips, forming a half smile. He didn't even try to resist. He leaned down and brushed his lips lightly over hers before dissolving into tiny molecules and streaking away. His resting place would be beneath the tree house, deep in the ground.

CHAPTER 10

She was a prisoner after all. Sarika woke two hours before sunset. She wasn't certain how she knew exactly what time it was, but she did know. She woke uneasy, with vague memories of nightmares, Tomas taking her blood, forcing her to drink his. Of a head rolling across the floor of an ancient temple to land at her feet, face up. It was the head of her mother. Or perhaps her. She couldn't tell the difference, only that the eyes were wide open, watching as her head was taken from her body. A roar of approval swept through the temple, and she could only look down in utter horror at that severed head.

Sarika dragged herself off the hammock, getting up too fast, her heart beating far too hard. She had to leave this place now, while she still could. If Tomas came back, or Luiz, or any of them, she was lost. She jammed her belongings into her backpack and rushed for the strange door made of vines. Just before she reached the door, she hit something solid, like an invisible wall, and fell back.

She was definitely a prisoner. There was no need to run around like a maniac checking every square inch. The Carpathians would have been thorough. She had gotten out of Luiz's safeguards because he'd made them one way only. This weave was far stronger and went both ways, inside and outside. She couldn't see the invisible barrier, but she felt surrounded by it. She'd always been sensitive to any item with power. She could feel the strength, and this particular barrier was extremely strong.

She sat on the floor for a moment, breathing deep, pushing beyond panic to look at the situation from more than one point of view. There was a convincing argument that the Carpathians had woven the safeguards for her protection.

She wasn't going to hide from the truth. She had been able to stall the male shifters, but she never could have defeated them in battle. She wouldn't have been able to prevent Rud from taking Sandrine. She believed he would have killed the child simply because he was thwarted in getting what he wanted. She couldn't have stopped him, not if Percy and Bacus entered the fray. She didn't trust either of them.

She wasn't certain how much help Jasmine would have been. She was ready to trade her life for that of her child. She was so terrified for Sandrine and so focused on keeping her alive, Sarika doubted if she would have gone against anything Rud said or did. She wanted to appease him and keep him in a good mood. Sarika couldn't blame her, but it wouldn't have been helpful.

So okay, Tomas was committed to her protection. If she looked at it like that and not that he'd made her a prisoner, she could have a conversation with him and point out what was wrong with his approach. He could have asked her to stay inside . . .

Sarika let out a groan and covered her face. Luiz had asked her to stay inside, but she hadn't done that when she heard a child crying. She could understand why Tomas might think she would leave, even if she agreed to stay. She'd done exactly that. But if she hadn't . . . what would have happened to Sandrine?

She forced herself to her feet, flung her pack behind one of the chairs and made her way to the bathroom. She was a little in love with the tub. She'd always wanted one that was deep and wide and where she could sink into the hot water, put her head back and just relax. A part of her found it difficult to see Luiz having the tub or even the large beautiful bathroom. There was no woman in his life to decorate, and yet the house looked like something out of a magazine, specifically to her taste. She liked that she and her cousin shared the same taste.

The water filled the tub abnormally fast. She still hadn't figured out how it did that or where the water came from, but she was grateful for it when she sank down into its depths. She loved that the faucet could be handheld, and she could wash her hair and rinse thoroughly after soaking.

Her body was still sore from travel, and weirdly, her neck throbbed and burned, making her aware of a spot right over her pulse. She found herself covering the spot over and over with her palm and then rubbing at it with her fingers. It was a strange sensation, but she found, after consideration, that she liked it.

She closed her eyes and tried to relax. That uneasy feeling hadn't left her. Usually, the hot water would help ease all tension, but she found herself becoming almost agitated. The only thing that soothed her was the way she stroked her fingers over that burning spot on the side of her neck.

Tomas. She couldn't get him out of her head. There was some part of her that kept wanting to reach out to him. To connect. To just touch him. They didn't even have to talk. She wanted to know he was close. She made herself take a deep breath, realizing panic was beginning to set in. She forced herself to analyze the situation. That was one of her greatest strengths. She could step back and look at a problem from various angles. Needing to touch base with Tomas was definitely a problem as far as she was concerned.

She might have written him a hundred letters over the years, but it was difficult to equate the living, breathing, larger-than-life man with the faceless figure she'd had so many discussions with on paper. Across oceans. Far away. What were the odds that he would be trying to put a claim on her?

"Trying?" she murmured aloud. Tomas had done something to

bind them together. She felt those ties. She felt them pulling at her now. The ritual words he'd spoken in his language and hers had bound them. She knew the power of words. She wore an ancient protection amulet and felt the weight of it each time she was in a dangerous situation. Words mattered.

There was no book to research the secretive Carpathian species. Nowhere to find information on them. They were an ancient race and yet had managed to hide themselves among civilizations for centuries. Not only had they managed to hide themselves, but they had hidden the fact that vampires weren't simply a myth as well.

Carpathians hunted vampires. That much information she'd gotten from Luiz. They could read minds. They could take blood and prevent a human—or jaguar shifter—from knowing. Thoughtfully, she stroked the pads of her fingers over her pulse point. Why was it burning right in that particular spot? Why did it soothe her when she touched it? Why had her nightmare included Tomas taking her blood?

She hit the surface with the flat of her hand and sent the water flashing high across the tub to splash against the wall. "He took my blood after I specifically told him no. Just like Luiz did. One thing we've learned about Carpathian males is they refuse to give their women choices." She hissed her conclusion aloud, certain she was right. Tomas had taken her blood despite her clear refusal. "Not a good start to this lifemate business."

Where was he? The need to reach out to him hit her again, this time even stronger than before. Sorrow welled up. Inexplicable grief. She kept taking deep breaths to stay calm and center herself. Tomas had warned her. At least he'd done that.

What was she going to do about all of this? She admitted to herself she was confused and even afraid. It was the fear that made her angry. There was a *lot* of fear. She was a woman who liked to make her own decisions. Maybe she didn't always make the right decision, but who did? She learned from those mistakes and tried to do better.

She also had to admit to herself that she was, for the first time in her life, physically attracted to a man. She had no idea if it was because she had a past with him. All those letters. All those candid discussions. Even when she was a child, when she wrote to him with her ideas, he'd never made fun of her or acted as if her opinion didn't matter. She didn't always get that from her colleagues, even with her extensive education, internships and the fact that she had a brain. A good one.

She had experienced wanting sex because when a jaguar went into heat, it was equally uncomfortable for their shifter counterpart. When it had happened, there were no jaguar shifters to satisfy her female, and she didn't want to randomly pick up a strange man, so she'd retreat into deep forest and ride it out. It hadn't been easy, and she had spent a great deal of time apologizing to her jaguar for the lack of ability to see to all her needs, but she'd done her best under the circumstances.

But there was Tomas, and if she just let everything go while she was soaking in the bathtub and allowed herself a few private moments, she could definitely have some amazing fantasies with him as the star. The temptation was strong, especially since she was stuck in the tree house and couldn't retreat. There was no running from the situation.

Information. Knowledge. That was the biggest source of power. The more she knew and understood, the more of an advantage she would have. She felt it was necessary to extricate herself from the situation. She wasn't a woman to have her choices taken from her. She wasn't a woman to be silenced. She needed to be in a partnership, one where she was respected.

It didn't seem to matter what her wishes were when it came to the Carpathians. They took away choices and felt that somehow that was their right. As men? As ancient beings? It didn't matter because that trait, clearly in every one of the five she'd met, was strong.

Sighing, she soaked her hair and began massaging the shampoo into her scalp. It hit her, as she used pressure to give herself a scalp massage, that the shampoo was her brand. She looked at the items on the sink. The conditioner waiting for her to use. She was careful with products. She had curly hair, and it could be wild and untamed, growing huge in any humidity. The shampoo and conditioner, along with several no-frizz products, were all her exact brands.

How could that be? How could Luiz have those exact products in his bathroom waiting for her to use? He couldn't have known ahead of time and bought them for her. Everything came in on boats. He would have had to arrange it far in advance. The more she looked around, the more she realized the design of the bathroom, the tub, even the detail of the handheld water faucet was exactly as she'd pictured in her own home—if she ever had one.

She stepped onto the thick mat Luiz had on the floor and wrapped herself in a towel before going to the cabinet to examine the contents on the shelves. Her heart nearly stopped beating when she saw the dryer. For her curls, she used a very specific diffuser. It was designed to work with her type of hair. She had very thick hair and a lot of curls. She kept her hair long; otherwise, her curls would be tight little ringlets all over her head.

There was no way to just get that diffuser. It was from a special company, and it took a while for them to ship it. She knew. She'd been in the United States, not the Peruvian rainforest, and yet there it was. Sitting on a shelf with half a dozen other, smaller products she liked for her skin.

"Okay," she whispered aloud. She spent a great deal of time alone and often spoke out loud.

"He was definitely in my mind, looking around at my memories. When was he able to do that and I wasn't aware? What about Tomas? He can do that as well."

She leaned into the mirror, turning her head slowly, and for the first time examined the mark on her neck. Two small spots that looked suspiciously like a snakebite. Or just a bite. Her heart went crazy as her hand crept up to cover the brand.

"You knew," she accused herself. "Don't act shocked. Don't get all panicky, because you've known all along—he took your blood after you said no to him. That's why you woke up and wanted to run."

What's with Carpathian males that they don't care in the least what their lifemate, or maybe it's any woman, thinks or feels? She sent that question out into the universe because she really wanted the answer.

Where is the disconnect happening? Why are women less to you? Why don't we have the same rights as you?

If she was being honest, the jaguar shifters were equally as bad. And human males around the world seemed often to have those same opinions. They were in charge, and the women were supposed to do whatever they said.

She shook out her hair and began to style it, completely on automatic, strangely grateful and yet resentful of having the products she needed at her fingertips.

Okay, not all men worldwide. She had to be fair. There were good men in the world, many of them. Men who respected women and had good relationships with them. Men who didn't treat women as sex objects or servants.

Was she crying? Did she actually have tears spilling over and running down her face? She peered closer into the mirror because her image was blurry. She wasn't a big crier, although she indulged occasionally when she was alone. Sorrow had welled up unexpectedly. Overwhelming grief. It was shocking in its raw intensity.

Her hands shook as she wiped at the tears and studied her pale face in the mirror. "What is wrong with you? You aren't in love with him. You have the brains to get yourself out of this if you think logically."

Emotions were visceral. Gutting her. It wasn't simply because she couldn't touch Tomas; it was because he was wrong for her. Dead to her, whether he was asleep beneath the ground or not.

Why are you so distressed, sivamet? *I warned you what to expect. I am coming to you at sunset. Only a short time away.*

Tomas flooded her mind—with him. Strong. Confident. Reassuring.

That gentle stroke of velvet like a caress. He seemed to do so effortlessly. His concern for her was apparent, and yet he was undisturbed by their separation. Only she seemed to have to suffer the consequences of his binding them together.

Perversely, she didn't want him to come to her. She hadn't decided what to do or how best to handle the situation. She detested that he could read her emotions, which were all over the place. That had been one of the reasons she didn't want him taking her blood. No one had the right to look into her personal thoughts or feel her emotions, confused or otherwise. She should be able to decide when and what she wanted to share.

Don't mistake my sorrow for me believing you are dead or being sad about our separation. Yes, I do feel sad. Very sad. I asked you not to take my blood, just as I asked Luiz. Neither of you respected me enough to listen. My choice didn't matter to you or to my cousin. Only what you wanted or needed. I needed time to learn about you and your ways. Neither of you was willing to give that time to me.

There was silence, but she felt him there, moving in her mind, stroking soothing caresses. She wasn't even certain he knew he was doing it as he absorbed her accusation.

I understand how you would think that. Your point of view does count, Sarika, far more than you know. In my culture, before all else, we must put the safety of our women first. That is an absolute rule. We cannot get around it. No manner of discussion or upset can remove that fundamental imperative obligation. It is bred into our bones. Far before our births it is imprinted on us, just as the ritual binding words are.

That is an excuse, not the reality of the situation. She wished he didn't sound so persuasive. He did. She didn't want to hear him, but she was a listener. When she listened, she tried not to form arguments while the other person was speaking. That allowed her to hear them and try to process what they were really saying.

You do not understand. You believe you have no choice, but the truth is

I have none when it comes to certain things, such as your safety and health. I wanted to give you the space you asked for so you could come to terms with the situation. I know you from your letters. I know you're a thoughtful person, who would give real consideration to our customs and ways. The binding ritual is not a custom. Neither is the need to protect you. Those two things are sacred in our society, and we are compelled to obey those decrees. It is compulsion, not just want or need.

Sarika did her best to hear him out. He sounded as if he spoke the truth when he said he wanted to give her the space to come to terms with everything on her own. She liked that he referred to her letters. He had always given consideration to her ideas. She had to admit that about him. He'd never been dismissive of the things she thought would be good for the big cats in various environments.

He would always assess what she said and then give her his thoughts. Sometimes he would point out why something wouldn't work, but then he would tell her that the idea she had for corridors went right along with his thinking. The jaguars needed to be able to move from one place to another in order to find mates.

But compulsion? What did that mean exactly? Had Tomas been unable to do anything else? Luiz had acted the same way about taking her blood.

Tell me about the binding ritual. What does that mean, and what did it do to me?

She felt his hesitation. That didn't bode well. She began to dress carefully in clothes that she could easily shed if she needed to. Clothes didn't work when one was shifting, and she had no idea what to expect once the sun went down.

I would prefer to explain it in person. It is a difficult concept, and the conversation needs to be in depth.

That was fair, but she felt different, as though something significant had changed in her body. Not just her body. Something fundamental that she couldn't change back.

I understand. I also think you feel that if you're here with me, you can console me. Why would I need consolation? In your world, doesn't everyone have a lifemate? Is it a good thing or a bad thing?

That was a challenge. She made it clear to him that she wanted the truth. She wasn't going to pretend she was on board with what he'd done or that she would accept his explanation, but she did expect him to provide her with one, whether he was there in person or not.

The lifemate binding ritual is imprinted on a male before he is born. When he is born, his soul is split; all darkness goes into him, and the light finds its way to his lifemate. She must guard that half of his soul from all enemies. Carpathian males, as they age, are very dangerous. They are incapable of feeling emotion or seeing in color. Only a true lifemate can restore those things to him. Carpathian women were raised to know they guarded the soul of a warrior, and one day he would find her and the ritual binding words would be said to them. The vows only work on a true lifemate. The soul is restored, and the warrior is safe from turning vampire.

Her heart thudded hard. Luiz had alluded to some of what Tomas was saying, but she hadn't really understood. *You could become a vampire?*

All Carpathian males spend centuries hunting and killing the undead. They remove all evidence of their existence. Sometimes the ones they hunt are family members. Or friends they grew up with. We have a strict code of honor, but when centuries pass without color or emotion, one looks for something, anything, to feel. It is necessary to find our lifemate and restore our soul to keep us from turning. Killing while taking blood can provide a rush.

Now she could barely breathe. *Stop for a moment and let me process what you're saying.* She was grateful he wasn't standing in front of her with this explanation. He might think it would have been easier for her to understand, but she wasn't Carpathian. She'd never heard of them—at least she didn't think she had. Carpathians terrified her, and the concept of them terrified her. The idea that they would kill while taking blood sent her mind reeling.

Sarika did deep breathing, trying to understand her reaction. She had expected the things Tomas would reveal to be huge. She didn't think the lifemate thing was trivial. Why was she reeling so badly? She could almost hear doors in her mind creaking. Rattling. Trying to open.

Those memories were sealed closed for many reasons. Her mind could never accept her nightmares as reality, and the nightmares were horrendous. The things she witnessed in those visions were so terrifying she couldn't face them. Especially if they were real and the culprits turned out to be Carpathian.

She didn't have panic attacks over most things, but she did when it came to those nightmares. She was incredibly strong. She believed in herself. In her training. And she'd trained hard in self-defense simply because she traveled the world, and going into other countries, some unstable, some dictated solely by men, she wanted to be able to depend on herself to escape any situation.

That wasn't the case here. This rainforest was triggering things best left alone. Tomas' explanation shouldn't have sent her into a full-blown panic, but it had. She needed to calm herself to allow Tomas to continue. She didn't want him there with her to observe her reactions to the things he was telling her. She'd asked him. No, made it a demand, insisting on learning her way, and he had given her enough respect to do so even though he felt that decision wasn't the best.

She always made tea for herself when she woke, no matter the time of day or night. On automatic pilot, she made her way into the kitchen. The ritual of making tea was as soothing to her as the actual drinking of it. She wasn't even surprised that Luiz had the kitchen stocked with her favorite brands of herbal teas. Chamomile was her tea of choice. It provided a soothing calm and combated anxiety. It was loose-leaf, her preference, and with the kettle and infuser set right out with the choices of tea, Luiz had made it easy for her to have whatever she needed at her fingertips.

She put the water on to boil and walked over to the window to look at the view. The tree house had an incredible panorama of the surrounding jungle. Tropical flowers climbed tree trunks, giving joyful, gorgeous splashes of color as a backdrop to the hundreds of various shades of green. What would it be like to travel through such beauty and never see it? Tomas and his brothers had frequented many rainforests in various countries. She knew because she followed T. Smolnycki Jr. and the good he was doing for those habitats. And if not seeing that beauty for centuries, what would it be like to suddenly have all that change? The shades of green were vivid. The flowers vibrant, even at night. Some of the plants came alive at night.

Did you remember the beauty of the rainforest?

Those memories were lost to us many centuries ago. My brothers helped to keep what we could alive, but eventually, over so long a time, those things fade until there are only gray shadows and the need to do battle with the enemy. We held out to find our lifemates when so many others succumbed to darkness. When judging my actions, I would like you to think of that. How long I have existed in a dull void. How long I refused to dishonor myself, my brothers, our people and especially you. You were that reason. That hope. The only safe haven I have. The only reason to keep my honor. Not only did you restore colors and give me my soul, but you gave me the ability to feel emotion. In turn, I can share those things with my brothers to help them stay on the path and keep to the code.

There was a lot to like about what he said. It did make her important to him. Perhaps too important. That would speak loudly to his making decisions that affected her life without giving her choices. That wasn't a good thing. She should still have a say, be given the time to process his needs, but she understood better why he took the action he had. She still didn't understand why those ritual binding words affected her the way they had and what changes in her they'd made.

I am doing my best not to be judgmental, Tomas. I will admit it is difficult to try to think in your point of view because your experiences are so different from mine. I understand a Carpathian woman growing up knowing she is a hunter's salvation. Because she has known, probably since birth, it must be far easier for her than for someone who has no concept of such a thing. Trying to put it in perspective, relating to your customs and imprints that become compulsions is extremely difficult for an outsider.

She didn't want to be judgmental about his species. She didn't know enough to pass judgment on him—not yet. It was difficult to push back her upbringing as an independent woman capable of making her own decisions. She was more human than anything else. Even her shifter side had been raised to be independent.

On the other hand, she felt Tomas' struggle. That was one of the advantages of speaking telepathically with him that she appreciated. He might be able to read her emotions and her intent, but in turn, she could read his. She saw glimpses of the other males who were shocked that he didn't do the things immediately necessary to bind her to him. That he hesitated to go against her wishes. He wanted to give her time, but whatever the reason he had come to Peru, he was under a severe time constraint, and he was walking into an extremely dangerous situation. Those were all factors that had persuaded him to go against his instincts to allow her time.

That knowledge helped her to step back from her own beliefs and arguments and listen to him. To truly try to comprehend his life and how hers was so entangled with his. She liked that he had hesitated. That he wanted her to make the decision to come to him of her own free will. She really liked that he wanted to be that man for her that would back her choices, even if his brethren didn't agree.

That didn't settle the problem of compulsive behaviors his species had imprinted on them. If he couldn't resist those behaviors, what would a future with him look like?

Your species can become vampire if they don't find their lifemate. She made that a statement.

Not a woman. She holds her own light as well as that of her partner. Most women are aware of this task, and it is often a huge one. Should an enemy become aware of the woman who holds the other half of a warrior's soul, they will do everything in their power to take it from her, including torture. They would slay everyone she loves to force her to turn over that soul. Should they achieve their goal, they can turn that very dangerous hunter into a pawn for their own use.

She poured the boiling water into the small teapot over the infuser and slid a cozy over it to keep it warm. Then she poured water into the tea mug to warm it.

Why wasn't I told I had this very unique and dangerous task? I had no idea. If some horrible vampire or one of your enemies I know nothing about had demanded I turn over your soul, I wouldn't have had the least bit of an idea what they were talking about.

I do not know. If you are reborn multiple times before I find you, there is some indication that you carry the soul of a warrior.

Tomas was genuinely puzzled and struggled with an unfamiliar anger that she hadn't been more carefully prepared—and guarded. He was very aware she had traveled the world in her capacity as an environmentalist, working to save habitats. She had focused on large animals, specifically cats, to do her veterinary work, but she had done so going into many dangerous situations. In his world, she would have been protected by every Carpathian, knowing she carried the soul of a warrior.

Perhaps the lack of knowledge was my protection, she ventured. *How would your enemies find me? How would they know I carried your soul?*

Vampires and others are capable of scanning memories of humans and shifters. It isn't always easy with Lycans, but it can be done, depending on the power wielded by the individual.

Do not say "Lycans." We're already dealing with far too many scary things. She wasn't kidding, and she could tell her little outburst left him amused.

No Lycans, he agreed promptly.

That made her smile. The thing was, she liked him. She'd liked him from the very first time he had gone to the trouble of answering her silly letter when she'd written to him with her concerns and ideas. A man, a busy one, one well respected in his field, would rarely take the time to give each line of her letter consideration and then follow through with answers.

Tomas had continued to correspond with her, although long gaps would occur between her letters and his answers. She would worry for his safety and wonder why he had disappeared for so long, but she came to believe he would always reach out to her when he had the chance—and he had. Somewhere along the line, she went from hero worship to thinking there was no one else like him on earth.

She hadn't considered his age. His father was the leading conservationist for so long, a part of her believed his son was perhaps ten years older than she was. That age gap didn't seem insurmountable to her, since they had such similar interests and ideas. She had no idea how she had turned her childhood hero worship into a full-blown fantasy that there could be more between them. It was just a little humiliating that he could find those girlish hopes. And maybe that was one of the reasons she had tried so hard to keep him out of her head.

If your enemies scanned my mind, they wouldn't find any memory or knowledge of such a thing, she pointed out. *That was protection right there. It might not be the protection afforded to your Carpathian women, but for someone like me, it was most likely for the best.*

He remained silent, giving her response thought before he answered. *I cannot argue with your logic. It goes against our customs, but you are not Carpathian yet, and no one, probably not even your uncle and aunt, was informed you held a Carpathian's soul. I cannot imagine that they would know and not prepare you to be a lifemate to an ancient hunter.*

Her mind shut down when he used the phrase "not Carpathian yet." She didn't want him to explain that to her. She had enough to process. The things he told her were true; she not only heard the honesty in his voice, but she could see it in the glimpses of his thoughts.

She poured out the water from her mug and added the tea. The aroma alone should have helped to soothe her, but the moment she smelled the tea, her stomach lurched. Her throat closed. All of a sudden, just the thought of drinking her beloved chamomile tea sickened her. She pushed the mug away from her and quickly left the kitchen.

What's wrong, sivamet?

His concern was instant and genuine. She liked that she mattered to someone. Right at that moment, when she didn't know her future and she was afraid of the species her lifemate was, she needed someone to care. To see her. To want to help her out of the mess she was in. She didn't think Tomas was so willing to help her leave, but he wanted to help her sort the confusing things out.

It's nothing, she reassured. *No danger.*

Tell me.

Tomas said it gently, stroking caresses in her mind, but there was a demand there, whether she wanted to acknowledge it or not. And what was her objection to his knowing the smell of her favorite tea made her sick? She wasn't used to sharing herself with anyone, but it would be silly not to tell him.

I drink tea every morning. Sometimes in the evening. I use it to calm me down when I'm feeling anxious, which, believe me, when I discovered I couldn't leave this place and that you had taken my blood regardless of my wishes, I felt that anxiety in abundance. So my favorite chamomile tea. Luiz had the brand I like and I made myself a cup. Just the smell of it made me sick. I've been traveling for days. Weeks before this. I lost my adoptive parents. Confronted male shifters for the first time and found you. It's been an anxious time for me, but I'll get through it. Feeling sick because I couldn't drink my tea is nothing in the grand scheme of things.

She felt him hesitate, and instantly her stomach rolled. Her heart plummeted. If there was a reason he knew that she couldn't handle her tea, she didn't want to know about it. She was all Carpathianed out. Done.

Don't say anything more. Not one single word.

He obliged her, and she was very thankful. She went out to the wraparound deck and sank into one of the gliders to wait for sunset.

CHAPTER 11

Tomas stood at the entrance of Dominic and Solange's home. He had hoped bringing Sarika somewhere she might feel safe, somewhere there were other women, might help to relieve the trepidation she was feeling over his species. His brothers accompanied them, as did Luiz. That wasn't in the least bit helpful. She had to think she was surrounded by an army when he wanted this to be a fun, upbeat visit for her.

Bringing Sarika into Dominic and Solange's home felt as if he were taking his woman into a dark lair where power shifted to those who were living there. He hesitated at the entrance and glanced back at his brothers.

Don't like the feel of this.

It is Dominic and Solange, Lojos pointed out even as he strode forward, moving in front of Tomas and Sarika. *Dominic will do all in his power to protect Solange just as she does for him. You had to know, when the invitation was accepted, that he would safeguard his lair.*

Tomas didn't like his brother going in front of him. That made him all the more uneasy.

"What's wrong?" Sarika asked.

He should have known she would feel the building tension in the air. "I wanted you to have a good time, be around other women, but I shouldn't have pushed for this. You were reluctant, and I decided that I knew more than you."

"I made the decision to come," Sarika corrected. "I'm nervous, yes, but I spend a great deal of my time alone. My understanding is that Jasmine and Sandrine will be here. It would be nice to see them and know they don't have any lasting effects from the encounter with Rud." She tilted her head to look up at him. "What's really wrong? I thought these people were your friends. Dominic came to Luiz's home, and everyone seemed to think he was a good man."

He could tell her the truth and hope she understood, or he could brush off her concerns. He gave her truth. "My brothers do not have lifemates. Luiz has a lifemate, but she is too young to anchor him. That means that all three could, if the circumstances were right, cross the line and become the very thing we hunt. Dominic and Solange will be acutely aware of it."

Her lashes swept down and then back up. "If your brothers share your memories, can't you anchor them? Keep them safe until they find their lifemates?"

"I try. I have been sharing color and emotion as best I can. It is you providing those things for me."

"You're saying I can give them those things, share with them enough to keep them safe? Can I do the same with my cousin?"

Tomas nodded slowly. "You have a gift, Sarika. You aren't aware of how special you are. Not just because you're my lifemate, but you seem to be able to ease any ancient when you're close to him. To my knowledge, there are only a few women who can do such a thing."

"How would I make it easier for Lojos, Mataias and Luiz?"

He took a deep breath, pulled her away from the entrance to the cave and gave her the truth he knew she wouldn't like. "In our world, everything is about blood. Luiz took your blood in order to better communicate with you from a distance so he could ensure your protection, but he didn't give you his blood."

Her lashes fluttered again, removing his ability to see her reaction. It took discipline not to look into her mind. She had a very real abhorrence to anyone taking her blood. It had to be worse to think she would have to ingest blood herself. She was silent for so long he almost interfered to tell her it was simply information.

No one expected her to or would want her to think she needed to aid the ancient warriors. They didn't think in those terms. They were solely there for the purpose of protecting her. To Luiz, she was his family. To his brothers, she was their little sister. They would give their lives for her.

"When I dreamt that day, I dreamt that you not only took my blood but you gave me yours. We haven't yet discussed it because I wasn't ready, but it wasn't a dream, was it?"

He shook his head. "No."

"But I was unaware while you did it, right?"

"Yes." They were in uncomfortable territory for both of them. He didn't like the fact that their first blood exchange had been without her consent. He would have to address that, along with his reasons, soon. His explanations for trampling on her rights had to be getting old.

"If I could actually agree to such a thing, would you be able to be with me? In my mind, I mean. Where I could feel you and not them? Could you keep me from knowing what they were doing? What I was doing?"

His heart reacted with physical pain. Sarika surprised him at every turn. Just the fact that she would consider such a thing when she was so terrified of having them take her blood astonished him. He especially loved that she wanted him to buffer her. He didn't deserve her faith in him, not yet. He needed to earn that.

"What you're offering is amazing, Sarika. A gift beyond any price, but you aren't ready for it. My brothers and Luiz will endure because that is what they do. You haven't yet come to terms with being my lifemate. You're asking far too much of yourself."

"The point is this, Tomas," she said, tilting her chin at him so her eyes met his. "I had no choice when it came to being a lifemate. There doesn't appear to be a way out, so I have a couple of choices. One is to fight you every step of the way, and the other is to do whatever I can to understand your customs and your needs to give us a better life together. I choose the second one. The more choices I make for myself, the more I feel in control of my life."

Every word of every letter she'd ever written to him was engraved in his mind. This was the woman he'd come to know through the many years of posts she'd sent to him. She always took time to process a situation, and then she came up with solutions. She was willing to learn and change her opinions if things made sense to her.

"Your brothers mean everything to you. They are good men, and they're willing to put their lives on the line for me. My cousin is the same. Annoying and intimidating, but he's my family, and he would have risked fighting with you for me even knowing he was outnumbered. If I won't have knowledge of it while it is being done, the blood exchanges, I mean, and you're there with me, my protection, I think it would be a good thing."

"Here? Now? Before we enter Dominic and Solange's home?"

"Yes. I think it is best to do it quickly, right here and now, especially if that will help to put Dominic and Solange at ease. I've made up my mind, and I don't want to think too much about it. So let's get it done."

What's the holdup? Dominic asked.

Sarika has offered a gift beyond price to my brothers and Luiz. He sent all of them her offer using the pathway of the ancients. Vampires had been Carpathians, and using the common communication could mean one chanced being overheard by the enemy.

There has been no coercion? She was terrified of all things Carpathian, in particular, taking of her blood, Dominic pointed out.

She still is, but she is determined to do this. Tomas couldn't help the surge of pride in his lifemate. She was much stronger than anyone gave her credit for. Even him. He had underestimated her.

Have you told her the repercussions? Mataias asked. *That we will always be able to find her? That if she tried to run, there would be no hope of escape?*

I have already made the first true blood exchange. She would be unable to hide from me, Tomas said. *This is her idea, and she is determined, but if we do this, it must take place immediately.*

Luiz gently took Sarika's elbow and drew her close to him. "Little cousin, we are ancients and have endured for centuries. We would not lose our honor at this late date. What you offer is an incredible gift, but not necessary when it is very frightening to you."

"I have no doubt that the three of you would never break your code, Luiz. That isn't why I want to do this. I believe if you can share color and emotion, even a small amount, it will ease you in times of trouble. And the three of you strike me as men who are always in trouble. Not to mention, recognizing your sense of humor will go a long way toward others not being so fearful of you. It's also important to me that your friends don't treat you with suspicion."

"The point of being me is to strike fear into their hearts," Luiz objected.

Tomas felt that spark of humor in him through his connection with Sarika. She had said she felt the emotions of the ancients when they couldn't, but he didn't understand until that moment. Luiz was a De La Cruz. He might have his jaguar, but he was wholly of that lineage. Every warrior long past had poured their knowledge and pain into him. He carried a very heavy burden, more so than most. Worse, the De La Cruz line had something twisted in it. Something that made them incredible predators, more so than most Carpathian hunters. There was very little civilized about them, and they didn't try to be. To find that humor was incredible. To realize Luiz had a sense of humor, that it was even there, was huge.

"Well, you'll have to strike a little less fear," Sarika said. "Because, for me, this is necessary."

Tomas liked that she stood up for herself. He didn't interfere or add to her arguments. She needed to feel in control, and if he stepped in, that control would be taken from her.

Don't allow her to do this yet. Solange is coming out and wishes to speak with her.

The point, Dominic, is not to use the word allow, Tomas objected. *She needs to feel in control, and this is a decision she made, not me. This came as a surprise. Taking it away from her would set us back weeks. As you well know, we are tracking Justice. We may have lost him and can afford to give my lifemate a few days to acclimate, but she has to have accepted all that being my lifemate entails.*

If this is her decision, Tomas, she will persuade Solange that it is hers alone.

Dominic's decree set Tomas' teeth on edge. That monster inside him burst forth, rearing up like a volcanic eruption. Lojos and Mataias immediately flanked him, ready to go to battle.

You are overstepping your perceived authority, Dominic, Tomas reminded. *You have no right to interfere with my lifemate. Consider this visit canceled. Give our regrets to your lifemate.*

He took Sarika's elbow. "We're leaving this place. Come with me now." He gave her no choice, taking her with him as his brothers and Luiz closed ranks around them.

On the path in front of them, the leaves blew into a wild eddy, whirling up like a small twister. A woman appeared out of the leaves. She was short with an hourglass figure but appeared all muscle. Her eyes were amber with hints of green. Her hair was very thick, evidence of her jaguar heritage, a dark sable with a few golden streaks. If one looked closely, they would see the tiny scars that covered her face and body.

"Solange," Tomas greeted. His voice wasn't welcoming, and Sarika frowned up at him uncertainly.

"Tomas," Solange answered him, her gaze sweeping over the group of men surrounding Sarika. "Ordinarily, my husband is the diplomatic one, and I tend to put my foot in it, but I think in this case, he did. He tends to be overprotective of me, which I appreciate most of the time. Your woman is a fellow jaguar, one from an incredible line. She saved my cousin and my niece, and I owe her. At the very least I wish to thank her for what she did. Jasmine tells me she put her life on the line with Rud."

She sent Sarika a tentative smile, but she didn't attempt to address her, waiting on Tomas' verdict. He knew, should he object, he would look churlish and guilty. He felt both. Rage remained, bubbling like a pool of magma below the surface.

Tell me what is wrong.

He was startled that Sarika reached out to him so confidently. She kept her head up, not looking in the least submissive or afraid. He recognized that her gifts were growing in strength.

Dominic and Solange are determined to manipulate this situation.

How? Why?

With Solange, it is probably genuine concern that you are being coerced into helping my brothers and Luiz. With Dominic, he will back Solange's play, whether he thinks she is right or not.

Sarika sent him a genuine smile. *Introduce us, please.*

Open the gate, Tomas commanded his brothers.

Lojos and Mataias stepped aside. Neither went far. As they had for centuries, they separated, giving plenty of fighting room, and slid back into the shadows of the larger trees until they faded from sight. Luiz remained behind Tomas and Sarika, guarding their backs, a silent reminder that if one took him on, they were taking on the entire De La Cruz family. It didn't matter that Solange, through her cousin Juliette's marriage, was a part of that family.

"Solange, this is my lifemate, Sarika Silva. Sarika, Solange Sangria Dragonseeker. If there is one true ruler of the jaguar, it is Solange."

"Who wants no part of ruling anything." Solange stepped forward without hesitation, right into the circle that Tomas and his brothers had created. She didn't appear to notice she was in a danger zone, but Tomas wasn't falling for it. Solange was a warrior through and through. She was cunning and fast, and aside from all her skills in the jaguar world, she had Dominic as a mentor for the Carpathian world.

There was no smile on Solange's face. She wasn't a girlie, feely kind of woman. She was skilled in battle, and those who knew her respected her abilities.

"Silva is a very respected name in our world," Solange said. "I want to personally thank you for your incredible bravery. You stepped in to save a complete stranger. Jasmine and Sandrine are very dear to us. We owe you quite a debt of gratitude."

"I think anyone hearing a child cry out in pain and fear would have rushed to aid them," Sarika said. "Jasmine was right there, determined to protect her child."

"She said she tried to trade her life for Sandrine's. Rud would have killed my niece out of sheer spite. He grew up under my father's regime and became every bit as cruel and brutal as Brodrick was. He believed in Brodrick's teachings, that women shifters were worth nothing, and the men had the right to their bodies anytime they wanted them. After Brodrick was killed, Rud took over, carrying on that same fanatical rhetoric. You saved them both. My sincere thanks. If there is anything I can ever do for you, please let me know."

"Sandrine is a beautiful child, and she was very brave under the circumstances. I am happy I was there to help." Sarika glanced over her shoulder to smile at her cousin. "I knew Luiz would come the moment he could. It was a surprise to have three other male hunters rise up right at our feet just in the nick of time."

"Jasmine and Sandrine are on their way with Jubal, Jasmine's husband. They would very much like to see you again. Please come in and visit. Let us show you a warm welcome after so much turmoil."

Sarika sent her a quick smile. "I have made a decision my brothers and cousin are wary of, and they think to persuade me from my chosen path. Once I do as I wish, I would very much like to take advantage of your hospitality."

At her declaration, there was a visible change in Solange's demeanor. Her eyes narrowed, did a quick scan of the surrounding area, and then once more focused on Sarika.

"If you don't mind my asking you, what are they pressuring you not to do?"

Sarika sent Solange a little frown. "I wouldn't use the word *pressuring*. I know very little of Carpathians and their customs. My lifemate, brothers and cousin all are aware I have this aversion to exchanging blood. It is taking some getting used to. But I also know if we exchange a small amount of blood, they would be able to share my emotions when needed. They would see in colors. Perhaps it would be dull colors, but it would ease their way while they search for their lifemates. We're a family. I need to feel empowered, and they are having a difficult time understanding when they want to protect me from anything that could distress me. I understand, but I don't agree."

"You came up with this idea on your own?"

"Yes. Tomas is doing his best to allow me to make choices so I feel in control. I will admit I don't understand why they're all upset with my decision. Perhaps you could enlighten me on the Carpathian male way of thinking, but after I complete my task."

"I can do that," Solange agreed, "although their logic and our logic are not ever going to be the same."

"Why is that?" Sarika curled her hand in the crook of Tomas' arm and leaned into him.

Tomas knew what she was doing, and he appreciated it. A show of solidarity. Tomas was her lifemate, and she was declaring she was with him to Solange.

"Because they are who they are. We'll talk inside. Good luck with your plan. Would you like me to stay with you?"

She smiled up at Tomas. "I asked him to promise to shield me, and I know he will." She spoke with every confidence.

Tomas was amazed at her ability to appear completely composed and confident when he knew she was very frightened of her decision. Determined—but afraid. Still, she gave Solange a bright, happy, all-too-confident smile and leaned into him even more.

Tomas recognized immediately that she was on overload. He

wrapped his arm around her and brought her front to his side, tucking her under his shoulder. "Let's do this," he said aloud.

She's reaching her limit. I need all three of you to cooperate with her. Luiz, you're up first. Just take over and get it done. I'll be with her, shielding her. She's very strong, and it won't be easy to get her to go under, even though she wants this and is cooperating. There is an ancient power fighting back, trying to keep her safe. More and more he was becoming aware of something ancient and very formidable growing in his lifemate.

He felt the power of the De La Cruz sweeping over Sarika. It was swift, no hesitation. He suppressed her ability to feel or know what was happening. Tomas extended her wrist toward Luiz, and again, he didn't hesitate. He wanted this over just as quickly as Tomas did. Tomas hadn't considered how he would feel having other men, even his brothers and Sarika's cousin, taking her blood and then giving her theirs. Every instinct as a lifemate told him to take her and run. To defend her. To shove the men away from her.

He had to admit they were quick and respectful, but his emotions were all over the place. Through it all, he kept the shield strong and steady. He poured himself into her mind, building a wall around her thoughts and memories so no other could intrude. She needed to feel safe, that she could rely on him when she was unaware of what was happening to her. Sarika was intelligent enough to know that being a lifemate to a Carpathian hunter would necessitate this very protection.

Dominic is here somewhere, Mataias advised. *He would never leave Solange out in the open without backing her up himself.*

He's here, Luiz confirmed. *The Dragonseeker fades into the shadows the way the three of you do, but his power is difficult to hide with his form.*

He is able to make the forest uneasy if he wishes, Lojos added.

Tomas was aware of the Dragonseeker's power. That lineage was the only one in Carpathian history where not a single warrior had ever turned vampire. Many of them had made enormous sacrifices, including Dominic, but they had held out against the whispers of darkness.

Dominic Dragonseeker was not only owed respect simply because of his lineage, but for all the things he had done for their people over the centuries. He had stopped a war, infiltrating the ranks of their enemies, suffering the agonizing pain of parasites and acid blood, to appear as if he had joined the fight against the prince.

Too much power corrupted. That was a fact of life. Living far past the time when even Carpathians should, without having a lifemate, forever changed them, and not in a good way. Becoming too close to men you respected and hunted with, when those males were without lifemates, was never a good move. At any time, those friends could become the very thing you were forced to hunt and kill.

Tomas understood why Dominic was wary, careful of his family. Not just Solange, but Jasmine, Sandrine and even Jubal. In his eyes, his first duty was to protect them, and he would do so with every weapon in his arsenal. He had known the triplets for centuries. Hunted with them. They had even saved one another's lives. He knew Luiz; they coexisted in the same territory. But that didn't reduce the risk to Dominic's family. If anything, it increased it.

That brought Tomas up short. Sarika had made an incredible offer. She knew so little about Carpathian ways, yet she had insisted, without really discussing it with him, that she do the very thing that had made her the most reluctant to become his lifemate.

She was a mystery. And she displayed incredible courage over and over. He knew she was afraid, and yet she'd faced Rud. She'd made a decision to aid his brothers and her cousin, but she'd also defused the situation with Dominic.

Look into her memories, Luiz advised.

Tomas brought Sarika out from under his compulsion very slowly, giving her body and brain time to adjust.

Look into your own, he said. He was tired of the male hunters expecting him to follow their advice when it came to his lifemate. She was his, not theirs, and that meant he needed to get to know her and follow his own instincts when it came to making her happy.

You have been far too long around humans, Mataias said with a long-suffering sigh.

So much easier if she'd obey you without question, Lojos added.

He knew his brothers were deliberately provoking him. He sent them a disgusted look, wrapping his arm around Sarika and pulling her into him. His larger body shielded her from the others.

"Do you feel dizzy? Uncomfortable?"

She leaned into him as if for support. That surprised him, but he'd take it. Any concession from her was good when they had so much to work out. They would have to leave in a few days to continue to track Justice. His brothers would be casting around, looking for signs of Justice's passing while he worked with Sarika to get her ready to travel with them. He hadn't gotten to that bit of information for her as of yet. Time was their enemy.

"I actually feel good, Tomas." She whispered her answer. "I just can't stop shaking, and that's embarrassing to me. I don't want anyone to think you made this choice for me, or your brothers and Luiz did."

"I think you were very clear that this was your choice, *sivamet*. I'm proud of you. Are you ready for that visit?"

Her hand slipped into his. "Stay close to me."

Again, she showed him she was willing to put her trust in him when he hadn't done much to earn it. He could become obsessed with her. He certainly understood Dominic's need to guard Solange. He would do the same. In fact, he would never be a good lifemate to a woman like Solange, who insisted she go into battle. She was not only good in a fight, but she was every bit as skilled as the Carpathian hunters, thanks to her lifemate, who had made certain she knew everything he did.

Tomas wasn't about to allow Sarika to go into a battle with the undead or any other monsters, not if he could help it. That didn't mean he wouldn't prepare her, but he saw no reason for her to risk her life.

"Solange, we've taken care of the task of ensuring you and your family are safe from everyone entering your home," he announced.

Solange gave him a little salute. "In truth, Tomas, I wasn't worried. I know Luiz very well, and he keeps to a strict code. You and your brothers have always had the respect of Dominic. That isn't something he gives lightly, so again, although I appreciate that Sarika was courageous enough to give aid to your family, I had no doubts that we would all be fine."

He didn't point out that Dominic hadn't been as sure because Dominic had been doing his job. Had he not been leery, Tomas would have lost respect for him. Solange was different. Hardened by her past. Skilled beyond imagination. Willing to put her life on the line over and over for the female jaguars she fought so hard to free. She might not be what everyone considered an ideal lifemate, but she was devoted to Dominic and he to her.

Solange led the way to the entrance to her home. Should anyone come across it, there appeared to be a crack in the boulders. Tomas felt the safeguards woven around the entire area. Lojos and Mataias followed closely behind Solange, staying in front of Tomas and Sarika as shields against any danger. Luiz was behind them, ensuring no enemy could creep up on them.

The overgrown bushes hiding the entrance were part illusion and part reality. The crack opened up to a very narrow opening. So narrow, Tomas' shoulders brushed either side of the corridor. This gave those inside an advantage in that an enemy would have to advance one at a time. It was a clever trap that appeared to be naturally formed, but Tomas knew it wasn't.

They traveled a few feet inside the cave, and the narrow opening suddenly widened to what appeared to be a spacious hallway. Sarika gasped and stopped walking for a moment, looking around her to take in the beauty. Sconces made of blown glass in soft shades of blue and purple were on the walls on either side, lighting up the floor beneath their feet. That floor was made up of stones in various shades of color. The same stones ran up the curved walls and were embedded in the ceiling. The floors and ceiling were works of art. The effect gave the feeling of entering a magnificent mansion.

The moment they entered the hallway, the feeling of the space changed to one of warm welcome. The hallway gave way to an extremely large chamber that had to be the great room, with high ceilings and gem-covered walls. Gold filigree held up the delicate blown-glass sconces that lit the gems in starburst patterns.

Diamonds, rubies, emeralds and sapphires in various colors sparkled when the lights from above played over them. The effect was breathtaking. The floor was made of great flat stones in various shades of gray, highly polished until they gleamed. There was nothing cave-like about the space. The great room was rare and lovely and a work of art. Massive trees crawled up the walls; the branches curved artfully, reaching to the cathedral ceiling. Flowers hung in bunches off the twisting limbs.

Even the furniture was different, several pod-like chairs that were either for one person or two, designed to invite anyone visiting to sink down into them and get comfortable. Sarika looked around her in obvious wonder.

"This is lovely," she said to Solange. "Incredibly beautiful."

Caves deep beneath the earth often hold incredible secrets and a beauty unseen by those aboveground. Carpathians weren't bothered by pressure or lack of air; they could go deep into the earth and often found treasure hidden below the surface. Sarika had never experienced the wonders of caves.

"Thank you," Solange answered, looking pleased. She waved toward the chairs. "Please make yourselves comfortable. Jubal and Jasmine own a furniture company together. These are their designs. Trust me, they are extremely comfortable. Their designs are becoming very popular."

Tomas walked his lifemate across the floor to one of the two-person chairs. The moment they sank down into it, the chair seemed to come to life, the back and sides adjusting to their height to make it very comfortable. Sarika cuddled into him, allowing his body to partially shield hers from those in the room. It wasn't an overt move, but should she become overwhelmed, he could easily protect her without seeming to. He really liked the chair for that reason alone.

"I can see why," Tomas said. "Very comfortable."

Dominic entered the room, just as if he'd been in another part of the house. He did it smoothly and silently. He went straight to Solange, who had positioned herself across the room so she could have a conversation facing her visitors.

"Sarika, it is good to see you again. I hope you're feeling better after a long rest." He stood behind his lifemate and casually wrapped one arm around her waist.

Tomas hadn't been expecting that intimate gesture. Solange's body language didn't invite intimacy. She seemed aloof, alone, completely self-sufficient. Dominic was so casual about his claim on her it was clear that the way he stood with her was something done often. Whatever restrictions Solange put on other relationships didn't include Dominic.

"I really needed to sleep. I'd lost my aunt and uncle within days of each other, and that was a horrible time. I needed to take care of the details of their estate and see to their cremation. There aren't a lot of shifters where I was raised. In fact, I only met a couple in all the years I was there, so I couldn't rely on anyone else to make certain our customs were followed."

Luiz frowned. "You didn't write to me immediately, Sarika. I would have gotten to you as quickly as possible. It isn't like we don't have planes available to us."

Tomas sensed how uncomfortable she was with Luiz's statement. Or rather, reprimand. Her cousin took his role as head of the family very seriously.

"I didn't know about you," she admitted, her voice filled with sorrow and guilt. "I wasn't told about the shifters here in Peru until about a year before they passed. This was the one place my aunt and uncle asked me not to come, and I respected their wishes. I suspected there would be shifters here, just because I knew I was born here and they were from here, but I would never have gone against their wishes while they lived."

Through her bond with Luiz, Tomas felt the man's smoldering reaction. Luiz's expression didn't change. He appeared calm, but there was anger on Sarika's behalf. Her aunt and uncle had done her a disservice by keeping so much of her past from her. And they had nearly deprived Luiz of the last of his family.

She is struggling to maintain in this unfamiliar situation, Luiz, Tomas cautioned. *Don't force her to defend her aunt and uncle in front of strangers.*

Sarika flicked her gaze up to his. She relaxed further against him and gave him a half smile before turning her attention back to Solange. "I understand there is to be a celebration of sorts. Luiz was telling me your friends and family were gathering together."

Solange made a little face and glanced up at Dominic. Tomas was aware the two had a quick, intimate exchange before Solange turned back to face Sarika.

"I am not really good in the spotlight. My cousins are insisting on a party to celebrate the fact that I am pregnant."

She didn't exactly make a face, she was far too stoic, but she may as well have. Dominic laughed, the sound rich and vibrant. His other arm swept around Solange, engulfing her smaller frame as he bent to brush a kiss on top of her head.

"As you can see, Solange loves to be the center of attention."

"Why is everyone making such a big deal about it? Jasmine had a baby and she's pregnant, too. I don't see everyone turning cartwheels. And what about Riley? She has a child, and although she hasn't said a word, I think she's in the same state." She turned her face up to glare at Dominic and then looked back to Sarika. "Don't drink the water, and don't be persuaded by *anything* that man says to you. It's a dangerous time right now."

Thanks to Sarika sharing her blood with his brothers and cousin, Tomas could feel the shared amusement in all of them.

CHAPTER 12

Balloons," Solange said. She pinned Sarika with a steely gaze. "What is it with balloons? Why is it necessary to put those things all over the house? Do you honestly think they're festive?" She gave a little shudder, which the males immediately found amusing.

Under Solange's stoic demeanor, Sarika could feel her blossoming need to run. It was Dominic keeping her there. Dominic ensuring she didn't do what Solange would have considered humiliating herself. Dominic protecting her in the way she needed and asked for. Solange was mimicking the other women under similar circumstances. Those weren't her own reactions at all. Deep down, she was horrified at the attention and wanted to conceal herself far away from whatever event was unfolding.

Sarika considered how best to aid her in the deception. She understood Solange's motives. She was attempting to fit in for her cousins, whom she deeply loved. She showed her love in the way she fought for them and their rights. She had no idea how to show a softer side. She trusted Dominic to help her, but it was extremely difficult for her.

Sarika wasn't certain the stress of trying to fit in was good for Solange or her baby. She didn't question why she was able to feel so deeply what the males in the room, true Carpathians, could not. She only knew that there was a well of concern deep inside her struggling to reach Solange to help her.

"It's funny you say that about balloons, Solange," Sarika said. "I've always had an aversion to them as well. I detest them floating through the air all over a room. When they pop, and kids often pop them, the sound freaks me out. And what's really a pain is when the kids or adults start hitting them toward your face and think it's funny."

"Bad for the environment," Tomas put in. "People release them into the air and birds get caught in them or poisoned by them."

"The voice of doom," Lojos joined in. "Sarika, Tomas is always the voice of doom when it comes to planet earth."

"That doesn't mean I'm wrong," Tomas pointed out.

"Here we go," Mataias said. "It has to be asked: Luiz, where do you stand on balloons?"

Sarika realized that Tomas and his brothers understood, through her, that something wasn't quite right in the situation and were taking their cue from her. She was grateful none of them delved into her mind and took information. Sarika wasn't adept at hiding anything, and she was certain Solange would view it as a betrayal if the men were suddenly aware of her deception.

"You want me to weigh in on the importance of balloons at a party?" Luiz asked, his voice that same monotone he used when he appeared aloof.

"Yeah, Luiz, you must have an opinion," Lojos prompted. "You're a De La Cruz. Does your family have opinions on the importance of balloons?"

Luiz lifted an eyebrow at Lojos, and Solange looked up at Dominic. Sarika was gratified to feel the woman's amusement. It didn't show on her face, but the conversation was helping.

"I have no idea what Zacarias would have to say about balloons. It has never come up in any family discussion. I suppose we didn't realize the importance of whether or not to include them in any female ceremony we don't take part in."

"Female ceremony?" Sarika deliberately echoed. "That's what you call a baby shower?"

"Carpathian babies don't take showers," Luiz said.

Solange laughed. Out loud. She looked up at Dominic again, her face soft. Sarika thought it was a beautiful look. She could actually feel the tension easing from Solange's body.

Again, Luiz's eyebrow shot up, and he directed his comments to Solange. "Well, they don't. My memories include warriors cognizant of our origins, and I see no recollection of Carpathian babies showering."

"The ceremony is called a baby shower," Dominic supplied, "because the baby and mother are showered with gifts."

Luiz shook his head. "This isn't logical. Carpathian mothers can give their children whatever is needed by simply manufacturing those things."

"Women have very little logic," Lojos stated, "when it comes to babies."

Sarika glared at him. "This is your informed *male* conclusion because you know so much about women?"

"Careful there, brother," Mataias said. "Sarika has been known to become violent in certain situations. This is likely one of them. I want to point out, *sisarke*, for the sake of family honor, we have an audience."

"Family honor?" Sarika bristled, glaring at him. "Are you implying I'm going to dishonor your family because I'm going to hit your misogynistic brother over the head?"

"One does have to protect him when he spouts his nonsense," Mataias pointed out.

"Tomas?" Sarika turned on him.

"I'm all for hitting Lojos over the head as often as possible," Tomas said and leaned down to feather a kiss across her nose. "He isn't an environmentalist."

"I want to point out that Luiz cleverly manipulated everyone by changing the subject so he wouldn't have to weigh in on his opinion of balloons," Lojos said.

"He did do that," Dominic agreed.

"Have you considered giving Lojos a good brotherly beating?" Luiz asked.

"Many times," Tomas answered. "But he often is right, and in this situation, I believe he is. You are deliberately trying to get out of answering. That means you do have an opinion. You just don't want any of us to know you do."

Sarika would have thought it meant Luiz didn't have an opinion, but she realized Tomas had read the situation correctly just by the way the other males were looking at Luiz. She could feel their shared amusement. Best, she could feel Solange's. That had been the ultimate goal: to get her to feel relaxed and even, maybe, to have fun.

Luiz waved a dismissive hand. "If it is necessary for me to share an opinion on the hideous and frivolous invention of the balloon for children, I know Riley and Dax's daughter, Maureen, is afraid of them. She becomes very anxious around them. She doesn't convey this to her parents as she should because she doesn't want to upset Riley, who always has balloons at any party."

"How would you know this if Riley and Dax don't know?" Solange asked immediately.

Sarika couldn't detect any humor in her. She'd gone into protective warrior mode. In that moment, Sarika saw the true woman. Solange wouldn't hesitate to take on an ancient warrior if it meant she was protecting a woman or child. The man standing behind her, with his good looks and scars, arms around her waist, would back her up without hesitation.

"I feel her when she is afraid, Solange," Luiz confessed. "I speak with her to calm her fears. Dax is aware of my connection with her."

There was a sudden silence as comprehension dawned. Solange pressed back into Dominic, one hand going to her throat as if protecting herself from an attack.

"Maureen, Dax and Riley's daughter, is your lifemate?" She whispered it. "Luiz."

"They know, but we do not want this getting out because she would be in more danger than she already is. Dax is a powerful Carpathian, very ancient, and he has enemies. Many of them. I stay close to help protect Maureen and Riley. So yes, when she has fears, I comfort her. I do so from a distance. She is far too young to give me back emotions and colors. It can be . . . difficult to be so close to her and know it will be many years before I will have my lifemate with me."

"Dimitri found Skyler when she was far too young," Dominic said.

Skyler is the adopted daughter of a legendary Carpathian, Gabriel Daratrazanoff. Her birth father is Razvan, a Dragonseeker like Dominic. She is unusual and is held in very high regard. She saved Dimitri when a faction of the Lycans took him prisoner and sentenced him to death by silver. A war was nearly started over that particular incident. But it is true, she was far too young when Dimitri found out she was his lifemate. Over time, they developed a very unique bond before he ever claimed her. That bond was what allowed her to save him when no one else could track him. She was very young, and no one even considered that she would mount a rescue with two of her friends.

Sarika wanted to meet the famous Skyler. She sounded courageous, a woman to be admired. The more she learned of women like Solange and Skyler, the more she felt she had a chance of being happy as Tomas' lifemate. It was clear the women weren't shut away in a safe house while their men went out to do battle.

Luiz nodded. "They have a good relationship. I have spoken to Dimitri often and am learning from him how best to keep my lifemate safe when enemies would target her should they know. Valentin Zhestokly has a young lifemate as well. She is protected by several Carpathians, but he stays close. It happens, and we have to take extra precautions. I am grateful for her existence and take her safety and well-being very seriously."

Sarika felt her cousin's heavy burden. She had thought it would be a good thing to know one's lifemate was close and in a few years could be claimed, but apparently that knowledge could increase the stress on the male. She understood he would be aware his lifemate was in even more jeopardy than most.

She knew the cost to the male wasn't sexual. She had been concerned by Solange's initial reaction that a male might develop those feelings for his lifemate, but it was an impossibility. She didn't quite understand it, but she was aware through Luiz that he didn't have those kinds of feelings. He had been a jaguar shifter with the urges of that species, yet once he had been converted to Carpathian, despite vague memories, he had no interest in sex.

Trying to understand Carpathian customs was going to be hard enough, but to understand who and what they were fundamentally was going to be much more difficult. How did one navigate through such things quickly?

"So, the answer to the balloons," Tomas said, taking the spotlight from Luiz, "is a resounding no. I think 'not good for the planet' is a good reason to use."

"That makes sense," Dominic said, backing him up. "Out of the eight hundred things on your list, we managed to resolve one. That's good news." He tipped up Solange's face toward his with two fingers under her chin. "See how easy that was? The logic of males."

Solange and Sarika both burst out laughing. That felt so good, to see and hear Solange's genuine laugh.

"So, Solange," Lojos said. "We have a pointless party so you can get things from people for your baby that you and Dominic can make yourselves anytime you want, but you've got a list of problems you have to take care of before this party takes place. Have I about covered it?"

Immediately, Sarika felt the distress rushing through Solange at the reminder of what she was supposed to be doing. Before the woman could answer, Sarika did it for her. "It's a celebration of life, Lojos. You have so much to learn. I have no idea if I have the time to educate you, not only about women but about life, in the time before you find your lifemate. Seriously, Tomas, your brother has been very poorly educated."

She heaved a long-suffering sigh and exchanged a long-suffering look with Solange. "You have one man to deal with; I have four. Two of the four seem to have zero knowledge of women. Zero. Can you believe that? I thought I'd be happily learning about Carpathians and customs, but I fear I will be needed to educate Lojos and Luiz in the ways of women."

Solange sent her a small smile, but it was clear that tension in her was rising just at the mention of solving other problems for the party. Sarika became aware of the child growing in Solange. She was further along than she looked, but the more upset she was, the more distressed the child was. The two beings were locked together, highly sensitive, and both unable to cope with the amount of stress.

Faintly, far away, Sarika heard a chant, the voice feminine, but it began to swell in volume. She hastily ensured she was cut off from the male Carpathians. Now she was highly stressed, as if she were one and the same with Solange and the unborn child. The more agitated Solange became, the more that emotion flooded Sarika until she was nearly shaking with the knowledge that she had to de-escalate the situation or Solange would lose the child. The knowledge was there, also that she had the ability to prevent the loss and aid Solange in coping. She just didn't know how yet.

It was there inside her. Deep. Unexplored. But she knew there was an untapped well of something unnamed that only she could provide. Not for the Carpathian in Solange. For the female jaguar. That was the side of Solange unable to cope with anything feminine. She'd had to reject that side of herself in order to fight her father's cruel regime. In doing so, she had perfected the warrior at the expense of her female jaguar shifter. Her shifter would never allow her to carry a child to full term—especially a female child.

Sarika had the knowledge, but she didn't have a clue what to do with it. Solange would be mortified if those in the room knew her secrets. She didn't have a clue that her female jaguar was working against her. Dominic didn't know, either. They both put her rising stress down to her reluctance to show her feminine side to the world.

Sarika's hand crept up to encompass the amulet. It was warm, growing hotter. She covered it with her palm, certain it wouldn't be welcomed without explanation, and she didn't have one to give them. She didn't understand anything that was happening. She could ask Tomas to take her back to the tree house, pleading that she felt unwell, or she could risk everything and try to aid Solange.

What's wrong, sivamet? Tomas' voice was a soothing balm in the middle of what she knew was a terrible crisis.

She had a decision to make. Could she trust him with her secrets? With Solange's? Would he know what to do? This was the man she was supposed to spend the rest of her life with. Either he was the right man, or he wasn't.

It is important that the others don't know what we are discussing. And I need your word that you won't expose Solange to the others.

Tomas was silent, his arm stealing around her shoulders, his hand urging her closer to him. She knew he was carefully deliberating. *I may have to share with Dominic anything you tell me about his lifemate. He has her best interests at heart. He sees to her health, her protection and her state of mind. I cannot promise you, if you tell me something that is harming his woman, that I will not share the information with him because my code of honor demands that I must.*

He may throw us out, she cautioned.

Tomas simply waited. He didn't urge her to tell him or demand it. He didn't look into her head to see her concerns. He simply waited for her to make up her own mind. She wanted to throw her arms around him and hug him close. It felt to her as if he "got" her. That her wishes counted for something.

I don't know how, but sometimes I can feel other people's emotions. I could feel your brothers and Luiz, but with women, especially shifters, it is far stronger. She's going to lose her baby. Her jaguar is inadvertently working against her. It's part of the reason she's so stressed.

Wouldn't her lifemate know?

I don't know much about that, Tomas. I don't even know how I know, only that there is something in me that sees it. I can fix it, I think, but I've never done such a thing to my knowledge, and it is terrifying to think I could be wrong. What should I do? Solange would never be able to handle the others knowing her business, especially something that makes her feel less. Or makes her feel vulnerable.

A part of her wanted him to tell her they would leave and go back to the tree house. If they remained, she wouldn't be able to stop herself from attempting to aid Solange. She finally understood why Tomas felt he had to slip into her mind and do the blood exchange the first time without her knowledge. The compulsion in her to help Solange and the unborn child was extremely strong, and truthfully, she didn't have a clue what she was doing. She didn't know if that place of healing came from somewhere good or bad. She only knew that if she stayed in the room with Solange, she would eventually give in to the need building so strongly inside her.

Let me reach out to Dominic and figure out a way to handle this without involving anyone else. He may want to look at your memories, Sarika. Before I allowed anyone near you, I would insist the same.

That had been one of her biggest fears. *I don't look at those memories. They're tied in with my nightmares. I have no idea what he would find, and I'm uncomfortable with him being inside my head.*

Even if I am with him?

She didn't know how to answer that. She barely knew Tomas. She knew he was a good man, but she'd only been with him in person a short time. He was asking for an entire level of trust she wasn't certain she could give.

This is such a mess. I want to run away from it, Tomas. How cowardly is that?

You are no coward. Let me reach out to Dominic.

Sarika glanced up at the man in question. His gaze was fixed on her and Tomas. He already knew something was up. If she didn't make up her mind soon, everyone in the room would know. Her distress level had risen to such heights that it was impossible to contain it. She nodded her head to give consent, but that freaked her out even more. Whatever was inside her, demanding she aid Solange, felt like a volcano bubbling with an ominous pool of magma ready to explode any moment.

Dominic smiled at the men in the room, his features totally relaxed, as if Tomas hadn't just shared what could be scary news. "Gentlemen, Jubal, Jasmine and Sandrine are on their way. If you would do me the favor of guarding the surrounding forest so they can safely reach their destination, I would appreciate it. It will also spare you the indignity of listening to the endless discussion on party favors."

That brought Lojos and Luiz instantly to their feet. Mataias glanced at Tomas. *Will you need one of us with you?*

Sarika should be fine, ekäm.

Mataias nodded, and the three men left the great room. Dominic waited until the ancient Carpathians had left the cave altogether before he seated Solange in the chair across from Tomas and Sarika. He took the chair beside his lifemate. Sarika knew Tomas thought it was significant that Dominic hadn't chosen the other double chair, nor was he holding Solange's hand.

Why is that putting you on alert, Tomas?

He is in a good fighting position, and I am not.

Do you need to be?

She had started this. Now she was uncertain what to say or do. She didn't want the ancients to fight. She looked Dominic directly in the eye. "I don't want you and Tomas to be at odds over something I can't help and am uncertain of. I want to help Solange, but I'm not even certain I know how. Perhaps I shouldn't have said anything and let nature take its course, but the feeling is so strong, I couldn't help it. I had to tell Tomas, and he thought it best to tell you. But really, if you are more comfortable with us leaving, I'll do so without continuing this conversation."

"How do you think you can help me?" Solange asked, curiosity more than anything else in her tone. "What do you think I need help with?"

"I have nightmares, Solange, terrible, horrific nightmares of human sacrifices, boys and girls, men and women. The nightmares have increased over the last few years, and sometimes I hear chanting." She reached for Tomas' hand, needing comfort, uncaring that it would put him in a position of having even less of an advantage with Dominic. "I've come to believe these nightmares depict real events that happened centuries ago. I was there. I don't know how, but I was there."

Solange didn't make fun of her. She simply nodded. "I have heard of such things."

"I've traveled to most of the rainforests in the world, and I've never had increased anxiety or felt the differences in me until I came here. I seem to be able to read emotions that ancient Carpathian males have but they don't feel. I can catch vignettes of their lives, even though they have shields up in their minds."

Dominic shifted in his chair, and Sarika's heart went crazy, pounding in fear. She didn't understand any of these people, and she certainly didn't understand herself or what was happening to her.

"Sarika," Dominic said, his voice gentle. "You have nothing to fear from me. It is clear to both Solange and me that you are struggling to understand what is happening to you. It is also very clear that it is difficult to disclose this information to complete strangers. Please don't fear me or Solange. We will take what you say into consideration, and we will not share it."

Sarika sighed. "This is going to sound even crazier. I did my best not to intrude, Solange. I don't want Tomas to get inside my head without my permission, so I feel extremely hesitant about taking away anyone's privacy. It's just that this thing inside me feels what others are feeling. When it comes to jaguar female shifters, it is really heightened."

Again, Solange didn't appear in the least concerned. "That's why you stepped in to help me. Thank you for that. You were amazing."

"I'm not quite finished, and you won't think I'm so amazing." She rubbed at her temples. Her head was beginning to hurt. That headache that came when her mind insisted on opening that door she never wanted to look behind. "It's your jaguar. She's fighting you on the baby. She's making it hard not only on you but on the baby. A female, by the way."

Dominic sat up straighter. He and Solange exchanged a long look. They knew the sex of the baby. They hadn't told anyone, so both wondered how she could know.

"I've been fully converted to Carpathian," Solange informed her. "I shift into my jaguar because I'm familiar with her, but I am fully Carpathian."

Sarika shook her head. "You're not. She's in you, and she doesn't know how to be what you've become. She has a tendency to fight you when you choose to be feminine and not strictly a warrior."

Dominic's eyes grew a metallic green, giving off a dragon feel for the first time. "I would know. She would know. We've been together a long time."

Sarika wanted to concede she was wrong. She didn't want to continue the conversation. She could be wrong. Maybe she had a vivid imagination. Whatever it was, she didn't want to continue. She had a very bad feeling it was all going to go wrong.

"You would know better than me," she conceded, and once more threaded her fingers through Tomas'.

Dominic studied her face for a long time. Too long. She had the feeling he saw far too much, things she didn't want him to see. Uneasiness grew into fear.

"There is a way to settle this," Dominic ventured. "If you would consent, I could examine your memories. I would see what you did in regard to Solange and her jaguar. I would be able to see into your nightmare and tell you what is real and what isn't. I have lived long and experienced many things. I would know the difference."

Sarika thought she was prepared for Dominic to do just that—

examine her memories. Tomas had tried to prepare her for the possibility, and it made sense. The moment Dominic so casually stated what he could do to see what she had, full-blown panic rose. It was a visceral reaction, sharp and raw. She nearly jumped out of the chair. She knew the color drained out of her face. She could barely breathe as she shook her head.

"He was there. The Carpathian. He took their blood. He forced them to do horrible things to each other. He sacrificed so many, practically killing everyone while he howled with laughter. He proclaimed he had a lifemate. He used that term. There was blood, so much blood, everywhere. He was hunting for a soul, he said. He knew someone had it, and unless they gave it up, he would kill everyone."

She turned grief-stricken eyes on Tomas. "His name was Mitro. He spoke the truth about having a lifemate. It didn't stop him from doing the terrible things he did. He thrust his mind into mine. I could see how rotten he was. I could feel his glee in the brutal killings. He had no mercy in him."

Now she was up out of the chair and backing away from Tomas. "I was there. I saw him. I felt him. He tried to find my jaguar power, but I was able to hide it from him."

Tomas came to his feet as well, following her across the room. "You aren't there, Sarika. You're here with me, and you're safe. Solange is true jaguar royalty. She would never allow anyone to betray you."

He spoke in his gentle, nonthreatening voice. She heard it, but the sounds and smells of the past were assaulting every one of her senses.

"I remember Mitro," Dominic said, his voice equally as gentle. "Dax and Mitro's lifemate, Arabejila, chased him for centuries and finally were able to lock him in a volcano. Dax was locked in that same volcano with him. When they broke free, Mitro went after Riley, Dax's lifemate. Dax was able to defeat him. Mitro is no longer alive."

Sarika pressed her hand to her mouth. She was trembling so badly, she could barely stand. "I want to go home. Back to the United States. I kept the family home in the forest. I can live there."

Solange pushed out of the chair and approached Sarika slowly, waving off the two men. "I'm sorry you had to endure the brutality of a crazed Carpathian. He never claimed his lifemate. Instead, he tried to kill her. Carpathians, like any species, are not immune to mental health issues. It's just that when one goes wrong and they have all that power, it can be horrendous. That's why ancients like Tomas and Dominic and Luiz spend centuries hunting those who have turned or the ones like Mitro."

She glided closer. "I know you're frightened, Sarika. Your only knowledge of Carpathians is not good, but you have looked into the minds of Lojos, Mataias and Tomas, and you know they are good men. The same with your cousin. And I need you. I'm scared, far more than I should be. Dominic and I discussed why I was so stressed. We're good together. I trust him implicitly, but you're right, I'm making myself so sick. If you have a way to make me understand why, if you could help me in any way, I would be forever grateful. I never forget a favor, and if you really think there is a chance I could lose this baby, I would be in your debt if you would help us."

Sarika allowed Solange's words to sink into her mind, to push back the memories threatening to overwhelm her. Just the revelation that Mitro had been real, that Dominic knew him, was terrifying. That meant she had been guarding Tomas' soul, and Mitro murdered an entire village of peaceful people to find it.

She had protected him. She'd tried to protect those in the village, find ways for them to escape. She had blocked his access to the routes she'd provided for the few she could get into the tunnels to escape. She'd done multiple things to thwart him, and he hadn't known it was her. He suspected. It was why he hadn't killed her, but he didn't realize she was countering his viciousness with her own feminine power.

She couldn't leave Solange alone in her fight to save her child. Dominic and Solange both had missed the connection to her shifter jaguar. She was royalty. Her royal blood would never allow any species to take her over completely. Solange had wanted to belong with Dominic so much she had convinced herself that she simply shifted into what she knew best.

"I want to help you," she admitted. She blinked rapidly, trying to bring herself completely into the present. "I do, I just . . ." She trailed off because she didn't know exactly what she was going to say. She looked around helplessly for Tomas.

He was at her side instantly. "I'm with you, *sivamet*. Tell us what you need. If you want to help Solange, we can find a way. If you want to leave, we'll do that."

She couldn't just leave Solange, not when neither she nor Dominic believed the baby was in danger. She had to convince them.

"I'm sorry I panicked. I must seem like a crazy person to you," she told Solange. "I felt like I had been thrown back centuries." She squared her shoulders. "I need you to believe me when I say your jaguar is causing you far too much anxiety. She doesn't know how to be feminine. Or soft. She really doesn't know how to have a child. It isn't that she is causing a problem on purpose; she just doesn't know how to fit into your life. She's all warrior, not the lifemate of a Carpathian male."

Solange turned toward Dominic and held out her hand. "What do you suggest we do, Sarika? How can Dominic and I see and feel what you have?"

Sarika scrubbed her hand down her face as if she could lower a mask to cover her terrified expression. "I don't know. Tomas suggested that I give consent to him and Dominic to look into my memories to see what I saw and felt from your jaguar." She answered tentatively, unsure she could follow through. "I just don't know if I can let them. I despise being a coward, but anytime I think about a Carpathian entering my mind, I panic."

Why are you feeling threatened? Luiz's voice pushed into Sarika's mind. It was echoed by Lojos and Mataias. *Tomas, the safeguards are up on Dominic's home. We cannot get in to aid Sarika. We will have to use our blood bond to see through her eyes to come to your aid.*

Sarika realized she had been broadcasting her fear rather than containing it. Her champions had taken that as a call to arms. Her champions. She had to think of them that way. They were Carpathian, and they would come for her. Fight for her. Just as she knew Tomas would. Her lifemate might be standing beside her, looking relaxed, giving off friendly vibes to Dominic, but he was in full protection mode. He wouldn't hesitate to take on Dominic and Solange in their home if he thought she was in trouble.

I'm sorry. Thank you for your concern, but I have just been confronting nightmares that seem all too real. Tomas is here with me. Dominic and Solange are being lovely over my panic attack.

The three men obviously consulted with Tomas, and then they faded from her mind.

In front of her, Solange nodded her acknowledgment of Sarika's fears. "I understand how you would feel that way. I did, too, for different reasons. All I can say to you is that we want this child. I never believed I could have one. To us, she is a miracle baby. If something is wrong, I would ask that you help us fix it."

Tomas, I can't allow a child to die because I fear someone looking into my memories. She felt desperate and turned to the only person she had any real trust in. She based that trust on all the letters she'd read of his over the years. No matter where he'd been in the world, no matter what he was doing when he'd disappeared for months—and now she knew he hunted vampires—he always answered her. Always made her a priority.

I will be with Dominic. I have ways of shielding you so only the things that need to be seen can be seen. Trust me to do this for you. You can show Solange and Dominic her jaguar so they can deal with her.

Sarika didn't think Solange and Dominic could deal with the jaguar. She had a nagging feeling she would have to. She knew they were waiting. Patiently. Calmly. All on the outside. Inside, she could hear Solange weeping and Dominic comforting her.

"I will, of course, give my consent to Dominic accompanying Tomas to look at my memories and see if he draws the same conclusion." She forced a smile at Solange. "I think we need to stick together when it comes to our jaguar sides."

Gripping Tomas' hand, she faced Dominic. "Tell me what you need me to do."

CHAPTER 13

Sarika is petrified, Tomas told Dominic.

You do not have to tell me to have a care for her, Dominic said. *I feel her fears, as does Solange. We are profoundly grateful, whether we come to the same conclusions as Sarika or not. We both realize the incredible gift she is giving us.*

Tomas led Sarika to a single chair, knowing the furniture would fit around her once she sank into its unique design. It would feel as if the chair were holding her close, keeping her safe. He couldn't sit with her and hold her the way he wanted, not when she needed to count on his protection.

He had known Dominic for centuries. He was a man of absolute honor. He was also completely devoted to his lifemate. Tomas understood. In the short time that his world had changed due to discovering her, Tomas knew he would do anything for Sarika.

"This won't take long. Do you want to be aware of us and what we're seeing, or would you prefer not to know?"

She caught his hand. "Thank you for giving me the choice." She knew his preference through their blood connection. He didn't want her aware. He didn't push his choice on her; he simply allowed her to decide. He wanted to shield her from every fear.

"I would like to be aware." She whispered her answer, not knowing if she was testing him or not. She only knew she was so scared of what was in her mind and how that would impact not only her but Tomas and everyone around her. Because whatever was inside her was powerful, and it was insisting on being acknowledged. Not only acknowledged, but it demanded she act on the compulsions it was placing on her. She needed to see for herself if that entity was for good or evil.

Her hand crept up to her amulet. It felt warm, the head of the jaguar pushing into her palm as if offering comfort. "I'm ready."

Solange seated herself directly across from Sarika. Despite her trepidation and fear at what would be revealed, Sarika felt her determination to offer her comfort and support. She chose solidarity with Sarika even before she knew what they would find. Tomas was able to feel all of that through Sarika.

Sarika felt the instant Dominic entered her mind, following Tomas. Tomas knew, to Sarika, he felt intimate, yet Dominic felt like a gentle intruder. Tomas couldn't change that and was grateful to Dominic for ensuring he showed Sarika respect and was as gentle as possible.

They both examined Sarika's earlier memories, the ones where she sat in the room with Solange and Dominic and felt every emotion Solange was feeling.

Highly unusual, Dominic commented to Tomas. *Disturbing in that I didn't detect her, and neither did Solange. I can see why she was reluctant to reveal what she is capable of. This kind of intrusion to a Carpathian couple could be considered an attack.*

Tomas was careful not to react to Dominic's concerns. He knew the ancient was right. Both also knew that Sarika hadn't tried to connect with Solange. It had happened, and it made her very uneasy. She'd considered leaving.

She is struggling with the need to help Solange, to ease her fears, Dominic said, continuing along the path Sarika's mind had taken.

Tomas and Dominic felt the punch of the powerful compulsion at the same time. Sarika had been nearly overwhelmed with the need to aid Solange.

She resisted, Dominic said. *Your lifemate knows nothing of our ways. She thinks of herself as human, not a shifter, because they raised her mostly human. She doesn't think she's particularly strong because she has panic attacks, but she resisted such a powerful compulsion that many Carpathians might have given in to.*

Tomas felt the same admiration Dominic did for Sarika. She hadn't understood what was happening, but she certainly felt the power of the need to invade Solange's mind and fix whatever was wrong.

She doesn't trust that what she has inside of her is purely good. She didn't want to chance harming Solange, and she didn't want to take Solange's choices from her, Tomas interpreted. He felt a deep pride in Sarika. She had to have been terrified, sitting in the room surrounded by virtual strangers, afraid whatever was inside of her would burst free.

This is where she saw the jaguar and recognized immediately that the cat was fighting Solange and the pregnancy. Tomas continued the dialogue with Dominic, needing to ensure that the ancient Dragonseeker was reading what he was. This was the crucial data Sarika had risked everything for in her effort to find a way to save the child and reduce the stress on Solange.

How could we have missed this? Solange shifts into her jaguar for every battle. We knew she was available, but both considered her a part of the Carpathian world, Dominic said. *Solange can walk in sunlight. This is the reason. Right here. Her jaguar.*

Tomas agreed. *This isn't an illusion such as we create. Her jaguar is very real.*

Dominic explained, wonder in his voice. *She is wholly intact, including all the memories of the battles Solange had rescuing the women from male shifters. The battles were sometimes fought against multiple male shifters. She had to think and act as a warrior at all times. In doing so, she was forced to repress every feminine quality she possessed in order to survive.*

Tomas was aware of that information, not from Dominic but because Sarika had communicated with the jaguar. Somehow, the animal had recognized her, and an exchange was made.

Sarika isn't fully aware she communicated with the jaguar. He wanted that on record, so Dominic would have to acknowledge it. Tomas knew that whatever he was finding, Dominic was sharing with Solange. Solange wouldn't like that her jaguar, the one she didn't think she had anymore, was confessing secrets to someone else.

Without that communication, we wouldn't know that our child is in jeopardy. I can see and feel the stress the jaguar is putting on Solange's body.

Will you be able to keep the child safe? Tomas asked the one question that was the most important. *You are a tremendous healer. Luiz is renowned for his healing abilities. Between the two of you, will you be able to save your daughter?*

Tomas didn't like that Dominic hesitated. Sarika had stayed silent, a small presence like a shadow, but she reacted with a faint moan of concern. He didn't know if that meant she didn't think the Carpathian males could save the baby or she was just overwhelmed with having to endure the distressing news a second time.

Sarika wasn't the only one reacting to that question. Dominic was relaying everything to his lifemate, and when Tomas asked if it was possible for the healers to keep Solange from losing the baby, Solange made a single sound of agonized pain, echoing Sarika's distress.

I will have to spend time examining what is actually happening. When Solange was converted, at the time we thought she retained her jaguar, but then when she shifted, she would build the illusion of the jaguar, so we came to believe she was wholly Carpathian.

Tomas tried to puzzle that out. How was it possible Dominic and Solange couldn't tell her jaguar had retreated from her? The bond between shifter counterparts was very close. Tomas was Carpathian, but he'd spent centuries around other species and had taken the time to study them.

This makes no sense, Dominic said. *When Solange went through the conversion, we were very careful. I monitored each stage, particularly of her* cat. She was concerned about losing her jaguar. The cat was calm throughout the entire procedure. Organs changed, reshaped with my blood, but her jaguar was still there. And she was Carpathian.

And yet she is not, Tomas pointed out.

Again, how could that be possible? Dominic asked.

Does Solange have any ideas?

She is as puzzled as I am, Dominic admitted. *If this is her true cat, jaguar royalty, and she is threatening harm to our child, what is the other jaguar? Where did she come from? I examined her multiple times. It was important to Solange that nothing harm her cat. We took extra precautions,* Dominic reiterated.

Tomas didn't know what to say. The evidence was very clear that Solange's cat resided within her and was causing problems.

It was Sarika who came up with the only idea that made sense. *Is it possible to examine the cat? See if organs have reshaped? If this cat is actually the one you monitored while Solange went through the conversion? I know it sounds crazy, but . . .* She trailed off.

Tomas felt her instant retreat. She didn't want to call attention to herself. She hadn't been able to stop herself when the two Carpathian males had come to a standstill, and Solange was becoming even more stressed.

Thank you, Sarika, Dominic said. *Ordinarily, Solange and I work out puzzles very quickly, but the threat to our child has us both off stride.*

Tomas stayed very still as, without preamble, Dominic surrounded the jaguar, engulfing it with his power. There was nowhere for it to go, but it fought back, refusing to give in, not that it did any good.

Tomas winced inwardly, knowing Sarika was observing the swift way Dominic took over the female jaguar. The animal had no chance to use its vicious skills on the hunter. She would be able to see how ruthless a Carpathian could be. Not only that, but she'd see evidence of how difficult it would be for any species to defeat him.

I already have this knowledge, Sarika told him. *My first memories of a Carpathian male are of Mitro and the havoc he wreaked in our temple. It was the temple of the jaguar. The female shifters would gather to bless the crops and farms. To help our people become more prosperous, better able to handle everyday life. Many problems were brought to us, and we helped our people. Never once did we use a blood sacrifice. That wasn't the source of the female power.*

You are remembering a great deal more of the past. He was careful to just make it a statement. As an ancient Carpathian, he and Dominic were both on shaky ground. Taking over a female jaguar would most likely come under the heading of "things never to do."

If the baby is to be saved, I have to face my past and the reasons I'm so afraid of Carpathians. The only way to do that is to examine the memories I've been too terrified to look at. It obviously did no good to close that door. The memories escaped in the form of nightmares. That only made me more afraid. That isn't going to help save a baby.

Tomas was so proud of her. Proud that she was his lifemate. She didn't think of herself as courageous, but once she made up her mind to fight for something or someone, she went ahead full throttle.

What do you think happened to Solange's jaguar? Or do you know?

I communicated with her. She recognized me as one of the three royal bloodlines. Memories of female shifters appear to be very much like your ancient lineages. You share information. We, apparently, do as well.

Tomas wasn't surprised at the revelation. The shifters were nearly as old as the Carpathians. They were nearly extinct now, but at one time, they thrived, particularly during the Inca period. They intermingled with the people, residing together in harmony.

Is the jaguar Carpathian? Was she converted when Solange was converted?

Dominic pulled out of Sarika's mind abruptly and went straight to Solange. He had stayed for a prolonged period of time in Sarika and would need blood to keep him at full fighting peak. Tomas hadn't considered he would need blood as well. His brothers and Luiz were outside, and apparently, Dominic had activated their safeguards.

What is it?

Sarika was becoming very sensitive to him. That was a good thing and yet not so much in that moment. She asked, and he was bound to answer honestly.

Staying a prolonged length of time outside my body takes energy. When I return to my body, I will be weak. Without blood to replenish me, I will be in a vulnerable position should I have to fight an enemy. Or fight to get us out of here.

Sarika did what she usually did: took her time, turning over his statement, trying to understand. It didn't take her long.

It isn't like it will be my first time giving you blood. I just did the same for your brothers and Luiz. Just do it fast, please, before I chicken out.

Knowing or not? He had to give her the option.

Not this time. Just do it fast.

That didn't bode well for them. She was definitely at her limit, and the situation wasn't resolved. Worse, Jasmine, Jubal and Sandrine were on their way. That hadn't been a ruse to get his brothers and Luiz out of the house; it was a very real excuse.

Tomas did as she requested, taking her over so she was unaware. He used the far less intimate way of taking blood—her wrist. It didn't seem to matter where he took her blood; the rush hit like a fireball. Her blood was definitely an aphrodisiac to him. His body reacted, and he had to put a strict control on that, something that in the long centuries had never been a necessity.

He sheltered her as best he could from the other two in the room before closing off her vein with a sweep of his tongue. At the same time, he brought her out from under the veil of separation so she could easily function again.

Thank you, sivamet. *I know that is one of your least favorite things to do.*

I am coming to terms with it.

She wasn't, though. Tomas knew she didn't think she was telling him a lie, but she was pulling away from him. It was subtle. He didn't think she realized she was doing it, but he was so tuned to her, he knew. More than anything, he needed time alone with her. This plan of bringing her to Solange's party planning had backfired in the worst kind of way. It was adding obstacles to his relationship with Sarika. That was the last thing he needed when he knew time was working against them.

"Sarika," Dominic said. "Solange and I are unsure what is happening with her jaguar, but when I examined her, the cat was not Carpathian in the same sense of the word that she should be. She is able to go to ground, but in every other sense, she is a shifter. And not a happy one."

Sarika nodded. "I'm aware. She feels she is protecting Solange, and she is uneasy with any changes in her. She believes Solange is a prisoner and forced to do your bidding as a woman."

"Why can't I connect with her?" Solange sounded forlorn. "Why would she talk to you, a stranger, but not me?"

"She fears for you. She doesn't understand and is doing the best she can without the knowledge she needs." Sarika hesitated and then put her head down, studying her hands where she had threaded her fingers together. "She recognized me. You must be aware female shifters can pass memories to one another. Some, anyway. Those from certain lineages. Yours, mine, one other."

She didn't look up, and that worried Tomas. He was beginning to feel a cross between desperate and alarm.

"Jubal's," Dominic said. "I find it interesting that fate has brought those lines together in one place. Over time, I have learned there is always a reason for the way fate shapes our destiny. The right people are in place at the right time. What they do with that is up to them, but opportunities present themselves."

"Sarika." Solange waited for Tomas' lifemate to meet her eyes. "Tell us how we can fix this. You must have some idea."

Tomas inhaled sharply. "I can take you home to rest, Sarika. We can address this problem another rising."

"It will be too late," she predicted, again without looking at him. "I fear the two of you will have to sift through my memories once again until you uncover my nightmare. I want to make absolutely certain that what is inside me is used purely for good. If it isn't, I'm walking away, sad that I can't help, but like your jaguar, I refuse to risk you, Solange, even for your child."

Solange placed both hands over her stomach protectively. "She's more important than anything."

Not to me, Dominic said to Tomas and Sarika. *I want my child to live. I will love her and protect her, but Solange must come first. I cannot survive intact without her. I would never want to live without her. Save our baby, if possible, but never make the choice between the two of them.*

Tomas knew Dominic wasn't being selfish. He wanted his child. He already loved her. But Solange was his world. Tomas hadn't had Sarika long, not if you counted only from when he'd first heard the sound of her voice, but he would be just as adamant as Dominic. Not solely because she was his lifemate but because she had become his world.

Tomas sent Dominic one look, and then he shed his body, his pure spirit moving into his lifemate's mind. He felt Dominic's presence like a white-hot streak of lightning, taking his back as he deliberately sought the earliest memories Sarika had. Ancient ones. Ones of a peaceful village where the people were farmers and potters and lived their everyday lives in harmony with the earth.

Then there was the temple made of limestone and some other material, an impressive structure. He recognized the tall statue of the jaguar made of that other material. That statue had somehow remained intact over hundreds of years while the temple was in ruins. Despite the temple being rubble, it was an impressive structure, even now, but in ancient times, the way Sarika remembered it, the sacred place was an imposing and joyful place. The massive temple joined sky, earth and the underworld together.

Tomas' heart nearly stopped beating. The underworld. Justice had lived centuries in the underworld. He sought an ancient weapon that could be used against their prince, and from what Gustov had told him, the weapon had a chance of working.

Both Dominic and he had lived centuries, and they were very aware of how the universe often came full circle. He shared his worry with Dominic.

This could be where a piece of the weapon Justice hunts for is located. It would explain his presence. Why he has come this way and recruited vampires to be his army, even though both you and Dax make your home here.

Dominic agreed with him. *Few enemies would deliberately come into our territory to challenge us. If this weapon is somewhere in the temple, it would be best for us to find it before he does.*

In present day, the ruins had nearly been reclaimed by the jungle. Thick vines and heavy brush wound around and through parts of the broken limestone. A great deal of the temple was still intact, however. The memory Sarika carried with her was of a temple in full glory. Looking around, both ancients were able to recognize the thriving farms and village.

Sarika loved the people. She was very involved in their everyday life. There were other female jaguar shifters, all of whom worked in the temple.

The Mayans were never supposed to have been in this part of Peru, yet there were three distinct ruins of temples, sites proclaiming they had lived and thrived for many years there. Tomas realized it was the jaguar. This particular tribe of people worshiped the jaguar. Where they originated from, he had no idea.

Several statues of the jaguar remained long after the temples were smashed into ruins. Sarika and the other female shifters had taken part in the ceremonies at each one. They were revered, although they didn't act as if they were any different from the other women. They aided in farmwork and taking care of the children. They helped carve the hieroglyphics into the temple walls. They aided in developing the astronomical system, particularly paying attention to Venus. The stars and planets were important, and the female jaguars spent a great deal of time studying them.

As far as Tomas could tell, there were three women of equal importance, ones regarded with the highest of honor. He recognized Sarika. She had the same features as the woman who was, in modern times, his lifemate. She seemed so like his Sarika, kind and sweet, ready to help even with the crops. She was *his*, and he recognized her as such.

Each time she came across a female jaguar shifter, Sarika had a private word with her—not just her, but her jaguar. She seemed very in tune to the animal. If the jaguar's health wasn't good, she was able to open a well of healing. But it was more than that. She had a special gift, one Tomas was certain the other two women had as well.

And then came Mitro with his brutality and vicious cruelty. He murdered the entire village, made them turn on one another, made fathers kill sons and mothers kill daughters. Blood ran in rivers, and those seeing to the temple wept. Mitro took great delight in torturing the three women who brought health and happiness to the jaguar shifters and the gentle people who worshiped the jaguar.

Sarika is not under his compulsions the way the other female shifters are. Neither are the other two women. They are aware of his intentions, and they are doing their best to counter him.

Dominic studied the memories for a period of time. *How is this possible?*

I have no idea, but you can see into her memories. See the carnage taking place around her, Tomas said. *She is being tortured just as the others are, but there is a part of her manipulating Mitro. He has no idea.*

Dominic reacted audibly, shocked that a female shifter could be more powerful than a Carpathian ancient. He was nearly thrown out of Sarika's mind, but he recovered swiftly.

They have tunnels that run beneath the temple and are stalling Mitro so they can get as many women and children to safety as possible. For Tomas, it was difficult to watch. The entire time Sarika and the other two women were aiding those to escape, they were forced to pretend they were under Mitro's spell.

She is using her connection with the jaguars, Tomas said, unable to keep the admiration from his voice. *The ones she is helping to leave are under Mitro's compulsion, so she bypassed the humans and called on the jaguars to herd them to the tunnels below.*

All three women are very connected to the jaguars. That connection feels sacred and strong. They aren't using any powers from the underworld, Dominic said. *Sarika was extremely concerned about that.*

I believe she'll be able to talk to Solange's jaguar and find a way to resolve the situation, Tomas said. *If you're satisfied, I cannot watch Mitro's gleeful killing of so many innocents. It is no wonder Sarika fears Carpathians.*

Dominic agreed. *It will be good when she meets Dax and realizes he was the one to stop Mitro permanently.*

About to slip out of Sarika's mind and back into his own body, Tomas felt a sudden shift in the feel of the events he was observing. Ancient Sarika's hand crept up to her amulet. The other two women mimicked her move. Tomas thought Mitro's actions pure evil. Everything about him felt foul and vile. But something else had entered the temple. Something far worse than Mitro.

Wait, Dominic, Tomas cautioned. *This is the true enemy and one Mitro knows well and serves. Is it possible he was the one promised the weapon to destroy the prince? He looks gleeful. Far too pleased and smug.*

Debris and body parts whirled through the temple, bathing everyone in the blood of the dead or dying. Evil laughter filled the temple, that sacred place that was now a slaughterhouse.

Mitro nearly convulsed with glee. He waved a hand encompassing the dead and dying. Those tortured and still suffering. "I've done everything we agreed on. You need to give me my reward."

Tomas held his breath. Mitro had struck a deal with the underworld. He should have suspected. The whirling debris settled just enough for him to make out a woman. It would have been impossible to describe her, not with the streaks of blood and brain matter dotting her face. She seemed to be bathing in the blood, her maniacal laughter piercing through him. She was so evil she put Mitro to shame.

"But you haven't. I've brought you one piece because you haven't fulfilled your part of our bargain. One. You will need to earn the other two."

Mitro's face burned with anger. Flames licked at his skin and appeared in his eyes. He snorted smoke and spat burning embers. "I have wiped out this entire civilization. It isn't the first and won't be the last, just as you demanded."

"But you didn't slay your lifemate, Mitro," the woman said, her voice sly. "That was part of our bargain. You had to kill her with your own two hands. Look into her eyes and smile while you kill her. Instead, she has gone to another man. They make you look weak. A joke in our world and yours. How does that earn you a weapon powerful enough to destroy the prince and take over ruling aboveground?"

"I killed hundreds for you. Carpathians. Jaguar. Lycan."

She waved her hand to encompass the temple. "These are your toys. You love to play with them. You're a sick man, Mitro. My kind of man, but you need to keep your word if you want to play my games. I don't give second chances. You have a job to complete, and it is important. If you are able to break the lifemate bond and kill your woman, others will be able to as well."

He never tied them together, Tomas reminded Dominic. *He refused to bind them. I think he feared if he said the ritual words to her, he wouldn't be able to kill her. He'd already made this bargain.*

That would explain a lot.

"Use your Carpathian skills on every jaguar around that has escaped or is within your range. Make them fear all Carpathians. All males. Send the male shifters into a frenzy of animalistic lust when they are around the females. The high mage is working to eradicate them, and with your help, it will happen sooner."

She waved her hand toward a small male child, and he screamed as Mitro's arm and hand became a sword, hacking the child's head off at the shoulder. The head flew across the temple to land at Sarika's feet.

That wasn't enough blood for the woman. She pointed to one of the sacred jaguar women. "Tear her apart, limb by limb. I want to see you play, Mitro. If you please me, I will give you the first part of the weapon. If you don't, I will take you back to the underworld with me. As I said, I do not give second chances."

Gleefully, Mitro kicked the smaller of the two women chained beside Sarika. She doubled over and then slipped in the puddles of blood. Mitro stuck his foot in her stomach and reached down to take one arm. Tomas saw Sarika close her eyes, but the sight was already there in her mind as Mitro ripped the arm away and threw it, hitting both Sarika and the other jaguar shifter prisoner.

The woman from the underworld cackled with joy. "More, Mitro."

He didn't hesitate but immediately pulled at the other arm, wrenching it free, and as he did, he cauterized the wound so she wouldn't bleed out. He was clearly enjoying himself.

"Broadcast your message to the jaguars," the woman instructed. "Do it while you play."

Tomas could feel Sarika's sudden stillness. She turned inward, reaching for that well of healing light she had deep inside her. As Mitro spewed forth his commands to all jaguars, she countered his ugly, vile orders. She did so carefully, spreading her power over his in a thin, undetectable layer. Even the woman commander from the underworld didn't feel the veil that shrouded Mitro's mandates.

"Finish her off," the woman said. She kicked at the jaguar shifter. "But make her suffer."

Sarika and the other prisoner locked gazes and then turned toward Litza as Mitro began to systematically stab down at her with the blade he'd made his arm and hand into. He didn't hit a single spot that would kill her, only the places that would hurt the most. He ripped at her clothing, and Tomas' heart nearly stopped beating, reading Mitro's intentions.

Without warning, Tomas heard the faint plea. *Now, before he touches me. Before he defiles my body. Let me go clean into the next world.*

Tomas and Dominic felt the exact moment when the healing power turned lethal. Both women stood in chains, tears running down their faces, looking with love at their fallen sister and stopping her heartbeat and brain function at the exact same time.

There was no spillover. No way for Mitro or the woman from the underworld to suspect either had a hand in the demise of Mitro's toy.

"She was weak," the woman said. She gave a sneer of contempt and pushed at the body with her foot. "These jaguar shifters revered the wrong ones."

Mitro licked his thick lips as she reached into one of the bloody tubes spinning close to her and pulled a triangular piece of metal from it.

"This is one of three. Once you have all three, they will snap together, and your weapon is complete. Nothing from this earth will be able to stop you because it is fashioned from material not from this earth. It is that powerful. The combined power of Dubrinsky and Daratrazanoff will be nothing in comparison."

Mitro reached for the triangular-shaped piece of metal almost reverently. "Where do I go to get the next piece?"

"Find your lifemate and dispense with her." She stepped back into one of the whirling tubes and disappeared.

The relief of her foul existence leaving had Tomas breathing again. He hadn't realized how badly the woman's presence affected him until he remembered he was sharing Sarika's mind and feeling her emotions.

Again, the two men had nearly left, both needing fresh air, when Tomas felt that same well of light rising in Sarika. He turned back.

Mitro had reached for the other woman, dragging her, chains and all, to force her to her knees in front of him. "Your turn," he said. "You are so happy to serve me in any way that I demand. Say it." He had shoved the piece of weapon into the front of his shirt.

Asiri, Sarika whispered. *Sister kin.*

Do not worry about me, the kneeling Asiri said. *I will cooperate and distract him. You must retrieve and hide the weapon where he will not be able to find it.*

Sarika gave a nearly imperceptible nod. What could she possibly do? Tomas and Dominic watched closely as the woman kneeling obeyed every foul thing Mitro instructed her to do. While she did, he roared with laughter and thought up even fouler, more vile things.

Sarika concentrated on the piece of metal. Her hands crept up to cover the amulet at her neck, cradling it in her palm as she matched the properties of the triangular piece of metal. She wasn't Carpathian. Shifters weren't able to change the composition of things or make them vanish into thin air, but somehow, she did.

Both men replayed that moment over and over, trying to see what she did to hide the weapon, but it was impossible. One moment she was all light and goodness, lifting the piece of metal from the *inside* of Mitro's shirt as if she were a member of the thief's guild. In the next, she and her friend combined their power and struck at Mitro's throat, closing it off, taking the air from his lungs, opening a thousand cuts all over his body.

Both ancients could have told the women this would not kill Mitro, but it appeared they knew. They distracted him enough that they had the time to stop their own hearts and shut down brain function, essentially dying to keep the secrets the two women held.

CHAPTER 14

I would say that answers the question of whether or not you have power and where it comes from," Tomas said, as he once more bent to Sarika's wrist.

Sarika looked up at him, not even wincing because he was taking her blood. Tomas should have taken that as a good sign, but he didn't. Sarika was exhausted. And confused. She had just allowed two Carpathian males into her mind when she was anything but on board with that. He'd rather she argue or at least discuss what they'd found, so he opened the discussion.

"I killed my friends and myself. How is that coming from a good place?"

"You saved lives, *sivamet*. You and your friends saved many lives."

"Perhaps." She looked across the room to Solange. "Now you know I'm not so squeaky clean. You'll have to make the decision whether you trust me to speak to your jaguar or even be acquainted with your family."

It was evident she knew Dominic had shared everything he'd observed with his lifemate. Sarika sounded tired and defeated, not at all like the woman Tomas was used to. Twice he'd removed her headache, but it was back in force. After looking into her memories, he understood exactly why she had reservations about Carpathians. She knew

Mitro was evil, and she was fully aware he had a lifemate. The bond between lifemates didn't stop him from the brutal cruelty he had exhibited when deliberately wiping out an entire population.

Tomas exchanged a long, telling look with Dominic, but as before, it was Solange who took the lead.

"I understand why you think the way you do, Sarika. You've been horribly traumatized and didn't even realize it. You suppressed those memories for a good reason. But I have killed far more male shifters than you can imagine. I planned their deaths and carried them out without any remorse. If there is one person in the room who should be condemned for the things they've done, it would be me. You are a saint by comparison. So I ask you, please, will you see what you can do to persuade my jaguar that I am not being held hostage? That I am still that ruthless warrior but have added to my arsenal by becoming Carpathian."

Solange spoke softly. Persuasively. Her gaze steady on Sarika. Sarika responded the way Tomas knew she would. It didn't matter that she was tired. Or still a little afraid of the power she wielded. She was going to help Solange because fundamentally, that was who she was.

She twisted her fingers together, took a deep breath and let it out. One hand crept up to the amulet she wore around her neck. Tomas felt the heat of it burning against her skin. It wasn't just warm; it was hot. The heat seemed to comfort his lifemate. He stayed very still in her mind, not wanting the jaguar to sense his presence and recoil. Tomas couldn't allow her to face this alone. If she needed him, he would be there.

Sarika didn't look for help. The moment she wrapped her fingers around the amulet, cradling the head of the jaguar in her palm, the state of exhaustion and fear left her. She closed her eyes and inhaled deeply, sending out a call, first to the baby.

Little one, you are very wanted. You're both jaguar and Carpathian. But most of all, you have a mother and father who want you. It is difficult right now, but you're strong. You will learn to overcome all obstacles. That is what your mother does. That is what your father does, and you will follow their lead and be a strong woman. No matter what happens in the next few minutes, know that they love and want you. It may not feel that way at first, but you know me. Your soul has always known my soul. Stay true to who you are and allow me to fight your battles for you at this time.

Tomas was astonished at the pure velvet magic of her voice. She spoke low, almost a whisper, as if the conversation were an intimate one between the child and Sarika. He felt the pull of that voice, the strong compulsion, but it wasn't so much a demand as it was pure love. She came from a place of purity.

Just as Carpathians could shed their bodies and egos and become pure spirit to heal, she wrapped up the baby in the purity of her essence. She wasn't asking for anything in return for herself. She wasn't looking for recognition. She felt humble to him. The more power she wielded, the more unassuming she seemed to be.

This power wasn't something she showed to the world. She kept it under wraps and used it for important situations. He realized she could use her gift to keep a male shifter focused on her rather than on what was happening around him. And she'd done just that. She'd manipulated Rud, Percy and even Bacus. She'd stalled them until help came in the form of Tomas and his brothers. She'd expected Luiz, but once the three Carpathian males were there, she still used the subtle power of her gift to aid them in holding off Percy and Bacus. That was a revelation.

This woman was his lifemate. He had been so worried that she was going to find out about the battles he and his brothers would face in the coming weeks as they tried to trace Justice and discover his plans, and she would realize they had little hope of defeating him. At the moment, it didn't look good for any of them, but Sarika would be an asset to them. That was the good news. The bad news was she had retreated to a place he was going to have to retrieve her from. She was still looking to find a way out of their bond. He could see that working at the back of her mind. She might not even be aware of it, but he was.

What was he offering her after all? He'd thought about that before he met her. He'd wanted his brothers to enter into a real discussion with him so he could work it out in his mind, but not even Mataias was willing to look at what the three ancients had become—or were still becoming. Evolving into. What was he offering her? He needed to know for certain because he knew he wouldn't give her up. He would follow her to the ends of the earth and try to make things right.

Sarika touched the jaguar, surrounded it with her beaming light. To him, the female jaguar felt feral. Dangerous. Extremely lethal and very hostile. The cat stared at Sarika with malevolent eyes. It even took a single stalking step toward her, but the light surrounding it acted like a powerful barrier.

You are angry. Sarika made it a statement.

You sit in the room with them. The jaguar spat the accusation at her. *You give them your blood to make them strong, knowing they hold Solange hostage.*

Sarika didn't bend under the accusation—or the veiled threat. Her energy felt serene. She faced the snarling cat with full compassion. From a place of love. Of peace. Tomas realized it would be difficult for any species to maintain anger and distrust for long in the light of her energy.

You had been Solange's only companion for years. You protected her from the moment of her birth. There was admiration and respect in Sarika's voice. In the warmth she showed the animal. *She has always been yours to look after.*

Her life was difficult from the time she was a child, the jaguar answered, somewhat mollified.

Sarika's praise was sincere, and it would be impossible for the jaguar not to feel that. *Not only was it difficult,* Sarika said, *but she was in danger from the moment of her birth. And you were the one to train her to fight. To give her the skills needed to carry out the important work she did, fighting her birth father and rescuing female shifters.*

She made it a statement, again giving the jaguar her due credit. Tomas could feel the shift in the animal's demeanor. Already she was far calmer and less accusing. The malevolence had faded from the eyes of the cat. She looked lost. Even forlorn. For the first time, Tomas felt empathy for the animal. It was clear she loved Solange and had done everything in her power to aid her human counterpart to survive.

There was such sorrow in her, the jaguar proclaimed. *So much and I couldn't do anything to change that. She lost everyone she loved.*

She loved you, Sarika corrected gently. *You've lost sight of that. She loved you and still does. She still needs you, especially now when she has a daughter coming. Think what that means. Who will teach her daughter's jaguar to keep the child safe? Solange has always relied on you.*

She chose to leave me and become something else.

The hurt the animal felt was devastating. So much so that Tomas felt the wrench, and he wasn't a man to feel emotions when he was prepared for a battle. He could easily compartmentalize, and he knew it was the only thing to do when hunting the vampire—or a monster such as ancients could become. Yet this jaguar's sorrow and hurt were so acute that she made his chest ache with pain. He couldn't imagine how someone as empathetic as Sarika felt. This was going to take a huge toll on her, and he couldn't do anything to stop it.

Well, he could, but he wouldn't. This was her woman power. Her magic. Her unique gift that few, if any, others had. It had occurred to him that the two women working in the temple with his lifemate could have been the lifemates of his brothers. It would make sense. The women were the same age. The three clearly had the same gifts and, when working together, were extremely powerful.

He should have taken a closer look at the other two women, but he'd been wholly focused on Sarika and her memories. What she'd gone through. He would have to revisit the memories. He had them locked in his mind. He would have to ask Sarika's permission to share them with his brothers. He'd always shared information—it was automatic—but Sarika's private thoughts and memories belonged to her. He didn't have the right to give them to anyone, not even the two men he loved and trusted the most in the world.

Sarika shifted in her chair, her gaze sweeping over him, eyes still distant and glazed with turning inward, but she saw him. That hit him like a punch. She felt the moment he realized he would be separate from his brothers. It was difficult to think he wouldn't have what he always had. Sarika was giving so much in the relationship, but perhaps that loss, for him, equaled what she would be losing.

He felt the wash of her female power, the love and compassion that she gave to the jaguar she gave to him. She shouldn't be aware of his presence, but she was. She was aware of his thoughts as well. He wasn't broadcasting. He was an ancient, and his kind were automatically careful. They didn't make mistakes because mistakes would cost them not only their lives but the lives of many others as well.

Yet she knew. She was aware. In whatever powerful state she was in, her feminine magic, that of selfless, unconditional love and compassion, enabled her to see him as well as the jaguar she was engaging. He felt at peace, a testament to her magic, when he'd felt such sadness just moments earlier. He was still struggling with coming to terms with having emotions, and for the most part, he held them at bay. That was impossible when he was in her mind, sharing the experience with her.

Tomas wanted to tell her that he thought she was magic. That she was an unbelievable being, and he was grateful she was his personal miracle. He couldn't do those things because she had her attention once more completely centered on the jaguar, and the cat couldn't know he was taking up even a tiny portion of her mind. He knew that would be a trigger for the animal. She would believe that the Carpathians were controlling not only Solange but Sarika as well.

The cat was nearly weeping, and Tomas felt the burn of tears behind his eyes. That had never happened to him before. Not ever. It was just that he was feeling the animal's pain amplified by what Sarika was feeling. That compassion and heartache for the lost jaguar.

I can imagine it feels that way to you, especially since there was no consulting with you. You two always found answers together. You always discussed where you would go and how you would handle problems. I see that so clearly, and I feel your sorrow for what you believe to be betrayal.

It was—is—betrayal unless he took her without her permission. Carpathians can take over anyone's mind. See into their thoughts. Direct their actions. That's what he's done. It has to be, or she wouldn't have left me.

That hurt, any way one looked at it. Tomas knew that, to some extent, Sarika felt the same way. That he was taking over her life. That he made decisions that affected her without getting her consent or talking it over with her. The worst of it was he knew it would happen in the future. When it came to safety and health, there would be no arguing. His duty was to protect her, and that was one of his greatest strengths—that instinct. His protective and extremely loyal nature. Those shared characteristics had always bound his brothers to him and kept all of them safe throughout the centuries.

His name is Dominic Dragonseeker. Are you aware of him? Deliberately, Sarika named him.

Tomas knew she was paving the way to make Dominic an ally. He didn't see it in her mind; there didn't appear to be any master plan, but he was beginning to know his lifemate and the way her brain worked out strategies. This mess required careful handling. Over the years, the wounds the cat felt had deepened and were thoroughly entrenched in her mind.

He is the enemy. I have studied everything about him.

Has he harmed Solange? She poured purity into the question. Not alarm. She asked it with that same calm serenity. No judgment. Just a thought-provoking question the jaguar would have to answer.

There was hesitation. The jaguar wanted to condemn the Dragonseeker, but it was clear that the animal was trying to be fair. To cooperate. That was a testament to Sarika's abilities. She didn't take over the cat with her power; she simply provided the animal with calm. There was no confrontation. Just acceptance of the jaguar's feelings. Tomas found himself feeling that same empathy and acceptance of the animal, despite the threat it presented not only to Sarika but to an unborn child.

He has changed her.

Did he? Or did Solange repress her feminine side to be the great warrior you helped develop? You said she was forced from a very young age to become a fighter. You are female. You have needs as a female. She might have set those needs aside, but that didn't mean she didn't feel them. Can you recall those times? She must have shared with you when she felt vulnerable. You were her beloved counsel and friend. You were her only family, the one she trusted to always have her best interests at heart. She trusted you to want the best for her. Did that mean she only confided in you about battle tactics? Help me to understand Solange's life. Her way of thinking.

Again, gentle pleading, as if Sarika believed the jaguar would *always* have understanding of Solange and would want what was best for her. Not what was best for the cat, or the two of them together, but what was truly best for Solange. In essence, the cat had acted like a mother, not just a mentor.

Sarika was able to convey those things to the jaguar because she seemed to genuinely have faith in the animal. Tomas was astonished at her patience and gentle guidance. She didn't try to push whatever she thought onto the animal; she waited for the jaguar to come to its own conclusions.

The jaguar was silent for a long time, and Sarika didn't interrupt her thoughts. She stayed quiet, respectful, just waiting.

She was very much afraid to show she had any vulnerabilities. She didn't want the shifters to ever see her as a woman. That scared her. She was royalty and the only hope for the female shifters in captivity. If she didn't rescue them and get them away safely, she knew those women were doomed to lives of torture and rape. She couldn't afford to be soft or vulnerable. She couldn't chance being attracted to a man.

The jaguar gave an honest answer.

Even with you guiding her, that must have been such a lonely life. And frightening every minute. She must have always felt she wasn't good enough. Would never be good enough.

The jaguar made a single sound of pain. *I tried to tell her that every being needed balance, but she couldn't hear me through her fear. And she had* reason to fear. More than any other, Brodrick searched for one with her blood. It didn't matter that she was his daughter, he would have imprisoned her just as he did the others.

But he thought he had killed all of his offspring.

The jaguar sighed. *There was a massacre, she was very young, but when he questioned her, she refused to give me up. He tried to tear out her throat.*

How did she survive? There was genuine interest in Sarika's gentle inquiry. Tomas was just as interested.

The jaguar looked uncomfortable. *When he tortured her to try to force me to show myself, she would position her body in such a way he didn't harm me. He stabbed her with the point of a knife multiple times. You can see the scars on her body. But she never allowed that knifepoint to touch me.*

There was admiration in the jaguar's thoughts. Wonder that a child could be so protective that she would endure torture and even certain death so Brodrick the Terrible couldn't get to her jaguar.

I was unhurt, and the moment he tossed her outside on the pile of dead and dying, I acted to stop her bleeding. I couldn't allow attention to be called to her. I didn't want them to know she still lived because they were in a killing frenzy. I just ensured she wouldn't bleed to death.

Sarika gave the cat a serene smile. One of admiration. *Again, you saved her life.*

She saved mine, the jaguar corrected.

As she grew, it is clear you wanted her to have a relationship as a woman. You encouraged her to allow herself to be feminine.

Again, the cat sighed. She sank down onto her haunches and then stretched out, no longer a threat. If anything, she was in a vulnerable position. *She wouldn't listen. I don't think she could listen. Being a woman made her feel too vulnerable. Jaguars submit to their mates. She was extremely submissive in that regard, and she despised that trait in herself. She saw it as weakness. She vowed a man would never have dominance over her.*

Sarika allowed that information to sink in. Allowed the jaguar to understand what she'd just revealed. *You wanted so much more for her, didn't you?*

The jaguar rested her head on her paws. *Yes. There were times I wanted her to have someone else watching over her. Comforting her. I couldn't hold her when she cried. More and more, she would stay in the jaguar form rather than her human one so she wouldn't have to cope with so much sorrow alone.*

And despite her insistence, and she probably was impatient and annoyed when you persisted, you continued to counsel her to allow herself to be a woman as well as a warrior, didn't you? You wanted the best for her.

Tomas went still inside. Sarika had led the cat to the only real conclusion that made sense. It was the jaguar who had persuaded Solange to accept Dominic. From the beginning, when Solange had come into her teens, the cat had worked on her to be more than one-sided.

He saw that exact moment when the jaguar realized she had been the one to open the door for Dominic. He was unfailingly gentle with Solange. In public, they presented as two equal warriors. He respected her abilities in a fight and didn't attempt to force her into staying at home and waiting for him. She fought at his side as an equal.

It is only at home that Solange shows him her feminine side. She still has trouble, even with him, and he is unfailingly gentle with her. He always allows her to choose what she will do for him when they are alone. What she will wear. When they are alone, he prefers a certain type of clothing, and she feels vulnerable in those garments, the jaguar conceded.

Does he know she is uncomfortable?

Yes. He never insists, and he always makes her feel beautiful. He always shows his appreciation of her as a woman and partner. I cannot fault him on that. The jaguar admitted it reluctantly.

Why do you feel she was coerced into becoming Carpathian? I am facing such a decision. If you don't mind, I would like the benefit of your wisdom. Frankly, I am afraid. Not of him, he is wonderful to me, but of a species I don't understand. Solange must have been terrified. How did you help her through it?

That was genius, sheer genius. The part that got to Tomas was that she was telling the jaguar the strict truth, making herself vulnerable, treating the jaguar as a respected elder. She wasn't playing the cat; she was sincere. That was part of Sarika's magic. She took the time and listened. She didn't judge. She heard and acknowledged another point of view, and she respected what others had to say.

The jaguar was silent again for a long time. Tomas realized that the animal was actually thoughtful. He had become a shadow in Sarika's mind because he had already judged the animal as being violent and harmful. He worried for Sarika's safety as well as that of the baby. But he was wrong. The animal not only was hurt with the feelings of betrayal but had genuinely convinced herself that Solange needed to be saved. She was a wise and deadly opponent, and she played the long game, not one of instant gratification.

I was present when he courted her, but to give her privacy, I stepped back. I trusted him with her at the time. The jaguar was thoughtful. Admitting the truth to herself for the first time. *I believed he was good for her.*

The cat lifted her head and stared directly into Sarika's eyes. *I told her to trust her heart. I give you the same advice. Trust your heart. Don't have your eyes closed. Try to see him for who he is, both good and bad traits. Do not love an illusion, a fantasy that is in your mind. See him for what he truly is, and if he is right, love him for that. That was my advice then, and it stands now.*

Sarika frowned, the expression as delicate as the emotion she portrayed. *But then you withdrew your approval. What did he do that made you suspicious of him?*

Solange always talked important matters over with me. Always. Even when I knew she had made up her mind, she would still discuss those things with me because I have always been important to her. She did not. Conversion can take away your jaguar—did he tell you that? If your cat is important to you, the conversion can change who and what you are. She accepted the risk that she would lose me without even talking it over with me.

The hurt of betrayal was once more weighing all three of them down, Carpathian ancient, Sarika with her feminine power and the jaguar. They weren't the only ones. A small cry came from a distance, so low as almost not to be heard. A baby calling out in pain.

The jaguar lifted her head alertly. *She is hurting.*

She feels your pain of betrayal and shares that with you. You are important to her because Solange has made you important to her. Or rather the imposter, the illusion of you. Did you ask Solange what happened at the time of the conversion?

Tomas felt the soothing warmth she surrounded the baby with. He also felt she was beginning to tire. She was putting out a great deal of energy, psychic energy, that cost her. She would need his blood to bolster her. She was unable to eat solid food and, to his knowledge, wasn't hydrating. The effect of blood exchanges often left an unconverted lifemate unable to keep food down.

He also felt the vicious headache pounding at her. He couldn't interfere and heal her as he would have wished. As that strong protective streak demanded. He would give away his presence, and everything Sarika had accomplished would be for nothing.

I did not ask, the jaguar admitted. *I was too hurt, and I convinced myself Dominic was to blame. There was no evidence of that, just that Solange had always protected me as I did her.*

You need to ask her. My understanding is she delayed the conversion over and over in order to ensure nothing would go wrong with you. Each blood exchange, it was you they both monitored, not her. She was used to protecting you, and she would not have gone through with it had there been a single sign that she would lose you. Or that you would be harmed. I wasn't there, but when she shared some of her memories with me, that was what I observed. I could have read it wrong, or her character incorrectly.

The jaguar female bristled in annoyance. *Solange's character is not in question. She leads her life with honor.*

Sarika inclined her head. *You taught her those things. You instilled those traits in her. She is counting on you to do the same for her daughter. It hasn't occurred to her that you would think she betrayed you. According to my cousin, Luiz, Solange spends quite a bit of her time as a jaguar. She believed the illusion because she knows you so well and gives the false jaguar everything she knows and loves of you.*

This will devastate her, the jaguar said. *She might view this as a betrayal of her.*

Would she? You know her better than anyone. What is going to be her honest reaction?

The jaguar sighed. *She will place the blame squarely on her shoulders. She wouldn't ever consider that I might have acted out of jealousy. I didn't consider it.*

The stress is threatening the life of the baby, Sarika said gently. *Solange will be a mother. You will be as well. It would be wonderful if Dominic and Solange could count on your wisdom in raising their daughter and helping to raise her jaguar as a strong yet loving warrior just as you did Solange.*

Visibly agitated, the jaguar leapt to her feet. Across the room, Solange gasped and reached out to Dominic. Tomas felt the moment when the cat reached for Solange. To give her waves of reassurance. To apologize and ask for forgiveness.

I thank you, the jaguar stated as Sarika withdrew.

Her hands were shaking as she slowly released the amulet. Tomas didn't care that they had an audience. At that moment, Solange and Dominic were occupied with their own drama, but it wouldn't have mattered. Tomas gathered Sarika into his arms and transferred her to his lap.

Let me take care of you.

He framed her face with his palms, fingertips pressing into her temple as he sent warmth and healing light into her to ease the pounding there. It took a few moments to remove the offending pain.

She leaned into him, so exhausted she didn't bother to respond with words. She just allowed him to take charge. Her lashes drifted down, and he feared she might actually fall asleep.

You need blood, Sarika. I know it isn't your favorite thing, but it will revive you enough to get you back to the tree house, where you can get some rest.

A small smile curved her mouth. "Can't you feel the energy rushing toward us? There isn't going to be any reprieve for the next couple of hours, Tomas."

She didn't raise her head or open her eyes. She just looked amused.

Tomas hadn't missed the incredible surge of joyous energy that seemed to crash through the forest, coming at them from three different sources. A male, much more somber than the female and child he traveled with, but happy and grateful nevertheless. That had to be Jubal. Tomas had met him on occasion and liked the man. He was a male jaguar shifter. He had two sisters, and both were lifemates to Carpathian males.

He knew Jasmine's energy. They all did. She had suffered greatly at the hands of the male shifters, and there were some obsessed with her. She was Solange's younger cousin and much loved by everyone. She was excited to see Sarika again. There were few things that made Jasmine feel young and happy, so it was good to feel her emotions of joy being broadcast so loudly. Just because his woman felt those things, Jubal was grateful. No Carpathian could miss the way Jubal loved and protected his wife.

And then there was Sandrine. She was the wildest, most expressive child Tomas had ever come across. Her aunts and uncles encouraged her to think for herself and solve as many problems as possible herself. She was intelligent and had a sense of humor. She'd been shy and reserved when Tomas had first noticed her years earlier. She was a product of rape, and it would stand to reason that her mother and cousins might not want her, but it was just the opposite. They treated her like royalty, lavishing love on her. That had brought her out of her shell in a big way.

"You had better hurry with the despicable blood thing. I don't want to know you're giving it to me. Just please do it before they come in."

"The safeguards are down," Dominic confirmed. "Sandrine will come running in and throw herself at Solange. Or possibly Sarika. I'm certain Jasmine has told her entire family how heroic you were, Sarika. There will be no getting away from the accolades they will shower on you. I won't be able to save you, and neither will Tomas."

Tomas noted he sounded cheerful about the entire business, probably because there were new targets for the child and the women in the family to annoy.

Sarika laughed softly. "Annoy? We annoy you?"

"You, in particular, annoy me." Tomas tried to sound gruff. "You are looking forward to seeing that wild child when you should be resting."

"I don't think I'll ever be able to pass up the opportunity to annoy you by refusing to bow down to your authority."

He was grateful he could share her amusement. That was new to him. The feeling washed over and into him, soaking into every cell in his body the way rich blood did.

"I have the feeling you don't acknowledge too many authority figures."

She tilted her chin at him. "According to my uncle, I don't." Her smile faded. "Tomas, I hope you know I'm only teasing you. Thank you for doing your best to give me choices. I feel the conflict warring inside you, and I know your brothers and Luiz have a very different point of view on how you should handle things with me, but seriously, I'm so grateful to you. I feel like you see me. That what I think and feel matters to you. So thank you."

"We'll find our way," Tomas reassured. "I'll do my best, when we have more time alone, to explain what is happening and why we are so pressed for time."

"Hurry with the blood thing. I'm so tired, and that darling child is coming closer every second we wait."

He knew she wouldn't want the others to observe her taking blood from him. She still had an aversion to it, and he didn't blame her. It wasn't like it was natural in her society. Not in human or shifter.

Tomas didn't wait. He curled her closer into him, shielding both from everyone's eyes, and opened a line on his chest with one lengthening fingernail. She didn't fight him at all when he pushed her to go under. That meant quite a bit to him. Her level of trust in him was growing. They would need that in the coming weeks as they hunted for the demon Carpathian who was plotting to destroy the Carpathian people.

He gave her as much blood as he dared. Had they been alone, he would have made certain he took enough back for a true exchange, but that wasn't for when she would be under the scrutiny of several shifters and eventually other Carpathians. He knew what was coming. Luiz had filled him in on the ridiculous party that was being planned.

Tomas supposed that was what it was like when two species got together and tried to combine customs. He'd never seen the need for showers and bathtubs until he saw what pleasure that deep sunken tub gave Sarika. He decided bathtubs were in their future. He liked the idea of washing her hair and lavishing attention on her, adding to the ritual of her bath.

There were other things she enjoyed that he would try to incorporate, just as Dominic so obviously did for Solange. His brothers were going to give him hell, but they might as well learn if they were going to be with a woman. The notion of cavemen wasn't as correct as people believed. Those women weren't pushovers. Many hunted and fished right alongside their mates.

He closed the wound in his chest. After ensuring there was no evidence that she had taken blood, he woke her.

CHAPTER 15

Sandrine burst into the room, arms outstretched, a smile of pure joy on her face as she raced across the room straight to Solange. She looked like a little tornado dressed in pink tulle, her dark hair a riot of curls. Someone had attempted to tame the mass by putting in bows, but the ribbons hung in streamers, adding to the effect of a little pixie come to vibrant life.

At the last moment, as Solange braced to be bowled over by the little dynamo, Dominic stepped in, swooped her up and spun her around, laughing as he made the interception.

"Ha, little one, I caught you."

Sarika could see that Sandrine was older than she'd first thought. She was very small, but she was more like six or seven than four or five, which was the age Sarika had originally thought her to be.

It is entirely possible Jubal and Jasmine keep her looking younger when they take her out in the forest to train her jaguar. They don't want the male shifters fixating on her, Tomas informed her.

They seemed more fixated on Jasmine. And that's just gross that they look at female children as potential breeders. Sarika was indignant as well as disgusted. *What is wrong with the males? How did they get the way they are?*

She watched the interaction between Dominic, Solange and Sandrine. The child hugged both and chattered about how she raced Jubal and her mom and *beat* them, she was so fast. Her laughter had a magic to it, lightening Sarika's heart. She had been feeling so lost and sad. Just having the child in the room changed everything.

Not all of them have been affected, but the high mage began to work against the jaguars, with the intention of destroying them. From your memories, the high mage wasn't the only one. I believe he made a deal with the underworld to aid him in his plan to destroy all other species. It was found, after centuries, that he was a triplet, and the other two conspired with him, Tomas explained.

The child turned in Solange's arms and immediately went still when she noticed Sarika and Tomas for the first time. She looked up at Solange. "I didn't see everything like you taught me. My jaguar didn't, either. That's a bad mistake."

"You weren't feeling a threat. You're in a safe place, and the people visiting us are friends. Your jaguar would have felt a threat and warned you," Solange stated gently. "But it is always good, when you enter any house, even your own, to take a moment to ensure you are completely safe. That will come with time, Sandrine."

Sarika smiled at the child, her heart hurting for her. She shouldn't have to worry about her safety every moment of her existence. She should be able to play and laugh and learn in a loving, safe environment. Sarika's childhood had been happy. She might have been alone quite a lot of the time, but she loved her life. She felt free and was encouraged to make decisions and solve problems for herself, but she always knew she had that safety net of her adoptive parents who loved her. They were never harsh. At no time did she feel threatened by outside sources the way Sandrine was.

This is why your father sent you to his brother, Tomas reminded.

She had been resentful of that. Resentful that her father had kept her brother with him but had sent her away. There was no contact with him or her brother after that. She'd asked her uncle and aunt numerous times, and the answer had always been the same. Now she knew why.

Her father had wanted her protected from what was happening to her people. Solange, with her scars and warrior's demeanor, had grown up in an environment that was virtually a war zone. Sandrine was, perhaps, a little safer, but she still had to be taught to be alert.

She wiped a hand down her face, trying to clear her thoughts. Would she want to bring a child into this environment? She understood Solange's concerns. She didn't want any part of the male jaguars, but after talking to Solange's jaguar, she worried for her own if she went through the conversion. She knew as far as Tomas was concerned, there was no *if*. What if she lost that inner well of healing that aided other jaguars? There were so many unanswered questions. So many concerns.

You're tired, sivamet. This was supposed to be a happy time for you. It has turned into something else. Jubal and Jasmine are entering now. As soon as we can leave without being rude, we'll do so. Once you've had time to rest, we can discuss your concerns.

That was so Tomas. He felt safe. He felt steady. He felt like a rock one could always count on. Yet when she thought about it, he was the source of her current problems.

Tomas' palm circled the nape of her neck, his fingers doing a slow massage to ease the tension from her as first Jubal and then Jasmine walked into the room at a much more sedate pace than their child.

The moment Jubal entered, Sarika recognized the jaguar in him, the bloodline, and her jaguar reacted as if they were old friends. She'd never met him. She was wary of male jaguars. But still . . .

He is so familiar to me, but I have never met him. My blood calls to his. She couldn't help but notice that the moment he entered, Jubal's gaze jumped to her. Not Tomas, the clear threat in the room, but her.

Jubal knows me, Sarika. He knows I am no threat to his family. Is it possible one of the women from your past was from the same bloodline? There were three of you. There is Solange's lineage, yours and Jubal's. Three distinct lines of royal blood. When you and the other two women worked in the temple, each of you had the same extraordinary gift.

Sarika hadn't considered that. She didn't ever look at those memories. They were too painful. She had never acknowledged that they were memories, not nightmares. Not until now.

Tomas stood to greet Jubal. Both hands gripped Jubal's forearms. *"Én jutta félet és ekämet."*

What does that mean? Sarika asked.

I greet a friend and brother, Tomas interpreted.

Jubal replied in kind, using the Carpathian language. Sarika realized he was comfortable around Carpathians, and he'd learned their language. That meant he was accepted by them. They were a secretive race, yet Jubal was included in their trusted circle.

Both sisters are lifemates to Carpathian males, Tomas supplied.

Sarika remembered that Tomas had mentioned that before. There was a story there, but now wasn't the time.

Tomas turned from Jubal toward Sarika. "Jubal, this is my lifemate, Sarika." He returned to her side, seating himself in the chair as close as he'd been before. He didn't seem to mind showing affection for her publicly. His actions seemed claiming, as if he were declaring to Jubal and Jasmine that he and Sarika were solid. Sarika wished they were, that she didn't have all the doubts pressing in.

It is natural that you have doubts, Sarika. And as concerning as this day has been with all the revelations, I think you're doing very well. Once again, Tomas' strong fingers found the knots of tension in her neck and began to work them out for her.

Jubal smiled at her. "Jasmine and Sandrine have talked of nothing but you and your extraordinary courage."

He gave her an old-fashioned bow, when Sarika could easily see he was anything but old-fashioned. This man was born and raised in the modern world, but he seemed to be successful at navigating between the old and the new. He was also clearly capable and comfortable in the human, jaguar and Carpathian worlds.

Around his wrist he wore what appeared to be a star-shaped charm. That place inside her that seemed to have connections with other jaguars knew immediately it was a weapon. A very deadly one—and it was made of the same material as her amulet.

"I think it was Jasmine and Sandrine displaying all the courage. I just helped stall until sunset. I knew Luiz, my cousin, would come. It was a bit of a shock to have three Carpathians come to our rescue. Fortunately, Jasmine and Sandrine clearly knew them."

"You know they would have taken us if not for you," Jasmine insisted. "Thank you again."

Sarika smiled at her, trying to be reassuring. "We've been discussing the party for Solange and only managed to agree on one thing. No balloons. That's it. That's as far as we got. Hopefully, you're a better party planner than I am."

Jubal swept his arm around Jasmine. "She's excellent at planning parties." He sounded immensely proud of her. "And Solange, we've brought news as well. Not that we want to steal your thunder."

Solange's eyes widened, and she turned to Dominic. He immediately caught her hand and pulled her beneath the shelter of his shoulder.

"Are you pregnant, Jasmine? Are you going to have another baby?" Solange whispered the question. She seemed both hopeful and fearful.

Is this a huge deal? Sarika asked Tomas.

Yes, it is, Tomas replied. *Jubal wanted more children, but Jasmine was afraid. No one blames her after what she went through. It took her forever to admit she loved Jubal and would agree to a life with him. From what I understand, he finally just railroaded her.*

I see there is a pattern with the men around here. She tried to make it a joke, but she was serious. There did seem to be a pattern. Make the decision for the woman, and she had to learn to live with it.

I know it feels that way.

It is that way, she corrected.

Then when she tried to have a baby, she lost it, Tomas continued. *That was so hard on both her and Jubal. Sandrine was devastated right along with them. She wanted to be a big sister so much.*

Sarika's heart went out to the two women. They'd gone through so much. She wanted the best for them, and she was grateful it appeared that Dominic and Jubal really loved and cared for their wives. The two women needed that, after all they had been through.

She glanced up at Tomas. She didn't want to fight with him. She wanted to share this moment with Solange and Jasmine, a new pregnancy, a new life beginning. She wanted to be able to feel their shared joy in that moment.

"We waited to tell you until we were certain I'd carry," Jasmine told Solange. "Our baby will be nearly the same age as yours. Cousins to play together. And Sandrine is so excited to be able to look after both." She smiled at her daughter, who began to jump up and down.

"I didn't give away the secret this time," she announced, her silky curls bouncing nearly over her head. She grinned mischievously at Sarika. "I always tell secrets. It is so hard to keep them. I try really hard, but they burst out of me all by themselves."

She looked up at Jubal. "Daddy never gets mad at me, though. He laughs about it and says I'll get better at not letting secrets escape, and I did this time. I didn't let it get away from me."

Jubal immediately reached down to lift her into his arms. "That's right, pixie. You did good. I'm so proud of you. Wrangling secrets and putting them behind locked doors is very difficult."

Sandrine's little arms snaked around Jubal's neck. She laid her head on his chest and squeezed hard, determined to give him the best hug she could.

"I think we need balloons, Daddy," she murmured, clearly a cajoling, manipulative move on her part. She looked innocent and even sounded it, but Sarika knew she was far from it. "Bright red ones."

Dominic groaned, and Solange covered her face with her hands.

Sarika laughed. "Sandrine, I'm sure bright red balloons would be wonderful, but did you know that they freak your aunt out? She doesn't like them, and neither does her jaguar. If you're planning the special party just for her, it might be a good thing to see what she likes and doesn't like. I have never planned a party, but if you have, is that the way you do it? Find out what your client likes?"

At once, Sandrine lifted her head and looked around the room. Suddenly looking important, she directed her question at Solange. "Are you my client, Auntie?"

Solange nodded. "I am. Dominic and I are both your clients," she added firmly.

Dominic put on a look of horror. "Wait. This is a girls' thing. Totally female. Dominic isn't any part of it. I can slay demons for you, but whatever you women are up to, that's far too scary for me."

That put Sandrine into a fit of laughter. Her giggles filled the room with joy. If Sarika could imagine such a thing, she would think there were incandescent bubbles floating throughout the house, all created by the one small child.

She wiggled until her father put her down, and then she danced in front of Dominic, making chicken noises until he chased her around the room. She let out several girlie screams and dove for the couch. "Safe. This is the safe zone."

"There is no safe zone." Dominic growled like a large bear. "This house is a big bear den and has no couches." He put his arms up and lumbered toward her. Illusion took over, and he did appear as a giant standing bear.

Instead of being frightened, Sandrine buried her face in the cushions, laughing so hard she snorted, which made her laugh even more. She put one little hand up to fend off the giant bear as it shuffled closer, making growly bear noises.

"Auntie Solange, Uncle Dominic is drooling. *Drooling.*" She burst out laughing again and rolled right off the couch to land on Dominic's gigantic paws.

"Bears drool, you little demon," Dominic told her in a bad-bear voice.

That sent her rolling across the floor, holding her sides. Sarika found herself laughing because, really, how could you not? On the other hand, the child was so high-energy, she couldn't imagine keeping up with her twenty-four seven. And a new one on the way?

Sandrine was up and dancing, rocking out to a beat only she could hear and calling to her mother to dance with her. "Since you're my client, Auntie, no balloons!" she called, wiggling her hips and bottom in a wide, gyrating circle.

Tomas tugged at Sarika's hair. *The only time I've seen that child quiet is when she's scared or asleep.*

"Sandrine, we need to sit down with Auntie Solange and write down the things that she wants for the party," Jasmine said. She glanced at Dominic, and he waved a hand toward the corner, where a small desk appeared with a little chair. There was a notebook and several glittery colored pens sitting invitingly on the desk.

The exchange was smooth, practiced, something the two had done many times. Sarika found she liked Dominic. He might be intimidating, but when it came to his family, he was all in. She risked a quick peek at Tomas. He would be like that. He was all in with his brothers. Protective of them. She knew he thought of them continuously and wanted the best for them.

Was he right about the three royal families being tied together by the temple? Just knowing the temple was there, in a place it shouldn't have been, made her think about what was the known truth and what was hidden. Historians were aware of the many Mayan communities, and supposedly, there weren't any in Peru. Yet the ruins of the temple were there, and they had a Mayan feel. The jaguar statues still stood, glaring, judging good or evil. The temple joined the sky, the earth and the underworld. *She* had been there, serving in that temple. Once she allowed that door to open in her memories and she could acknowledge to herself that the things in her past were real, she was remembering more and more.

The temple was more than a place of worship. It was sacred for many reasons, not the least of which was that the women came together to visit and help one another. There was always laughter and singing. Young children ran and played and danced with abandon, just as Sandrine had done. There were art projects and mathematics and much teaching going on. It was always busy and always a place of joy.

Sandrine ran to the desk and arranged her paper and pens, then sat with a red gel pen poised in her hand while she looked expectantly at her client.

Solange indicated the paper. "Write down 'no balloons.'"

Sandrine sighed, looked about to protest, but then squared her little shoulders and began to painstakingly write "No balloons. Not even red ones."

She showed the paper to Solange, looking very mournful. "What else?"

"What do you suggest we have at the party?"

Sandrine's face lit up. "We should do a princess party. We can all wear tiaras. The glittery kind. The baby is a girl. She'll like that. I'll wear a pink princess dress."

Sarika expected Solange to object, but instead, she looked very somber, nodding her head. "I think princess is a great theme—thank you, Sandrine. I would never have thought of that."

Sarika fell in love with Solange right then. The woman might be the fiercest female warrior on the planet, but she was the *best* auntie of all time. She didn't like parties, and she certainly didn't do princess, but to make her niece happy and build her confidence and self-esteem, she would have a princess-themed party.

She's amazing. She had to tell Tomas. *Solange. She's absolutely amazing. She isn't letting on that just a few minutes before Sandrine got here, she was afraid of losing her baby. She isn't letting on that she has no clue what to do with a party for her baby. Or that she doesn't want to have a party. She's doing it for Sandrine.*

And Jasmine, Tomas pointed out. *Solange has another cousin, Juliette. She'll be coming as well. Probably already on the way. Solange would do anything for Jasmine and Juliette.*

Do you know Juliette's lifemate? More Carpathian men. Wonderful. She thought there were enough running around the forest without adding to the mix.

She is lifemate to Riordan De La Cruz. He's the youngest of the De La Cruz brothers but no less lethal.

The family Luiz is now part of.

Tomas nodded solemnly, his fingers tightening on the nape of her neck. *They take family very seriously. You are Luiz's only family on his jaguar side. He is fully a De La Cruz and considered a full brother. The blood of their line runs in his veins. That means,* sivamet, *they will take you being a member of their family very seriously.*

She turned to him to raise her eyebrow. *I thought I was your family. Lojos and Mataias certainly treat me as such. I don't need to be a De La Cruz. Luiz is scary enough.*

No one is as scary as Zacarias. Technically, Luiz is considered older, but Zacarias has led the family for centuries. He's the one who made the decision to turn Luiz and offer him the gift of the family. Luiz, like the other brothers, follows his lead.

She couldn't imagine Luiz following anyone's lead. She decided it was best to put off meeting Zacarias.

Where does he stay?

He has a cattle ranch on the outskirts of the forest. There was the slightest bit of humor in his voice. *His lifemate, Marguarita, was raised there and is very entrenched with the ranch people. They make their home base there. He is good friends with Dominic.*

There was a small part of her listening to Sandrine and Jasmine give more ideas for the baby shower, but mostly she was interested in the things Tomas was telling her. This was jaguar territory, but it seemed that several Carpathians made their homes here. Was that to keep the jaguar women safe?

Sarika believed in destiny. She found it odd that so many Carpathians had gathered in one area. Was fate orchestrating such a thing because something big was happening?

Is it common for so many Carpathians to be together in one place?

It is more common in the Carpathian Mountains, where the prince resides. Hunters, as a rule, are alone. Tomas had an inquiring note at the end of his statement.

Everything is odd about this, Tomas, beginning with the tribe of Mayans finding their way here. And were they Mayans? Why do we think that? Their existence has been kept a huge secret.

That wouldn't be unusual, Tomas objected. *Jaguars are a secretive society. The animals have been decreasing in number, let alone shifters. The temple was considered a sacred place to the jaguar shifters, regardless that it is in ruins. If anything, the remaining shifters wanted to conceal the ruins so there wouldn't be an influx of those robbing the temple or archaeologists digging up a sacred site. Not that they had to worry; the temple conceals itself.*

Sarika considered Tomas' response. He traveled throughout the world's rainforests. He knew the changing environments better than most because he'd experienced them. The shifters were a secretive society, so much so that her aunt and uncle didn't tell her anything about what was happening in the forests with the shifters. They wanted her to avoid her birthplace at all costs. The information she did have came from Luiz, and it wasn't much.

Even with what Tomas said, she still had an uneasy feeling. "Solange, will there be very many people at this party? Women? Children?"

"We're keeping it small," Solange answered.

Sandrine gave a protest screech, but Jasmine shook her head and pointed to the list. "That is not the way we express ourselves, Sandrine. Use your words, not noises."

"Who will be coming?" Tomas asked.

Solange and Dominic exchanged a look. Sarika was certain they were communicating telepathically, the way she did with Tomas.

Is something wrong? Dominic asked.

Sarika shook her head. *I'm just trying to figure some things out.*

Solange sent her a tentative smile. "Jasmine, Sandrine and Jubal, of course. We have to have the party planners. My cousin Juliette is on the way with her lifemate, Riordan. They have a son, little Hunter. He's only eighteen months old. Dax and Riley are coming. They have a daughter, Maureen, who is three, and there is a rumor that Riley might be expecting as well."

"Zacarias and Marguarita will also be attending," Dominic said. "If she is expecting, Zacarias would never tell a soul."

"I have three wonderful friends, jaguar shifters, who will attend," Solange added. "Adele and Lucy will come with Tara and her husband, Finn. Tara and Finn have a daughter, Bianca. She's six and best friends with Sandrine."

"Solange rescued all three women from Brodrick years ago," Dominic said. "They've been friends for years. The women have already heard of your bravery." He seemed to be trying to reassure Sarika that everyone would welcome her.

Sarika reached for Tomas' hand, threading her fingers through his. That feminine place inside her, the one with the power to envision good or evil, was studying the situation with great trepidation. These were Carpathian children. Carpathian lifemates.

Tomas, what happens if your lifemate is killed?

His gaze narrowed. His entire demeanor changed. Not just his demeanor, his energy. Everything about him. He went from sweet Tomas, sitting quietly with her, a little amused by the unexpected chaos of Dominic's home, to a lethal predator within seconds.

Lojos and Mataias instantly slipped into her mind. She felt them enter, a swift takeover. They had become as lethal as Tomas. And Luiz seemed even worse. He poured into her mind aggressively, clearly looking for threats.

Tomas, it was just a question. I need to know these things. She tried to defuse the situation. Both Dominic and Solange had gone on alert. She was a little shocked that Jubal had as well. Everyone was looking at her. She felt the glare of a white-hot spotlight.

"What is it, Sarika?" Dominic asked. His voice was very, very gentle.

"I just asked a question about lifemates. I don't know enough about the Carpathian culture, and in asking, I got a very scary reaction." She went for strict honesty because she didn't understand how a simple question could trigger such a visceral reaction.

"Your question was?" Dominic prompted.

She glanced warily at Tomas. He wasn't leaning into her, taking her weight, gently easing the tension out of her; he was on alert. He'd shut down his emotions and had become fully a predator. A hunter. His brothers and Luiz had as well.

"I want to go home." She was being a coward again, and she didn't even care who knew it. She didn't belong with these people. Maybe she was afraid something big was happening outside their control, but they could figure it out. Not her. She just didn't have enough information.

Sarika made a move to get to her feet. Jasmine went straight to her and put her arm around her. "If you're not used to their intensity, it can be really scary, Sarika. I know. When I first was rescued, I could barely be in the same room with any of them."

Her glare encompassed everyone in the room. Sandrine, for once, had gone very sober. She slid off the chair and came to Sarika, wrapping her arms around Sarika's leg protectively.

"My daddy can do anything, Sarika. He won't let anyone hurt you—will you?" She looked at Jubal as if he were a superhero. Not only did she look at him that way, but she felt that way, and her emotions filled the room.

"I would never allow Sarika to be harmed," Jubal confirmed. "No one in this room would ever allow any harm to come to Sarika. She's family, and she saved you and Jasmine."

Sandrine nodded solemnly and then smiled up at Sarika. "We always tell the truth, even if we're going to get into trouble."

"I just asked a question," Sarika said. "That's all. I needed to know the answer."

Dominic's head went up alertly. He exchanged a long look with Tomas. It was obvious he had asked Tomas what had triggered the alarm.

"Sarika." Tomas used his softest voice, aware she was on the verge of flight. That would be a disaster on every level. He would have to stop her, and that would undo every bit of trust he'd built up with her. "Do you realize what you just said? You *need* to know the answer. You weren't simply looking for information. There was a reason behind the question."

Sarika shook her head. "I just asked, Tomas."

"What is it you need to know?" Jasmine asked. She led Sarika across the room to Solange.

Woman power. Woman magic. The terrible threat Sarika felt lessened just by being in their circle. Solange gave her an encouraging smile. "Hopefully, I can answer any questions you have about Carpathians, Sarika. Like you, I am jaguar. I was before the conversion, and I still am. She's here with me, and thanks to you, we found our connection again. We're working everything out, and she's helping me with the baby. In return, I'd like to help you."

"What if I want to leave? Go back to the States? Would you help me do that?" Sarika knew it wasn't fair to challenge Solange, but she couldn't help it. She felt as though she was a prisoner, and the feeling was growing stronger with every passing minute.

"Is that what you really want?" Solange countered. "I don't believe it's what you want. Your fear is deep. Just as it was when Dominic and Tomas were looking at your memories. There's something else that is scaring you." She waved a hand toward the men in the room. "It isn't those you know who would lay down their lives for you. It's something else, something you know deep where none of us can go."

Sarika's hand crept up to her amulet. She'd had her fill of monsters. She had seen people she loved brutally murdered. Women, men and children who were peaceful people. Loving people. She'd lost her "sisters," maybe not by birth but certainly of the heart. She'd helped to kill one of them.

"Mommy, she's crying," Sandrine whispered.

"Crying is a good thing sometimes," Jasmine said.

Tomas made a move to go to Sarika, needing to comfort her, but Solange shook her head, and he backed off. A part of her noticed and was a little shocked that he would take direction from a woman.

"Ask me your question, Sarika," Solange said.

She took a deep breath to bring herself under control. "I asked what happens when one lifemate dies and the other is left behind."

"You mean the woman?"

Sarika nodded. "Yes. What happens if the Carpathian male loses his lifemate?" She spoke very softly, but it was clear the men in the room heard. Not only them, but Tomas' brothers and Luiz also heard the question.

"Some men will choose to follow their lifemate into the next realm. They have only seconds to decide," Solange said. "Without their anchor, they can be lost."

"By 'lost,' do you mean they would become a vampire?" she persisted. Sarika didn't know why it was so important to understand, but it was. She clutched the amulet tighter. The head of the jaguar pressed into her palm, nearly burning her, but she couldn't let go.

"Yes," Solange confirmed. "After hundreds of years living with honor, some would be unable to make the choice to follow their lifemate. They immediately go into what is known in their world as a *thrall*. They turn vampire and are lost."

Sarika took a deep breath, her mind spinning with the information, trying to sort through what it all meant. Jubal wasn't Carpathian, but counting Jasmine and herself, that was six women, five of whom had ancient Carpathians for lifemates. She wasn't pregnant, but at least four of the other women were.

That number didn't sound huge until she considered that Luiz had indicated the Carpathian people had been on the verge of collapse when their prince discovered a human psychic woman could be a lifemate. So how many couples were there? How many children? If those women were targeted and killed, how many of their lifemates would choose to follow them, which would rid the world of the ancient hunters, and how many would become vampire?

Her mind raced with the possibilities of what could be happening. What was orchestrating the events? Was it really simply a joyful gathering to celebrate a highly anticipated pregnancy, or was something very sinister happening beneath the surface? If that was the case, how could it be stopped?

The sorrow in her, weighing her down, led her to believe something was terribly wrong. But if that was so, why didn't the Carpathian males feel the threat? Why was she the only one feeling it? That didn't make sense. She needed to be alone to figure out whether her imagination was working overtime, she was going insane, or there was something evil threatening the women and children of the Carpathian people. She was rather terrified that it was the latter.

"Sarika." Tomas used that voice that seemed to play over her skin and soothe her when she was so troubled. "You have many secrets buried in your mind. They are rising now and cause you great fear. Do you believe there is really a conspiracy happening?"

"I wish I knew. You can see into my mind. I can't calm it down. I told you, sometimes my mind starts working on a problem, and it won't let it go. I need to be somewhere quiet so I can solve this puzzle."

Tomas gave her his gentle smile. "I'll take you home, and we'll work it out together. Solange, Jasmine, Sandrine, we'll return this next rising."

He and Dominic exchanged another long look. Sarika heard a soft murmur as if they were speaking. To her surprise, she heard Jubal's voice, which meant he could speak telepathically. She didn't try to hear what they were saying. She just wanted to lie down to let her brain rest.

CHAPTER 16

Tomas watched his lifemate pacing back and forth across the wide wraparound porch. He knew his brothers and Luiz watched her as well. They were in the shadows, keeping guard, but they were upset with him because he didn't take over her mind and find out what was bothering her so much.

They each tried to persuade him that a lifemate didn't allow his woman to suffer as Sarika clearly was. Every cell in his body demanded he do just that, wave his hand and stop her in her tracks, slide into her mind when she was unaware and ferret out the problem.

He was Sarika's lifemate, and his brothers and her cousin were right. His number one priority had to be to see to her health and happiness, not just her protection.

How you handle your lifemates is for you to decide. You are the ones who must get to know what makes her happy. What scares her. If you feel that taking away all freedom of choice can be justified, that is what you must do with your woman. I know if I take that path with Sarika, she would be a long time forgiving me.

The point is, Lojos objected, *she wouldn't know.*

You believe in deceiving your lifemate? It was difficult enough to feel

Sarika in turmoil without his brothers pushing their ideas at him so relentlessly.

How is it deception? She won't know, so therefore won't ask. You've removed any threat to her, and she's calm and accepting of her fate rather than questioning every custom and ritual we have, Lojos said.

No. Mataias, always the thoughtful one, suddenly backed up Tomas. *It is deceiving, and eventually it would come out. Are you looking to have a puppet for a lifemate, Lojos?*

There was silence as Lojos considered his answer. *I am not like either of you. You know that. If my lifemate is a Carpathian woman raised in our traditions, I doubt there would be conflict. But Sarika isn't my lifemate. She is my little sister, and I can't bear the thought of her in danger. Or the way she becomes so fearful after examining one of her memories. Why should she suffer if we can prevent it? How would I be able to endure these things from my own lifemate without intervening?*

That was what came of sharing emotions with his brothers. They felt Sarika's fears. They felt her need to run. The way she vacillated between trust in him and fear of him. Tomas understood his brother. The compulsion to protect was overwhelming in all of them, but Lojos was the one who was weighed down by that need. He put himself in the most dangerous position during battles with their enemies to keep them off Mataias and Tomas. Tomas understood what was happening to Lojos, because it was happening to all three of them.

The triplets had stayed alive and sane, keeping to the code by weaving their spirits together and sharing every scrap of information possible. They knew the moment one was injured or in trouble simply because they'd lived too long and none of them truly believed they had a lifemate. Until the tarot cards had revealed that somewhere in the world, in this life cycle, they would be able to find her.

That revelation had been a shock, but more importantly, none of them truly believed. They'd seen the evidence of their fellow ancients finding lifemates, and it was still inconceivable that it would happen to one or all of them. Sarika was sacred. She made it real. She represented the hope they'd lost centuries earlier. It wasn't just his hope, his miracle; she was that for Lojos and Mataias as well.

Tomas had to acknowledge that his brothers could feel emotion through Sarika. They saw in faint color, more like memories of color, but it had changed their lives. It also was a heavy burden. Away from her, those colors and emotions would fade, making it more difficult to accept the gray nothingness of their existence.

That was when they would turn to battle, actively hunting for vampires, aggressively hunting them. They had made a pact with one another that they wouldn't go off alone when they realized they all felt a rush when they took on the undead. So far, all three had kept their word.

Tomas' intention was to remain with his brothers throughout their journeys to find their lifemates. That meant Sarika would be traveling with him. She couldn't be aboveground in unfamiliar and dangerous territory while he was sleeping the rejuvenating sleep of his kind.

They hunted Justice. Tracking him was extremely difficult, and Gustov and his followers weren't the first vampires to be thrown in their path. Now it was imperative to find this weapon Gustov had told him about. They had to get to it before Justice and find a way to destroy it for good. It couldn't be allowed to exist on earth because sooner or later the enemy would find a way to acquire it and use it against their people.

Tomas turned his attention to Sarika. She had taken that first piece from Mitro. He had been so caught up in his vicious, brutal behavior that she had been able to steal the piece from him. Tomas tried more than once to replay the details back from his memory, first to identify the features of the two women who had been with Sarika, and second to see where she had secreted the piece of weapon.

The women's faces were hidden from him, always in the shadows. That was strange. He couldn't identify them, and he should have been able to. He had excellent vision in the dark. He knew what Mitro was forcing the one woman to do to him, all the while torturing her. But she held out so Sarika would be able to take the weapon from him. It was very courageous in the face of the brutality he knew Mitro had done to women over the centuries. It was also odd that he couldn't see her. He could only see Sarika clearly.

He knew his brothers struggled to find details, especially after Sarika noted that there were three families with royal bloodlines. Solange's lineage was considered the top of the royal bloodlines. Luiz's family and then Jubal's were both branches of royal blood. As far as anyone knew, Solange, Luiz and Jubal had been the last of their kind. Others might have a small percentage of their bloodlines, but no one else alive had that pure blood that gifted them with speed, agility and cunning.

Jubal had two sisters. They were fast and more than capable, just as Solange's cousins were, but it wasn't the same. Jubal had a different father from his sisters, although they had not been told that until their mother tried to kill Jubal. Tomas turned that information over and over in his mind.

He knew Sarika was concerned that they were all missing the larger picture. That a threat was developing, yet the Carpathians were not feeling it. If that were true, it would be another first for Tomas and his brothers to experience in centuries of battling the enemy. They were ancients and well tuned to the presence of evil in any form.

Are you certain Sarika is right? She's overwrought with everything that has gone on the last few days, Mataias said.

Tomas didn't think *overwrought* was a good word choice. He wouldn't describe his lifemate as being overwrought. She had a right to her feelings, even the panic attacks. There was more working here than met the eye. Sarika seemed to be the only one feeling those underlying currents, the threat to the women and children and therefore the ancients.

Tomas, listen to yourself, Lojos said. *This could be her imagination. She is fearful of your claim on her, and unpleasant memories of her past have surfaced.*

Unpleasant memories? he echoed. *You don't have to believe she is right, but it would be negligent to ignore the possibility.*

He was angry with his brother, an unfamiliar emotion. Lojos always countered each topic with an opposite point of view. He shouldn't be bothered by his brother's casual assessment of Sarika, but he was.

She is your lifemate, Luiz pointed out. *She is the one who guarded your soul for centuries. She gave you back life. She is giving that same hope and life to your brothers. And she is extraordinary. All the traits you most admire, Sarika has in abundance. She has every reason for panic attacks. Unlike your brother, I believe there is something evil here, and it is orchestrating a strike against our women.*

There was comfort that he wasn't alone in that belief. Sarika had calmed and was still pacing, but she seemed to have managed to overcome the fears she had been dealing with. That allowed Tomas to breathe easier. He hadn't realized how difficult adjusting to emotions would be. Normally, he would have shared that information with his brothers, but he was thinking about Luiz's assessment of the situation.

Luiz was jaguar. He was from the same line as Sarika. Truthfully, no one thought of Luiz as jaguar, and they hadn't for some time. He was fully Carpathian and from one of the most powerful families. He exuded power. No one who came near him would think him anything but one of the most powerful of ancients. But unlike the other ancients, he felt uneasy, just as Sarika did. Tomas felt that same dread *through* Sarika. It wasn't his own warning system; it was hers. And now Luiz's.

Did you ask Dominic if Solange was feeling the same uneasiness? Tomas asked Luiz.

He said she was, but they both are putting it down to her nervousness around large groups of people. Solange doesn't normally interact with more than one or two people, and she has to know them very well to be comfortable.

Tomas turned that information over in his mind, pondering it, wondering what it meant. Luiz and Solange and Sarika. *What of Jubal?*

Jubal was always a question mark in Tomas' mind. He wasn't Carpathian, yet he knew every aspect of Carpathian life. He knew the language. He knew the prince. He fought alongside the Carpathians against any and all enemies. He was fiercely jaguar, protecting Jasmine and Sandrine. He knew the ways of the jaguar people, yet he had come into his own quite late. His mother had tried to murder him because he was a jaguar male. And he was human. He'd grown up in that world and was equally at ease there as he was anywhere. Tomas liked him. How could he not? He respected him and knew Jubal was the kind of man to always have his back in a fight.

Jubal keeps his own counsel, Luiz said.

Can you read him? Tomas asked, suddenly curious. Jubal seemed to have some kind of built-in protection that prevented even an in-depth scan from reading him. Tomas had no doubt he could push past the shields, but it wouldn't be easy and might cause harm if Jubal fought it.

The prince himself aided Jubal in protecting himself.

Tomas and his brothers traveled the world. Luiz mostly stayed in the rainforest, away from others. How did he get the information he always seemed to have?

I have several brothers. They never mind their own business. Don't say I didn't warn you when they come around asking what appear to be innocent questions but aren't.

Tomas found it interesting that Sarika was correct in that Luiz had a sense of humor; he just didn't acknowledge it. That had to be the way of the Carpathian ancients. He had noticed when his brothers weren't sharing Sarika's emotions, they had a touch of humor in them, but it was suppressed and deep. Hidden from them.

The brothers had spent a great deal of time deliberately ensuring they would remember as much as possible. They explored the idea of color, trying to reach back into their memories to find various colors and what they appeared to be like.

Having had colors restored to him, Tomas could testify that they'd had it all wrong. The dull, lifeless grayish colors they had tried to remember were nothing like the real thing. Especially in the rainforest.

He had spent most of his life in various jungles, and never once did he notice the vibrant shades of green, so many, some subtle, some vivid, but all in amazing shades.

Then there was simply the bark on the trees. Every color of brown, black and ash mixed with rich caramels and soft tans. Who knew there were so many shades of color that made up the trunks of trees? And that was without even counting the flowers winding their way up the trunks, or the tree frogs, lizards and snakes. That didn't even count the birds with their brilliant colors. Sarika had given that to him. He was able to share it with his brothers. Real, bold, larger-than-life colors.

He didn't want to admit that he often had to mute the colors because they were too much for him after centuries without, but there were moments he would just stare in awe, taking the jungle in for its unrivaled beauty.

The sounds of the night were soothing to him. Music played through the trees brought by the slight breeze that was always in the canopy but often didn't reach the forest floor. Bats dipped and wheeled, performing an aerial ballet while catching insects. Fruit bats swooped down on the night-blooming dragon fruit, epiphytic cacti, plants that used other structures for support rather than growing in the soil. The bats loved the fruit and descended on the plant in record numbers when the fruit was ripe.

He wanted Sarika to feel the magic of the night, view it the way he did. He wanted her to see the beauty that was there and feel peace and serenity in the familiar sounds and colors of the night. If she could view that time as he did, she wouldn't miss the day so much.

Tomas watched as she sighed and leaned over the rail to look down at what appeared to be steps of fungus leading up to the tree house. She rubbed at her temples, and he immediately caught the beginnings of the nagging headache that wouldn't quite leave her alone. He could go to her and take it away, but he sensed she wasn't quite ready to talk to him about the very important things they needed to discuss.

He had never thought much about the human ritual of bathing. Of soaking in a hot tub. As a Carpathian, there was never a need for it. But if there was one thing he knew for certain Sarika enjoyed, it was her bath. She took one every night. He was pretty sure she often took one in the morning as well. The more he considered taking part in her ritual, the more he liked the idea of it.

Tomas had always been the leader in accepting new ideas. He was a conservationist. An environmentalist. He wanted to preserve the animals and their habitats for future generations. He believed that there were many lifesaving and disease-altering plants in the rainforest as yet to be discovered.

So he was going to learn every ritual his woman enjoyed, and he'd do his best to make it even more enjoyable. He filled the deep tub with hot water and laid out the products Sarika liked to use. The flames on the candles he set around the room flickered and jumped, and fragrance filled the room.

He found the thick bath towels folded neatly on a shelf. He studied them, ensuring he would know how to manufacture them for his lifemate each time she wanted to take a bath. He hoped they would establish their own ritual.

"Sarika." He walked out onto the porch and held out his hand to her. "I've run your bath."

Her face lit up. That alone was worth the time he'd spent deciding her bathing ritual would be a good idea to share. She slipped her hand into his, and his heart clenched. It was such a simple gesture. One he'd never considered. Like most ancients, he'd observed a multitude of relationships down through the ages, but he didn't understand until that moment why that simple connection was so important.

Tomas drew her against his side, her smaller hand in his, the feeling of intimacy nearly overwhelming. He liked being with her. No matter the circumstance, when they were together, a sense of peace stole over him. Not just peace, belonging.

"I know you aren't aware of it, Sarika, but you've given me so much already." He led her into the dim bathroom, lit only by the flames of the candles.

She looked around her and then tilted her face up to his. "Thank you, this was so thoughtful of you. I use the bathtub to relax. Sometimes my mind is very chaotic, trying to piece together puzzles, and I have to shut it down. This is the only way I've found to do it."

He found himself smiling down at her as he reached for the hem of her shirt. "Let me consider other ways that might help you relax. In the meantime, I'd like to wash your hair and give you a massage. It will be a first for me. You've given me quite a few already, but this is important to me."

She let him pull her shirt over her head. Next, she kicked off her shoes and dropped her hands to the cargo pants she was wearing.

"Let me." He nudged her hands aside gently and found the waistband of the cargo pants.

"You want to undress me?"

It wasn't exactly a protest, but there was trepidation in her voice.

"Yes. I would like that privilege. I want to savor every single thing about your bath ritual and share it with you. If this is something you love, we will need to incorporate it into our daily life. Just preparing the room and bath for you gave me tremendous and unexpected pleasure. Undressing you would be a gift."

"But you can take off clothes with just a thought, can't you?"

"Yes, but I am discovering that your ways have value. This is one of those times when I believe it is important for me to experience every aspect of this ritual, including taking your clothes off. It is a powerful aphrodisiac even thinking about it, let alone doing it." He made the confession sincerely, hoping she understood she was safe with him. That this meant a great deal to him.

She studied him from under her lashes, her expression thoughtful, and then she nodded slowly. He bent his head to brush a kiss along her temple before he pushed the cargo pants over her hips. His fingers trailed over her bare skin, lingering. Taking her into his mind, absorbing the way all that soft skin felt under his palm, the pads of his fingers, he knew he would never forget this first time.

He felt the small tremor that went through her as he removed her bra. "You're safe with me, Sarika. I'm not going to push you any faster than you want to go."

He led her to the tub and helped her step in. The water was deep and steaming. Because the room was lit with candles, the surface took on a glow, but beneath that layer, there was a purple effect, much like the color of midnight.

Sarika made a small sound of content. "This is heaven."

He picked up the handheld sprayer, checked the temperature of the water and instructed her to lie back against the wall of the tub. He thoroughly rinsed her hair before pouring a small amount of the shampoo into his hands so he could massage it into her hair.

Tomas allowed himself to read her thoughts. She was relaxed, enjoying herself, eyes closed and hopeful he would massage her scalp. He did so, taking his time, tuning to her every reaction.

"I love this, Tomas, thank you." She murmured it with her head back, eyes closed, and a feeling of peace stole into the room. "I try not to be afraid of us, but that fear creeps in. I tell myself I've made up my mind to be your lifemate, and then something happens, and I want to run. I don't like that trait in myself, but I can't seem to stop the behavior."

His fingers were strong, massaging her scalp, producing the sensations his lifemate needed. "You have to be kinder to yourself, Sarika." He liked that she felt comfortable enough to tell him how she was feeling. "You're putting too high a demand on yourself. You expect to learn our ways and accept the way we exchange blood without having the time to process. I think you're amazing." He poured his genuine admiration into her mind.

"Do you intend to do another blood exchange with me?"

"I do." He was truthful with her. She was his lifemate, and one never deceived one's lifemate. "It takes three blood exchanges to bring you fully into our world. If you have two and we are attacked and you're hurt, I would be able to save you by giving you the third exchange."

She was silent while she contemplated what he said. "I think we are going to be attacked, Tomas. I know none of you feel the threat the way I do, and I don't blame you for not believing me, but I know in my gut I'm right."

"I've never said I don't believe you. I am in your mind, *sivamet*. I can see this worry and feel the growing dread in you. I have searched your mind to find the source of your fears and cannot find it. Have you discovered who or what is going to attack us?"

She kept her eyes closed, enjoying the feel of the warm water as he rinsed her hair. "They will attack the women, not any of you. Or at least, that's my first guess."

Tomas' gut tightened. He felt that the threat to his lifemate was very real. He not only believed her that they would be attacked, but after being in her mind, his warning radar had gone off with equal strength.

"How would that be possible if we are always with you?" Tomas wanted to hear her theory. He knew she had one. She had an intelligent mind. He'd read every letter she wrote to him, and even as a child she had grasped a problem and come up with not only one solution but several. She would have considered how the enemy might try to get to the women and children.

"I've given it quite a bit of thought," she admitted. "If they are going to strike, they must realize they would have to kill all of us in one fast blow. If they missed, the Carpathian males would be on them, and they wouldn't stand a chance."

Tomas couldn't conceive how the enemy would be able to get to the women and children. It just didn't seem possible. "Dominic and Solange's home is safeguarded," he pointed out. "With the threat and all the women gathered in one place, all Carpathian ancients will add to the safeguards. There would be no possibility of getting through those protections."

"I disagree, Tomas. You're very used to being so powerful that no one ever really challenges you. It doesn't always have to be a big thing that is the downfall of the strong. It can be so small one can't see it."

She was making sense when he didn't want her to. He wanted to believe that with so many ancients close by, nothing could ever harm their women—in particular, his lifemate. A part of him wanted to catch her up in his arms and vanish from the forest until all threats had passed.

"You are very sure, Sarika. With each passing minute, you seem to get even more certain." He made it a statement, not an accusation. She was coming back to herself, that courageous woman who had the self-confidence to face down a jaguar who was both angry and hurt.

"I think I was born at least once before, centuries ago, and it didn't end well for me."

"I agree," he validated, hearing the note of doubt in her voice. She didn't doubt she was right; she doubted he would believe her. "I looked at your memories and saw you. I recognized you. After witnessing Mitro's reprehensible behavior, you have every reason to fear Carpathians."

"If I can be reborn over and over, carrying your soul with me, wouldn't it stand to reason that some of our greatest enemies could be as well?"

His hands stilled in her hair. He had been brushing it out, but he stopped, and Sarika turned her head to look up at him.

"I have never thought in terms of our enemies being reborn. We hunt vampires. When they are destroyed, they do not return."

"What if they did? What if they were in the underworld and somehow they were able to return?"

Tomas couldn't conceive of such a thing. "How could we live for centuries and not notice such a phenomenon? If I was able to defeat a vampire and he reappeared, even a century later, I would recognize him." He shook his head. "That goes against the rules of our world."

"Maybe, but over the centuries, has every rule remained exactly the same?"

Tomas had always admired the young girl and then, when she was a little older, the young woman who wrote to him and asked him interesting and thoughtful questions. He had learned she thought outside the norm. In taking the time to examine her questions and ideas, he found it had always expanded his way of thinking.

"Now that you ask that question, no, the rules have changed over the centuries. In the beginning, no vampire would associate with other vampires. Their egos wouldn't allow it. They didn't want to share the blood of any of their victims. There were all sorts of reasons why vampires didn't form coalitions."

She reached out a hand for a towel, stood and wrapped it around her. "But that changed?"

Tomas nodded. "Over time, vampires began to collect the newer ones and use them as pawns. They would sacrifice them in battle. The master vampire would recruit lesser vampires that had managed to stay alive and have them be their line of defense after the pawns."

"Like an army."

"Yes, like an army. A lone hunter would find himself facing multiple vampires, not just one. They were often very skilled in battle." Tomas kept his voice very matter-of-fact. Sarika was puzzling things out. She had a mind that once started on a path would continue working until it came up with a conclusion. He had the feeling that whatever conclusion she came up with would give them the direction they needed to prevent a massacre.

Sarika dressed in a racerback tee and thin capri pants. Tomas found himself enjoying the sight of her feminine form and the graceful way she moved, almost like a dancer. He had observed thousands of women over the years, and not a single one had captured his interest, certainly not as a male interested in a female.

Everything was entirely different with Sarika. He was aware of every movement she made. Every expression that crossed her face. The way her hair fell in a riot of curls and coils around her face and down her back. When she gestured or moved her hands, for him it seemed as if she were weaving magical spells, mesmerizing him. Her voice was beautiful, a soft, low melody that played over his nerve endings, setting them on fire.

He could hear her heartbeat calling to him. At times, their hearts beat in the same rhythm. And there was her blood. The taste of her was always in his mouth. In his mind. It was unforgettable and addicting.

"Tomas, you have to stop looking at me that way." There was a trace of amusement in her voice. She sent him a look, her green eyes holding that same humor, but there was a trace of desire. A hint of need. Of hunger.

"I was thinking how beautiful you are. And remembering the taste of your blood."

Her fingers stroked over the pulse in her neck where he'd left his first mark on her. The touch was gentle, almost reverent. "I know. I was thinking the same thing. It's kind of scary to me how often I've thought about the way you taste when I wasn't aware of exchanging blood with you. I woke up with the taste of you in my mouth."

Tomas found it very sexy that she would admit it to him that she thought about their blood exchange, and she felt she was as addicted as he. He had never thought in terms of sexy. He never had the experience of just thinking of or looking at a woman turning his body to fire.

He liked the fact that she was courageous. She didn't think she was because she had panic attacks, but he found her astonishingly brave. That not only made him proud of her, but he found her courage sexy as well.

He gave her a faint grin. "Can't stop looking at you this way. I've never, in my life, found a woman sexy until you. I like looking at you. To a man who had no feelings or emotions, when I look at you and you give me a slow, burning heat, or a rush of flames through my veins, I know it would be impossible to ever stop."

A blush stole up her neck into her face. That dusting of freckles stood out against the soft rose color. "Weirdly, I was never attracted to any of the men I was around. I traveled quite a bit, and mostly, the groups I went with were all men. I can't remember a single time I found any of them physically attractive."

He gave her an old-fashioned bow. One that was courtly and showed respect. "I believe we were created for each other. Every man wants purpose. I thought it would always be my duty to our people as a hunter. But since meeting you, I realize my purpose on this earth was to be your man."

She pressed her hand over her heart. "One would think you were very experienced in the art of seducing a woman. Everything you say makes me want to stay with you."

"Don't sound as if that's a bad thing. I swear to you, I'll make you happy you chose me."

"The strange thing is I feel like I've known you all my life, that we're close and that I can totally trust you, but the truth is we've only known each other a couple of days."

Tomas didn't correct her language. The Carpathian people would use the term *risings* for the passage of time. "You have known me all of your life. T. Smolnycki Sr. was me. I just changed from father to son when it became clear that my findings were being viewed as academic, and I began to make a name. You wrote to me when you were just a very little girl."

"That seems so strange."

"Carpathians do not keep anything that would identify age. No photos, no letters, nothing that would allow anyone to think they lived longer than a normal human. I have every single letter you sent me. I keep them in a cave deep beneath the earth, not yet discovered by humans. Those letters were sacred to me, and I did not want to give them up." He gave her another faint grin. "That is kind of silly when I could quote each letter word for word. I carry them here." He put his hand over his heart.

That meant something to her; he could see it on her face. She walked past him, her fingers brushing his face. He followed her to the hammock in the bedroom. "When you say things like that to me, I don't know what to do with you."

"Fall in love with me." He said it before he could censor the words. There was no taking them back, no hiding the longing that weighed down every word.

She stood beside the hammock, fingers of one hand tangled in the weave, and studied his face. "I think it would be very easy to fall in love with you, Tomas. You seem to know when to say the things I need to hear. You don't push me the way the others are urging you to do. You take care with me when I'm falling apart. Those are all the things that sneak up on a woman and capture her heart. You see me. You seem to see what I need. I can feel there is urgency in this situation. The others know you have to leave here soon and hunt the enemy threatening to destroy your prince, but you refused to listen to them in regard to me."

Her eyes met his steadily. "I felt as if you stood up for me, even when they were deliberately trying to make you feel as if you weren't taking care of me."

Tomas could see his decisions had meant a great deal to her. "We'll sort it all out between us," he assured her. "We don't need the others to interfere, although they will continue to do their best to try." He stepped closer to her, one hand tucking stray curls behind her ear. "You know why, don't you? Lojos and Mataias feel the same driving need to protect you and keep you from harm. Like Luiz, they just feel they should put you somewhere safe and ensure nothing harmful can get near you. They actually are able to feel through you. That's the gift you've given them. You are their sister, and they would lay down their lives for you."

There was shyness in her eyes when she looked up at him, turning his heart over. Her expression was soft and open. Her mind was open to him. "I'm aware they do so out of affection, even when they are not," she confirmed.

CHAPTER 17

Sarika collapsed back onto the hammock, her legs shaking too much to hold her up. Tomas was the most attractive man she'd ever met. Everything about him appealed to her. She couldn't help feeling nervous. He had a way of looking at her as if he might devour her entirely. The saddest part of that was she didn't think she'd mind.

Sometimes she fixated on his mouth. She had never thought a man's mouth could be sensual, but his was. And then he had those eyes. Sometimes he looked more predator than human. She didn't want to dwell too much on that, or why she wasn't as bothered as she should be at the thought of Tomas taking her blood.

Tomas waved his hand and his shoes were gone. He floated to the hammock and lay down, drawing her beside him. "Nothing is going to happen that you don't want. We have time, Sarika," he assured her to allay any fears that he might ask for more than she was willing to give. "If you prefer not to know when the actual exchange is being made, I'll make certain you don't feel anything. If you're curious, we take it very slow, and I'll help you with anything that's difficult."

She curled into his side, grateful he didn't try to kiss her. She needed a little more time to adjust to her decision. It was strange to be at war with herself. Her head screamed warnings at her, but her body and heart said just the opposite. Tomas seemed to understand, and he didn't push her, just let her cuddle into the rock that was his body. He put one arm around her waist, tucking her as close as possible.

"I know you looked into my memories several times in an effort to find where I hid the piece of weapon I took from Mitro. Do you have any ideas?"

"You don't remember at all?"

"I died right after. Since you found that memory, I've tried to revisit it, although when I try without you being close in my mind, I can't do it. I think that time was so traumatizing that my mind rejects any recollection of it. In any case, I have no memory of where I could have hidden the piece of metal."

Sarika did what she always did when she was uncomfortable. Her hand crept up to wrap around the familiar jaguar head on her necklace. She'd been using the amulet to soothe herself since she was a small child. Sometimes she thought she could picture her mother's face, when she didn't have a single memory of her. Or photo of her. Even as a toddler, when she'd wrapped her fingers around the pendant, she felt her mother close when she needed her.

"Woman magic," Tomas murmured, reading her thoughts, letting her know he was still close in her mind. "Over centuries of living, I've witnessed the power women have when they get together and combine their gifts and strengths. When I accessed your memories, in truth, Sarika, I had never seen such power in three women as I did then. I felt it, and it was centuries past. I couldn't even see the other two women clearly, their faces were hidden in the shadows, and I realized it was the combination of the three of you shielding one another so others could not see the depravity or vileness Mitro perpetuated on you."

"I have dreamt of it, but those nightmares never seemed real to me," she admitted, pleased that an ancient as formidable as Tomas would acknowledge the power of her and her friends. She had found that the more she traveled the world, the less a woman was acknowledged as intelligent and important.

"Unfortunately, now we both know how real they are. I knew Mitro as well as his lifemate, Arabejila. Mitro destroyed so many lives. Dax and Arabejila would catch up to him, there would be a terrible battle, and then Mitro would slip away. It was one of the worst times in our history. Every hunter tried to find him, to destroy him, but no one ever got close, other than Dax. He felt responsible for the carnage Mitro left behind everywhere he went."

"Dax was able to find him through Arabejila," Sarika guessed.

"She was unclaimed, but the bond was still there, and she could track him when no one else could," Tomas said. "The bond between lifemates has always been unbreakable. It was shocking that Mitro didn't claim her when he knew she was his. He killed her mother, but he couldn't kill her. Down through the centuries, he tried more than once, but the bond held. He could not defeat her."

"How terrible for her." Sarika felt such compassion for the woman she could feel tears burning behind her eyes. She couldn't imagine Tomas attempting to kill her, let alone murdering hundreds of innocent men, women and children. Arabejila must have lived her life in a kind of hell.

"Both Dax and Arabejila blamed themselves for every death, every massacre. I know Dax is unable to integrate back into our society. He stays here in the rainforest unless he feels Riley, who was human, needs outside company. He does not use the illusion of a dragon, nor did he recruit a dragon as many of us did. In the volcano, there was an old one who believed he was the last of his kind. He had resolved to stay there, once more becoming part of the earth."

Sarika couldn't help the little thrill that ran through her. "I always loved every mythical tale of dragons. It didn't matter to me whether I believed them to be real, and there was some slight evidence they may have been, at least I clung to that belief because I wanted them to be."

She made the confession with a small self-effacing smile. "Are you saying this Dax ran into the real thing in that volcano?"

"He did. I'll give you a ride on Kinta, my dragon companion, this next rising. Once you're fully Carpathian, you will find the right dragon to suit you."

"Tell me more about Dax and his dragon," Sarika urged.

"The old one is most likely the oldest dragon on earth. There are several, but he appears to date far back, further than we do. He was becoming part of the volcano when Dax awakened him. There was a battle for supremacy, the dragon determined to destroy Dax, but in the end, their souls merged."

She turned into him, rubbing her face on his shoulder, needing the contact. "If Dax's soul is merged with a dragon, what does that do to Riley? Isn't her soul merged with Dax's?"

"You always manage to ask the hard questions. I didn't give that a thought. Riley and Dax seem happy together. I know that, for her, he pushes himself to take her into the world for short periods of time, but it is difficult, especially because of the old dragon."

"Does Riley know it is difficult for him to leave the rainforest?" Sarika was curious. What did lifemates do when one wasn't as happy as their vows proclaimed they would be?

"Of course she knows. You're already tuning yourself to me, and we haven't completed the ritual. We don't keep anything from our lifemates. Riley knows when things are difficult for Dax, and she never stays long when they are away from home."

"Why doesn't she just go visiting her friends by herself?" Sarika tried not to make that sound like a challenge. Women were independent and quite capable of visiting friends and family by themselves. She couldn't imagine having to wait for Tomas to give her permission to go where she wanted to go.

Tomas stroked a long caress over her hair. His fingers settled into the thick strands, and he did what he often did, began a slow massage.

Sarika found that was one of her favorite things about Tomas. He knew when she was tense. He didn't spend time trying to talk her out of her anxiety. He didn't arbitrarily remove the knots and tightness from her body using his ability as a Carpathian. Instead, he eased as much tension from her as possible with his own two hands. Physically. And it felt good. Not just mildly good; she could curl into him and purr like a cat. That was how good it felt.

"It is difficult to be away from one's lifemate," Tomas revealed. "The bond is soul to soul. I am not certain how to explain it in your language. The only Carpathian I know that is able to leave his woman behind for any length of time is Zacarias. Zacarias and Marguarita have a very unique bond."

She was fascinated. The sounds of the night were all around them, flooding the tree house with music from the night. Her hearing was even more acute than it had been, and the various creatures calling back and forth added to the beauty surrounding her.

"Tell me about them," she encouraged. To her, it felt as though Tomas was giving her even more gifts, more adventures. It was surreal lying on the hammock tucked in close to him, breathing him in with every inhale.

"Zacarias is one of our greatest hunters. He's legendary in our world. He has a shadow in him, a darkness, if you will. He saw to it that his brothers found their lifemates, and he left them with the intention of meeting the dawn. He was drawn to one of the family's estates. He'd been there months earlier when a vampire attacked. It killed Marguarita's father and tore out her throat because she refused to give up Zacarias' resting place. He wasn't even there at the time, but the family is completely loyal to the De La Cruz family. In any case, Zacarias saved Marguarita's life, but she isn't able to speak. Hearing one's lifemate's voice is what restores emotions and colors. In their case, that didn't happen immediately because Zacarias never heard her voice."

"How horribly tragic." She felt for the couple, particularly Marguarita. Unable to speak. Unable to voice to a very scary Carpathian what she might need.

"It worked itself out over time, but Zacarias carries a shadow in him. Without Marguarita close, colors and emotions are lost to him. He becomes the relentless hunter. He insists that his lifemate is stashed somewhere safe. I know his father used to take his mother along when he was hunting. If he had that same shadow, it would make sense."

"But Zacarias doesn't take his lifemate."

"No, he won't risk her. She once told Riordan's lifemate that she knew Zacarias was safer hunting without emotion. She's right. When I'm in the rainforest without you close, I shut down all ability to feel. If I were battling a vampire, I wouldn't want him to even know about you. The risk would be too great."

"But you intend to leave here." Sarika finally got to the subject she was very afraid of. Strangely, leaving the rainforest felt more difficult to her than accepting that she would become Carpathian. She wanted to ensure that her jaguar was safe, the way Solange's had been. She intended to talk to hers and explain every step of the way. If it became apparent that she would lose that well of feminine magic she attributed to her jaguar birth, she wouldn't go through with the decision to become Carpathian.

"Yes, we can't stay. I promise to bring you back as soon as the situation with Justice is resolved."

There was that name again. Justice. He was the reason the Carpathians were on edge. He was the person they believed was planning to kill the prince and destroy the Carpathian people. He wasn't vampire, but he was *more*. She knew he had escaped the underworld after being held there for centuries. He was feared by those above- and belowground. The strange thing was, she could never actually catch a glimpse of him in any of their minds. As if he were a phantom they all chased.

"You don't think Justice is vampire, yet he somehow is able to get vampires to do his bidding?" She caught glimpses of the battle with Gustov and Tomas' conclusions.

"If Justice has turned vampire, there would be the kind of brutality that you saw with Mitro."

"But Mitro was still Carpathian, not vampire, during the time he was committing such atrocities." Sarika struggled to understand. She also realized the conversation was making Tomas increasingly uncomfortable. Was he hiding something important from her? He had been careful to tell her the strict truth and answer any question she'd asked. It occurred to her she hadn't asked the right questions.

"He had not turned vampire, although many said he was acting like a vampire."

She listened carefully to his neutral tone. He wasn't giving anything away. "But he wasn't yet vampire." The jaguar amulet grew warm against her skin. Her hand crept up to cover it, to hold it against her. "What is it that you're not telling me, Tomas? I know you're holding something very important back from me."

His arm tightened around her, an involuntary movement, as if he thought she might run from him when he revealed the important detail he had kept hidden.

"A Carpathian leads a very long life. It isn't true that we can't be killed. We can. It is just extremely difficult. Most hunters who do not find their lifemates seek the dawn rather than risk turning vampire. It is an accepted practice."

"By seeking the dawn, you mean they stay out in the sun, and that kills them," she clarified. She tried not to think of those honorable hunters living centuries and then choosing such a horrific death to ensure they kept that honor. It hurt.

The amulet pulsed in her palm, grew hotter as if trying to protect her from the overwhelming wave of empathy she experienced. She didn't know any of the men who had faced that decision, but the grief overpowering her made it seem very personal. It took her a few moments to realize it wasn't just her empathy; she was feeling Tomas' grief. He didn't seem to be aware he felt so deeply about those lost brethren.

A part of her acknowledged that she felt even more for Tomas, knowing he was grief-stricken losing so many of his friends.

"Yes, that is how they die," Tomas acknowledged. "Not all of us believed that was the right thing to do if we truly had a lifemate. It was our duty to find our lifemate even if she was reborn several times throughout the centuries. That meant finding ways to stay alive and keep our honor no matter how difficult. A number of us chose to continue long past the time we should have ended our lives."

Sarika listened to every nuance of his voice. He sounded matter-of-fact. He always spoke in a low, velvety tone. The way he talked appealed to her. Everything about Tomas appealed to her. The reluctance to continue was there, but she felt she knew him far better than either of them realized. He would tell her the things he would prefer she didn't know, and he would do so honestly. It was something that was desperately important to her in their relationship. She could handle bad news as long as her partner shared with her and allowed her the necessary time to process. She wanted to be heard in their relationship. And respected. Tomas, despite the advice from his brothers and Luiz, seemed to do both.

"Those of us who chose to remain found strange changes taking place. Where before, we continually heard the whisper of temptation, voices insisting if we killed while feeding, we would feel something, a rush after centuries of nothing, those whispers ceased. Completely and utterly stopped. What was worse? Hearing the continual temptation, or the absolute silence that followed for centuries? We found ourselves living in a complete void."

Sarika deliberately used her ability to see into others to merge with Tomas, tuning her energy to his to allow her to feel what he had experienced for so many centuries—what his brothers and Luiz were still suffering. Most of the time when she connected with those close around her, she didn't do so deliberately. It just happened, usually when they were experiencing strong emotions. Or there was danger.

She didn't want her privacy invaded without consent, so she was as careful as she could be not to intrude on anyone else's privacy as a rule. This was so important, too important not to miss whatever it was that Tomas was feeling. He distanced himself so much, and she understood why he would. Emotions weren't helpful when battling a vampire. After centuries with no awareness of feeling, the intensity was overwhelming. Toning them down, or putting them aside altogether, was the intelligent thing to do.

"We noticed as we continued to hunt our enemies that our skills, reflexes and awareness became more and more acute. We could heal our wounds faster. We seemed to be evolving, although it was slow, and we didn't notice immediately. And then, little by little, we found that we could feel when in battle. It was a rush unlike anything we remembered. There was joy in battle. The longer the fight lasted, the longer that rush. The temptation, obviously, was to prolong the battle, draw it out so we could continue to experience emotion as long as possible. That rush was addicting, much, I'm certain, as it is for vampires when they kill while feeding."

She felt that emotion, that high, with him as he was recalling the various master vampires he had hunted and destroyed. After the centuries-long emptiness, that feeling was impossible to ignore. She caught glimpses of the discussions the triplets had over the best ways to stay safe as well as keep to their code of honor. She saw their struggles, felt them, that pull, the need of battle—and she understood.

"It would have been bad enough had it ended there, but we realized there were changes taking place in us as well when we destroyed our enemies. Before, we were aware we were sacrificing pieces of our soul, but we knew our lifemate could make it all right. The scarring the kills are leaving on us is different, and it appears to be permanent. What that means for our future, I don't know."

Tomas sighed and stroked another caress along the left side of her face. "I don't know what it means for us as a couple or for future generations. I tried to have a discussion with my brothers about the possibility of not claiming our lifemates because we didn't have a clear future, but the moment I heard you, I saw you, all good intentions went out the window."

She felt the conflict in him. The worry. The guilt. He had claimed her because the compulsion to do so was too strong to overcome. She could have told him it wasn't just a compulsion. It was centuries of conditioning. Of culture. Of believing in the Carpathian bond between a man and a woman. She was struggling to understand it and could testify how complex that bond really was. She wasn't Carpathian, but she was as caught in it as Tomas.

"I intended to reveal all of this before our third blood exchange, but I should have done so before making my claim."

Sarika didn't like the way he held himself so responsible for events he had little control over. In theory, it sounded good that he wanted to have a perfect code of honor, but that was never going to be reality for anyone. She was grateful. She could never live up to such perfection. She was anything but that.

"I'm happy with you the way you are, Tomas. I hope you see the real me. I have panic attacks at the worst possible moments. I charge into the fire when I see something is wrong and I want to fix it. I do a lot of things that may make you wish you had a different lifemate. And as much as I'm committed to this path, I don't want to risk my jaguar or my ability to help my people. I expect you to help me monitor those things when the time comes. If things go awry, I would want to talk over with you how we can fix things before we proceed."

Any other man, she doubted if she would trust, when he had the ability to compel her obedience and then hide from her what he'd done. She felt, in such a short time of using the intimate telepathic communication and the letters they had shared over the years, that she knew the heart of him.

"I see the real you, Sarika," he assured.

"Since we agree that we're going to continue forward, you might want to prepare me for what to expect. I caught glimpses of Solange after her third blood exchange, but not too much seemed to transpire. That doesn't fit with the shadows I see in your mind."

"My brothers, Luiz and the others will aid you, but it is painful. Your organs will be reshaped, and you must die as a human and be reborn as a Carpathian."

Sarika pressed her lips together to keep from blurting out her first response, which would have been *hell* no. "Put like that, it doesn't sound like much fun." She went for levity, because really, what could one say to that revelation? "And for your information, I look human, but I'm fully jaguar shifter. I have a jaguar and a legacy to protect." She was adamant, hoping he would listen to her. She needed him to hear her when she stated she wouldn't allow anything to happen to her jaguar side.

"I know of two people—one is Solange and her jaguar—who remained nearly the same. She is Carpathian in that she can go to ground, but she also can walk in the sun, and no Carpathian can do that. It's said her blood can extend our time in the early morning hours or allow us to rise an hour before sunset. Dominic said it is 'iffy' and can't be relied on."

"And the second one?"

"Her name is MaryAnn. She isn't jaguar; she's Lycan. When she was converted, she remained both. I believe you will as well. You have a gift, Sarika, one that I don't understand, but I know it's very powerful. I think that gift is a very integral part of who you are and can't be taken from you."

She liked that, mostly because she knew he meant it. If his belief in her was that strong, she wanted to believe as well. Her gift had always been a part of her. It had grown stronger as she got older, but she couldn't imagine not having it. When she was around other formidable women, that wonderful power in her magnified and spread, responding to feminine supremacy.

She knew the empowerment had little to do with gender. If she tried to use her gift for her own gain, it would fail every time, and there would most likely be repercussions falling back on her. While she knew her gift was potent enough to be a weapon, again, she couldn't use it for personal power or gain.

"When we make our second exchange, Sarika, it will only add to our need to be together. You are still aboveground, and if you wake before sunset, you will feel grief. Your mind will reach for mine, and if I don't respond, you will believe me to be deceased. That is your mind playing tricks on you. You'll have to be very strong. I will attempt to wake as early as possible, even if I cannot rise, so if you're in need, I will be able to communicate with you."

"We're going to do the second exchange tonight?" She tried to push down the trepidation, reminding herself she wanted this. She didn't want to give herself too much time to think about it. She needed to continue on the path of commitment.

He stroked another long caress down the back of her head. Her heart tripped. Stuttered. Even her stomach did a slow roll.

Sarika made up her mind. If she could at least control a small part of it, if she felt it was her decision as well as what was necessary, she knew she would do so much better. She took a deep breath and let it out. Another one for clarity and then she made her daring suggestion.

"I think you need to give me the full effect of Carpathian abilities, Tomas," she ventured, trying not to blush. Just making the suggestion made her feel not only empowered but sexy, something she'd never felt in her life.

His thumb traced her jaw gently. "What would that entail?"

"A real bed, not a hammock. Lots of my favorite candles. Wave your hand and do the clothes thing. I wanted to experience that the moment I heard about it. If we're going to do this, shouldn't we do it right?"

"I told you that you'd be safe with me. In a bed, with candles and without clothes, you aren't safe. There is no way, especially when we exchange blood, that things aren't going to get out of hand."

Sarika managed to look him in the eye, even if it was very brief. "I was rather hoping for the part where things get out of hand."

"I always accommodate my lady," Tomas said. "Show me what you like in the way of beds and candles and the room setup. Your wildest dreams."

Sarika hadn't thought in terms of a room being in her wildest dreams. The best she'd been able to do was dream of being with Tomas. *He* was her wildest dream. She tried to think of what the bedroom had been like. She loved candles, and she had pictured a room lit with many candles and a wide, very comfortable bed with four posters. She had always liked the way a bed looked with sturdy columns for posts. She shared that with him.

Tomas waved his hand, and instantly the bedroom was transformed. They were no longer lying together on the hammock. The dark blue sheets covering the bed were luxurious, woven of bamboo, cooling, perfect for the tropical setting. Sarika was very happy they were still in their clothes. She had asked for this. She wanted this, but she wasn't quite ready.

Dozens of flames flickered throughout the room, some lit up in sconces on the walls, while other candles were set in pillars around the room. Those flames cast shadows on the ceiling. Even the sconces lit the ceiling and didn't shine on the walls so that the room seemed to be huge, a dark, mysterious cavern with the bed as the focus.

Tomas turned her into his arms, his mouth on hers, gentle, coaxing a response rather than demanding one. Instantly, she felt feverish, burning everywhere, flames as hot as the candles, spreading through her body in a maelstrom of desire like she'd never known. His lips feathered lightly over hers, strayed toward her high cheekbones and then down to her chin, leaving a trail of fire wherever he ventured.

He took his time, a leisurely assault, but when he returned to her mouth, it was with more precise pressure. His tongue slid along the seam of her lips, and she instinctively parted them slightly so she felt the silken tip touch her like a hot brand.

Tomas cradled her cheek as he teased and nibbled, catching her lower lip between his teeth to tug and bite with exquisite gentleness. Everywhere he feathered those kisses, he left a burning flame behind.

Sarika caught at the nape of his neck and exerted enough pressure, urging him to kiss her again on her mouth. Her lips. A real kiss. She needed that from him. Tomas didn't disappoint; his mouth took hers in a long, passionate kiss that poured those same flames down her throat. She couldn't breathe. Couldn't find air. Her lungs felt raw and burning.

She tore her mouth from his and buried her face against his shoulder. The hot rush of his breath stirred tendrils of her hair as his thick chest rose and fell. He grasped the mass of hair that was suddenly loose from her braids, pulled her head back to expose her throat. Her heart stuttered and then began to pound as his lips burned a path, beginning at the hollow just beneath her left ear. Every nerve ending came alive as he traced the line of her vein with his tongue.

His fingers slid over the top of her shoulder, his thumb finding the wing of her collarbone, his palm exploring the curves of her body. It was only when he nuzzled the side of her throat right over her pounding pulse that she realized she didn't have a single stitch covering her body.

Sarika gasped, already on fire. Already anticipating. She hadn't been aware during the blood exchange, but her body remembered. He kissed her again, distracting her as his palm brushed the curve of her breast. Her nipple peaked, pushing against him. Just that slight touch sent heat waves rushing through her straight to her core. He stroked caresses with the backs of his fingers over her nipple, keeping her attention centered on the fire he created.

She lost her awareness of time. Of where they were. Of the fact that she was naked and moaning, exposing her throat to him when he once more licked over her pounding pulse. His mouth traveled from her throat to the tip of her breast. She found herself gasping, arching at the gentle tugs of his mouth. His tongue flicked her nipple and another moan escaped. She couldn't lie still, parting her legs involuntarily. He slid one thigh into that space, and that was when she realized he wasn't wearing clothes, either. She felt the rough hair sliding against the inside of her thigh, another brand marking her.

Sarika brought both hands to his head, her fingers sliding through his hair while he brushed those featherlight kisses on her inner wrists and elbows. His mouth wandered lower, finding the shallow depressions between her ribs, exploring every inch of her. Claiming every inch of her.

She was lost in the feel of the shadow of his beard scraping along her breasts and down her stomach to her navel. His fingers drifted down her body as his knee widened the angle between her thighs. She felt the stroke of his knuckles through her feminine curls before he parted her to caress her most sensitive button.

Sarika gasped as his finger slid gently into her slick heat. Her heart pounded out of control as pleasure burst through her. His mouth continued exploring, following his hands, kissing his way down her body until he was directly between her thighs. He gripped her hips, holding her still.

"You have to be ready for me, *sivamet*. I don't want to hurt you."

The room around Sarika blurred into mysterious shadows and flickering flames. There was nothing but sheer feeling. A kind of bliss, of rapture she had never experienced. She didn't attempt to hide her reaction to his demanding mouth and insistent hands. She heard herself give a low cry as waves of heat rushed through her.

Tomas gently pushed her thighs wider apart. The broad crown of his shaft nudged her slick entrance. "You look incredibly beautiful," he told her, one hand smoothing back the hair from her forehead.

"I feel incredibly beautiful," she admitted.

He increased the pressure, pushing relentlessly into her. She tried to relax for him as he continued in little starts and stops to get her body to accept his invasion. It hurt at first, and that faded to a burn as her silken tunnel allowed him deeper. She felt his heart beating deep inside her, and the sensation was so amazing she forgot to be scared.

Each time he moved, his hips surging forward, flames streaked through her. Then his mouth was on the curve of her breast, and she felt his teeth pierce her skin. She cried out as the bite of pain gave way to the most erotic, addictive sensation she could imagine.

Tomas shared the way she made him feel, the ecstasy, the pleasure beyond anything his centuries of existing had given him. Her slick, silken tunnel was tight, nearly strangling his shaft as her blood filled his mouth and spread through every organ, adding to the wild firestorm roaring through him.

His tongue slid over the twin holes he'd made in her skin, and he pressed his lips over the burning, throbbing mark. His body continued to move, his hips like a piston, burying him deep and withdrawing to create friction over her sensitive nerve endings.

Tomas used one hand, his fingernail growing to slide over the heavy muscles of his chest. A thin line of bright crimson beads appeared. His palm shaped the back of her head, and he gently guided her mouth to the temptation of his offering.

The memory of the addicting taste of him burst through her mind and added to the pleasure his body was producing in hers. She licked along those beads, savoring the taste that was hers alone. She wanted this. She wished she could take his blood without his help. It didn't matter, though; the pleasure wasn't any less as his blood filled her, and his body took hers higher than she ever thought possible.

Time slowed down. The shadows of the room took on layers of beauty. The candles flickered and crackled, the sudden drifting breeze allowing them to illuminate Tomas' face and the lines cut deep there with a mixture of love and lust. It was sheer beauty.

He gently stopped her from taking more of the perfect elixir. She had thought he was serious before, but now his body moved in hers in a wild rhythm that sent streaks of fire spreading to every part of her.

The pressure grew and grew, and then she felt her body bite down on his, dragging at him, milking him. The waves roared through her and, with her, Tomas.

He buried his face against her throat as the tension gradually left his body. He let out a long hiss of pleasure as he withdrew from her.

"I think this bed will be my favorite place," he informed her, rolling to the side to remove his weight and then fitting her body into the side of his.

She liked that he wanted her close. She felt drowsy and sated. That moment, when he brushed a kiss across her mouth, was as perfect as she could have imagined.

CHAPTER 18

Sarika woke uneasy. She'd had nightmares. The residue from her terrifying dreams carried over the moment she opened her eyes. Her first thought was for Tomas, and just as he'd warned her, her mind reached for him and found . . . nothing. Emptiness.

She sat up, clutching the sheet to her, her lungs burning for air. Cold chills crept down her spine. She couldn't stop the tremors. Grief welled up, so overwhelming her throat closed down. It was as if her body reacted to the absence of Tomas before her brain could catch up.

Wrapping her arms around her middle, she rocked herself back and forth in a self-soothing manner, trying to stop the chaos in her mind so she could think clearly. Not react. She was very grateful that Tomas had warned her what might happen. In all honesty, she hadn't believed she would have such a severe reaction. She was strong. She was logical. Just him telling her what to expect should have prepared her.

She continued to breathe as deeply as possible, counting in her head to stop the noise of false grief. It took a few minutes, but eventually, she was able to calm her brain enough to think much more clearly. That allowed her body to regain control.

Sarika forced herself to listen to the soothing sounds of the forest.

She inhaled the scent of the various flowers. Her world was slowly righting itself. Determinedly she performed her ritual, filling the bathtub while she made a cup of tea, although her stomach rebelled at the idea of actually drinking anything. Tomas had warned her about that as well. She sank into the soothing hot water, grateful for whatever Luiz did to give her such a luxury.

While she soaked in the hot water, she reached for her jaguar, sharing as much information as she'd learned. Her female was always thoughtful, taking her time before she responded. Over the years, Sarika was grateful for her guidance. Now she understood. Her jaguar, like her, had been reborn more than once over the centuries as they guarded Tomas' soul.

"I worry that when the conversion takes place, we will both be different. I don't want to chance anything happening to you," she murmured aloud to the jaguar.

We have always known you were going to be Carpathian. We just didn't know when.

The royal *we*. "You were aware of this all along?"

Of course. I remember every life cycle. And the waiting for our mate.

"Why didn't you tell me?"

You suppressed everything after the Carpathian killed all of our people. You didn't even allow yourself to remember the ones you saved, sending them deep beneath the earth into the tunnels. The knowledge of your lifemate was always there, but when you refused to see it, I knew your mind was protecting you for a reason. I watched over you.

Sarika knew her jaguar was very pragmatic but also extremely protective. If she believed Sarika wasn't able to handle information, she would keep the specifics locked away to protect her.

"You are certain if we go through the conversion, you will remain the same."

I will be more, as will you. Our gifts, already powerful, will be enhanced, but we will remain Sarika and Coh.

"You aren't afraid?"

We are very powerful together. Now her jaguar sounded as if she were speaking to a child. *There is no need for fear. Others should fear us.*

Sarika didn't want anyone to fear her, nor did she want to be afraid. "I am still getting panic attacks. It's humiliating."

Your lifemate does not think less of you. If anything, he respects you more. It has never mattered; when you have what you refer to as a panic attack, you do whatever needs to be done.

That much was true. She pushed past when she was panicking so she could get the job done, whatever it happened to be. She'd never noticed the admiration and respect Coh gave her in those moments. She'd been too busy holding it together.

"Thanks, Coh," she said, meaning it.

Sarika dressed carefully for the party. It wasn't just about trying to look as if she belonged with the other women; she still believed they would be attacked. She knew the Carpathian males believed they were too strong for such a thing to happen. Too many of them gathered together in one place. They would weave safeguards that would be impenetrable. She knew every single argument against such an attack. It would be suicide for any individual or group to try. But Sarika's warning alarms were blaring at her. She dressed in clothes that allowed her to go into combat if necessary or quickly shift. She wanted to be ready for anything.

Her hair was always a wild mess. She had naturally curly hair, and no matter how long she grew it or how heavy it was, it curled in thick coils and unruly spirals interspersed with waves. Most of the time, she braided it in an attempt to tame it. She found herself staring in the mirror, literally feeling Tomas' hands in her hair. He liked her hair. And he liked it wild.

She exposed the twin marks where Tomas had bitten her. She could feel him there, too, his mouth, his tongue, the pads of his fingers. She covered the mark with her palm, holding him to her, needing to feel him close. Today was going to be a very difficult day. She was in the minority when it came to worrying that there was a credible threat to all the women and children at the party. Tomas had made it clear that if the women were killed, the ancients would either suicide or turn vampire. It would be a coup beyond anything ever done in their history.

Sarika pressed a hand to her temple and reached out to Tomas. It was close to sunset, and she was certain he would hear her. *I am surer than ever that there is a plan in place to harm all the women and children. The longer I am awake, the more the dread is growing in me.* She willed him to believe her.

There was a long silence. At first, she wasn't certain she'd reached him, but then she felt him pouring into her mind. Filling her. Every lonely place. *Tomas.* The moment he was in her mind, she felt whole. Complete. She had always been alone, and she was used to it. She thought she preferred a solitary state, but now she had Tomas.

Not just Tomas, he corrected. *You inherited a family, such as it is.*

She loved the sound of his voice. The way it felt like a caress smoothing over the uncertainty in her mind. She heard the soft note of amusement, as if he found his brothers and Luiz humorous.

They do like to give their opinions, she said, allowing him to feel her laughter.

Just that fast, with Tomas touching her mind, she felt better. Lighter. The warning signals hadn't lessened, but she wasn't going to be alone facing the threat. Tomas would listen to her. That was one of the things she could count on with him. He heard her, and he paid attention to what she had to say.

You're very worried about the baby shower. Tomas made it a statement. *You absolutely believe the women and children will be attacked.*

She walked to the railing to watch the sun sink from the sky. The shadows in the forest turned several shades of purple and blended with darker shadows. A chill slid down her spine. It wasn't particularly cold, but she shivered nevertheless.

Yes. I feel it, Tomas. I know there is great danger here. It makes sense that your enemies would strike at the ancients through the women. Do you feel what I feel? That was her greatest hope—that Tomas wouldn't have to simply believe her and then try to convince the others; he would feel the growing threat looming over the day that should have been one of great joy.

Yes. There is no doubt that you have gifts, Sarika. In this case, we are all going to be the beneficiaries of those gifts. We have advance warning of the impending attack, and therefore, we can be ready.

Wouldn't it be better to cancel the baby shower? Sarika found herself gripping the verandah rail so tight her knuckles turned white. She knew the Carpathians wouldn't cancel. Individually, they were powerful. Together, that power would be beyond imagination. They would believe they were nearly invincible when together.

You know they will not do so. Dominic knows Solange has trouble with events such as this one. She wants to have a celebration for their child, and he is determined to give this to her.

The lifemate bond. She couldn't imagine that Solange ever asked for anything. If she asked Dominic for this, he would move heaven and earth to give it to her.

There will be many of us inside Dominic's home and more outside. Even if we're wrong about the intended targets, the hunters will be able to stop our enemies.

Sarika wanted to be reassured, but that growing dread continued to spread, casting ominous shadows in every direction. *Can you rise?*

Will come to you after I hunt this rising. Need to feed and take a look around. Touch base with Kinta, my dragon.

Her heart stuttered at the idea of meeting his dragon. *What does your dragon look like?*

Kinta looks as if he is made of stone at times, but his color is violet, so he blends with the nighttime shadows. He will be happy if you find a dragon you like to match his. You may be able to call one to you. Or if you allow me to make you one, I can do that as well.

I'm not certain how one can make a dragon, but if it is at all possible, I want a real one.

My brothers and I made dragons from stones for children in the States. It was necessary to fly them out of danger. They loved the dragons. We were able to place them as statues on the grounds of their home, and the children can awaken the dragons when they want to play with them. They are real now. The spirits of long-lost dragons moved into the stone dragons at the call and needs of the children. It was always the choice of the lost dragon, not ours. I don't know if every stone dragon we made has the spirit of a lost dragon dwelling in it, but those that do are very real.

Sarika pressed a hand to her chest, over her heart. *You have a way of making my dreams come true.*

There was a short silence. *That is the nicest thing you could say to me. I worry I'm bringing you into a nightmare world. I don't know what the future holds for me or how I will continue to evolve. I only know I want the world for you, the one in your dreams, not the nightmare life I may be offering you.*

I know you don't think I have a choice, Tomas. You bound us together in the way of your people, but that doesn't mean I don't have choices. I do. I made you my choice. Whatever happens in your world happens in mine, and I believe we're stronger together. I believe we will be able to face anything in our future as a couple.

I am grateful you feel that way, sivamet. *It is humbling to have your support when you haven't been given the time needed to process our world fully.*

I know things. I don't know how I do. I believe it is my jaguar. I believe in her wisdom. She has memories I closed myself off from, but her gifts, the incredible warning system as well as her ability to feel when something is right, have always been shared with me.

She wanted the reassurance that should anything affect her jaguar, they wouldn't proceed with the current plan of converting her. *What would we do if things go wrong with Coh?* She made certain her mind was open to any possible solutions he might make. *I try to plan for any contingency. This is huge for me. It is the only thing that would stop me from going through with becoming fully Carpathian.*

Sarika waited, trying not to hold her breath. Trying to give Tomas complete trust.

Solange's jaguar remained intact. I believe that yours will as well. If we can see there is a problem, we will stop what we're doing and wait to consult with our greatest healers. Luiz has much skill. It will be uncomfortable for us, and certainly the others will think it is an inconvenience when we must travel, but your safety and that of your jaguar must come first.

Tears were suddenly burning in her eyes, and Sarika was grateful no one was there to witness the tremendous relief that washed through her at Tomas' response. He was the right man for her. Steady and careful thinking. He seemed to truly put her needs first.

They had been connected mind to mind, and she caught glimpses of the problems—and there would be numerous ones—Tomas and his brothers would encounter if she wasn't able to go to ground during daylight hours. They would have to find a way to keep her safe while she remained aboveground and they were rejuvenating in the soil. Vampires would not be able to get to her, but they created puppets, humans that were no longer capable of thinking for themselves. They only served their masters. Those puppets ate human flesh.

A little shudder went through her body. She didn't think it would be a very pleasant way to go, eaten by a puppet of the vampires.

You are not going to be eaten by puppets.

There was definite male amusement not only in his voice but pouring through her mind. She had to admit, she liked the smooth sound. She could listen to his voice forever.

First of all, you are quite capable of defending yourself even from something as vile as a puppet.

Sarika really liked his belief in her. It was no wonder she found him attractive. He treated her with respect, and she needed that.

Thank you for believing I could defeat a flesh-eating puppet of the vampire, but I think I'd prefer to faint and let you take care of it. I'll put aside my badass status and try the fainting, fragile flower approach.

I see. You'll play that card whenever you see something you don't want to do?

Of course, kind of like asking the husband to take out the trash because it's so heavy, when in reality it's just smelly and not a good job to have to do.

His laughter played through her mind, lightening her spirit. Sarika stepped back from the rail. She didn't feel a threat to her. There were no jaguar males waiting to pounce on her should she leave the safety of Luiz's tree house. Not that she could. She frowned, trying to decide if she should be happy at Tomas' concern or annoyed. She chose to be happy.

Hurry to me, Tomas. This is going to be a long day. Right at this moment, everything is beautiful. The sky, the trees, the animals. All of it is astonishingly beautiful. I want to share the beauty with you before everything falls apart.

There was a short silence. Her stomach did a slow roll. He liked what she'd said to him. She wasn't the best at relationships. She was feeling her way, but she knew he was pleased, and that made her very happy. She tipped her head back to look up at the canopy, at the various leaves and branches gently swaying.

Family wasn't about perfection. They could have differences of opinion. They could argue and disagree, but they stood with one another. Luiz, Lojos and Mataias would stand with her because they considered her family. She'd come to Peru hoping for just such a connection. She'd nearly missed it because she had been so afraid of it.

She had vowed, before she'd made the journey to Peru, to be open to a relationship with Luiz, her cousin. She hadn't expected that she would meet the man she'd corresponded with for years, or that she would be introduced to several women who were or had been jaguar. She hadn't known she would be challenged to face her past, the scariest memories she'd always called nightmares. She hadn't known she would feel so *alive*.

The first thing Sarika noticed as she entered Dominic and Solange's home was the feel of it. The joy that spread through the rooms like wildfire. The sound of children laughing together and talking in conspiratorial whispers, running through the various rooms she couldn't see, their little feet making happy noises on the floor.

Growing up, I was never around children, she confessed to Tomas. *Listen to them. I love the way they laugh together. They don't walk anywhere, they run. It makes me feel happy just to hear them, and I haven't laid eyes on them yet.*

Tomas tightened his arm around her shoulders and leaned in to brush a kiss on top of her head. *I have not had emotions in centuries. I forgot what joy a child brings. You've given me back that gift. Thank you,* sivamet.

From the moment Tomas had risen, the night had taken on a different feel from when she'd first awakened with such dread. She'd spent time with Tomas—not much, but enough that he made her feel beautiful, intelligent and secure, giving her the confidence to face numerous strangers.

Sarika had always been a seemingly confident woman on the outside, able to hold her own in the many circumstances where she was surrounded by men dominating whatever field she was working in at the time. She knew she was intelligent and that her ideas were solid. Tomas had instilled that confidence in her when she was very, very young. She hadn't realized how much he'd shaped her life and her belief in herself. He'd been a major influence on her from that early age, making her feel important and that her ideas counted.

She hadn't realized until this evening just how often Tomas had given confidence to a young girl by simply acknowledging her ideas. He hadn't dismissed a child's rambling ideas even when she was far too young to know about habitats and what affected them long-term. He read every word she said and validated her concerns.

You will make an amazing father. He would. She was lucky that he would be her partner. She didn't know how to be a mother or wife, but she would try her best. And she felt better knowing she would have Tomas to rely on. He wasn't flashy or showy; he was steady and kind. He was thoughtful, considerate and deliberate. Sarika realized Tomas had all the qualities she sought in a man. She didn't need a peacock or a falcon; she needed quiet and reliable.

Thank you, Sarika. Tomas flooded her mind with caresses. She felt every single one and hugged them to her.

"Sarika. Tomas." Solange hurried across the expanse of the great room with its high cathedral ceilings to greet them.

Solange's home was underground, but it didn't feel that way at all. Trees and branches had become part of the walls and ceiling, looking decorative and bringing aboveground nature into the massive chambers that made up her home. Sarika could see the branches of the trees curving upward and dipping downward, making arboreal traveling easy should Solange be in jaguar form.

Sarika greeted Solange with a smile, a little shocked that the introverted woman was so welcoming.

Her jaguar is happy to see you, Tomas pointed out. *You resolved the issues between them, allowing them to talk things out. Solange is very grateful. You saved her cousin and niece, and then her baby, and put things right with her jaguar. I would say she considers you a true friend.*

Sarika didn't feel as if she'd really earned that friendship—she barely knew Solange—but she was willing to accept the offering. It meant quite a bit since Solange held herself apart from most others.

"I want you to meet my friends, Sarika." Solange indicated the three women seated across the room in a small grouping with Jasmine. She caught Sarika's hand and tugged until she followed the other woman.

Immediately, the four women looked up, greeting her with smiles. Jasmine jumped up and flung her arms around Sarika, startling her and everyone else.

"I'm so glad you came. Solange told me you saved her baby. She didn't say how, but I believe you can move mountains, so I'm sure she was right."

"Good evening to you, too," Sarika said. "I didn't really do all that, but it's nice Solange thinks I did."

"These are our friends." Jasmine waved toward the three women she was seated with. "Adele, Lucy, Tara, meet Sarika. She's Luiz's cousin. And she faced down the jaguar males when they came for Sandrine and me. We've known these three since we were children. Tara is married to Finn. He's around here somewhere." She looked around the room a little helplessly and then turned back with enthusiasm.

"So nice to meet you," Tara said. "I had no idea Luiz had a cousin."

"He must be thrilled," Lucy added.

Sarika laughed. "I don't know how thrilled he is. He likes obedience. So far, I've been an utter disaster for him."

"Our daughter, Bianca, is running around with Sandrine. They're the best of friends. Bianca is six, a year younger than Sandrine," Tara explained.

Sarika looked at her with jaguar vision. Inhaled her scent. Tara hadn't said so, but she was pregnant with her second child.

I think the other two jaguar females are also pregnant, Tomas. That was extremely concerning. She'd been feeling the joy in the room, but now a single thread of apprehension crept in.

Tomas shared the information with the other Carpathians. None of them reacted, but she felt the measure of protective surveillance go up a level.

Riordan De La Cruz walked his wife over to the table, gave the briefest of smiles to the women without really looking at them and seemingly melted away, leaving the women looking after him.

"Good grief, he's good-looking," Lucy said. "Juliette, it's been too long since we've seen you. Where have you been hiding?"

Solange made the introductions. Juliette was her cousin. Right away, Sarika recognized the jaguar in her.

"Having a baby is *exhausting*," Juliette announced and flung herself in the chair that Dominic provided. "Solange, I love you, but you should have waited until Hunter was a full year before you decided to follow in my footsteps. And all of you"—she swirled her finger encompassing the women seated at the table—"lied your asses off telling me it would be a walk in the park. Hunter can't be still for a single minute."

The women burst out laughing as Juliette slumped in her chair dramatically. Sarika found herself smiling with the others. Juliette was being somewhat honest about the exhaustion she felt, but she clearly wouldn't change a thing.

"Thank the universe for Sandrine and Bianca. They're watching over Hunter so I can get some much-needed female time," Juliette continued. "Riordan was looking forward to seeing Zacarias today. He's bringing Marguarita."

There was a long silence, and the women looked at one another with concern. Juliette immediately sat up. "Please remember that Marguarita is alone for long periods of time. Zacarias is an exceptional hunter and he leaves her to chase after the worst of the vampires. Her throat was torn out by a vampire, and she's never been able to speak, even after the conversion. She needs friends."

"Of course, she's always welcome here," Solange said. "She's family."

"It's just that Zacarias can be . . . disturbing," Jasmine said. "More so even than Luiz. Forgive me, Sarika, but your cousin can be all kinds of intimidating."

She felt Tomas' amusement. These women were in the room with several ancient hunters, all of whom were apex predators, yet they were relaxed around them.

"One just needs to take a firm hand with Luiz," Sarika said deliberately, sharing her amusement with her cousin. "By any chance, is Marguarita pregnant?" Sarika asked, suddenly suspicious. Juliette was ensuring these women would accept her sister-in-law when it was doubtful Marguarita had asked to be championed.

Juliette glanced at Solange. "If she is, Zacarias would not want anyone to speak of it. He is the most hunted of our ancients. He is hated by every vampire, and often they conspire to kill him. If they knew of Marguarita, which is doubtful, they would move heaven and earth to take her from him. Knowing she was bringing his child into the world would create a frenzy of hatred and conspiracy to kill her and the child. We shouldn't speculate."

That meant, without a doubt, that Juliette knew Marguarita had a baby on the way. It didn't take long to confirm it. The atmosphere in the house went from easy, joyful fun to high alert and uneasiness, as if a prowling, very hungry tiger had entered. There were no soft edges to Zacarias De La Cruz. None. His sweeping gaze took in everything and everyone, leaving them feeling as if he'd stripped them bare and uncovered every secret they had. His burning gaze settled on Sarika.

He halted in the center of the room, halfway to the women's table, Marguarita behind him. Ordinarily, that would have annoyed Sarika. She never liked when a woman trailed behind a man as if she weren't equal to him. As much as Zacarias' attention was centered on her, she knew his every instinct was to shield his lifemate, not lessen her importance.

Sarika smiled at the terrifying Carpathian. "I had hoped to meet with you and your lifemate. Luiz is my cousin and speaks very highly of you."

"Luiz didn't tell me you have many powerful gifts. He focused on your courage and your inability to stay out of harm's way."

The tone was the casual arrogance that ordinarily could set her teeth on edge. Absolutely in command. Implying he could and would remedy what might be perceived as failings. Because she had a thread to him through her jaguar, she felt his humor. More, he shared that humor with his lifemate. He hadn't let go of the woman's mind for even a small moment. It was as if Marguarita anchored him into the world of civilization.

"Luiz does seem to have a teeny problem with modern-day independent women. He told me you were head of the family. You might want to have a little discussion with him about it and clue him in."

Dominic burst out laughing. Tomas did as well. Marguarita came out from behind Zacarias and offered her hand.

"Do you prefer to speak telepathically, with notes or sign?" Sarika asked. She was willing to use any of Marguarita's preferences. Just the fact that she could be lifemate to a man as dark and shadowed as Zacarias elevated her to star status. The moment their hands came together, she knew it was a fact that Marguarita was pregnant and much further along than she appeared. There was no evidence in her feminine form.

Dominic put another chair up to the table. "Sit, Marguarita, before Zacarias loses what little civility he has left."

That little taunt told Sarika that Dominic and Zacarias were very old friends, and if Zacarias trusted anyone with his lifemate, it was Dominic.

She was beginning to get a feel for those in the room. They might be very powerful individuals, but they were good people, and all of them seemed willing to bring her into the family circle. Even Zacarias, who found it amusing that her cousin was having a difficult time reining her in.

As Marguarita sank into the very comfortable chair Dominic had added to the women's table, Zacarias, like the other men, seemed to fade into the background. There was the briefest of pauses as a little girl raced into the room.

Her hair was in fiery curls, her eyes a deep velvety gold ringed with reddish-gold lashes. She was dressed like a little dragon rider, but the little black jacket had ruffles down the back, trimmed in rose and gold sparkles. The jodhpurs were cuffed with the same rose and gold sparkles. Under the jacket was a little tank top of rose and gold.

"Auntie Solange! I'm here. I'm here." She skidded to a halt to look around the room, her gaze taking in Sarika, and then her face lit up when she looked past her. "Luiz! You came. I hoped you'd come. I'm looking for Sandrine and Bianca, but I'll give you a hug, too."

The child couldn't have been more than three, but she was extremely intelligent for her age and spoke very articulately. There wasn't even a hint of baby talk.

"Maureen." A male voice came from the doorway to the room. "What have I told you about security?"

"I scanned carefully, Daddy, while I was running," the child said. She smiled winningly. "And *everyone* is here. I was late."

"Perhaps because you threw a fit about your hair ribbons."

This, then, was the legendary Dax, who shared his soul with a real dragon. Sarika could see evidence of the fire-breathing soulmate in the Carpathian's eyes. The man had looked beyond his daughter to find Luiz. Sarika could see he was very conflicted. He was a Carpathian male and would want to know his daughter had added protection. But Luiz was now one of the controversial De La Cruz family. And he wasn't in the least modern.

"Thank you for ridding the world of Mitro," she said to Dax, once more regaining his attention. She was certain Tomas had shared information with Dax as soon as her memories became known. Dax lived close, and Mitro had been a larger-than-life monster that haunted her.

Dax gave her a short old-world bow. "I regret that I was unable to rid the world of him before he destroyed the people you loved."

She felt his regret. His guilt. It was the last thing she wanted. She certainly didn't blame Dax for the terrible things Mitro had done. "At the time, I didn't think there was anyone in this world who could rid the world of such a monster."

Maureen went over to her father to take his hand. "Mama says Daddy is a hero, but we're not supposed to call him that when he's around." She stated it proudly to Sarika in an overly loud whisper.

Riley came through the door just in time to hear her daughter's declaration and receive the burning, piercing glare from her lifemate. She laughed, the sound moving through the room to dispel any doubt that she thought her man was a hero.

"But you are, honey," she said and circled his neck with her arm. "At least to me."

"And me," Maureen said staunchly.

"And me," Sarika chimed in, enjoying the Carpathian male's discomfort just a little too much. She liked that the women weren't intimidated by their own lifemates, not even Marguarita.

Dominic brought chairs, this time for Riley and Sarika. She found herself seated at the women's table. The men faded into the background, and the party began in earnest. Maureen ran into the next room to find the other children. She seemed to be a little force of nature. Her hair was several shades of red, emphasized by the corkscrew curls. Secretly, Sarika was very pleased that Luiz's lifemate was a little tornado and already very self-assured.

Sarika wasn't certain how the males did it, but they faded so much into the background that she nearly forgot they were there. She didn't ask questions about being Carpathian. The talk was mostly about babies and being a mother. Solange was clearly nervous but very happy, and the others wanted to support her.

An hour of fun and silly games had gone by when, without warning, the shadow hit Sarika hard, dropping over her, into her, until she could barely breathe. The threat came out of nowhere, in the midst of children's laughter and women's excited murmurs as they talked of new babies and the love and joy they brought.

The atmosphere in Solange's home had been joyful. Bright. Filled with hope and friendship. She had relaxed, believing that with all the male Carpathians there, she had been wrong. The women and children were protected, not only by those inside the house but also by the roving patrols outside.

In that one heartbeat, everything changed. Shadows shifted in the room. In her mind, she saw the shadows growing on the walls, reaching to the high ceilings to loom over the children and the women laughing and talking as if none of that threat touched them.

CHAPTER 19

Sarika looked around the room, a long, slow scan, trying to see with more than her eyes. The little girls sat at the craft table, their heads together, glitter falling around them like pixie dust. Sandrine had pink and green frosting smeared across her face and in her hair. Bianca was much cleaner, but glitter sparkled over her hair and outfit. Hunter's face was covered in frosting. Little Maureen was chattering away, wiping at Hunter's face with a napkin, smearing the frosting into his hair. Her hands sparkled with glitter, but shockingly, there wasn't any in the bright red of her curls.

One moment Sarika was laughing, totally absorbed in the antics of the children, and the next, a terrible shadow spread like a cancer, creeping across the artful branches and shimmering leaves on the walls and ceiling until the ominous portent engulfed the entire upper half of the room. The shadows began to creep downward, inch by slow inch.

Instinctively, she reached out for Tomas. *The danger is here. They are gathering for the attack. Do you feel them?*

Instantly, Luiz was on the alert, showing himself, where before he had been part of the walls. She hadn't forgotten his presence, but apparently, everyone else had. He crossed the room with blurring speed and positioned himself in front of young Maureen, who immediately smiled at him and offered him a glittery cupcake.

The moment Luiz stood in front of the table to guard the children, Dax joined him. He looked warily around the room. "What is it?"

"I can only feel the threat through Sarika," Luiz admitted. "It is very real, but why I can't identify it, I have no idea."

Dax scanned the room and then turned his gaze on Sarika. "You are certain of her?"

Tomas rose in one fluid motion, his body partially shielding Sarika from the scrutiny of the two legendary Carpathians. "I am certain of her, Dax," he said simply. "There is a threat to our women and children."

"Yet some of the most powerful Carpathian hunters are gathered together, and they cannot feel this threat. Only she can," Dax persisted.

Luiz turned cold eyes on Dax. "I feel it as well. It is very real. Should you prefer to ignore it, know that I will keep your lifemate and daughter safe."

Flames flickered in Dax's eyes. Sarika could see the dragon eyeing Luiz like prey.

"Do not think you are safe because you believe you have a claim on my daughter."

She tilted her chin at the two men. "Seriously? That's called divide and conquer, a very old tactic I would have thought all of you were long past." She glanced up at Tomas. "Is there a subtle influence I'm missing? Something to pit the men against each other?"

Jasmine started to go to the children's table, anxiety on her face, but Jubal stepped in front of her, blocking the way. "We are not going to panic or alarm the children. At present, everyone is still safe. Stay with the other women. We'll be better able to protect you."

"Since no one feels this threat other than you, Sarika, will you open your mind to all of the hunters?" Tomas asked.

Sarika considered it. "If I open my mind to all of them, would I be opening my mind to the enemy? We're only going to have one chance to shut them down."

"I believe you are safe enough," Tomas said. "We've established a blood bond. You have one with Lojos and Mataias as well. Luiz and Dominic are familiar with the path. The others will see it through us."

He was calm. Reassuring. Certain. Sarika was so grateful for him. The other Carpathians in the house seemed much more menacing, yet Tomas exuded a quiet confidence that left her feeling he had no trouble taking the lead in a battle with any enemy. She felt she could rely on him for anything.

Sarika immediately opened her mind to those she had developed a relationship with, trusting them to allow the others access to their impressions. She felt the difference instantly as the men processed the looming threat.

With the safeguards we've woven, Dominic reassured, *it would be impossible to penetrate our home should our outside guardians fall.*

Tomas moved into the center of the room, his body still between the others and Sarika. He turned in a full circle, trying to find the threat. *The enemy has somehow managed to get into your home already. There is no other explanation.* Tomas stated it as fact.

Tomas must be correct, Lojos added. *There is nothing outside that any of us can find. Even following Sarika's mind along the path of alarm, there is no obvious danger.*

The other hunters spread out and began to search the rooms for any place an enemy might be concealed. Jubal moved very casually over to the table with the women and engaged them in quiet conversation. He sounded reassuring and gentle, but Sarika knew he was listening for one note that would give away an enemy. The thing she found the most fascinating about Jubal was he spoke with charm to every single woman, jaguar and Carpathian alike. He didn't automatically assume the enemy had arrived in the form of a jaguar shifter.

Finn, Tara's husband, joined Jubal and the women. Sarika watched the interaction carefully. Finn's palm circled the nape of Tara's neck, and he moved his body close to hers, a gesture of protection. He didn't feel "off" to Sarika or to her jaguar.

Her hand crept up to wrap around her amulet. It was growing warmer, the head of the jaguar pressing into the center of her palm. Her breath hissed out of her lungs as her sense of hearing became even more acute, so acute that she would be able to pick up the rustle of leaves in a very dense forest, to track the subtle movements of prey even on the darkest night.

Sarika blocked out all sounds of children, women and the males in the room. She needed to focus her attention on her pursuit of the enemy. She was no longer Sarika. She was jaguar, and she embraced every aspect of who and what she was. An apex predator. She could detect the faintest of sounds through the network of cells and organs located at the roof of her ear. That network directed sounds into her ear canal, allowing her to accurately locate prey.

She had never been the type of woman to depend on anyone else in a tense situation. She used every resource, so if that meant Tomas or Luiz, as far as she was concerned, it was just an intelligent decision.

It took a few moments to hone in on the sound she needed to isolate. It was extremely subtle, almost like the flutter of wings sliding against the walls in a delicate fanning motion. She instantly felt the stillness in the hunters around her. Through her, through their telepathic connections, they all heard that delicate sound.

Mage, Tomas identified. *Feel the vibrations, there is mage magic at work.*

Underworld, Zacarias added. *Feel the connection to Lilith and her army.*

Xavier and his brothers reside in the underworld, Mataias reminded. *They serve Lilith.*

Justice spent centuries in the underworld, Lojos added. *We tracked him to this area and stumbled across Gustov, who told us his master has a plan to destroy the Carpathians.*

We do not know for certain if Gustov's master is Justice. Tomas was always the cautious one in judging others.

Sarika felt Tomas struggling to be fair. He didn't want to jump to conclusions when they had no proof. The evidence seemed damning, but he had centuries of experience to know one needed actual proof if they were condemning a fellow Carpathian to death. She found herself taking a moment to soothe him, to send him warmth and reaffirm her conviction that he was the one she was meant to be with.

The women and children can be put in the safe room, Dominic suggested.

Instantly, every instinct screamed no. That was certain death for all of them. The safe room wasn't any safer than where they were.

Better to keep them together in a tight circle, children in the middle, their mothers surrounding them, warriors ringing them, she said hastily. The amulet was nearly burning her hand. *Watch the ceiling. They'll drop down from above. Can you construct an impenetrable dome around them? A shield that cannot be penetrated from above, below or any direction.*

The sense of urgency was on her. They had only a few precious seconds. The male Carpathians indicated for the women to circle the children. It was Dominic and Zacarias who wove the protective bubble around their loved ones. Solange objected to remaining inside, but Dominic was adamant that should danger break through, the women were the last protection for the children. He was smart enough not to mention that she was pregnant.

I would prefer you to be inside, Tomas said.

I would not be as useful to you, she pointed out. A silly part of her was pleased that he wanted her protected, just as the other women were.

Before he could reply, she heard the wings and the scratching of clawed feet. *They are coming.*

Mage-born from the underworld, Luiz reminded. *Expect anything and know they were made specifically to kill our women and children, so venom will be lethal.*

What are we facing, Sarika? Tomas asked calmly. *Identify them now.*

The confidence he had in her, that she could do such a thing, astounded her and at the same time galvanized her into further action. The scraping was louder. She listened with her acute hearing.

Beetles, she identified. Then the knowledge swept through her. She'd seen this before. Mitro had used such a clever and diabolical trick against her people. Swarms of the insects had descended on them from below the ground, the trees, the dirt. *Bombardier beetles.*

The beetles normally wouldn't kill a human being. The explosive material they mixed in their double abdomens to become a chemical to defeat their enemies was irritating to humans but not, as a rule, deadly. Unless a mage added to the potency. She had seen the results of the tiny insects swarming over children and infants, their exploding bombs shot with deadly accuracy to burn their victims.

As a rule, the beetles could be the size of a fingertip or up to one inch in length. They most often had red heads, legs and antennae and dark abdomens. She had encountered such beetles on two different treks in Africa, but she knew they were common throughout the world.

They can shoot their chemical bombs in rapid bursts from a distance or slow, precise blasts. The material is caustic, very hot, an acid-like substance. At best, without a mage enhancing these beetles, it would burn and irritate your skin. But I witnessed the damage they caused. The blasts killed anyone the material touched in a very painful way.

She felt the slight disdain of the ancient Carpathian hunters. They fought vampires and demons. Hellhounds and mages. They had fought Lilith's army from hell on several occasions. She found it strange that she knew their emotions when they had no knowledge of those feelings—in fact, didn't believe they had them. It was clearly a disconnect that happened as the Carpathian male aged. From what little information she'd gathered, their emotions began to fade and then completely disappear. Some far quicker than others.

The idea that they would be battling insects had to be laughable to them when they had spent so much time fighting larger-than-life enemies. A beetle, compared to a hellhound, did not seem very dangerous.

The walls and floor erupted with armies of beetles—so many, hundreds, perhaps a thousand, maybe even more. They were everywhere, crawling across the floor like a relentless wave of red, eyes fixed on their prey. They appeared to be a moving carpet as they assumed a formation of side-by-side rows.

On the trees above their heads, more beetles emerged, running along the leaves, working to get their bombs mixed, no easy task. Two chemicals, hydrogen peroxide and hydroquinone, are stored in separate reservoirs in the abdomen. The chemicals pass through a valve to mix in a special chamber along with a special enzyme that effectuates the reaction. Gases rapidly expand and give off heat. The beetles are able to open and close the valves so fast they could produce five hundred bursts in a second.

Sarika thought the bombardier beetles looked as if they were on steroids.

Jubal, they aren't attacking you or me, only Carpathians. They've been programmed to kill Carpathian men, women and children. I assumed because several of the women are jaguar that they were targets. But it is anyone Carpathian.

Jubal's head came up alertly, and he swung around to first look at her and then at the attacking insects. So many of them. The ancients had set shields around themselves, but the bombs were acid and, after so many hits, seemed to be weakening the protective layers around the hunters. Clearly, the mages responsible for mutating the beetles were prepared for the kinds of shields the Carpathians would use. She knew there were vampires in the underworld. They would have knowledge of what kinds of protections the ancients would use, and they would prepare their beetles to get through those defenses.

Jubal stood right in front of the women and children, and the insects rushed around him as if they couldn't see he was there. A few went over his boots to attack the bubble, but not one speck of the chemicals touched him. Not one beetle perceived him as a threat.

How do we defeat them, Sarika? Tomas' voice was calm, accepting of her evaluation. He didn't point out that there were master strategists in the room. He believed in her and the ancient power of the jaguar. What Sarika got from that calm acceptance was that in no way did he feel superior to her. She swore, in that moment, the power in her amplified.

We will join together, every jaguar in this room. I'll reach for others. We can destroy them. Just make certain that everyone continues to keep their shields strong.

Sarika didn't hesitate. She moved out from behind Tomas' body. Just the movement alone should have attracted the attention of the bombardiers, but none of them followed her. Not a single one. They swarmed around her just as they had done with Jubal.

I have had two blood exchanges with you, Tomas, yet they don't recognize that blood in me. They sense only jaguar.

The raised face of the jaguar burned into the center of her palm. It pulsed with a rhythm she recognized, although, to her knowledge, the amulet had never sprung to such life in all the time she'd had it.

She reached for the three jaguar women, touched their jaguars with her own, and the creatures, without consulting their human counterparts, turned over all power to her. Solange's jaguar joined them. Then Jasmine's. Juliette's was next. Power crackled all around her, but the bombardier beetles didn't appear to notice as streaks of light raced around the massive room.

Finn stood beside Jubal, placing his body between the beetles and the ancient Carpathians. Luiz abruptly stepped out of his protective shell to stand with him. The boost of power was so strong, Sarika could barely contain it. How Luiz managed to suppress his Carpathian legacy, when he was truly of the De La Cruz line, Sarika couldn't begin to fathom, but she only felt his jaguar, a powerful animal from a royal lineage. Jubal was from one as well. And Solange's cat was perhaps the most powerful of all.

The bombs exploded everywhere so that the entire room smelled caustic and white acid was flung on every possible surface. Even Finn, Jubal and Luiz had to protect themselves from the explosions as the beetles marched relentlessly toward the ancients. They dropped down from above and crawled all over the walls and trees.

Sarika blocked out the sounds of the loud explosions and let go of all thoughts of herself. Power filled her. Jaguar power. She drew on it, pulled it to her. Jubal, Finn and Luiz gave freely of their power. She felt the difference in the male power and used it to reach out, to send for every available female shifter close or far.

Streaks of blue and white arced throughout the room, building an electrical storm. Each time the lights flashed, they became even more brilliant, zipping throughout the space from the high ceiling to strike the floor. Everywhere the incandescent light touched as it traveled, it cut through the mass of beetles, reducing them to ash.

Sarika unleashed more power, building the blue-and-white jagged electrical arcs so more and more flashed throughout the room, burning through the invaders, finding them in the trees, the ceiling, the walls, and destroying the ones on the floor. She had no idea of time passing. She was only aware of the combined power moving through her to find its way to the electrical storm.

When it seemed as if the beetles were annihilated, she changed the blue-and-white storm to piercing spears, illuminating every leaf, layers of walls and ceiling, paying special attention to the floors to ensure not a single insect was left.

Tomas caught her before she fell, her body completely drained. He simply cradled her in his arms.

"You can do the cleanup," he told the other ancients. "I'm taking her to Luiz's. She needs to rest."

Sarika was more than happy to have Tomas carry her back to the tree house. She was utterly drained. She didn't even hear or acknowledge the women calling out to her as Tomas took her out of Dominic and Solange's home and far away from the celebration that had turned so ugly.

"This women's empowerment business is exhausting," she informed him, circling his neck with her arms. She buried her face against his chest. "I can barely keep my eyes open."

"We'll get you tucked into bed," he assured her. "You can sleep until next rising."

She felt as if she were floating through the clouds. If she weren't so brain-dead, she might have been afraid as he took her across the sky toward Luiz's tree house. She wasn't used to their ability to carry another being as they flew. The idea that she might be able to fly after the conversion would have been exhilarating if she weren't so tired.

"I don't think I can manage the conversion tonight," she whispered, knowing it was true. "I just want to sleep. Not dream. No nightmares. Do you think you can manage that for me this one time?"

"Anything you need," he assured.

She thought she could actually be in love with him. If not, she was on her way to falling hard. He was a good man. Steady. A rock she could always count on. She especially liked that he wasn't a man to posture or make demands.

His soft laughter teased her hair. "I'm no saint. I will always make certain decisions regarding your safety and health without your consent, and no doubt, you won't be happy with me."

She made a face he couldn't see. "I'm not into bossy, arrogant men."

"You're into me."

She was. She *so* was. That made her laugh. Here he was admitting he would do something that would annoy her, and yet she found him endearing.

"I'm too tired to make sense of how I feel about you," she said as he gained the wraparound verandah and took her straight through the house.

"You know how you feel about me."

She wasn't about to argue.

"Are you too tired for your bath? It's already waiting for you."

She'd forgotten Carpathians waved their hands and magic happened. The magic of a hot bath. She could get used to Carpathian ways. She tightened her arms around him and rubbed her face against his chest. "That sounds perfect. Thank you for thinking of it."

She found it amazing that despite everything that had happened, he would remember her nighttime ritual of relaxing in a bathtub. It wasn't something Carpathians did, she'd gleaned that much, yet it was important to him.

"You're important to me," Tomas said, nuzzling the nape of her neck as he entered the bathroom, which was set up like a spa. "I'm removing your clothes and setting you in the tub."

She liked that he always warned her when he was about to do something different, something unfamiliar and maybe a little freaky to her but entirely normal to him. She found him thoughtful of her when she'd had it in her head after first meeting Luiz that Tomas would trample all over her.

"I shouldn't have judged you so harshly, Tomas," she admitted as she sank into the steaming water. The scent of lavender was soothing as it permeated the air, driving the stench of the bombs from her mind.

The moment she was settled in the tub, he had her hair in a messy knot on top of her head. "Lie back, close your eyes and relax."

There was that voice, a mesmerizing dark velvet caress stroking over her skin. She loved his voice. The water stirred, and she lifted her lashes just enough to see that Tomas had joined her, his back resting against the sloped wall of the tub opposite her. He reached for her foot, drew it into his lap and began a mind-numbing massage that sent shivers of pleasure throughout her entire body. She hadn't known her arches hurt so much.

"Your hands should be insured," she murmured, allowing her lashes to drift back down.

His laughter was soft, pouring into her mind and filling her with joy. With peace. She had faced her worst nightmares with him and, in doing so, found that as she embraced her past, those memories unlocked more and more of her abilities. Tomas had given her that. He'd given her so much in the years she had corresponded with him. Now with him in person, she felt so much more empowered as a woman and partner. So much more seen.

"Sarika, I love that you believe those things of me. You have always been strong. Always intelligent. I did not give you those things. In our relationship, you will be giving up so much more than I am. My life will be forever enhanced and beautiful because you're my lifemate, but the truth is it will remain the same. My customs. My rituals. My language. My brothers. You will have to conform to my way of life. What you give to me is beyond any price, and I will never be able to balance the scales between us."

She could feel his sincerity. Tomas melted her heart. He'd slipped inside and was stamped deep into her bones when she hadn't even been aware it was possible.

"People always say that a marriage or partnership should be fifty-fifty," she murmured, not for a moment opening her eyes. The water, his hands on her and the sounds of the rainforest created a perfect peace. "It never really is. It never can be. Sometimes one person needs more than another. Sometimes they both do."

"What do you think is a solution when both parties need seventy percent?"

"I think it's important to communicate one's needs and listen to what their partner needs. If you trust that your partner is always going to do their best to put you first, then, looking at any situation with that trust, you're both going to come out better for it."

Sarika did believe that communication was all-important. Not just listening but hearing what was said and processing it without bias and judgment.

"I think my lifemate is a very wise woman," Tomas said and drew her other foot into his lap.

They both fell into a companionable silence that was soothing and peaceful. He continued to massage her foot and calf, adding to the beauty and magic of the night. The sound of the wind fluttering leaves in the trees. The drone of the insects. The occasional flutter of wings. It was a symphony of rainforest music lulling her to sleep while her man used his amazing skills to get out every single painful knotted muscle in her feet and calves.

As if in a dream, she had a hazy recollection of him carrying her to the bed and tucking the sheet around her. He stretched out beside her, his body warm and relaxed, as he murmured softly to her. She barely caught the words, ones of safeguards to keep away nightmares, to only have sweet dreams. To awaken when the sun went down the following rising. She went completely under, feeling encompassed with what could only be love.

The small convoy trekking through the rainforest toward the ancient ruins of the jaguar temple consisted of Luiz, Lojos, Mataias, Tomas and Sarika. She was surprised that Jubal was also with them. They had flown through the jungle, staying high above the canopy. Tomas had carried her, and Luiz had taken Jubal. That also surprised her, that her cousin was so clearly involved with the jaguars when he identified as a De La Cruz.

Having met Zacarias and his brother Riordan, she knew the bloodline had embraced Luiz, taken him as a true family member. He wasn't adopted. He wasn't half. He was fully their true bloodline and as intimidating as hell, yet he carried Jubal as if Jubal were his family. He was an enigma, one she doubted she would ever solve.

As they neared the ruins, she began to get uneasy, a feeling of dread filling her when she'd been comfortable and safe in Tomas' arms.

We need to be on the forest floor, Luiz said, just as the exact same thought burst through her.

Something wasn't right. They were very high, and no one should have been able to detect them, yet there seemed to be more danger to them above the canopy than inside the darkened interior. The uneasiness spread to the others.

It is impossible to see the ruins from the sky, Luiz told them. *It is as if it is protected even from the latest technology. When others come to explore, they do not see the ruins of the temple. All jaguar know the way, but outsiders have not found it.*

We know the way, Lojos said. *We're outsiders.*

The temple recognizes Carpathians, Luiz said.

Sarika gasped, her hand sliding to her amulet. That was how Mitro had found her people centuries ago. He was Carpathian, and the temple regarded him as such.

Tomas set her feet gently on the forest floor. The interior was extremely dark, little light penetrating the thick canopy above. The moon was barely a sliver she could occasionally glimpse through the filter of leaves overhead. She relied on her night vision just as the others did.

The trek through the jungle carried a pall of gloom over it, a warning to turn back. With every step they took, the dread grew. The shadows moved ominously. There was no drone of insects or monkeys overhead. The forest was utterly still and eerily silent, as if holding its breath. No movement. No scurrying lizards or voles.

Sarika reached for the memories she kept locked away. Not all of them were nightmares, but she hadn't separated the bad from the good until then.

"It is a safeguard, much like Carpathians weave," Sarika said. "It was meant to allow the people to live in peace. That was all they wanted, to live out their lives in peace."

"Is it your safeguard?" Jubal asked.

Sarika shook her head. "No, the people had established their village and constructed the temple before my time."

"They called themselves Mayans?" Tomas asked. "Because as far as I know, Incas were in this rainforest but not Mayans."

"We called them Mayans," Jubal said. "Shifters did, because the ruins were close to the same type of structures the Mayans built."

Sarika drew on the memories she had so carefully avoided. This time she chose to uncover the happier moments she'd spent with the gentle villagers. "The people never referred to themselves as Mayans," Sarika confirmed.

"That makes much more sense," Tomas agreed. "The little I've seen or heard makes me believe these people were separate from the Incas and the Mayans."

Huge leaves like elephant ears flapped along the narrow path they trekked. Hundreds of vines hung down, thick ropes of twisted wood covered with hair, making them feel as if the legs of spiders brushed their faces as they passed. Long-stemmed liana, a woody vine rooted in soil, twisted into many alien shapes as it climbed the various trees.

They rounded a bend, pushing aside the overgrown abundance of leaves and brush to view ruins of more modern homes that had been burned to the ground. The jungle had reclaimed most of the area. That didn't lessen the impact of sorrow, of blood spilled, a slaughter of men, women and children. Sarika was so sensitive, she *heard* the cries, the screams, the sounds of the massacre.

Solange. She felt the woman's energy all around her. The terrible sorrow. The guilt of survival. The horrific knowledge that she couldn't prevent the slaughter of everyone she loved. This was the site of Solange's home before her father, Brodrick the Terrible, and his shifters had murdered every man, woman and child they deemed beneath them. This was where he had tried to kill Solange when she was just a child but hadn't succeeded.

"She comes here often," Jubal said, his voice almost reverent. "Dominic makes it better for her, but the pain of that day has never left her."

Blood had soaked into the ground. The pain penetrated deep into the recollections of the forest. It would always be there, the memory of the slaughter of a village. This hadn't been the only massacre committed on these grounds. The memories rose from under the more modern-time murders, choking Sarika.

The screams and wails of the dying, the tortured innocent people, came from beneath the layers of Solange's massacred village. Sarika couldn't block them out. She tried everything, but the closer they got to the actual ruins of the temple, the louder the screams were, reminding her she hadn't saved those gentle people. Her stomach lurched, knotted into tight fists of pain. There was no way to stop the rush of memories invading her mind and flooding her body with a sickening physical reaction.

The temple ruins were nearly overgrown with moss, vines and liana, making it nearly impossible to see until one was right up on it. The statue of the jaguar with its piercing eyes seemingly watched them from any angle of approach. Moss and liana climbed her body, but not her face. There wasn't a speck of green on her head. Her gaze was fierce, the eyes of a predator judging their intent.

Sarika felt the power emanating from the statue. Through her, the others felt it as well.

"What is it made of?" Tomas asked. He got very close to inspect the statue, but he didn't touch it. Sarika had been prepared to push him away. The statue was sacred. It was protected.

"Look at this," Tomas invited his brothers. "This material is not from our planet. Like Sarika's amulet, it is made from either an asteroid or a meteor. To make a statue this size, it would have been one huge chunk falling from the sky. Most are very small."

Tomas looked at Sarika. "Could these people have come from a different planet?"

"I don't know. They were highly intelligent and very advanced. Very peaceful people. They wanted to stay to themselves and live out their lives in harmony with the earth, sky and below. The temple was the connection between all three dimensions."

"Was it a female-dominated society?" Lojos asked Sarika. "The jaguar statue feels feminine, and you have the ability to bind power to you."

"They worshiped the jaguar," she said. "I was a shifter in those times and regarded as a sort of priestess. My life was one of service to the people."

"Were they shifters?" Mataias asked.

Sarika shook her head. They were entering the temple. On the outside, the building looked as if it were broken and sunken into the ground, but the moment they entered, walls shimmered around them, great blocks of stone. There were two chambers one could conceal themselves in, but Sarika pushed on what appeared to be a solid wall, knowing the actual temple was belowground. She did it instinctively, as if she'd done so many, many times.

She led the way with confidence, down the narrow stairs and through the various rooms used for rituals. They were looking for the weapon she had stolen from Mitro. She hadn't had time to take it down into the extensive underground tunnels. She had hidden it there in the chamber where Mitro so gleefully tortured and murdered the innocent, peaceful people she had come to love.

No one spoke. The chamber was far too soaked in blood and death. Heaviness invaded their minds and hearts. The Carpathian males automatically shut down their feelings, but Jubal and Sarika had no choice but to endure. She couldn't help admiring the strength in Jubal. He had come to pay tribute to these people as well as to Solange's. When he knew Solange was making her pilgrimage, he joined her to give her support and to let her know that her people would not be forgotten. He was making that same statement about Sarika's people.

With each step leading to the platform where her life had ended, Sarika found herself going further back in time. The coppery scent of blood that had permeated the ritual chamber. The stench of the fires Mitro had scattered around to throw live children into to watch them burn for his own amusement. The flicker of the orange-and-red flames built on the walls of the chamber. She felt the stone under her feet.

Her fingers circled the amulet until it grew so hot it burned the image of the jaguar into her palm just as it had done once before. She barely felt it as she deliberately took a deep breath and stepped from reality to her past. Her goal was to find the hidden piece of the weapon that could destroy the Carpathian people.

She felt the impact of connecting with her two best friends, women she called sister. Both wore the same amulet, and both carried the immense power of the jaguar. Even together, they could not defeat Mitro. They weren't prepared for such evil, or for the trauma their too-sensitive hearts would have to endure seeing the brutal torture and murder of a peaceful people.

She had to get past what was happening all around her and to her sisters, to focus completely on Mitro and the pie-shaped metal he had shoved inside his shirt. While her sisters distracted him, she had to steal the weapon and hide it before they suicided. They could never chance telling him where they had hidden what he considered the ultimate prize.

Her mind worked at rapid speed. She was all too aware of Mitro defiling Litza while Sarika combined their power to remove the weapon. With only seconds to hide it, she used every ounce of power she had to embed it deep in the hieroglyphics on the wall behind Mitro. As she did, she replicated the design throughout all the walls, inside and out of the temple. The hieroglyphics told the stories of the past, the star people who had come to live in peace and died in a horrendous and senseless slaughter.

As she relayed the information to the others, all eyes went to the spot behind where Mitro had stood to see that the wall had been broken open, as if someone had taken a hatchet to it. Small and large pieces of stone were scattered all over the floor, along with dirt and particles of dust. Great cracks ran up and down the wall, fanning outward from the gaping hole where the piece had been ripped from the wall.

Sarika collapsed on the platform, dissolving into tears, overwhelmed with grief, with too many memories, but uppermost, guilt. They'd given their lives for that small piece of a weapon. All three of them. How had it been found? Why hadn't she allowed herself to see into her nightmares and know they were real? This catastrophe was on her.

CHAPTER 20

"It's my fault." Sarika couldn't stop sobbing.

She became aware of Tomas holding her in his lap. Somehow, he'd gotten her back to the safety of Luiz's tree house, but her reality continued to flicker between the past and present.

"If I hadn't been such a coward and had just accessed my memories instead of hiding from them, we would have the first piece of the weapon they plan to use to destroy your people. Now your enemies have it."

Tomas rocked her gently, his arms providing a fortress, but even he couldn't stop the flood of tears and condemnation she heaped on herself. He let her cry for a long while, and then he caught her hair and tipped her head back.

"Enough, *sivamet*. There is only so much of this I can take. You know you aren't responsible for any of this. You take on too much. You began having nightmares as a child and believed those memories to be just that. In your human world, most don't believe there are past lives. And for many people there are not. There was a significant reason for you to be born over and over. If you must place blame, put it squarely on my shoulders."

She blinked at him, her long lashes wet and sticky. "Why would you even say that?" She hiccupped as she tried to stop the sobs choking her.

"I didn't find you. I looked, but I couldn't find you. And I opted to remain alive." His answer was simple—and truthful. She had to be born, live her lifespan, die and be reborn with his soul until he was gone from earth. He hadn't given her the chance at peace.

Sarika shook her head and pressed trembling fingers to her lips. "This is a huge mess because I couldn't face my past, Tomas. I didn't even know there was a weapon that has the potential to destroy your people until you told me. I had no idea I was the one who stole it from Mitro until you gave me the courage to face the memories I had buried and turned into nightmares. If anyone is *not* to blame, it is you."

"There was evidence of Justice being in the temple. I am very familiar with the few tracks he leaves behind. But he wasn't alone, or someone else was in the temple before him. Lojos and Mataias are insistent that Justice is the mastermind behind organizing an attempt to kill Prince Mikhail and Gregori. I still think we need to reserve judgment. What do you think?"

Tomas needed her to focus on solutions. He had little time to convert her and get them both in the ground so they could follow Justice and hopefully figure out where the second piece of the weapon would be. With all that, the most important thing to him was getting her to realize she had no blame for the weapon getting into the hands of the enemy.

He had talked it over with the others, and they hadn't wanted to draw attention to the temple by going there. Had they recovered the weapon, they would have had to leave the area immediately, and he couldn't leave without converting his lifemate. The Carpathian ancients had all agreed they would go to the temple after the women had their party. If they were able to recover the weapon, Luiz would carry it to the Carpathian Mountains, and it would be guarded until they figured out a way to destroy it.

Blaming herself wasn't going to help, especially since it wasn't true that she had anything to do with the fiasco of them arriving too late. Sarika had been pulled back in time, thrown into the abyss of the worst times in her life cycle, yet she'd done it to aid the Carpathian people. She had to do so selflessly, letting go of her present self in order to access the past, and she'd done so knowing what she would be facing.

"I'm proud of you. Proud that you're my lifemate. Proud of your strength and courage. The way you allow yourself to be vulnerable, that you trust me enough to show that to me."

Tomas nuzzled her neck, sliding her hair out of the way so he could brush kisses down the side of her face, from her temple to her delicate jaw. "We can do this together. We're good together, Sarika. Come into my world. Choose me of your own free will."

He wanted to be her choice, when she really didn't have one, not if he were to survive. But still, he knew she was his choice, and he wanted her to feel as strongly about him as he did about her. He'd claimed her in the way of his people. He hadn't even tried to fight the compulsion, and he knew that had upset her. She was human and a shifter. Neither would understand his society and the strict rules they had to follow. The code of honor that dictated their lives. Or how a Carpathian would feel about the woman who was nothing short of a miracle to him.

Sarika turned in his lap, both hands framing his face. Her tear-drenched eyes stared directly into his. "You will always be my choice, Tomas. Always. I know it took time for me to come to terms with what you are, but I have. I'm determined, as long as Coh will be okay, to go into your world."

He kissed her. He couldn't stop himself. He felt her sincerity. She wasn't saying she'd chosen him because she felt she had no other choice. His mouth wandered down to her chin, his teeth nibbling, his tongue tasting her skin. Everything about Sarika appealed to him.

I've checked with your jaguar multiple times after each blood exchange. Even after you exchanged blood with my brothers and Luiz. She seemed content and unafraid, he assured her.

His mouth moved over her pulse point, that temptation, beckoning to him. A siren's call. He sank his teeth deep, connecting them, feeling the rush of heated pleasure sweeping through his body. Only Sarika could make every nerve ending come alive. Her blood was his aphrodisiac, solely for him. He craved her taste. Craved her soft skin and curves. Her kisses. The sensation, the wonder, of physical desire was a new experience and one very profound.

It took discipline to only take the amount of blood needed for a true exchange. She moved on him continually, her soft body grinding into his as she sat on his lap.

I'm doing the clothes thing, Sarika.

It would be nice if you could hurry.

Her soft little plea sent heat rushing down his spine. He lifted her carefully, turning her to face him.

Straddle me.

He did the clothes thing while she put her legs over his. Without clothes, it was much easier for her body to slide over his, engulfing him in heat, surrounding him with tight, silken fire. She didn't even hesitate. Her body had to work to allow him in, and twice he whispered to her to relax.

I am relaxed. You just keep getting bigger.

That made him smile. He kissed her, his mouth as gentle as he could make it when he wanted to crush her to him. *Take my blood, Sarika. Come into my world all the way.*

There was no hesitation. Her mouth went to the offering he had opened on his chest, and the world, for him, tilted and spun. She made the earth move. He had never really experienced the sun, but he felt that the radiant brightness she shone over him had to rival it.

Sarika made little noises, soft moans, compelling cries, that sang through his veins like a symphony of fire. His body moved in hers. Her body rose and fell over his. They shared the same skin, the same soul. For him, it was a cosmic experience. So unexpected and beautiful.

It was difficult to force himself to stop her feeding when it felt so right and enhanced their lovemaking, but stopping it was necessary. He took over, surging into her, looking into her eyes, drowning there, feeling like they were one.

Sarika gasped out her climax, clutching his shoulders, her heart beating wildly as he found his own release. She buried her face on his shoulder. "I'm very, very fond of your ability to deal with clothes, Tomas."

He found himself laughing. "Happy to oblige."

She grew quiet, and he held her tighter, waiting . . . Twice he checked in with her jaguar. Coh was complacent. Seemingly unaffected. When the cramps began, they seemed far milder than Tomas anticipated, so mild they could have been nonexistent. Still, he opened his mind to his brothers and Luiz. They would help ease her into their world.

He nuzzled the top of her head, aching. Worried. He'd witnessed the conversion, and it was brutal as a rule. Time passed. He rocked her gently, but she didn't seem to be uncomfortable. The conversion was taking far too long. He shed his body and entered hers to see for himself what was taking place.

Her organs were reshaping just as they should have been, but her blood was *not* being taken over by his. It was as if the blood cells bonded together to create something else. His were fully Carpathian, and hers appeared to still be jaguar, but their cells clung to one another.

Tomas shared his findings with his brothers and Luiz. Luiz reached out to Dominic for reassurance. It appeared that the same thing had happened when Dominic converted Solange. She was Carpathian, but still jaguar.

Tomas checked on Coh. The jaguar seemed bored with the entire business, although, he realized, she was watchful over Sarika.

Are you hurting? he asked Sarika.

She shook her head. *I'm just very, very tired.*

I will allow you to sleep in just a little while. I want to ensure you are completely converted with no repercussions before we go to ground.

It only took another half hour. Sarika dozed in his arms as he took her beneath the tree house, where he opened the earth and floated her down into the soil's welcoming arms.

His brothers and Luiz met him on the tree house verandah. He explained in detail what happened with Sarika's blood. "She seems fully Carpathian and yet at the same time is fully jaguar."

"And you? What has her blood done to you?" Mataias asked.

"That's a good question," Tomas conceded. "Time will give us that answer."

"We have to follow Justice," Lojos said. "We can't allow him to get to the second piece of the weapon. I have a couple of ideas about how to track him."

"Go on ahead. I will wake Sarika in three risings, and we will catch up to you," he told his brothers. "We can go much faster than you because we won't be looking for signs of his passing. Keep me informed on where you are at all times."

"I will stay here," Luiz added. "When Tomas and Sarika rise, I will accompany them to you."

Tomas wasn't surprised. Luiz took his role as Sarika's family very seriously. They were chasing after who every hunter considered to be the most powerful Carpathian alive. If they caught up to him and a battle ensued, no single hunter would defeat him.

"Are you certain, Luiz? You have much to lose," Tomas pointed out.

"I have my duty to our people," Luiz said. "And to Sarika. I go with you."

Tomas gripped his brothers' forearms, first Mataias and then Lojos. "Safe journey," he murmured.

"Keep our girl safe," his brothers said simultaneously.

Tomas watched his brothers leave. They had spent centuries together, looking after one another, and it felt wrong to stay behind.

"You'll catch up soon enough," Luiz said. "I'll guard your sleeping chamber, and when you rise, we will be able to cover the distance in a rising. Maybe two at most."

Tomas nodded. "Thank you, Luiz."

He hurried back to Sarika. She was sleeping, but not as peacefully as he would have liked. Floating down into deep earth, he checked her and her jaguar again. Both seemed to be healthy. Sarika wasn't as far under his compulsion as he thought she should be.

Stop fighting sleep, sivamet. *It is the healing sleep of our people.*

To his shock, she answered him. *I was waiting for you to return to me. If I'm sleeping in the ground, I want you right next to me.* There was the slightest edge of humor to her voice. Humor and trepidation. His woman wasn't quite as sure of this particular custom as she wanted him to think.

Tomas wrapped his arms around her, pulling her into his body. *I love you, Sarika. Sleep now. In a few nights, we'll rise and join our brothers.*

Sarika cuddled close to him. *I love you, too.*

APPENDIX 1

CARPATHIAN HEALING CHANTS

To rightly understand Carpathian healing chants, background is required in several areas:

1. The Carpathian view on healing
2. The Lesser Healing Chant of the Carpathians
3. The Great Healing Chant of the Carpathians
4. Carpathian musical aesthetics
5. Lullaby
6. Song to Heal the Earth
7. Carpathian chanting technique

1. THE CARPATHIAN VIEW ON HEALING

The Carpathians are a nomadic people whose geographic origins can be traced at least as far as the Southern Ural Mountains (near the steppes of modern-day Kazakhstan), on the border between Europe and Asia. (For this reason, modern-day linguists call their language "proto-Uralic," without knowing that this is the language of the Carpathians.) Unlike most nomadic peoples, the Carpathians did not wander due to the need to find new grazing lands as the seasons and climate shifted, or to search for better trade. Instead, the Carpathians' movements were driven by a great purpose: to find a land that would have the right earth, a soil with the kind of richness that would greatly enhance their rejuvenative powers.

Over the centuries, they migrated westward (some six thousand years ago), until they at last found their perfect homeland—their *susu*—in the Carpathian Mountains, whose long arc cradled the lush plains of the kingdom of Hungary. (The kingdom of Hungary flourished for over a millennium—making Hungarian the dominant language of the Carpathian Basin—until the kingdom's lands were split among several countries after World War I: Austria, Czechoslovakia, Romania, Yugoslavia and modern Hungary.)

Other peoples from the Southern Urals (who shared the Carpathian language but were not Carpathians) migrated in different directions. Some ended up in Finland, which explains why the modern

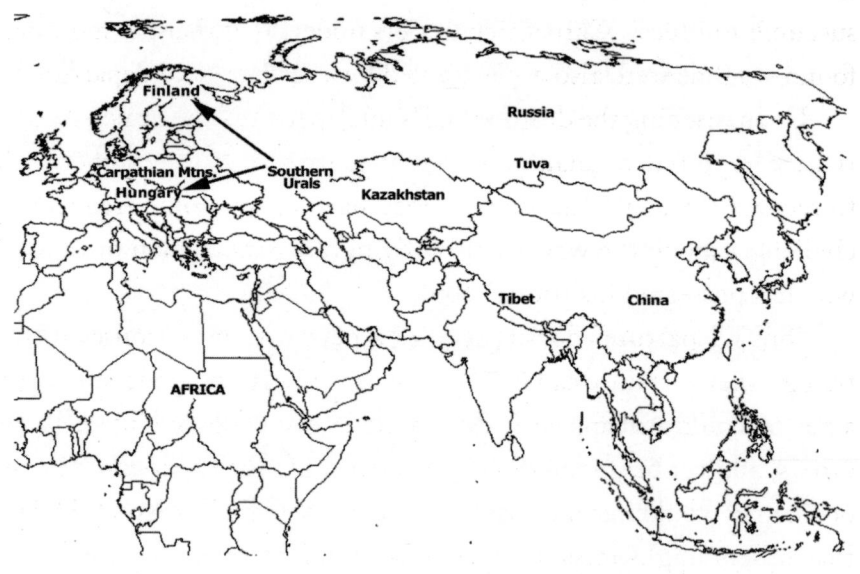

Hungarian and Finnish languages are among the contemporary descendants of the ancient Carpathian language. Even though they are tied forever to their chosen Carpathian homeland, the Carpathians continue to wander as they search the world for the answers that will enable them to bear and raise their offspring without difficulty.

Because of their geographic origins, the Carpathian views on healing share much with the larger Eurasian shamanistic tradition. Probably the closest modern representative of that tradition is based in Tuva (and is referred to as "Tuvinian Shamanism")—see the map on the previous page.

The Eurasian shamanistic tradition—from the Carpathians to the Siberian shamans—held that illness originated in the human soul, and only later manifested as various physical conditions. Therefore, shamanistic healing, while not neglecting the body, focused on the soul and its healing. The most profound illnesses were understood to be caused by "soul departure," where all or some part of the sick person's soul has wandered away from the body (into the nether realms) or has been captured or possessed by an evil spirit, or both.

The Carpathians belong to this greater Eurasian shamanistic tradition and share its viewpoints. While the Carpathians themselves did not succumb to illness, Carpathian healers understood that the most profound wounds were also accompanied by a similar "soul departure."

Upon reaching the diagnosis of "soul departure," the healer-shaman is then required to make a spiritual journey into the netherworld to recover the soul. The shaman may have to overcome tremendous challenges along the way, particularly fighting the demon or vampire who has possessed his friend's soul.

"Soul departure" doesn't require a person to be unconscious (although that certainly can be the case as well). It was understood that a person could still appear to be conscious, even talk and interact with others, and yet be missing a part of their soul. The experienced healer or shaman would instantly see the problem nonetheless, in subtle signs that others might miss: the person's attention wandering every now and then, a lessening in their enthusiasm about life, chronic depression, a diminishment in the brightness of their "aura" and the like.

2. THE LESSER HEALING CHANT OF THE CARPATHIANS

Kepä Sarna Pus **(The Lesser Healing Chant)** is used for wounds that are merely physical in nature. The Carpathian healer leaves his body and enters the wounded Carpathian's body to heal great mortal wounds from the inside out using pure energy. He proclaims, "I offer freely my life for your life," as he gives his blood to the injured Carpathian. Because the Carpathians are of the earth and bound to the soil, they are healed by the soil of their homeland. Their saliva is also often used for its rejuvenative powers.

It is also very common for the Carpathian chants (both the Lesser and the Great) to be accompanied by the use of healing herbs, aromas from Carpathian candles and crystals. The crystals (when combined with the Carpathians' empathic, psychic connection to the entire universe) are used to gather positive energy from their surroundings, which is then used to accelerate the healing. Caves are sometimes used as the setting for the healing.

The Lesser Healing Chant was used by Vikirnoff Von Shrieder and Colby Jansen to heal Rafael De La Cruz, whose heart had been ripped out by a vampire, as described in *Dark Secret*.

Kepä Sarna Pus **(The Lesser Healing Chant)**
The same chant is used for all physical wounds. "Sívadaba" (into your heart) would be changed to refer to whatever part of the body is wounded.

Kuńasz, nélkül sívdobbanás, nélkül fesztelen löyly.
You lie as if asleep, without beat of heart, without airy breath.

Ot élidamet andam szabadon élidadért.
I offer freely my life for your life.

O jelä sielam jörem ot ainamet és soŋe ot élidadet.
My spirit of light forgets my body and enters your body.

O jelä sielam pukta kinn minden szelemeket belső.
My spirit of light sends all the dark spirits within fleeing without.

Pajńak o susu hanyet és o nyelv nyálamet sívadaba.
I press the earth of our homeland and the spit of my tongue into your heart.

Vii, o verim soŋe o verid andam.
At last, I give you my blood for your blood.

To hear this chant, visit christinefeehan.com/members/.

3. THE GREAT HEALING CHANT OF THE CARPATHIANS

The most well-known—and most dramatic—of the Carpathian healing chants is **En Sarna Pus (The Great Healing Chant)**. This chant is reserved for recovering the wounded or unconscious Carpathian's soul.

Typically a group of men would form a circle around the sick Carpathian (to "encircle him with our care and compassion") and begin the chant. The shaman or healer or leader is the prime actor in this healing ceremony. It is he who will actually make the spiritual journey into the netherworld, aided by his clanspeople. Their purpose is to ecstatically dance, sing, drum and chant, all the while visualizing (through the words of the chant) the journey itself—every step of it, over and over again—to the point where the shaman, in trance, leaves his body and makes that very journey. (Indeed, the word *ecstasy* is from the Latin *ex statis*, which literally means "out of the body.")

One advantage that the Carpathian healer has over many other shamans is his telepathic link to his lost brother. Most shamans must wander in the dark of the nether realms in search of their lost brother. But the Carpathian healer directly "hears" in his mind the voice of his lost brother calling to him, and can thus "zero in on" his soul like a homing beacon. For this reason, Carpathian healing tends to have a higher success rate than most other traditions of this sort.

Something of the geography of the "other world" is useful for us to examine in order to fully understand the words of the Great Healing Chant. A reference is made to the "Great Tree" (in Carpathian: *En Puwe*). Many ancient traditions, including the Carpathian tradition, understood the worlds—the heaven worlds, our world and the nether realms—to be "hung" upon a great pole, or axis, or tree. Here on earth, we are positioned halfway up this tree, on one of its branches. Hence, many ancient texts referred to the material world as "middle earth": midway between heaven and hell. Climbing the tree would lead one to the heaven worlds. Descending the tree to its roots would lead to the nether realms. The shaman was necessarily a master of movement up and down the Great Tree, sometimes moving unaided and sometimes assisted by (or even mounted upon the back of) an animal spirit guide. In various traditions, this Great Tree was known as the *axis mundi* (the "axis of the worlds"), Yggdrasil (in Norse mythology), Mount Meru (the sacred world mountain of Tibetan tradition), etc. The Christian cosmos, with its heaven, purgatory/earth and hell, is also worth comparing. It is even given a similar topography in Dante's *Divine Comedy*: Dante is led on a journey first to hell, at the center of the earth; then upward to Mount Purgatory, which sits on the earth's surface directly opposite Jerusalem; then farther upward to Eden, the earthly paradise, at the summit of Mount Purgatory; and then upward at last to Heaven.

In the shamanistic tradition, it was understood that the small always reflects the large; the personal always reflects the cosmic. A movement in the greater dimensions of the cosmos also coincides with an internal movement. For example, the *axis mundi* of the cosmos corresponds with the spinal column of the individual. Journeys up and down the *axis mundi* often coincided with the movements of natural and spiritual energies (sometimes called *kundalini* or *shakti*) in the spinal column of the shaman or mystic.

En Sarna Pus (The Great Healing Chant)
In this chant, ekä ("brother") would be replaced by "sister," "father," "mother," depending on the person to be healed.

Ot ekäm ainajanak hany, jama.
My brother's body is a lump of earth, close to death.

Me, ot ekäm kuntajanak, pirädak ekäm, gond és irgalom türe.
We, the clan of my brother, encircle him with our care and compassion.

O pus wäkenkek, ot oma šarnank, és ot pus fünk, álnak ekäm ainajanak, pitänak ekäm ainajanak elävä.
Our healing energies, ancient words of magic and healing herbs bless my brother's body, keep it alive.

Ot ekäm sielanak pälä. Ot omboće päläja juta alatt o jüti, kinta, és szelemek lamtijaknak.
But my brother's soul is only half. His other half wanders in the netherworld.

Ot en mekem ŋamaŋ: kulkedak otti ot ekäm omboće päläjanak.
My great deed is this: I travel to find my brother's other half.

Rekatüre, saradak, tappadak, odam, kaŋa o numa waram, és avaa owe o lewl mahoz.
We dance, we chant, we dream ecstatically, to call my spirit bird, and to open the door to the other world.

Ntak o numa waram, és mozdulak; jomadak.
I mount my spirit bird and we begin to move; we are underway.

Piwtädak ot En Puwe tyvinak, ećidak alatt o jüti, kinta, és szelemek lamtijaknak.
Following the trunk of the Great Tree, we fall into the netherworld.

Fázak, fázak nó o śaro.
It is cold, very cold.

Juttadak ot ekäm o akarataban, o sívaban és o sielaban.
My brother and I are linked in mind, heart and soul.

Ot ekäm sielanak kaŋa engem.
My brother's soul calls to me.

Kuledak és piwtädak ot ekäm.
I hear and follow his track.

Saγedak és tuledak ot ekäm kulyanak.
I encounter the demon who is devouring my brother's soul.

Nenäm ćoro, o kuly torodak.
In anger, I fight the demon.

O kuly pél engem.
He is afraid of me.

Lejkkadak o kaŋka salamaval.
I strike his throat with a lightning bolt.

Molodak ot ainaja komakamal.
I break his body with my bare hands.

Toja és molanâ.
He is bent over, and falls apart.

Hän ćaδa.
He runs away.

Manedak ot ekäm sielanak.
I rescue my brother's soul.

Alǝdak ot ekam sielanak o komamban.
I lift my brother's soul in the hollow of my hand.

Alǝdam ot ekam numa waramra.
I lift him onto my spirit bird.

Piwtädak ot En Puwe tyvijanak és saγedak jälleen ot elävä ainak majaknak.
Following up the Great Tree, we return to the land of the living.

Ot ekäm elä jälleen.
My brother lives again.

Ot ekäm weńća jälleen.
He is complete again.

To hear this chant, visit christinefeehan.com/members/.

4. CARPATHIAN MUSICAL AESTHETICS

In the sung Carpathian pieces (such as the "Lullaby" and the "Song to Heal the Earth"), you'll hear elements that are shared by many of the musical traditions in the Uralic geographical region, some of which still exist—from Eastern European (Bulgarian, Romanian, Hungarian, Croatian) to Romany ("gypsy"). These elements include:

- the rapid alternation between major and minor modalities, including a sudden switch (called a "Picardy third") from minor to major to end a piece or section (as at the end of the "Lullaby")
- the use of close (tight) harmonies
- the use of *ritardi* (slowing down the pace) and *crescendi* (swelling in volume) for brief periods
- the use of *glissandi* (slides) in the singing tradition
- the use of trills in the singing tradition (as in the final invocation of the "Song to Heal the Earth")—similar to Celtic, a singing tradition more familiar to many of us
- the use of parallel fifths (as in the final invocation of the "Song to Heal the Earth")
- controlled use of dissonance
- "call-and-response" chanting (typical of many of the world's chanting traditions)
- extending the length of a musical line (by adding a couple of bars) to heighten dramatic effect
- and many more

"Lullaby" and "Song to Heal the Earth" illustrate two rather different forms of Carpathian music (a quiet, intimate piece and an energetic ensemble piece)—but whatever the form, Carpathian music is full of feeling.

5. LULLABY

This song is sung by a woman while a child is still in the womb or when the threat of a miscarriage is apparent. The baby can hear the song while inside the mother, and the mother can connect with the child telepathically as well. The lullaby is meant to reassure the child, to encourage the baby to hold on, to stay—to reassure the child that he or she will be protected by love even from inside until birth. The last line literally means that the mother's love will protect her child until the child is born ("rise").

Musically, the Carpathian "Lullaby" is in three-quarter time ("waltz time"), as are a significant portion of the world's various traditional lullabies (perhaps the most famous of which is Brahms's Lullaby). The arrangement for solo voice is the original context: a mother singing to her child, unaccompanied. The arrangement for chorus and violin ensemble illustrates how musical even the simplest Carpathian pieces often are, and how easily they lend themselves to contemporary instrumental or orchestral arrangements. (A wide range of contemporary composers, including Dvořák and Smetana, have taken advantage of a similar discovery, working other traditional Eastern European music into their symphonic poems.)

Odam-Sarna Kondak (Lullaby)

Tumtesz o wäke ku pitasz belső.
Feel the strength you hold inside.

Hiszasz sívadet. Én olenam gæidnod.
Trust your heart. I'll be your guide.

Sas csecsemőm; kuńasz.
Hush, my baby; close your eyes.

Rauho joŋe ted.
Peace will come to you.

Tumtesz o sívdobbanás ku olen lamt3ad belső.
Feel the rhythm deep inside.

Gond-kumpadek ku kim te.
Waves of love that cover you.

Pesänak te, asti o jüti, kidüsz.
Protect, until the night you rise.

To hear this song, visit christinefeehan.com/members/.

6. SONG TO HEAL THE EARTH

This is the earth-healing song that is used by the Carpathian women to heal soil filled with various toxins. The women take a position on four sides and call to the universe to draw on the healing energy with love and respect. The soil of the earth is their resting place, the place where they rejuvenate, and they must make it safe not only for themselves but for their unborn children, as well as their men and living children. This is a beautiful ritual performed by the women together, raising their voices in harmony and calling on the earth's minerals and healing properties to come forth and help them save their children. They literally dance and sing to heal the earth in a ceremony as old as their species. The dance and notes of the song are adjusted according to the toxins felt through the healers' bare feet. The feet are placed in a certain pattern, and the hands gracefully weave a healing spell while the dance is performed. They must be especially careful when the soil is prepared for babies. This is a ceremony of love and healing.

Musically, the ritual is divided into several sections:

- **First verse:** A "call-and-response" section, where the chant leader sings the "call" solo, and then some or all of the women sing the "response" in the close harmony style typical of the Carpathian musical tradition. The repeated response—*Ai, Emä Maγe*—is an invocation of the source of power for the healing ritual: "Oh, Mother Nature."

- **First chorus:** This section is filled with clapping, dancing, ancient horns and other means used to invoke and heighten the energies upon which the ritual is drawing.
- **Second verse**
- **Second chorus**
- **Closing invocation:** In this closing part, two song leaders, in close harmony, take all the energy gathered by the earlier portions of the song/ritual and focus it entirely on the healing purpose.

What you will be listening to are brief tastes of what would typically be a significantly longer ritual, in which the verse and chorus parts are developed and repeated many times, to be closed by a single rendition of the closing invocation.

Sarna Pusm O Maɣet (Song to Heal the Earth)

First verse
Ai, Emä Maɣe,
Oh, Mother Nature,

Me sívadbin lañaak.
We are your beloved daughters.

Me tappadak, me pusmak o maɣet.
We dance to heal the earth.

Me sarnadak, me pusmak o hanyet.
We sing to heal the earth.

Sielanket jutta tedet it,
We join with you now,

Sívank és akaratank és sielank juttanak.
Our hearts and minds and spirits become one.

Second verse
Ai, Emä Maɣe,
Oh, Mother Nature,

Me sívadbin lañaak.
We are your beloved daughters.

Me andak arwadet emänked és me kaŋank o
We pay homage to our mother and call upon the

Pōhi és Lōuna, Ida és Lääs.
North and South, East and West.

Pide és aldyn és myös belső.
Above and below and within as well.

Gondank o maɣenak pusm hän ku olen jama.
Our love of the land heals that which is in need.

Juttanak teval it,
We join with you now,

Maɣe maɣeval.
Earth to earth.

O pirä elidak weńća.
The circle of life is complete.

To hear this chant, visit christinefeehan.com/members/.

7. CARPATHIAN CHANTING TECHNIQUE

As with their healing techniques, the actual "chanting technique" of the Carpathians has much in common with the other shamanistic traditions of the Central Asian steppes. The primary mode of chanting was throat chanting using overtones. Modern examples of this manner of singing can still be found in the Mongolian, Tuvan and Tibetan traditions. You can find an audio example of the Gyuto Tibetan Buddhist monks engaged in throat chanting at christinefeehan.com/carpathian_chanting/.

As with Tuva, note on the map the geographical proximity of Tibet to Kazakhstan and the Southern Urals.

The beginning part of the Tibetan chant emphasizes synchronizing all the voices around a single tone, aimed at healing a particular "chakra" of the body. This is fairly typical of the Gyuto throat-chanting tradition, but it is not a significant part of the Carpathian tradition. Nonetheless, it serves as an interesting contrast.

The part of the Gyuto chanting example that is most similar to the Carpathian style of chanting is the midsection, where the men are chanting the words together with great force. The purpose here is not to generate a "healing tone" that will affect a particular "chakra" but rather to generate as much power as possible for initiating "out-of-body" travel and for fighting the demonic forces that the healer/traveler must face and overcome.

The songs of the Carpathian women (illustrated by their "Lullaby" and their "Song to Heal the Earth") are part of the same ancient musical and healing tradition as the Lesser and Great Healing Chants of the warrior males. You can hear some of the same instruments in both the male warriors' healing chants and the women's "Song to Heal the Earth." Also, they share the common purpose of generating and directing power. However, the women's songs are distinctively feminine in character. One immediately noticeable difference is that while the men speak their words in the manner of a chant, the women sing songs with melodies and harmonies, softening the overall performance. A feminine, nurturing quality is especially evident in the "Lullaby."

APPENDIX 2

THE CARPATHIAN LANGUAGE

Like all human languages, the language of the Carpathians contains the richness and nuance that can only come from a long history of use. At best we can only touch on some of the main features of the language in this brief appendix:

1. The history of the Carpathian language
2. Carpathian grammar and other characteristics of the language
3. Examples of the Carpathian language (including the Ritual Words and the Warriors' Chant)
4. A much-abridged Carpathian dictionary

1. THE HISTORY OF THE CARPATHIAN LANGUAGE

The Carpathian language of today is essentially identical to the Carpathian language of thousands of years ago. A "dead" language like the Latin of two thousand years ago has evolved into a significantly different modern language (Italian) because of countless generations of speakers and great historical fluctuations. In contrast, many of the speakers of Carpathian from thousands of years ago are still alive. Their presence—coupled with the deliberate isolation of the Carpathians from the other major forces of change in the world—has acted (and continues to act) as a stabilizing force that has preserved the integrity of the language over the centuries. Carpathian culture has also acted as a stabilizing force. For instance, the Ritual Words, the various healing chants (see Appendix 1) and other cultural artifacts have been passed down through the centuries with great fidelity.

One small exception should be noted: the splintering of the Carpathians into separate geographic regions has led to some minor dialectization. However, the telepathic link among all Carpathians (as well as each Carpathian's regular return to his or her homeland) has ensured that the differences among dialects are relatively superficial (small numbers of new words, minor differences in pronunciation, etc.), since the deeper internal language of mind-forms has remained the same because of continuous use across space and time.

The Carpathian language was (and still is) the proto-language for the Uralic (or Finno-Ugric) family of languages. Today, the Uralic languages are spoken in northern, eastern and central Europe and in Siberia. More than twenty-three million people in the world speak languages that can trace their ancestry to Carpathian. Magyar or Hungarian (about fourteen million speakers), Finnish (about five million speakers) and Estonian (about one million speakers) are the three major contemporary descendants of this proto-language. The only factor that unites the more than twenty languages in the Uralic family is that their ancestry can be traced back to a common proto-language—Carpathian—that split (starting some six thousand years ago) into the various languages in the Uralic family. In the same way, European languages such as English and French belong to the better-known Indo-European family and also evolved from a common proto-language ancestor (a different one from Carpathian).

The following table provides a sense of some of the similarities in the language family.

Note: The Finnic/Carpathian "k" shows up often as the Hungarian "h." Similarly, the Finnic/Carpathian "p" often corresponds to the Hungarian "f."

THE CARPATHIAN LANGUAGE

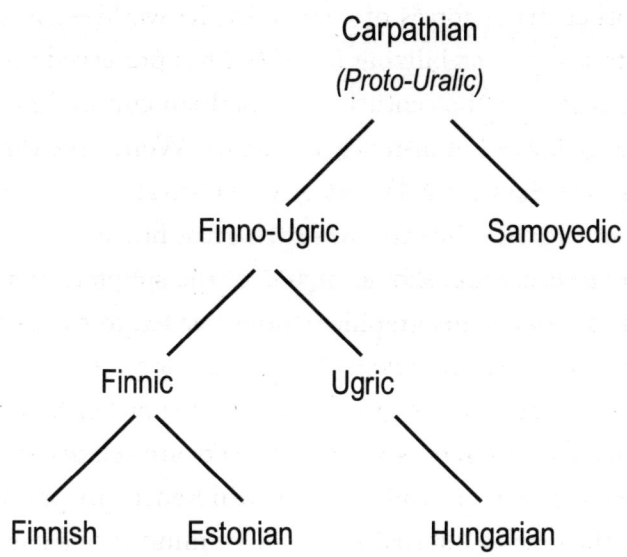

Carpathian (proto-Uralic)	Finnish (Suomi)	Hungarian (Magyar)
elä—live	*elä*—live	*él*—live
elid—life	*elinikä*—life	*élet*—life
pesä—nest	*pesä*—nest	*fészek*—nest
kola—die	*kuole*—die	*hal*—die
pälä—half, side	*pieltä*—tilt, tip to the side	*fél, fele*—fellow human, friend (half; one side of two) *feleség*—wife
and—give	*anta, antaa*—give	*ad*—give
koje—husband, man	*koira*—dog, the male (of animals)	*here*—drone, testicle
wäke—power	*väki*—folks, people, men; force	*val/-vel*—with (instrumental suffix)
	väkevä—powerful, strong	*vele*—with him/her/it
wete—water	*vesi*—water	*viz*—water

2. CARPATHIAN GRAMMAR AND OTHER CHARACTERISTICS OF THE LANGUAGE

Idioms. As both an ancient language and a language of an earth people, Carpathian is more inclined toward the use of idioms constructed from concrete, "earthy" terms rather than abstractions. For instance, our modern abstraction "to cherish" is expressed more concretely in Carpathian as "to hold in one's heart"; the "netherworld" is, in Carpathian, "the land of night, fog and ghosts"; etc.

Word order. The order of words in a sentence is determined not by syntactic roles (like subject, verb and object) but rather by pragmatic, discourse-driven factors. Examples: *"Tied vagyok."* ("Yours am I."); *"Sívamet andam."* ("My heart I give you.")

Agglutination. The Carpathian language is agglutinative; that is, longer words are constructed from smaller components. An agglutinating language uses suffixes or prefixes whose meanings are generally unique and that are concatenated one after another without overlap. In Carpathian, words typically consist of a stem that is followed by one or more suffixes. For example, *sívambam* derives from the stem *"sív"* ("heart"), followed by *"am"* ("my," making it "my heart"), followed by *"bam"* ("in," making it "in my heart"). As you might imagine, agglutination in Carpathian can sometimes produce very long words, or words that are very difficult to pronounce. Vowels often get inserted between suffixes to prevent too many consonants from appearing in a row (which can make a word unpronounceable).

Noun cases. Like all languages, Carpathian has many noun cases; the same noun will be "spelled" differently depending on its role in a sentence. The noun cases include nominative (when the noun is the subject of the sentence), accusative (when the noun is a direct object of the verb), dative (indirect object), genitive (or possessive), instrumental, final, suppressive, inessive, elative, terminative and delative.

We will use the possessive (or genitive) case as an example to illustrate how all noun cases in Carpathian involve adding standard suffixes to the noun stems. Thus, expressing possession in Carpathian—"my lifemate," "your lifemate," "his lifemate," "her lifemate," etc.—involves adding a particular suffix (such as "*-am*") to the noun stem (*"päläfertiil"*) to produce the possessive (*"päläfertiilam"*—"my lifemate"). Which suffix to use depends on which person ("my," "your," "his," etc.) and whether the noun ends in a consonant or a vowel. The following table shows the suffixes for singular nouns only (not plural), and also shows the similarity to the suffixes used in contemporary Hungarian. (Hungarian is actually a little more complex, in that it also requires "vowel rhyming": which suffix to use also depends on the last vowel in the noun, hence the multiple choices in the table, where Carpathian has only a single choice.)

person	Carpathian (proto-Uralic)		Contemporary Hungarian	
	noun ends in vowel	**noun ends in consonant**	**noun ends in vowel**	**noun ends in consonant**
1st singular (my)	-m	-am	-m	-om, -em, -öm
2nd singular (your)	-d	-ad	-d	-od, -ed, -öd
3rd singular (his, her, its)	-ja	-a	-ja/-je	-a, -e
1st plural (our)	-nk	-ank	-nk	-unk, -ünk
2nd plural (your)	-tak	-atak	-tok, -tek, -tök	-otok, -etek, -ötök
3rd plural (their)	-jak	-ak	-juk, -jük	-uk, -ük

Note: As mentioned earlier, vowels often get inserted between the word and its suffix so as to prevent too many consonants from appearing in a row (which would produce unpronounceable words). For example, in the table on the previous page, all nouns that end in a consonant are followed by suffixes beginning with "a."

Verb conjugation. Like its modern descendants (such as Finnish and Hungarian), Carpathian has many verb tenses, far too many to describe here. We will just focus on the conjugation of the present tense. Again, we will place contemporary Hungarian side by side with Carpathian because of the marked similarity between the two.

As with the possessive case for nouns, the conjugation of verbs is done by adding a suffix onto the verb stem:

Person	Carpathian (proto-Uralic)	Contemporary Hungarian
1st singular (I give)	-am (andam), -ak	-ok, -ek, -ök
2nd singular (you give)	-sz (andsz)	-sz
3rd singular (he/she/it gives)	— (and)	—
1st plural (we give)	-ak (andak)	-unk, -ünk
2nd plural (you give)	-tak (andtak)	-tok, -tek, -tök
3rd plural (they give)	-nak (andnak)	-nak, -nek

As with all languages, there are many "irregular verbs" in Carpathian that don't exactly fit this pattern. But the table is still a useful guide for most verbs.

3. EXAMPLES OF THE CARPATHIAN LANGUAGE

Here are some brief examples of conversational Carpathian, used in the Dark books. We include the literal translation in square brackets.

It is interestingly different from the most appropriate English translation.

Susu.
I am home.
["home/birthplace." "I am" is understood, as is often the case in Carpathian.]

Möért?
What for?

csitri
little one
["little slip of a thing," "little slip of a girl"]

ainaak enyém
forever mine

ainaak sívamet jutta
forever mine (another form)
["forever to-my-heart connected/fixed"]

sívamet
my love
["of-my-heart," "to-my-heart"]

Tet vigyázam.
I love you.
["you-love-I"]

Sarna Rituaali (**The Ritual Words**) is a longer example and an example of chanted rather than conversational Carpathian. Note the recurring use of *"andam"* ("I give") to give the chant musicality and force through repetition.

Sarna Rituaali (The Ritual Words)

Te avio päläfertiilam.
You are my lifemate.

Éntölam kuulua, avio päläfertiilam.
I claim you as my lifemate.

Ted kuuluak, kacad, kojed.
I belong to you.

Élidamet andam.
I offer my life for you.

Pesämet andam.
I give you my protection.

Uskolfertiilamet andam.
I give you my allegiance.

Sívamet andam.
I give you my heart.

Sielamet andam.
I give you my soul.

Ainamet andam.
I give you my body.

Sívamet kuuluak kaik että a ted.
I take into my keeping the same that is yours.

Ainaak olenszal sívambin.
Your life will be cherished by me for all my time.

Te élidet ainaak pide minan.
Your life will be placed above my own for all time.

Te avio päläfertiilam.
You are my lifemate.

Ainaak sívamet jutta oleny.
You are bound to me for all eternity.

Ainaak terád vigyázak.
You are always in my care.

To hear these words pronounced (and for more about Carpathian pronunciation altogether), please visit christinefeehan.com/members/.

Sarna Kontakawk (The Warriors' Chant) is another, longer example of the Carpathian language. The warriors' council takes place deep beneath the earth in a chamber of crystals with magma far below it, so the steam is natural and the wisdom of their ancestors is clear and focused. This is a sacred place where they bloodswear to their prince and people and affirm their code of honor as warriors and brothers. It is also where battle strategies are born and all dissension is discussed, as well as any concerns the warriors have that they wish to bring to the council and open for discussion.

Sarna Kontakawk (The Warriors' Chant)

Veri isäakank—veri ekäakank.
Blood of our fathers—blood of our brothers.

Veri olen elid.
Blood is life.

*Andak veri-elidet Karpatiiakank, és wäke-sarna ku meke arwa-arvo,
irgalom, hän ku agba, és wäke kutni, ku manaak verival.*
We offer that life to our people with a bloodsworn vow of honor,
mercy, integrity and endurance.

Verink sokta; verink kaŋa terád.
Our blood mingles and calls to you.

Akasz énak ku kaŋa és juttasz kuntatak it.
Heed our summons and join with us now.

To hear these words pronounced (and for more about Carpathian pronunciation altogether), please visit christinefeehan.com/members/.

See **Appendix 1** for Carpathian healing chants, including the *Kepä Sarna Pus* (The Lesser Healing Chant), the *En Sarna Pus* (The Great Healing Chant), the *Odam-Sarna Kondak* (Lullaby) and the *Sarna Pusm O Mayet* (Song to Heal the Earth).

4. A MUCH-ABRIDGED CARPATHIAN DICTIONARY

This very-much-abridged Carpathian dictionary contains most of the Carpathian words used in the Dark books. Of course, a full Carpathian dictionary would be as large as the usual dictionary for an entire language (typically more than a hundred thousand words).

Note: The Carpathian nouns and verbs that follow are word **stems**. They generally do not appear in their isolated "stem" form. Instead, they usually appear with suffixes (e.g., *andam—I give*, rather than just the root, *and*).

a—verb negation (*prefix*); not (*adverb*).
aćke—pace, step.

aćke éntölem it—take another step toward me.
agba—to be seemly; to be proper (*verb*). True; seemly; proper (*adj.*).
ai—oh.
aina—body (*noun*).
ainaak—always; forever.
o ainaak jelä peje emnimet ŋamaŋ—sun scorch that woman forever (*Carpathian swear words*).
ainaakä—never.
ainaakfél—old friend.
ak—suffix added after a noun ending in a consonant to make it plural.
aka—to give heed; to hearken; to listen.
aka-arvo—respect (*noun*).
akarat—mind; will (*noun*).
ál—to bless; to attach to.
alatt—through.
aldyn—under; underneath.
alə—to lift; to raise.
alte—to bless; to curse.
amaŋ—this; this one here; that; that one there.
and—to give.
and sielet, arwa-arvomet, és jelämet, kuulua huvémet ku feaj és ködet ainaak—to trade soul, honor and salvation for momentary pleasure and endless damnation.
andasz éntölem irgalomet!—have mercy!
arvo—value; price (*noun*).
arwa—praise (*noun*).
arwa-arvo olen gæidnod, ekäm—honor guide you, my brother (*greeting*).
arwa-arvo olen isäntä, ekäm—honor keep you, my brother (*greeting*).
arwa-arvo pile sívadet—may honor light your heart (*greeting*).
arwa-arvod—honor (*noun*).
arwa-arvod mäne me ködak—may your honor hold back the dark (*greeting*).

aš—no (*exclamation*).

ašša—no (before a noun); not (with a verb that is not in the imperative); not (with an adjective).

aššatotello—disobedient.

asti—until.

avaa—to open.

avio—wedded.

avio päläfertiil—lifemate.

avoi—uncover; show; reveal.

baszú—revenge; vengeance.

belső—within; inside.

bur—good; well.

bur tule ekämet kuntamak—well met, brother-kin (*greeting*).

ćaδa—to flee; to run; to escape.

čač3—to be born; to grow.

ćoro—to flow; to run like rain.

csecsemõ—baby (*noun*).

csitri—little one (*female*).

csitrim—my little one (*female*).

diutal—triumph; victory.

džinõt—brief; short.

eći—to fall.

ej—not (*adverb, suffix*); *nej* when preceding syllable ends in a vowel.

ek—suffix added after a noun ending in a consonant to make it plural.

ekä—brother.

ekäm—my brother.

elä—to live.

eläsz arwa-arvoval—may you live with honor; live nobly (*greeting*).

eläsz jeläbam ainaak—long may you live in the light (*greeting*).

elävä—alive.

elävä ainak majaknak—land of the living.

elid—life.

emä—mother (*noun*).

Emä Maγe—Mother Nature.
emäen—grandmother.
embε—if; when.
embε karmasz—please.
emni—wife; woman.
emni hän ku köd alte—cursed woman.
emni kuŋenak ku aššatotello—disobedient lunatic.
emnim—my wife; my woman.
emninuma—goddess.
én—I.
en—great; many; big.
en hän ku pesä—the protector (literally: the great protector).
én jutta félet és ekämet—I greet a friend and brother (*greeting*).
en Karpatii—the prince (literally: the great Carpathian).
én maγenak—I am of the earth.
Én olenam jelä—I am the light.
Én olenam teval it—I am with you now.
én oma maγeka—I am as old as time (literally: as old as the earth).
En Puwe—The Great Tree. Related to the legends of Yggdrasil, the *axis mundi*, Mount Meru, heaven and hell, etc.
enä—most.
engem—of me.
enkojra—wolf.
és—and.
ete—before; in front of.
että—that.
év—year.
évsatz—century.
ewal—sweet; tender.
fáz—to feel cold or chilly.
fél—fellow; friend.
fél ku kuuluaak sívam belső—beloved.
fél ku vigyázak—dear one.

feldolgaz—prepare.
fertiil—fertile one.
fesztelen—airy.
fü—herbs; grass.
gæidno—road; way.
gapâd—free; idle; unoccupied; easy; petty; small; trifling.
gond—care; worry; love (*noun*).
gyenge—weak; frail; slight; infirm.
hän—he; she; it; one.
hän agba—it is so.
hän ku—prefix: one who; he who; that which.
hän ku agba—truth.
hän ku kaświa o numamet—sky-owner.
hän ku kuula siela—keeper of his soul.
hän ku kuulua sívamet—keeper of my heart.
hän ku lejkka wäke-sarnat—traitor.
hän ku meke pirämet—defender.
hän ku meke sarnaakmet—mage.
hän ku pelkgapâd és meke pirämet—fearless defender. (*Pelkgapâd és Meke Pirämet*: "Fearless Defender" used as a nickname.)
hän ku pesä—protector.
hän ku pesä sieladet—guardian of your soul.
hän ku pesäk kaikak—guardians of all.
hän ku piwtä—predator; hunter; tracker.
hän ku pusm—healer.
hän ku saa kuć3aket—star-reacher.
hän ku tappa—killer; violent person (*noun*). Deadly; violent (*adj.*).
hän ku tappa kulyak—demon killer. (*Ku Tappa Kulyak*: "Demon Killer" used as a nickname.)
hän ku tuulmahl elidet—vampire (literally: life-stealer).
hän ku vie elidet—vampire (literally: thief of life).
hän ku vigyáz sielamet—keeper of my soul.
hän ku vigyáz sívamet és sielamet—keeper of my heart and soul.

THE CARPATHIAN LANGUAGE

hän sívamak—beloved.
hängem—him; her; it.
hank—they.
hany—clod; lump of earth.
hisz—to believe; to trust.
ho—how.
ida—east.
igazág—justice.
ila—to shine.
inan—mine; my own (*endearment*).
irgalom—compassion; pity; mercy.
isä—father (*noun*).
isäntä—master of the house.
it—now.
jaguár—jaguar.
jaka—to cut; to divide; to separate.
jakam—wound; cut; injury.
jalka—leg.
jälleen—again.
jama—to be sick, infected, wounded or dying; to be near death.
jamatan—fallen; wounded; near death.
jelä—sunlight; day, sun; light.
jelä keje terád—light sear you (*Carpathian swear words*).
o jelä peje emnimet—sun scorch the woman (*Carpathian swear words*).
o jelä peje kaik hänkanak—sun scorch them all (*Carpathian swear words*).
o jelä peje terád—sun scorch you (*Carpathian swear words*).
o jelä peje terád, emni—sun scorch you, woman (*Carpathian swear words*).
o jelä sielamak—light of my soul.
joma—to be underway; to go.
joŋe—to come; to return.

joŋesz arwa-arvoval—return with honor (*greeting*).
joŋesz éntölem, fél ku kuuluaak sívam belsö—come to me, beloved.
jŏrem—to forget; to lose one's way; to make a mistake.
jotka—gap; middle; space.
jotkan—between.
juo—to drink.
juosz és eläsz—drink and live (*greeting*).
juosz és olen ainaak sielamet jutta—drink and become one with me (*greeting*).
juta—to go; to wander.
jüti—night; evening.
jutta—connected; fixed (*adj.*). To connect; to join; to fix; to bind (*verb*).
k—suffix added after a noun ending in a vowel to make it plural.
kać3—gift.
kaca—male lover.
kadi—judge.
kaik—all.
käktä—two; many.
käktäverit—mixed blood (literally: two bloods).
kalma—corpse; death; grave.
kaŋa—to call; to invite; to summon; to request; to beg.
kaŋk—windpipe; Adam's apple; throat.
karma—want.
Karpatii—Carpathian.
karpatii ku köd—liar.
Karpatiikunta—the Carpathian people.
käsi—hand.
kaśwa—to own.
kaδa—to abandon; to leave; to remain.
kaδa wäkeva óv o köd—stand fast against the dark (*greeting*).
kat—house; family (*noun*).
katt3—to move; to penetrate; to proceed.
keje—to cook; to burn; to sear.

THE CARPATHIAN LANGUAGE

kepä—lesser; small; easy; few.
kessa—cat.
kessa ku toro—wildcat.
kessake—little cat.
kidü—to wake up; to arise (*intransitive verb*).
kim—to cover an entire object with some sort of covering.
kinn—out; outdoors; outside; without.
kinta—fog; mist; smoke.
kislány—little girl.
kislány hän ku meke sarnaakmet—little mage.
kislány kuŋenak—little lunatic.
kislány kuŋenak minan—my little lunatic.
köd—fog; mist; darkness; evil (*noun*). Foggy, dark; evil (*adj.*).
köd alte hän—darkness curse it (*Carpathian swear words*).
o köd belső—darkness take it (*Carpathian swear words*).
köd elävä és köd nime kutni nimet—evil lives and has a name.
köd jutasz belső—shadow take you (*Carpathian swear words*).
koj—let; allow; decree; establish; order.
koje—man; husband; drone.
kola—to die.
kolasz arwa-arvoval—may you die with honor (*greeting*).
kolatan—dead; departed.
koma—empty hand; bare hand; palm of the hand; hollow of the hand.
kond—all of a family's or clan's children.
kont—warrior; man.
kont ku votjak—knight.
kont o sívanak—strong heart (literally: heart of the warrior).
kor3—basket; container made of birch bark.
kor3nat—containing; including.
ku—who; which; that; where; which; what.
kuć3—star.
kuć3ak!—stars! (exclamation).
kudeje—descent; generation.

kuja—day; sun.
kule—to hear.
kulke—to go or to travel (on land or water).
kulkesz arwa-arvoval, ekäm—walk with honor, my brother (*greeting*).
kulkesz arwaval, joŋesz arwa arvoval—go with glory, return with honor (*greeting*).
kuly—intestinal worm; tapeworm; demon who possesses and devours souls.
küm—human male.
kumala—to sacrifice; to offer; to pray.
kumpa—wave (*noun*).
kuńa—to lie as if asleep; to close or cover the eyes in a game of hide-and-seek; to die.
kuŋe—moon; month.
kuŋe kont—moon warrior.
kuŋe kont ku votjak—moon knight.
kuŋe s3c3—moon monster.
kunta—band; clan; tribe; family; people; lineage; line.
kuras—sword; large knife.
kure—bind; tie.
kuš—worker; servant.
kutenken—however.
kutni—to be able to bear, carry, endure, stand or take.
kutnisz ainaak—long may you endure (*greeting*).
kuulua—to belong; to hold.
kužŏ—long.
lääs—west.
lamti (or lamt3)—lowland; meadow; deep; depth.
lamti ból jüti, kinta, ja szelem—the netherworld (literally: the meadow of night, mists and ghosts).
lańa—daughter.
lejkka—crack; fissure; split (*noun*). To cut; to hit; to strike forcefully (*verb*).

THE CARPATHIAN LANGUAGE

lewl—spirit (*noun*).

lewl ma—the other world (literally: spirit land). *Lewl ma* includes *lamti ból jüti, kinta, ja szelem*: the netherworld, but also includes the worlds higher up *En Puwe*, the Great Tree.

liha—flesh.

lõuna—south.

löyly—breath; steam (related to *lewl*: spirit).

luwe—bone.

ma—land; forest; world.

magköszun—thank.

mana—to abuse; to curse; to ruin.

mäne—to rescue; to save.

maɣe—land; earth; territory; place; nature.

mboće—other; second (*adj.*).

me—we.

megem—us.

meke—deed; work (*noun*). To do; to make; to work (*verb*).

mić (or mića)—beautiful.

mića emni kuŋenak minan—my beautiful lunatic.

minan—mine; my own (*endearment*).

minden—every; all (*adj.*).

möért?—what for? (*exclamation*).

molanâ—to crumble; to fall apart.

molo—to crush; to break into bits.

moo—why; reason.

mozdul—to begin to move; to enter into movement.

muonì—appoint; order; prescribe; command.

muonìak te avoisz te—I command you to reveal yourself.

musta—memory.

myös—also.

m8—thing; what.

na—close; near.

nä—for.

nâbbŏ—so, then.
ŋamaŋ—this; this one here; that; that one there.
ŋamaŋak—these; these ones here; those; those ones there.
nautish—to enjoy.
nélkül—without.
nenä—anger.
nime—name.
ńiŋ3—worm; maggot.
ńiŋ3 ködak—shadow worm.
nó—like; in the same way as; as.
nókunta—kinship.
numa—god; sky; top; upper part; highest (related to the English word *numinous*).
numatorkuld—thunder (literally: sky struggle).
ńůp@l—for; to; toward.
ńůp@l mam—toward my world.
nyál—saliva; spit (related to *nyelv*: tongue).
nyelv—tongue.
o—the (used before a noun beginning with a consonant).
ó—like; in the same way as; as.
odam—to dream; to sleep.
odam-sarna kondak—lullaby (literally: sleep-song of children).
odam wäke emni—mistress of illusions.
olen—to be.
oma—old; ancient; last; previous.
omas—stand.
omboće—other; second (*adj.*).
ŏrem—to forget; to lose one's way; to make a mistake.
ot—the (used before a noun beginning with a vowel).
ot (or t)—past participle (*suffix*).
otti—to look; to see; to find.
óv—to protect against.
owe—door.

päämoro—aim; target.

pajna—to press.

pälä—half; side.

päläfertiil—mate or wife.

päläpälä—side by side.

palj3—more.

palj3 na éntölem—closer.

partiolen—scout (*noun*).

peje—to burn; scorch.

peje!—burn! (*Carpathian swear word*).

peje terád—get burned (*Carpathian swear words*).

pél—to be afraid; to be scared of.

pelk—fear (*noun*).

pelkgapâ—fearless.

pesä—nest (*literal; noun*); protection (*figurative; noun*).

pesä—nest; stay (*literal*); protect (*figurative*).

pesäd te engemal—you are safe with me.

pesäsz jeläbam ainaak—long may you stay in the light (*greeting*).

pide—above.

pile—to ignite; to light up.

piŋe—little bird.

piŋe sarnanak—little songbird.

pion—soon.

pirä—circle; ring (*noun*). To surround; to enclose (*verb*).

piros—red.

pitä—to keep; to hold; to have; to possess.

pitäam mustaakad sielpesäambam—I hold your memories safe in my soul.

pitäsz baszú, piwtäsz igazáget—no vengeance, only justice.

piwtä—to seek; to follow; to follow the track of game; to hunt; to prey upon.

poår—bit; piece.

põhi—north.

pohoopa—vigorous.
pukta—to drive away; to persecute; to put to flight.
pus—healthy; healing.
pusm—to heal; to be restored to health.
puwe—tree; wood.
rambsolg—slave.
rauho—peace.
reka—ecstasy; trance.
rituaali—ritual.
s3c3—lizard; monster.
sa—sinew; tendon; cord.
sa4—to call; to name.
saa—arrive, come; become; get, receive.
saasz hän ku andam szabadon—take what I freely offer.
saɣe—to arrive; to come; to reach.
salama—lightning; lightning bolt.
sapar—tail.
sapar bin jalkak—coward (literally: tail between legs).
sapar bin jalkak nélkül mogal—spineless coward.
sarna—words; speech; song; magic incantation (*noun*). To chant; to sing; to celebrate (*verb*).
sarna hän agba—claim.
sarna kontakawk—warriors' chant.
sarna kunta—alliance (literally: single tribe through sacred words).
śaro—frozen snow.
sas—shoosh (*to a child or baby*).
satz—hundred.
siel—soul.
sielad sielamed—soul to soul (literally: your soul to my soul).
sielam—my soul.
sielam pitwä sielad—my soul searches for your soul.
sielam sieladed—my soul to your soul.
sieljelä isäntä—purity of soul triumphs.

sisar—sister.
sisarak sivak—sisters of the heart.
sisarke—little sister.
sív—heart.
sív pide köd—love transcends evil.
sív pide minden köd—love transcends all evil.
sívad olen wäkeva, hän ku piwtä—may your heart stay strong, hunter (*greeting*).
sívam és sielam—my heart and soul.
sívamet—my heart.
sívdobbanás—heartbeat (*literal*); rhythm (*figurative*).
sokta—to mix; to stir around.
sõl—dare, venture.
sõl olen engemal, sarna sívametak—dare to be with me, song of my heart.
soŋe—to enter; to penetrate; to compensate; to replace.
Susiküm—Lycan.
susu—home; birthplace (*noun*). At home (*adv.*).
szabadon—freely.
szelem—ghost.
ször—time; occasion.
t (or ot)—past participle (*suffix*).
taj—to be worth.
taka—behind; beyond.
takka—to hang; to remain stuck.
takkap—obstacle; challenge; difficulty; ordeal; trial.
tappa—to dance; to stamp with the feet; to kill.
tasa—even so; just the same.
te—you.
te kalma, te jama ńiŋ3kval, te apitäsz arwa-arvo—you are nothing but a walking maggot-infected corpse, without honor.
te magköszunam nä ŋamaŋ kać3 taka arvo—thank you for this gift beyond price.

ted—yours.

terád keje—get scorched (*Carpathian swear words*).

tõd—to know.

tõdak pitäsz wäke bekimet mekesz kaiket—I know you have the courage to face anything.

tõdhän—knowledge.

tõdhän lõ kuraset agbapäämoroam—knowledge flies the sword true to its aim.

toja—to bend; to bow; to break.

toro—to fight; to quarrel.

torosz wäkeval—fight fiercely (*greeting*).

totello—obey.

tsak—only.

t'śuva vni—period of time.

tti—to look; to see; to find.

tuhanos—thousand.

tuhanos löylyak türelamak saγe diutalet—a thousand patient breaths bring victory.

tule—to meet; to come.

tuli—fire.

tumte—to feel; to touch; to touch upon.

türe—full; satiated; accomplished.

türelam—patience.

türelam agba kontsalamaval—patience is the warrior's true weapon.

tyvi—stem; base; trunk.

ul3—very; exceedingly; quite.

umuš—wisdom; discernment.

und—past participle (*suffix*).

uskol—faithful.

uskolfertiil—allegiance; loyalty.

usm—to heal; to be restored to health.

vad—savage.

vár—to wait.
varolind—dangerous.
veri—blood.
veri ekäakank—blood of our brothers.
veri-elidet—blood-life.
veri isäakank—blood of our fathers.
veri olen piros, ekäm—literally: blood be red, my brother; figuratively: find your lifemate (*greeting*).
veriak ot en Karpatiiak—by the blood of the prince (literally: by the blood of the great Carpathian; *Carpathian swear words*).
veridet peje—may your blood burn (*Carpathian swear words*).
vigyáz—to love; to care for; to take care of.
vii—last; at last; finally.
votjak—to harness (a horse).
wäke—power; strength.
wäke beki—strength; courage.
wäke kaða—steadfastness.
wäke kutni—endurance.
wäke-sarna—vow; curse; blessing (literally: power words).
wäkeva—powerful; strong.
wäkeva csitrim ku pesä—my fierce little protector.
wara—bird; crow.
weńća—complete; whole.
wete—water (*noun*).

ACKNOWLEDGMENTS

As always, there are many people to thank. This book was written during a particularly difficult time in my life. Thank you to Brian Feehan for keeping me on track. Sheila English for coming through with quick research when I needed it instantly. Karen Brownfield Houtman, my amazing researcher. Diane Trudeau, who goes through each book numerous times in an effort to catch my many mistakes. Denise Tucker for holding down the fort while I worked. My wonderful Shylah for helping me through it all.